HOME BEYOND HELL

BOOK 1 OF THE HOME BEYOND HELL SERIES

KAREN YAKEY

RIVERHAUNT PRESS
RIVERHAUNT PRESS, LLC

COPYRIGHT

CHAPTER ONE

VANESSA

"Look, I like a raging case of dysentery as much as the next girl"—Vanessa Brouwer wrapped her arms around the branch to pull herself up—"but I'm throwing my rubber underwear at the next amateur cook who gets free rein in our kitchen."

She grunted, swung her leg, and straddled the narrow limb like a seesaw. Its bark—still cool to the touch, thanks to North Holland's version of late summer—scraped her bare thighs under the skirt, which was skimpy this morning even by her own standards.

"I'd like to actually live to see the end of 2066, now that I've made it to twenty-two—whoa!" She clamped the branch with both hands as she teetered in the tree. "Twenty-two years." She sighed. "Guess the ladder would have been better."

She looked down at the black-and-white bunny, who sat up on his haunches in the grass and wriggled his nose at her feet dangling a meter and a half above him. His right ear stuck out to the side at a ninety-degree angle from his left, which didn't help the half-wit appearance his single upper-front tooth gave him, poor guy. But the other residents were wrong: he wasn't ugly; he was…exotic.

She leaned back against the trunk and strained her fingers toward the wicker basket she'd already nestled in a crook of the apple tree boughs. "Anyway"—she managed to jerk the basket onto her lap without losing her balance—"I only need to gnaw my way through Marien's casserole surprise at dinner, and then I'll be leaving the compound for good this time. Tonight." She wagged a finger at the bunny. "My only regret is that my garden will be at the mercy of that bottomless pit of yours."

The Havana stared up at her with his big brown eyes, the picture of innocence—though his left eye was fittingly set within a black patch of fur like a little pirate. She swiped at an apple hanging far to her right, and all the fruit in the basket tumbled to one end. She caught herself against the tree trunk as the un-gotten apple went flying into the orchard somewhere. The rabbit's left white-tipped ear pricked forward, but then he hunkered down in the grass.

"I know, I know." She grimaced at him as she tugged up the shoulders of her peasant blouse. "Ladder: better."

She squirmed on the branch to scratch an itch on her inner thigh. *Okay, and maybe pants.*

Today she was decked out in a flouncy-skirted blue ensemble that would highlight her green eyes and blond tresses. She was going for a "free spirit" kind of look. But admittedly—perched in a tree and unintentionally exhibiting her undies—she probably reinforced the other residents' image of her as better suited to waitress at the Haarloze Hond bar than to act as chief gardener and kitchen help.

Nearby, the early sunshine danced across the panes of the two greenhouses, wherein her hydroponic experiments and tropical fruit trees cast foggy shadows like a phantom army of flora. A breeze carried the earthy sweet scent of leaves past her as it curled through the branches of the apple trees. It was not a huge orchard, by any means, because there was only so much space inside the old stone compound, but it had always been her favorite part of the garden.

She set the basket on her knee and draped an arm over the branch by her head to scan the surrounding gray walls of the crumbling eighteenth-century Fort Van Doorn, where she and so many other residents had grown up. Honestly, she did love her home, as ridiculously anachronistic as it was. But there was a real world out there to explore, with people who thought nothing of driving a car or surfing the internet.

She hooked an elbow around the basket handle and scooped up one of the red-skinned apple varieties that had ripened earlier than usual.

Unfortunately, that real world also held roving, pillaging gangs that had cropped up ever since the Netherlands had closed its borders and sunk into isolationism like all the nations around it, which had only stoked the growing turmoil. But such marauders preyed on the bigger inhabited villages, where there was more stuff to steal and people to abuse. This was a remote part of the country that used to be crowded with life, but which had been forcibly abandoned by a Dutch population who feared what the new era of governmental corruption would bring to the province. Now, much of this northern area near the coast was vacant, leaving nature to overrun and reclaim what it had once shared. Things were safer here.

Vanessa took a bite of the red prince apple and swung her legs to bump her heels rhythmically against the tree trunk.

Well, safety was overrated. And safety kept a person from the simple thrill of having choices. And it certainly erased the possibility of finding the elusive "soul mate" she always read about in her books who made the main character so blissfully happy.

Her smile widened as she chewed, and she bumped her heels harder.

She could brave a little dystopian chaos if it meant a meaningful make-out session with a tall, dark stranger. Considering it had been two years since she'd even dated a guy, her libido might pose more of a threat than any band of pirates out there. And a new life would be exciting. A new life would mean fresh faces and open landscapes, instead of old walls closing in on her with constant reminders that—

That I killed my parents.

She took a shallow bite of the apple, but all the flavor seemed to have drained from it.

They'd brought her here as a child, to keep her safe. To protect her from the people who were hunting them. And it had taken only a few short years for her to betray them. Both Cornelis and Rhetta insisted it wasn't her fault. They said the man had tricked her into giving her parents away. But it didn't matter. She'd been angry with her mom and dad at the time because they'd grounded her when they'd caught her doing something reckless. They'd done it to make her learn from her mistakes. So in an infantile snit, she'd pointed him their way, when he'd said he was coming to collect a debt. No one would let her see what the man had done, once he'd found them. No one would tell her about the way he'd torn them apart, slaughtered them—

Don't, Vanessa.

She swallowed the tasteless fruit. "De molen gaat niet om met wind die voorbij is," she mumbled. "The windmill doesn't turn from wind that has already blown by." It was one of the few proverbs she could actually recite in Dutch, because Rhetta had drilled it into her since she was twelve, when it happened: the past is gone, and no one can change it.

She'd opened her mouth to take another bite when something shot past the leaves with the sound of scissors through wrapping paper and slammed into her wicker basket.

The world spun and tilted. Branch after branch whacked her body all the way down until she landed flat on her back. She wheezed and fought for air as if a ten-kilo bag of sand had been dropped on her chest.

Her heart pounded in her ears, and her mind screamed at her. *What the hell?*

The rabbit—at first spooked by her sudden decision to rejoin him—promptly settled next to her and began to nibble on the apple still clutched in her hand. She struggled up onto one elbow and pushed his face away, gasping for breath. "Not…helpful."

She arched her back to feel for anything broken and then flopped onto her stomach in the dew-dipped grass, her lungs burning with the effort. She wheezed again, and goose bumps skipped down her arms. She got to all fours and scrambled backward until she rammed into the tree. She sat up and pressed herself to the slender trunk, finally managing to catch her breath.

The wicker basket sat lopsided on the ground nearby. Juice oozed out around an arrow embedded deep in the basket's side. Had it struck a few centimeters to the left, it would have pierced her like mutton on a spit.

She shifted against the trunk to peer behind her, but none of the other residents seemed to pay her any attention as they meandered along the covered corridors that encircled the garden's perimeter. She tugged on her skirt hem as she crouched against the tree. Everyone else wore pants and long-sleeved T-shirts this late in August, while there she was, publicizing her purple panties to any casual observer. But then, she hadn't planned on diving for cover to avoid becoming a pincushion!

She yanked on her skirt again and swept her eyes along the top of the battlements, where a few of the younger residents usually hung out. But there was no bow-wielding culprit in sight, so the arrow had not come from there. The back field. Had to be from the back field. That would have been the right direction, the way it came tearing through her poor Elstar apple tree.

She tried to flag down some passersby. "Hey! Did you see that?" she rasped. "Hey, listen!" When a few of the women stopped and stared at her, she gestured toward her wicker basket. "Did any of you see that?"

They continued to stare.

She dug her nails into the half-eaten apple she still held. "It was attempted homicide! How could you not notice?"

Their gazes moved to her legs. Then all of the women exchanged smirks.

Vanessa's face heated. *Really? We're going to ignore the Arrow of Death but not my fashion choices?* But just as she opened her mouth again, they bustled away. *Wait, did they just—?*

Vanessa snapped her mouth closed and shoved herself away from the tree to stand up. She flung the apple to the ground and leaned down to wrench the arrow from the side of the basket. She gripped it above her like a club, and her voice echoed off the stone walls. "Does anyone care that someone just tried to screw me from behind?"

With that, people did pause and look at her again.

She blinked. "I mean, skewer. Someone tried to skewer me from behind. From behind the fort, I mean."

A few more residents emerged from the surrounding hallways and stood between the arched columns of the perimeter, glancing at one another.

She shook the arrow at a cluster of elderly women to her right. "Damn it, I'm not crazy! If you want proof, just look at my backside!" Her cheeks flared, and she squeezed her eyes shut. "My basket. I meant basket. It was a sneak attack from the rear...uh, from the back field and right into my...I mean—"

Stop. Just stop, Vanessa.

No one else in the garden even paused after that. Big surprise. Her unpredictable yap often made her easy to ignore. But come on, this was different!

A bead of wetness rolled down her right wrist. She lowered the arrow to look at it. Wrapped around the shaft was a piece of paper, soggy from the juice of the pierced apples. She tucked a stray lock of hair behind one ear and unrolled the sticky sheet to detach it. There was big bold writing across the page: Knock, knock!

She shook her head. Had to be one of the kids from the town pulling a prank, especially if it came in from the outside. The people of Achterwaartsstad already thought the compound residents were a bunch of freaks for making their home in a rundown military fort from the seventeen hundreds, so not a shocker if this had been a random joke. Vanessa examined the bright red fletches. The arrow was finely made and was, in fact, too long for a child to handle with any accuracy.

She gave a wry smile. Too bad it hadn't landed in Caretaker Dijkstra's scrawny ass. The so-called leader of the compound would make a tempting target for anyone acquainted with the pretentious Dutchman. He was convinced that his knowledge and importance far outweighed his youth, despite the fact that he had the temperament of a candy-fueled toddler.

And then she heard it: that cringeworthy sound of the caretaker's voice as it whined through one of the perimeter passageways. Vanessa looked over the low wall that ran the length of the orchard to separate it from the rest of the garden. And there was Dijkstra making his way toward the rear entrance, his angular face pinched and covered with sweat. Several members of his personal kiss-ass brigade followed closely on his heels.

"People? What do you mean there are people out back?" Dijkstra demanded, the "v" and "d" sounds in his speech thicker under his overt bad mood so that it came out as "*Vut* do you mean *der* are people…" His accent was more pronounced than a lot of the other residents. It was a little jarring, considering her parents had raised her to speak English with more precise articulation.

The caretaker tugged on the collar of his embroidered tunic, while his aide scuttled alongside him. He had obviously deluded himself into thinking he was a feudal lord, out of place in this day and age, but still dressed as if he were a duke lounging in his pajamas. No one else would be caught dead in something that looked like their ancient ancestor's muumuu. Just because the residents all lived in an archaic dump didn't mean they had no sense of modern vogue.

"Sir, there are a great many of them." The assistant's hands flailed. "Fifty, I think. Maybe even a hundred. They appeared by the back woods ten minutes ago. They do not look friendly."

The several residents who trailed the caretaker bobbed their heads in agreement like a covey of quail.

"Vell, vut do dey vahnt?"

Vanessa squinted. Whatever was going on, it really had Dijkstra's tunic in a twist, because she had to work harder at translating. *Got it: "Well, what do they want?"*

The caretaker wiped his hands on his chest and left streaks of white powder that had most assuredly come from his interrupted breakfast of oliebollen. His obsession with the fried raisin-stuffed dough balls was notorious. "Schiet op!" Dijkstra barked at the aide and waved his hands ahead of him.

The aide picked up his pace. "We don't know what they want. They haven't approached yet so we could ask." The aide snatched Dijkstra's sleeve. "Sir, they're armed. Every one of them."

Even from far away, the note of hysteria in the assistant's voice was clear. Something simmering in the back of Vanessa's brain made her look down at the handwritten message:

Knock, knock!

An object buzzed by above, and she jerked her head up. A small spidery-looking drone circled briefly and then hovered over the fort. She winced as bright beams of orange light cascaded outward from all sides of the tiny black aircraft and created a burning, crackling dome over the entire compound. All the people who now wandered out from every corner of the fort stopped and stared above them at the glowing vault of light.

She glanced again at the paper note. *No, not a prank. A warning.*

Vanessa kicked her basket out of the way and hurled herself through one of the openings in the long wall. She wove her way around the fruit and vegetable beds as she headed for the rear gates. Maybe she could make it in time to intercept the caretaker and his entourage now that they had all slowed down to gape at the pulsating orange ceiling.

"Caretaker! Wait a minute!" She waved the arrow in front of her. "Caretaker, hold on! Something's not—"

He didn't hear her.

Or he's ignoring me.

She pressed her lips together and ran faster. She was only meters away, close enough to count the number of white pastry-powder handprints on the caretaker's tunic, when the sound of a low, muffled boom in the distance stopped her in mid-step.

Apprehensive silence gripped the compound.

Then an explosion burst the massive double doors off their hinges.

CHAPTER TWO

VANESSA

The shock wave spun Vanessa so hard that she hit the ground on her knees. Something rough grazed her arm while the repeated thud of falling debris surrounded her. She opened her eyes and felt along her jaw with her fingers, afraid her teeth had rattled out of her skull. She shook her head as a dull ringing grew in her ears.

What the hell? What the hell? What the hell?

Coughing, Vanessa climbed to her feet, her legs wobbly. She turned to look at the rear gates. One of the doors lay flat, split halfway down the center, while the other had crashed against the opposite side of the archway. Jagged splinters of wood and chunks of stone littered the ground and corridor. The quiet that followed seemed unreal, every sound wiped out by that single deafening blast. It was like childhood stories in which a dark predator, so deadly, would enter an area of the forest, and every scratching wood mouse, every songbird, every insect would fall mute as it neared.

Her skin went cold. *What kind of monster is making its way toward us?*

More residents rushed into the garden to see what the noise was about. They burbled to each other at the sight of the glowing orange dome overhead and the heavy oak gates torn away from the rear entrance. The acrid smell of smoke and dust floated through the air. The caretaker had clambered to his feet but stayed back among the others, as if he too were merely a bystander and not the undaunted hero of the compound that he professed to be.

Vanessa's breath caught in her throat as a huge hulk of a man stepped through the hazy doorway and eyed the small crowd in the corridor. His thick black mustache and smooth bald head made him a surreal character, like a baleful genie materializing from an old oil lamp. More men filed in, led by a burly brown-bearded stranger wearing a kilt and walking with a mechanical prosthetic leg—the length of it painted red and crisscrossed by green lines—that whirred and clunked with each step. Then a few other armed men in contrasting uniforms trotted by and sprinted up the nearby stairs to position themselves along the battlements above. What a diverse crew they were, like someone had shaken all the countries together in a bowl, grabbed a handful of people, and flung them at the compound. And there was something careful and calculated about how all this was playing out. They had done this before.

Fear, like a finger of ice, traced its way down Vanessa's spine.

Marauders.

But why would they attack here, in this tiny rural corner of Europe? There was food and money in the fort, but not gobs of either.

What happens when they find out that we don't even have electricity or creature comforts? What happens when a bunch of bandits get angry?

She stiffened.

And why am I standing so close to all of them?

She was about to back up, when another man appeared through the smoky gateway. He was tall and lean, but well-built. His hair was cropped short and raven-black, the same inky shade as his mustache and goatee. He motioned silently to two men behind him with rifles slung over their shoulders. He nodded toward both ends of the garden, where some of the residents were getting hysterical. The armed men took off and expertly corralled the panicked people who'd tried to flee back into the halls of the fort. Apparently, fifty-some-odd residents were no match for one pair of experienced invaders. These guys knew what they were doing, all right.

The raven-haired man stopped to survey the garden, but then his gaze rested on her. Again, she was standing way too close, because she could clearly make out the color of those eyes that now riveted her in place: deep bluish gray, like a storm darkening the North Sea sky.

Then behind the raven-haired man appeared a strange apparition. Vanessa stared at the newcomer as one of the resident women nearby emitted a frightened "God allemachtig!" The hooded figure seemed to be male and was dressed in a long robe of impenetrable blackness. Like an unholy monk, come to damn them all. Though he did wear a long-sleeved shirt beneath it, the robe itself had no sleeves, and so the black grip of a gun poked into view at his left hip. Maybe the open-sided robe gave him the freedom to draw his weapon at a moment's notice. And blow someone's head off. That thought made her shoulders go rigid.

Damn, why was she still standing there? If ever there was a time to belt out a healthy scream and run for the hills, it was then.

Don't notice me. Please don't notice me.

He didn't. He focused instead on Dijkstra, who cowered with his followers. The robed man stopped in front of the caretaker and tugged on the bottom of each of his black gloves. Since the sleeveless robe gave visibility to the long-sleeved black shirt beneath it, it highlighted how much the muscles on the stranger's arms stretched the shirt's fabric when he moved. Okay. Evil druid guy. But a very buff evil druid guy who could probably hold his own in hand-to-hand combat. She scanned him from his black boots to the top of his hooded head. And very tall. An uber-druid.

She gripped the arrow tighter and wrapped her arms around herself as she debated again about the best way to back up without drawing attention to herself. She glanced away from the towering hooded figure, but her stomach clenched when she saw that the raven-haired man still watched her.

"Are you in charge?" the robed man asked Dijkstra.

Finally, he speaks.

Mr. Tall-Dark-and-Violent was evidently a fan of huge dramatic pauses, considering how long they had all been staring at each other. The caretaker, however, couldn't *stop* staring. His aide nudged him in the back, and Dijkstra jumped. Then he inched forward.

"I am Caretaker Dijkstra." He glanced around at all the residents, who watched him expectantly. He held his chin higher and injected a tone of arrogance into his words...though not enough to hide the tremor in his voice. "I demand to know who you are and why you have attacked us!"

The tall figure pushed back his hood. His head was completely covered by a black cloth, with openings only for his eyes and mouth. He glanced once to the side, away from her, showing that the cloth had been crudely pinned together in the back. He had apparently spared *every* expense on a decent mask.

"If we had actually attacked you, Caretaker, then you wouldn't be alive to have this conversation." Uber-Druid had no discernible accent, but there was a certain subtle cadence to the rhythm of his speech that was oddly compelling. The quiet menace in his voice, however, cut through the hope that he would be tolerant of anyone who stood in his way. "Don't make me change my mind. I don't have time to drag all your corpses out of my new base."

The caretaker's mouth dropped open. "New base?"

Vanessa's mouth dropped open in turn. *That's* the part he was worried about? Had he totally missed the word "corpses"?

"N-no," Dijkstra said. "No, you can't do this. I-I won't allow it."

"Then we'll have to get rid of you." The masked

intruder's voice was low, the rumble of it seeming to ripple the air around him. "You choose: in the head or in the chest."

A distinct click came from the other side of the robed figure, where the giant bald genie stood. The caretaker paled as the mustached strongman pointed a long, brightly chromed pistol at him.

"But I'm the one who holds this compound together." Sweat began to flow in sheets down Dijkstra's neck. "It can't function without me."

"Head or chest?" the robed man asked more firmly.

Vanessa's eyes jumped between the stony faces that hovered near the strange leader.

Uber-Druid held back his shoulders. "Morgan!"

With one smooth step, the raven-haired man stood silently at his commander's side.

"Flip a coin."

"Please, wait!" Caretaker Dijkstra held up his palms and then clasped them in front of himself. "There doesn't need to be bloodshed. We'll open our home to you. I'm sure we can find a way to accommodate all your men. We'll share whatever we have!"

"This compound became mine when we blew your doors to shit," Uber-Druid said sharply. "We don't need your permission or your hospitality."

At that, the man named Morgan nodded at the shaven-headed stranger still pointing the chromed gun. The huge man stepped forward and pressed the muzzle of his weapon to the caretaker's temple.

Vanessa stumbled forward. "He's a giant pain in the ass, but he's not worth killing!"

All heads turned in her direction.

The edges of the crumpled note cut into her palm, and her heartbeat pounded in her throat. *Oh no. Why did I do that?*

She couldn't even blink. Everyone's focus was on her. Some men's gazes traveled the length of her body with more than mere curiosity, and her face roasted under the inspection. But the breath rushed from her lungs when

Uber-Druid fixed his gaze on her.

His eyes. So green, they couldn't be real. Bright and burning. A tiger's stare from the depths of wooded shadows. She locked her knees.

And now I have the beast's attention.

The robed man spoke directly to her then, and there was a clear growl in his voice. "Maybe you'd like to take his place instead."

Her legs grew numb. Morgan stared steadily at her and then gave a subtle shake of his head. A warning to keep quiet. But it didn't work.

"It wouldn't matter anyway," she said, her voice shaking. "It would still be a mistake you can't fix."

The back of her neck tingled painfully, and she squeezed her eyes shut. *What is wrong with you, Vanessa?*

At last, as the ensuing silence closed around her like a vise, she pried open one eye. The robed man watched her for a few seconds longer. Then her knees weakened in relief when he turned back to Dijkstra.

"Well, Caretaker Pain-in-the-Ass, evidently you have one advocate." The man paused, and he must have shifted his gaze to the people behind Dijkstra by the way they all flinched. "Unless someone else wants to vouch for you."

The caretaker's tongue flashed, lizard-like, across his lips. He looked around, but not even the brownnosers behind him made a sound.

"Looks like you're taking a trip. Sergeant Maxwell"—Uber-Druid signaled the man in the kilt forward—"if you don't mind…"

"Aye, Captain!" The bearded man seized the caretaker so hard that the brawny sergeant's long, braided ponytail whipped up over one shoulder. He held a basket-handled broadsword in his other fist, like he'd been extracted mid-charge from some battle in the dreary Scottish moors. His mechanical leg clunked with each footfall as he half-walked, half-dragged Dijkstra toward the rear archway, which still smoked from whatever explosive the marauders had used. The Scotsman shoved the caretaker out through the opening.

The captain stood in the gateway while Dijkstra regained his balance. The volume of the captain's voice rose just enough that it carried. "Show your face here again, or contact the town authorities, and *I'll* decide where to put the bullet. And I'll make sure you bleed out slowly."

The caretaker turned and visibly trembled at the mass of men—maybe thirty to forty soldiers who seemed to be of all races and nationalities. Some reclined against military-type cars dotting the expansive back field, and others hung out from what looked like a huge brown-camouflaged transport vehicle. But all of them silently awaited orders from their robed leader.

One tall and heavily muscled Black man with a clean-shaven head stood in the front of the group and leaned on a gun with a revolving canister in the middle of it. It did not seem to be a normal kind of weapon, like the hunting rifle her father had owned when she was a kid. This thing looked like it could lob small bombs with each trigger pull. Judging by the markings on the man's sleeve, he was some kind of high-ranking officer. He scratched his chin and flipped the weapon up to rest on his shoulder as he chewed his gum. He was probably the one responsible for the well-aimed strike to the old doors, since he maneuvered the mammoth gun as effortlessly as she handled a garden trowel. But what kind of marauders went to the trouble of smashing their way in, when they could have just taken one look around the decrepit fort and walked through the gaping hole already in the east wall? These guys were either impetuous or unobservant.

Caretaker Dijkstra whirled, and his mouth swung open and closed a few times like a dumbfounded marionette. He spread his hands wordlessly toward his former sycophants, who were huddled far back from the strangers. Then, with one last glance at the captain, Dijkstra seemed to wither inside his lordly tunic before he trudged out of sight. He was no doubt making his way toward the front of the compound, since the small town to the south seemed the only logical refuge.

The captain pulled his hood back up and rotated to

face her. Even from afar, his green eyes glowed in the gloom of the cowl. She held her breath. But then he pivoted again, and his polished black boots sent his footfalls ricocheting off the corridor walls as he strode away.

His men did not follow but instead exited the compound, where Morgan shouted instructions to the assembled marauders in a surprisingly refined English accent. She turned her head when a new voice echoed through the garden.

"Hey, me cocks, luh! A welcome basket!" A young man with a wild nest of dishwater-blond hair—like a scarecrow wearing a messy wig—stood in the orchard and hefted her basket high to show his comrades. Then he caught sight of Vanessa and bounded toward her with a broad smile. "Is this from you, ducky?" he called out. "That was a right thoughtful thing!" By his accent, he obviously wasn't Dutch either.

He sauntered to meet her as he adjusted the old-timey curvy bow that was slung over his shoulder. He pulled a long red-fletched arrow out of the quiver on his back and halted in front of her.

"We don't usually be gettin' presents, eh?" He stabbed the arrow's head into one of the green-skinned apples in her basket and took a bite from the speared fruit. "I'm Thomas Mercer, best point man booze can buy." A fleck of apple flew past her head as he forced the garbled words out. "Who do you belong to?"

She shifted her weight to one foot. "Uh…"

He pointed the impaled apple at the paper still clutched in her hand and spoke as he chewed. "I sees you got our message: knock, knock! Pretty good joke, wha'?" He swung the apple around to point it at the mustached man who now made his way across the garden. "That was Frank's idea. Russian sense o' humor. He's a real comedian!"

Well, that was unlikely. Tucking his chrome-barreled gun in his waistband, the bald giant glowered at every person he passed, as if they had woken him from a sound sleep and made him come down off his beanstalk.

Thomas clamped the apple-ended arrow between his jaws and pulled the message arrow through her fist. "Thanks for keepin' this warm, trout," he said through his teeth as he slipped it into the quiver behind him. He spat the apple-arrow into his hand and shoved the wicker basket at her. She grabbed the handle as she tottered back a step. Thomas caught her arm and tossed a grin toward the orchard. "Ay b'y, you got any other of those kinds of apples over there? Like McIntosh or Gravenstein? Used to have them ones back home in Newfoundland."

Ay b'y? What does that even mean?

Once more, intelligent speech escaped her. "Uh…"

He took another bite from his fruit-on-a-stick and talked around his mouthful. "Loves to score me a couple fresh off the tree, I would. Have a right good scoff, some quick. I'd have 'em back to me room…wherever that ends up being." He stopped chewing, and his face lit up. "Hey, maybe we'll gets to be roomies!"

When she didn't move, Thomas jiggled her arm and nodded at the orchard. Still hugging the basket against her chest like a child with a teddy bear, she led him toward the center of the garden.

Well, congratulations, Vanessa. You got your "adventure."

Because now this place was anything but safe.

CHAPTER THREE

ETHAN

Like we're stuck in a goddamn time warp.

Captain Ethan Evans pulled his robe's hood forward to block the late-afternoon light that flashed at him through a rough-cut window as he turned down another dank hallway. The layout of the stronghold was unusual, but his gut told him this was the way back to the central area of the compound where the spacious garden lay. It was only day one of his occupation, but he had an affinity for learning his environment quickly. Adaptability was key to survival. He had already located the caretaker's quarters and chucked his well-worn rucksack onto the bed. The temptation to collapse beside it and close his eyes for a few minutes had been hard as hell to resist. But he needed to keep moving so he could evaluate their surroundings.

Next on the agenda was to assess the size of the armory. It would probably be located near the garden for easy access. Most likely, the room would not be big enough to accommodate his army's heavier artillery. But this was the first time he had ever commandeered a fort— or any structure built for battle, ancient though it was—so it might surprise him. Regardless, it was a lesser concern than the many vulnerabilities inherent in a decaying building full of potential dissidents. Above all, he needed to keep the flock in check.

That busty blond girl from this morning required a little further scrutiny, though. He could read the unrest in many of the others' faces, but she had been the only one to attempt defiance—even if her words had been half-hearted. The caretaker didn't strike him as a man that people gave two real shits about. But the fact that she'd been able to stay Ethan's hand and defend the incompetent fuck showed she had more backbone than the rest of them. And that could make her useful.

He could certainly make use of those long legs of hers, were circumstances different. His success rate with women had always been gratifyingly high, back when he had the benefit of his old face. But even if he had any inclination to bed someone in his present condition, he'd had his fill of floozies who were interested only in ingratiating themselves with a man in power. And she was probably the same breed of bimbo.

He pushed the robe's hood back off his head and smoothed his mask with a hand. He returned the salutes of two of his soldiers but disregarded the timid looks he received from the residents he swept past. They were a low-grade threat compared to the hostiles who had been dogging his steps for the past two years.

The Ukrainians were still out there, nipping at his army's heels. Though they had not shown themselves in months, their absence proved nothing. At any point, one of their runners could start baying at Ethan's back and alert the larger enemy contingent. The runner would no doubt be a carbon copy of the first one Ethan's men had ever captured, back in Belarus: vindictive, single-minded, and righteous. In that initial encounter—before the bastard even finished choking down the poison pill hidden in his teeth—he'd delivered with a sneer the same English-memorized message that would later be uttered by every runner to follow. It was directed at Ethan alone and each time worded exactly: *You cannot burn us. You cannot kill us. We will bury you screaming beneath the bodies of your men.*

Ethan's army was then left with a useless carcass and no way to find the implanted tracking device so they could cut it out and silence the signal. Cracking open a can of gas and tossing a match on the dead fucker worked well enough. Turned out they still *could* burn after all. But the flames that ate away those bodies were probably nothing compared with the fate his pursuers were planning for him, if they ever got their hands on him. Because he'd gone too far, reached too deep inside his well of rage so that he'd drowned himself in it. What he'd done to them in Ukraine wasn't his only sin in life, by far. But it was the one that he might not survive.

The light was brighter up ahead. He was finally closer to the garden. But he paused at a door left partially open. He nudged the heavy slab of oak, and it swung inward with a slow creak. He scanned the room.

It was obviously a resident's cubbyhole. There was a bed covered with a checkered quilt, a small soot-filled fireplace, and personal effects strewn about. He frowned at a faint whiff of lavender from an air freshener. This, like so many other rooms he'd passed, was evidently once part of the original barracks that had been partitioned into separate quarters. Every room against the outside of the compound also boasted a glass window that could be unlatched and opened to the cool autumn breezes. But exterior windows were a weakness and therefore uncommon in historic military forts. Just one more item on his list of things that were wrong with this place. It was strange that these people had decided to make their home in a ramshackle fortress, but maybe they were more concerned with living under the radar than living in comfort.

At least that's one thing we all have in common.

He continued toward the end of the hallway. But as he emerged and turned to walk along one of the garden's perimeter corridors, he missed a step and did a double-take. In the middle of the garden, a pair of his soldiers, Liam and Thomas, huddled together. They were intent on something in the grass in front of them. Thomas—his blond hair, as usual, in the same disarray as a mongrel puppy—was bent over with his hands on his knees. Liam squatted on the ground and extended his arm with something white in his hand. There was movement in front of them, where a small, furry, black-and-white creature sat nestled amid the green blades. The animal rose up on its haunches as Liam waved the chunk of white at it.

Ethan ground his teeth. Perfect. Now he was running an army *and* a petting zoo.

"What the hell are you two doing?" Ethan said as he stalked across the garden toward them.

The rabbit took off in a dead run, and the men groaned.

"Aw, Cap, you scared 'im!" Thomas said as he straightened.

"Sure, look at the ugly little fella go." Liam hung his hand with the piece of parsnip over his knee and shook his head. "And what a trail of pellets you made him leave, the poor wee lad."

Ethan crossed his arms and directed a hard look at the young Irishman. Liam, getting the message, jumped to his feet. Both soldiers hastily saluted him.

"Why are you men not up on the ramparts at your posts?" he asked crisply.

"It's just that we'ms both of us done double duty this whole past week on the road, Cap." Thomas rubbed a hand in the back of his disheveled hair. "I mean, sweet Elijah's balls, we's all lookin' like we gone and been hauled through knotholes, but Donegan and me's is sure feelin' it now, b'y."

"Lieutenant Winchester seen how knackered we were and relieved us for the day with replacements." Liam nodded up at the battlement walkway, where several armed men paced and kept watch on the surrounding land.

Ethan ground his teeth harder. "And did Morgan also give you permission to stand around with your thumbs up your asses?"

"Well"—Thomas glanced at Liam—"not in so many words, exactly, but—"

"This isn't summer camp and you're not on vacation." Ethan narrowed his eyes at each of them. "If you need rest, then get some sleep. Otherwise, if you're going to wander around, then I'll find something for you to do." He'd started to turn away when Liam piped up.

"Actually, Cap, since you're of a mind to mention it, there's somethin' we'd like to talk to you about."

"Yes?"

"Any way we can put an extra bed in our room?" Liam's spirited accent was dampened by the tentative question. "I mean, I know we've been doublin' up wherever we go, but it'd be fuckin' great if I could have a bed to myself for once."

"We won't be here more than a couple of months, Private. Make do with what you have."

Thomas stepped forward. "But, Cap—"

"He gets randy in his sleep!" Liam waved a thumb at the Canadian soldier. "One time, I woke up with his one hand on my arse and the other grabbin' my—"

Thomas pointed at Liam. "He farts."

"That's a fuckin' lie!"

"Peels the paint off the walls, by Jibber," Thomas said with a grimace.

Liam whirled on him. "Jaysus Christ, Newfie, I'm gonna lamp you if you say another word!"

Thomas calmly gave Liam the finger.

So help me, if I don't put them both in front of a firing squad—

"One of you sleep on the floor," Ethan grated. "Are we done here?"

"Ya hear that, Tommy?" Liam motioned at Ethan with his head. "Cap says you have to sleep on the floor."

"Oh no, I gets the bed! I had to sleep on the floor the last place we was at, eh?"

"We *all* had to sleep on the fuckin' floor the last place we were at—"

"Enough!" Ethan uncrossed his arms. "Gentlemen, I don't give a shit how you do it, but work it out."

The two men fell silent as they knitted their brows and

exchanged looks like scolded schoolboys.

Ethan jerked his hood back up over his head. "And stop playing with the wildlife."

"Whoa now, stall the ball there, Cap." Liam held up his hands, the parsnip still pinched between his fingers. "That rabbit's not just wildlife, ya know. He's a mascot."

"Ands he's got a name now, too," Thomas added.

Ethan felt a headache spread into his temples. If his concentration had not been interrupted before this, it was fucking blown apart now.

"There are those who call him"—Liam cocked his head—"Tim."

Thomas put the back of his hand against his mouth and crooked two of his fingers. "A wee rabbit with big, pointy, scary teeth." He paused and folded back one finger. "Well, tooth."

Ethan tugged on the chin of his mask. "Well, the next time I see Tim, he'd better be in a stew."

Both men gasped and recoiled with a hand to their chest.

"But you can't cook Tim," Liam sputtered.

"Both of you report to Lieutenant Okusanya," Ethan said, ignoring the frowns on their faces. "We're not sending out recon teams till tomorrow, but I'm sure Mabayoje can run you through some drills to keep you busy in the meantime." With a shake of his head, he turned and started back across the garden to resume his search for the armory.

Several residents milled within the halls and talked in whispers as they glanced at the guards who trooped past them on their rounds. He looked over every face, but the blond girl was not among them. She seemed to have disappeared since that morning. Ethan tapped his fingers against his leg as he walked. His soldiers better keep their distance from her. It had been a long time since any of them had come across a piece of eye candy that sweet, so he didn't need them distracted. Her parts were fitted in a perfect assembly that could keep a man's imagination running in high gear...enough to burn out his engine before he even thought to put the brakes on.

And you'll have smoke pouring out from under your own hood, Evans, if you don't fucking snap to.

Ethan pulled the sleeveless sides of his robe up farther on his shoulders and flexed his hands. They all needed to get their heads straight after weeks of hauling ass. The old Dutch fort was a gift, considering how remote it was, stuck in a largely ignored speck of North Holland after the country's government dickheads had cleared out so many of its people. He'd been right to head directly for it in the hopes that it would throw off any Ukrainian runners trying to sniff him out. But his sentries would be ready to eliminate any stranger wearing the telltale bloodred "badge": a strip of nylon fabric tied around an arm. As one captured runner had proudly revealed, each of them had torn a piece from the mostly incinerated banner that had hung outside their little civilian community. A community that Ethan had, with one fateful command, decimated. Two years had passed, and yet the memory of that building exploding around him was a fresh fucking purgatory.

The gnarled, burned flesh beneath his robe crawled, and he pushed aside the sickening image of his own butchered anatomy. It was the consequence of savagery. He had reforged himself in fire, in the most literal sense, and man had become monster. All because he had needed his vengeance. His vision clouded, despite the bright day.

And now vengeance was serving a new master.

A loud *pop!* interrupted his thoughts. He snapped his head up just as the bright orange alarm shield encasing the compound vanished. The hovering drone wobbled and dropped like a dead spider into one of the nearby apple trees.

Ethan peered at the black-legged bot as it dangled from a limb. *Goddamn it.*

He jerked on the cuffs of his gloves to pull them tighter and walked to the orchard. He strained over the long, low wall and wrenched the jittering drone from the tree. The broken gears of the small aircraft clicked and whirred as he held it out beside him and started for the rear entrance.

He'd told Nicolo this piece of shit wasn't worth tinkering with anymore, even though the mechanic had insisted it still had some life left in it. And, sure enough, all the effort spent on bio-coding the drone's laser streams to each soldier's DNA signature had been a fucking waste of time. Now, instead of letting the drone's security shield do most of the work of detecting when one of the residents passed through it, he would have to double-up the perimeter so his sentries could stop any runaways. Morgan often ragged on Ethan about his Welsh-born temper, but this particular fuck-up demanded a serious ass-reaming.

On his way to give Nicolo an earful, he swept his eyes by the open door of the kitchen, where a girl was bending over to pick something off the floor. He slowed. There was something very familiar about those legs, even from the back. When she straightened and turned, he stopped walking altogether.

It was the blond girl from that morning. And she was still dressed like a barmaid angling for tips. Showing so much skin was a bold move, considering all the new eyes around her now. Unless she was naïve enough to think it didn't matter. She used a small brush to clear crumbs off a table into a dustpan, and Ethan let his gaze loiter on the parts of her that jiggled with her movements.

I bet she can't hide those curves even if she tried.

The girl glanced up. They stood for a moment with their eyes locked. She gave him a feeble wave with her brush. But the motion tipped the dustpan in her other hand and she bobbled the tools, spilling dust and clumps of food down the front of her clothes. She held the items against herself, her face reddening. Then she backed away and disappeared into the rear of the kitchen.

Ethan stood for a moment longer. *So. Ballsy when she wants to be. But not exactly a threat.*

He was long past military training. A weaponized nomad trying to survive the political neurosis gripping the world. But her youth and vulnerability gave him an edge, as long as she was bright enough not to challenge him again. He needed information. She was a resource, much like this compound and the food and shelter it provided. And as for her other qualities…

Wouldn't hurt to get a close-up reconnaissance of those later.

He looked down when the drone made a grinding noise and bumped insistently against his thigh. Ethan gave the chin of his mask a tug and held the vibrating aircraft out to the side. He strode to the fort's broken back entrance, where the Boxer MRAV sat idling while his men unloaded the last of the munitions from the armored transport.

Once he got everything squared away with his men for the night, he and that quirky blond were going to have a little meeting.

CHAPTER FOUR

VANESSA

Vanessa stood outside the kitchen in the evening gloom and fiddled with the buttons undone at her cleavage as she watched all the strangers pass through the garden and along the passageways in the distance. She had changed out of her favorite peasant top that morning, after her crash landing had smeared it with dirt, grass, and rabbit fur. But because her clothes rarely went unpunished, she had then managed to coat herself with hairballs and table scraps later in the afternoon.

She fished a piece of lint from between her breasts and glared at it before flicking it away. *It was all his fault, sneaking up on me like that. I should dump the next dustpan on his dinner instead.*

But as much as she would have liked to give him her best stink-eye for having to re-sweep the kitchen floor, there was no sign of the enigmatic Captain Evans tonight. She had discerned by watching him throughout the day that he was the brooding keep-to-himself type. He was probably off sulking in a dark closet somewhere counting his bullets.

She wrapped a hand over her shoulder to massage it as she stretched her neck from one side to the other. That tumble from the tree had finally caught up with her. *Thanks a ton, Thomas. Hope those apples give you gas.*

But the bruise on her backside was nothing compared with the black eye the compound had just gotten. Her plans to leave had changed drastically, but now everyone was under the same lockdown. She was no longer the only prisoner there.

A small huddle of residents pushed past without so much as excusing themselves when they bumped her aside. She scowled at their backs as they shuffled into the dining room. Inside the cooking area, Rhetta was a blur of brown apron and gray hair, issuing orders and stirring a wobbly pot of canned tomato sauce—which Vanessa knew the head cook regarded with scorn, as it was beneath her standards. The whole staff was on hand to prep more food to accommodate the unwelcome arrivals who had now turned the small world within the residents' home upside down.

Vanessa plucked at her bottom lip with her teeth. The soldiers looked so comfortable with cementing their control, as if they had done this a hundred times before. They were businesslike and alert, moving with practiced efficiency as they set up an outer perimeter around the compound and mounted guns along the parapets above. The modern weapons looked odd next to the fort's collection of old rusted cannon. And although each man had different markings on his uniform, with the exception of Morgan and the captain, they all bore the same colorful patch sewn onto their sleeves or chests: a red dragon and a golden lion standing back-to-back on their hind legs against a deep ocean-blue background. Some kind of flag that they all rallied around? But they didn't seem to be zealots, just a united team.

Vanessa straightened back against the corridor wall as two older male residents sidled past.

Overall, this takeover appeared to be more of a routine chore for them, as if the residents were not a major factor in any of it, only something the invaders needed to secure. Like shuttering one's windows during a storm so that everything stayed in place and was safely contained. Their fancy techno light show must have gone on the fritz, though, since the orange dome had winked out of existence sometime that afternoon. It wasn't clear what its purpose had been, but it probably had something to do with keeping the residents penned in like mindless cattle.

She slapped her palms in a rhythm against the stone wall to either side of her as she ran her gaze along the ramparts, where several soldiers in a variety of uniforms briskly patrolled.

But their captain was the real mystery. What was with the unnecessarily destructive grand entrance he'd made? If he had intended to get their attention, then blindly shooting that arrow into the compound, where it could have caused some serious head trauma, should have been enough. Hell, simply standing on the doorstep in his crazy Grim Reaper getup would have done the trick.

After all, the robe was a bit much. Not everyone endured the crispness of the North Holland climate like she did, but it was hardly the Arctic. It was as over-the-top as his hokey homemade mask…though the blackness of the cloth certainly highlighted those razor-sharp green eyes. As soon as they'd sliced toward her, they'd carved her up like a melon. Like he'd wanted to eat her alive. She shivered and rubbed her arms. But as much as the captain glowered at everyone and floated solemnly through the halls of his newly conquered domicile, the soldiers' fearsome leader seemed more preoccupied with control than persecution.

"I know that look."

She turned. Cornelis had settled himself against the wall beside her.

Vanessa wrinkled her brow at him. "What look?"

He nodded up at the shadows gliding along the ramparts. "The one that says, 'Maybe they're not so bad after all. People are people.' "

She frowned at him. "I'm trying to figure them out, that's all."

He propped himself on a forearm. "There's not much to figure out, Ness. They attacked us. They threatened to murder the caretaker and would have done the same to any one of us, if we had resisted. And now they've taken over our home. How is this a puzzle?"

"But they haven't actually hurt anyone."

"Yet."

Cornelis fixed her in his gaze. His naturally gray hair—the color of emerging moonlight—curled close against his head, making his chiseled features seem deceptively older than his twenty-four years. She had spent many nights cuddled close to him in his bed, letting her fingers trail through those soft silver curls, back when they'd been dating. Each one of his smiles was so familiar. But so were every one of his frowns. Right then, he was giving her his *I-know-what's-best-for-you* frown. It was the one that annoyed her the most.

"Listen to me and take this seriously." He paused, as if to make sure he had her full attention. "This is a hostile occupation. These are not good guys. You need to be careful around them. Don't do what you always do."

She pushed away from the wall. "What is that supposed to mean?"

He straightened, and his crystal-blue eyes appeared to flash when they caught the light from the kitchen doorway. "Godverdomme, Ness! Don't be so damn accommodating to every stranger you meet."

A sudden cramp in her chest made her voice tremble. "You mean like how I was to the man who came looking for my parents?"

The sharp light in Cornie's eyes immediately dimmed. "That's not what I meant," he said more gently. "That was not your fault."

She shook her head and glanced down at her fingers as she picked at her apron. "That's what you always say."

"All I mean is that these viezeriken aren't even trying to hide their intentions. You can't trust them. They are not like us, and they do not care about us. They are enemies. Remember that." He glanced at a pair of soldiers passing close to them in the corridor. When he focused on her again, the corners of his mouth dipped. "And will you please button up?"

Vanessa put a hand over her cleavage. "I'm hot."

"In more ways than one. So don't advertise."

She leveled her shoulders. "No one's noticed but you."

He huffed a laugh. "You know better than that."

Vanessa folded her arms and bowed her head.

Cornelis's shadow darkened the stone walkway when he came to stand in front of her. "Look, I'm only trying to watch out for you, schatje." He squeezed her arms as his voice softened. "You know that I care about you."

Yes, she did. But though her conscience stung at breaking up with him, she had made the right decision. She'd known he had been on the verge of proposing to her that night long ago, but she'd been unable to ignore the nagging voice inside her that had whispered that he wasn't the one. She did miss him. She wouldn't deny that. But someone else—the right someone—was out there looking for her. She'd felt it then, and she felt it now. And the best way for her to help that nameless person find her was to leave this place far behind. Of course, that stratagem had gone out the window, thanks to recent events.

Cornelis sighed. "Are you even listening?"

"I don't need protection." She stiffened her shoulders when he furrowed his forehead. "I *don't*."

"But sometimes you need saving from yourself. Stop getting these random notions in your head. You've already drawn enough attention to yourself with that little stunt you pulled this morning, to save the caretaker."

Vanessa's stomach pinched at the thought of the captain's gaze cutting through her, dissecting her. She had certainly gotten *his* attention.

"Ness," Cornelis said, "promise me you'll be careful."

"I'll be fine, Cornie."

He angled his head. "You know I hate when you call me that."

She smiled slightly. "I know."

He mirrored her expression, though his jaw tightened like it always did when he was worried. "Just stay out of trouble. I mean it."

At last, she nodded. He caressed her cheek—his fingers gentle and lingering—and then he entered the kitchen to join the others.

Vanessa sighed and looked across the garden, where the dour-faced Frank stood seemingly as tall as her apple trees within the fort walls. The glowing orange dot of a lit cigar bobbed in front of the bald giant's mouth as he spoke to the equally towering, muscled Black man—Maba-something-or-other—who had blown up the compound gates. Dutch people had a reputation for being a tall bunch, but these foreigners were marching mountains! A group of male residents skirted around them and speed-walked past the orchard and toward the kitchen.

She shook her head. It was like two gargantuan Gullivers shooting the breeze while the Lilliputians gaped up at them, threw down their tiny ropes, and declared, "Screw this!"

She shook her head again and jerked at the knot on the back of her apron. Don't get into trouble, Cornelis had warned. Vanessa wadded up her apron like she was beating a ball of dough. She was not a pushover. Sure, maybe she was sheltered, but she wasn't naïve. And she was as concerned as anyone else about the danger to the compound. Not that any of them were bothering to do anything about it.

She bunched the apron against her belly. *Well then, Miss I'm-Not-a-Pushover…why don't* you *do something about it?*

Back when she still had a choice in the matter, she had planned to leave tonight anyway, as soon as her chores were done. Her bag was packed and waiting in the kitchen's walk-in pantry, shoved out of sight under a bottom shelf. No use altering her course. It would simply be a trickier approach this time: rather than traipse out the front gates, she could sneak through the hole in the east wall that the caretaker had neglected to have repaired. Once she made it to Achterwaartsstad, she could alert the constable.

A surge of acid soured her stomach. *I don't want to be*

more than a meter close to that bastard. Not after the way he—

Forget it. She would go directly to Mayor Visser instead.

She glanced down the hallway and then up at the battlement walkways where there were fewer soldiers than before. If the intruders were, in fact, overconfident that their captives were all complacent, then that would be to her advantage. And whatever that orange laser dome had been, its absence was probably a bonus to her escape plan.

She stepped through the kitchen door and started toward the pantry. She halted. No. Leave the packed bag. Lugging it along would slow her down. She could always retrieve it after the captain and his army were arrested and taken away. And then she could finally get as much distance from the compound as a few hitchhiked rides would take her. She hurled her apron at a nearby table and accidentally bopped one of the male residents in the back of the head with it. She hurried out before he could turn around.

Okay, Vanessa. Time to run. Her legs momentarily froze as her heart tripped over itself. It felt like there was a marble in her throat. *You can do this. You can do this. You can—Damn it, just go!*

She slipped down the one-sided corridor. She stayed in the shadows as much as possible as she made her way around the entire perimeter of the garden complex. Her nerves on edge, it felt like hours before she reached the east side of the fort, where the wall had long ago begun to crumble. In the three years since he had taken over in 2063, Caretaker Dijkstra had never bothered to have the enormous hole fixed. But praise his lazy ass! His failure had become her salvation. And hopefully the captain's army was ignoring the breach now in the same way as earlier, when they blew up the gates in fireball fashion!

Vanessa took a breath and peeked out the jagged opening. *Okay, no guards nearby. Now or never.* She started to duck through...

And then yelped as an arm wrapped around her waist and hauled her backward. The male body that pressed against her was lean and solid. His arm squeezed her tighter, and she let out a squeak. A deeply masculine voice came from right beside her ear, and it held the calm intensity of a steady-burning flame.

"Our marksmen are the most highly skilled in the continent, and they have a decided aversion to allowing their charges to flee." His words rolled with a rich English accent.

Morgan.

He let go and spun her onto her back against the stone wall. He leaned on his hands and caged her between his arms as she stared up into those dark, storm-blue eyes. He was clad in black jeans and a long-sleeved shirt—evidently in kinship with the captain—but his trim-fitting vest at least suggested a personal flair.

"Now what do you suppose your chances would have been, had your strategy succeeded?" Morgan asked, his gaze cool and statue-like.

She took a breath and held it for a second before puffing it out. "Considering the way this first part crashed and burned, I suppose the answer is…zilch?"

"Indeed." Though his face was expressionless, his voice carried a sensual tone, like a hypnotist about to lull her into a trance.

To tell the truth, she *was* mesmerized by him. The ink-black sheen of Morgan's hair was like a pond's surface at midnight—sleek and gleaming—mirroring the sable hue of his mustache and goatee. Those raven locks probably would have fallen in graceful waves, had they not been cut short. She bet if she reached out, his hair would be soft against her fingertips. The urge sent an abrupt quiver through her stomach.

She cleared her throat weakly. They'd been staring at each other in silence, his hands still flat on the wall behind her. "So, Lieutenant uh…"

"Winchester."

"So Lieutenant Winchester"—she clutched the sides of her skirt—"how many lashes do I get?"

"You're fortunate. We ceased that practice months

ago."

Part of her was not so sure that was a joke. She eyed the knife sheathed at his left side that counterbalanced the gun holstered on his right. *Don't any of these guys just carry one weapon at a time?* Her attention snapped back when he spoke again.

"You shall, instead, receive but one warning: do not attempt escape."

"That's it?" she said slowly. "You're not even going to tie me up?"

He flexed his arms against her shoulders. "Unless that is your preference."

Her mouth hung open as she hesitated. *What kind of restraints does he have in mind? Something silky would be nice…*

She shook herself. "But if I told you I wouldn't try it again," she said, "why would you even believe me?"

He tilted his head, and the corner of his mouth curled upward. "Because I am trusting that your capacity for deceit is no more worrisome than your aptitude for stealth."

Well, he was right about that.

His eyes continued to hold hers, and their depths shifted in the dim light like smoke drifting through an evening sky. And even though he let that stoic mask slip only marginally, there was an energy emanating from his body that coiled around her like a vine embracing a trellis. She struggled to slow her breathing when he shifted nearer, and she could feel that invisible vine starting to work its way into her every crevice.

"Fine, I'll stay put," she told him. "Cross my heart."

He dropped his gaze to her chest as she drew an X between her breasts with an index finger. But when he kept it there, she glanced down to see what he was staring at. Her face flared like a struck match.

Okay, so she'd truly meant to button her shirt back up. But then *this* stroke of genius had landed her here: captured, half-dressed, and in the very inviting hands of Lieutenant Lancelot. And to top it all off, a small snarl of hair with a cookie crumb stuck to it was still trapped in her cleavage, from where she had dumped the dustpan on herself earlier.

Well done, Vanessa. Make this as awkward as you possibly can.

Morgan raised his eyes, and the shadows in the corridor turned their color an even smokier blue. "Very well. I shall take you at your word." He straightened and lowered his hands to his sides. "But you are not free of me yet. Your presence has been requested."

She flattened herself against the wall. "It has?"

"The captain awaits you in his quarters. I have been sent to escort you."

Her stomach did a somersault. "And if I decline?"

This time the lieutenant showed no trace of a smile. "I advise you do not."

"Oh. Okay, then." She imagined the Englishman throwing her over his shoulder like a sack of grain if she said otherwise.

And would that be so bad?

"Cut it out," she muttered under her breath.

"Pardon?"

"I said…let's head out." She shrugged one shoulder. "Obviously, my schedule has lightened up for the evening."

At that, Morgan stepped closer and placed his hands on her hips.

"Hey!" She jerked back as he moved his fingers down the outsides of her thighs.

"Merely a precaution," he murmured as he continued his exploration to her skirt hem. His hands moved up to press across her stomach. Oh. He was patting her down for weapons. She held her breath when he stopped beneath her breasts.

Okay, but if he tries to pat those—

Morgan circled his arms around her and firmly glided his palms up the length of her back. All the while, his gaze never left hers. And her pulse never slowed down. At last, he stepped back and extended an arm toward the end of the passageway. "Shall we?"

She did not move at first. But then she sidled past him to start down the corridor. She glanced once over her shoulder. Morgan's tall figure passed languidly in and out of the deeper shadows cast by the stone pillars lining the open side of the walkway. She fumbled with her shirt to re-button it and then gripped her hands together as she stared ahead of her.

Now to find out what the hell Captain Creepy wanted.

CHAPTER FIVE

ETHAN

Ethan sat at the desk in the caretaker's bedroom and flipped through the packets of documents he'd found buried in a few boxes between some sacks of flour and jugs of cooking oil in one of the fort's commissaries. The caretaker's room now served as the captain's quarters...even though the state of it made him wish his mask came without eyeholes.

His gaze drilled across the décor. Overwrought wooden furniture spanned every stone-block wall. Plush scarlet pillows climbed the height of the bed's headboard, while immense gold tassels dangled from kelly-green velvet curtains that were tied back at the corners of the four-poster migraine. The same kind of draperies adorned the window of the room, the textiles so threadbare in places that they'd glowed like patchy pond scum when the sun had backlit them earlier that day. And he had been trying for the last hour to ignore the room-size oval rug that leaked over the wooden floor like a lumpy puddle. Its pattern was chaotic, with geometric shapes and fluorescent colors that had been testing his gag reflex since he walked in. At the moment, there was nothing to be done about the rug...

Or the throne-like chair angled against one corner...

Or the figurines of unicorns and scepter-waving wizards that cluttered the fireplace mantel…

Ethan pushed back the hood of his robe and sighed. First thing tomorrow, he'd order Morgan to throw every bejeweled and velveted eyesore onto a bonfire.

He opened his jaw wide to stretch his face against the mask and blinked back his exhaustion. He tossed a bundle of Fort Van Doorn brochures into the open box by his foot and leafed through the blank postcards depicting the compound from the air—sprawling and irregularly shaped, with spiky edges forming the double-storied bastions along its perimeter. He picked up a plastic-sealed pack of flyers that declared in English "We've Got Fort-itude!" in orange letters on a background of the red, white, and blue horizontal bars of the Netherlands flag. He shook his head and dropped them to pick up a rubber-banded stack of maps. Finally, something useful. He peeled one off and pulled open the glossy accordion folds:

Fort Adventure Map—Discover the Past and Declare Your Victory!

A cartoon rendering of the compound overwhelmed the page, spotted with dark blue bubbles containing orange numbers. In the corner was a small tally sheet labeled with the words "Find all 50 and win a free return ticket!" Ethan crumpled the map into a ball and swept everything back into the box on the floor.

He reached up and gripped his right shoulder when a cramp tightened the flesh and left it tingling. His scars were sore tonight due to all the constant movement. The sooner he could tunnel through the mountain of red pillows on the mattress and rip the sequined comforter out of his way, the sooner he could strip off every layer of clothing and let his body shut down for the night. The very feel of his garments was nothing more than a reminder of the disfigurement beneath them. Wearing anything to bed always made his dreams worse, and the last thing he needed was another rough night's sleep.

He'd have to push himself harder during his morning workout, to keep his toughened tissues flexible. Well before the sun broke the horizon, he would don his fatigues and leave the robe behind to start calisthenics. Since Morgan often joined him in his laps through whatever countryside they had set up camp in, he'd see if the lieutenant was up for it tomorrow. At least this place was equipped with adequate facilities, so that as soon as the sky began to brighten he could hit the showers…before he resigned himself to the familiar weight of his black armor.

Hearing footsteps, Ethan rose from the chair and pulled his hood up over his head as he rounded the desk. He expected Morgan back at any moment, since he had asked his friend to bring the blond girl to him. But when she stepped into the room with the lieutenant behind her, the need to make use of her took a back seat to a different desire: making her squirm. Despite her outward bravery from earlier, she looked ready to blush the minute he made her uncomfortable. And he could imagine how far under those clothes that blush might extend.

Her legs were still bare up to the middle of her thighs, her wispy skirt revealing the same undulating terrain of flesh that his mind had been mapping all day. Her long golden hair tumbled about her shoulders, but it was mussed, like she had been twirling it around her fingers as she'd walked with Morgan to meet him. A single button was undone on her blouse, which did nothing but accentuate how much the fabric strained against her bust. If she had been trying to cover herself out of caution, she had sorely underestimated the effects that a few modest centimeters of skin could have. His gaze snagged on a bit of gray fluff that clung to the front of her bosom. He held back a soft snort. Maybe she'd had another run-in with a dustpan.

He looked at Morgan. "What took so long?"

His second-in-command ran a hand down his goatee, and Ethan swore the Englishman was hiding a smile. "A minor distraction absorbed my attention," Morgan answered and glanced at the girl. "Nothing worth noting."

She dropped her gaze to the floor. Whatever Morgan had meant, it confirmed that it didn't take much to set her to blushing.

He nodded at the lieutenant in dismissal and approached her. She wiped her palms on her skirt and glanced back at Morgan as he closed the door behind him. Then she looked up at Ethan as he stopped and loomed over her. Though she twisted her fingers together at her stomach, her eyes did not shy from his. They were a dark shade of green, so much deeper than his own. But not cold, like his always seemed whenever he caught sight of his reflection. Hers gathered the lamplight and buried its warm glow until only traces of it glimmered when she blinked.

He stepped closer. Her pupils dilated, and her breathing grew shallow. Good. He had her attention. "How long have you lived at this compound?"

"Too long."

"Excuse me?"

"I-I mean…nothing." She started to pick at a button on her blouse, almost dislodging the bit of fluff, but quickly put her hands behind her instead. "Sorry, but could you tell me why you want me?" Her lips remained parted, and her eyes widened. "I mean, not that I think you want—but, uh, why did you bring me here?"

His voice went flat. "Did you have other plans?"

Her shoulders drooped as she glanced toward the door. "Not anymore." She dragged her eyes back to his. "I mean, I…just finished my shift in the kitchen."

"Good"—he moved even closer so that his robe brushed against her—"because this might take some time."

She lifted her hands as if to hold him back. "What might?"

"Getting what I need from you. And I expect your cooperation." He canted his head when she stiffened. "Is that a problem?"

"Do I have a choice?"

"No."

She took a breath, and his eyes followed the gray dust

ball that still adhered to her breast. He wanted more than ever to stroke his thumb across that piece of fuzz…and see if his touch could raise her nipple behind the cloth.

He balled his left hand into a fist and focused on her face again. "How long have you lived here?"

"We're back to that? So this is more like…an interview?"

"How long?"

"Don't you want to know my name?"

He narrowed his eyes. "Fine."

"Vanessa Brouwer."

"Now. How long?"

"Nice to meet you too," she mumbled.

"Try it again without the attitude."

Her cheeks regained some of their flush. "My parents brought me when I was six"—her words were hesitant, though her gaze was steady—"so I've grown up here."

"Strange place to rear a child."

"Well, they weren't picky about ambience. Not when they had government henchmen coming after them." She paused and scanned his masked face. "You probably know what that's like."

"Who said I'm running from anything?" His tone caused her to flinch.

"I thought—"

"I don't want you to think. I want you to answer my questions." Waves of nervous heat rolled off her body, tempting him to close the scant space between them. "Who were your parents? Why did the government want them?"

"My dad was an artist and musician, so the Council of Ministers wasn't interested in him. But my mother was a scientist."

"So?"

She shrugged and tucked the tip of her tongue against a corner of her mouth. The sight of that unconscious motion made the groin of his jeans tighten beneath the heavy robe. "So…after the government started restricting and regulating what the labs could work on, the Ministerraad planned to move a bunch of scientists onto projects for the military."

He nodded. "They took a page from Belgium and Denmark."

Vanessa's nod was a weaker version of his. "That was the rumor, at least. My mom was a biochemist, so she was worried the Ministry of Defense would force her to do a lot of…horrible things. That's when she and my dad ditched their jobs in Utrecht and started running. A lot of Mom's colleagues went with them and—and they kept heading north until they came across this abandoned fort."

The centimeters that separated him and her were becoming smaller with each deeper breath she took. If he ran a gloved hand up between her thighs, he might get to make those lovely eyes widen again. The front of his jeans constricted further, and he flexed his left hand beside him. "How long have all the other residents been here?"

"Some of them came here not long after we did, but most moved in from town within the last ten years. Once our old caretaker left, Dijkstra showed up. That was just a few years ago." She paused and glanced around the room. "Probably after he flunked out of interior design school."

Cute.

"Is there anyone else in a position of authority here?"

"Not really. One person takes charge. My mom was more or less the first caretaker we had, but it's always been mostly an administrative thing." Her eyes fixed on the throne-like chair in the corner, whose ornate wooden back culminated in a crown-shaped golden spire. "Although some people take it way too seriously."

She caught a lock of her hair and twined it around a finger, and Ethan's gaze was drawn once more to the stray piece of lint that refused to let go of that delectable feminine curve of hers. Not that he blamed it.

Goddamn it, tighten your shot group, Captain. This is an interrogation, not a jack-off session.

He stepped backward, and she visibly relaxed. But his own body could not. It was a mistake to get that close to her, because now every muscle was wound tight. Going without some trim for this long had taken its toll. But he had been able to control his impulses well enough before this, considering he looked like a fucking nightmare of melted meat. No female would stomach the sight, and he was not inclined to get his rocks off in spite of it. But with this girl, he had to ignore every natural instinct that her presence was unearthing by the shovelful. He had a mission to keep his men alive, and she was a distraction from that. In another few weeks, she would not even be a memory. A pretty face forgotten.

She peeked sideways at him and twirled the lock of hair faster. His shoulders loosened slightly.

Maybe not completely forgotten.

He jerked on the chin of his mask and walked to his desk to lean back against the edge. He pushed the glowing oil lamp aside and crossed one boot over the other. "What skills do you have?"

She shrugged. "I can read, write, clean, cook a little. I have most of the periodic table of elements memorized. On a good day, I can do a couple of cartwheels and pretend I know sign language—"

"And act like a smart-ass, apparently."

She fell silent, dropping her hand from her hair. Either she was trying to push his buttons, or her mouth really did have a mind of its own.

She fidgeted with her skirt hem as she glanced around. "So, uh…you chose this room on purpose, huh?"

Ethan folded his arms. "Something wrong with it?"

She choked on a laugh and covered her mouth. "Sorry. It's just that…I've heard rumors about Dijkstra's room." She ventured toward a dresser placed near the bed. "But this—" She flicked the dangling bronze pulls of the ornate drawers and shook her head. "It's like someone gave their pet monkey a bag of money and let it wander through a flea market."

"You have a lot of opinions about things that don't concern you."

She pulled down a small elephant figurine from on top of the dresser and turned it over in her hands. "I'm just saying that if these are going to be your new digs for a while, you may want to consider redecorating." She paired the elephant with a miniature frog and pranced them through the air toward him. "Unless you've always wanted a place that screams, 'I'm a cheeseball!' "

He glared wordlessly at her until she quickly replaced the figurines.

She's getting too comfortable.

"Are you really a captain or is it an honorary title? I'm guessing your robe isn't standard military issue."

"Every man in this outfit earned his rank in his own country's army," he said, nettled at her dismissive tone. "No one ever handed anything to any of us."

She glanced at him. "Well, that makes more sense, then." She wandered along the edge of the canopied bed and examined the green velvet drapes festooning the four posts. "Because you seem disciplined, not like some evil, deranged marauder." She slapped one of the heavy tassels and sent it swinging. "Unless you hide that part well."

He shoved himself away from the desk and strode to the bed. Vanessa shrank back as he grabbed the tassel in his fist and leaned down to her. "I think the last thing you want to do is piss me off and find out."

She stared up at him, her mouth falling open. The front of her blouse—its buttons already struggling to do their job—was now only a hand's breadth away. The rapid rise and fall of her chest forced his gaze to go deeper, seeking out that single tantalizing glimpse of cleavage. And that damn piece of fluff still rode the front of her breast, no matter how hard he made her breathe. He should reach out and brush it off, so he could cup his palm around her soft, sweet—

That's it, I'm out. Time to shut this shit down.

He stepped past her. "Report back to me tomorrow at zero seven hundred hours."

He halted as soon as the words left his mouth.

Fuck.

"What?" she asked faintly.

Didn't matter that he hadn't meant to say it. And that

out of all the residents, she had become the wrong choice for this exercise. He was in it now.

He continued toward his desk. "I want someone who's familiar with all aspects of this facility to show it to me. That's your assignment." He paused and tapped his fingers thoughtfully against his leg while he kept his back to her. "I'll also expect you to draw up diagrams of the compound so that I have a reference for later."

That'll keep her busy.

When he looked back over his shoulder, he judged she was doing everything she could not to let her mouth hang open again.

She trudged toward him. "Me? But I'm no—ow!" She caught herself against the edge of his desk as she rammed into it. She winced and rubbed a hand savagely against her hip. "I'm no architect. And I'm certainly not the artist my father was. And there are plenty of others to show you around. Our building maintenance man knows every mildewy nook and broken cranny of—"

"Be on time." He picked up the pen from the stack of papers lying on his desk. "And wear something more suitable than that." He pointed the ballpoint at her skirt.

She stood up straighter. "I like how I dress."

He slid his gaze up the length of her. "It wasn't a complaint."

She wavered for a few seconds, but then lifted her chin. "What I mean is"—she steered herself around his desk to bustle toward him—"I shouldn't have to change for anyone. If you want me, then you'll have to take me without pants."

"Fine. Even better."

Her cheeks colored cherry-red. "Um, okay, that's not what I—"

"Zero seven hundred." He walked to the door and waited for her to trail after him.

"Seriously, you don't need a tour guide. The compound's a big place, but it's not the Royal Palace of Amsterdam." Her voice was pleading as he opened the door. "You don't need me."

He held her gaze silently. Finally, she shook her head and mumbled something under her breath. But before she stepped over the threshold, she met his stare and her eyes reflected the barest twinkle from the lamplight, like uncut emeralds. "Look, I know you're all Mister Grand Pooh-Bah and everything now," she said in a shaky voice, "but you shouldn't push people around like this. We're not...not...*pushovers*, you know. And—and moreover"—she made a hesitant move as if to poke a finger into his chest—"if I agree to show you around, then I expect to get...breakfast. Something special. That's *your* assignment." With that, she gave him a firm nod and backed away.

He glanced at Morgan, who stood next to the doorway with his hands clasped behind him. Morgan watched her hurry down the dimly lit hallway and then looked at Ethan with a half smile. "Is she going to be trouble?"

Ethan tapped a finger against his leg as his eyes followed her until she turned the corner. "Absolutely."

CHAPTER SIX

VANESSA

Vanessa ducked when one of the soldiers swung a rolled-up tapestry onto his shoulder and strolled by her.

She shook her head and dodged the rest of the men carrying furniture out of the captain's room. Both residents and soldiers filled the hallway that morning, each person burdened with some ornamental accessory plucked from the caretaker's old quarters. She skittered out of the way as Frank—the giant Russian's mustache as massive as his glower—walked toward her hugging a host of garish red pillows. But as she pushed upstream through the flow of bodies, every soldier eyed her legs on the way past.

She shouldn't have slacked off on her laundry. Her only pair of jeans was still balled up next to her wardrobe, along with all her longer garments, so she was left with nothing but short skirts to choose from. Ordinarily, that would have been her preference anyway for what should have been a carefree summer day. But nothing was ordinary anymore.

Inside the captain's room there was a flurry of activity as several women pulled the sheets from the mattress and detached the heavy vomit-green curtains from the four bed posts. There was nothing to be done about the red damask canopy, but it honestly didn't look so bad once the tasteless trappings were removed. She hopped out of the way as two women dropped to their knees and started to roll up the enormous glow-in-the-dark patterned carpet.

Good riddance!

The rug that the caretaker had bought for his quarters—using the residents' money, of course—now left behind a stained outline as the only thing to have marked its presence at all. The floors were wooden and worn, the deeply colored and heavily grained boards having been installed there long before she could remember. An odor like moldy logs surrounded her as she wandered farther into the room. She rubbed her nose as the smell grew stronger the closer she came to spots where Dijkstra's flashy furniture had once crowded together. The stone fireplace on the right side of the room sat unlit, despite the chilly morning. Vanessa rubbed her arms. Today, September was apparently impatient to hint at its imminent approach.

As she hovered in the middle of the wooden floor, several of the captain's men blatantly appraised her cream-colored button blouse while they toted paintings and furniture by her. She glanced down. Clamping her mouth shut, she crossed her arms over her chest. Her nipples were standing out clearly under the fabric. Perfect. A fat lot of good it had done to wear the bra that was "padded for warmth and discretion," according to the merchandise tag. So far, this day was going as well as she'd expected. How long had she stood like that on full display?

She looked at the captain to ascertain whether he, too, had been feasting his eyes. He certainly couldn't seem to keep his attention off her breasts last night, despite his whole ooga-booga Scary-Man-in-Charge act. But this time, he was turned away from her as he sorted through a collection of yellowed papers at his desk.

She approached him, interrupted only by a young soldier who dashed by in front of her with a gold-painted footstool in each hand. The holstered gun at the captain's left hip caught her eyes when it peeked up through the opening of his sleeveless robe. She had seen last night that he also had a gun in a shoulder holster on his right side. Like with Morgan, who needs that many weapons at the same time?

Evidently, Captain Compulsive does.

When she was just near enough, she leaned out to snag his shirtsleeve. He turned his head. And his gaze did appear to skim over her breasts, though the deep shadows inside his hood made that debatable. She crossed her arms again anyway.

He folded back a glove cuff to look at his watch. "Evidently, telling time fell off your list of skills," he said, the bad temper undisguised.

She stared at him. "It's only five minutes past seven."

He inclined his head so that she could see his eyes more clearly within the hood. "And that's not when I told you to be here. I said zero seven hundred hours. That means zero six forty-five."

"What? What sense does that make?"

"It's called being on time."

"I did the best I could."

"No. You didn't."

"What does it matter?"

"It matters to me." He set down the papers, and his eyes—almost acid green in the dark of the cowl—etched into hers. "I don't like having my time wasted."

"Well, who in their right mind wants to be up and at 'em by seven in the freaking morning? I can't even feel my legs under me until eight."

"The rest of us have been up since before zero five hundred. I can see to it that you're put on the same schedule."

She didn't respond but tucked her arms tighter around her chest.

"Here." He reached behind himself and tossed her a white cardboard container. "Breakfast."

She caught it with a start and opened the lid.

"You made your demands very clear last night." He walked around to the back of his desk and pulled a notepad and pen from a drawer. "Hope it's 'special' enough for you."

As she stared into the box, she pressed her lips together. She raised her head to fix him in a glare. "You found these stashed somewhere in this room, didn't you?"

He walked toward her, adjusting the open sleeves of his robe farther up on his shoulders. He stopped in front of her, leaned over to peer into the box, and then picked up one of the powdered oliebollen. "You weren't specific." When she opened her mouth to protest, he stuffed the pastry into it. "I'll just be glad for the quiet."

He headed toward the door, and she spat the sweet oliebol into the box as she pictured Caretaker Dijkstra's spindly fingers spider-walking their way over the doughy treats. She tossed the container onto the desk and wiped the back of her hand across her mouth. "I think I lost my appetite. Permanently."

The captain did not slow down to wait for her, so she had to scurry to catch up with him. He strode through the hallway, and the men all parted for him regardless of what heavy load they bore.

"I see you didn't bother to dress sensibly this morning," he said as she walked beside him. "Thanks for the show."

She missed a step. So! She had been right about his eyes getting their fill!

She hunched her shoulders as she hugged herself. "I'm used to working in the kitchen first thing in the morning." She was tired of crossing her arms constantly, but she invited the comfort—and the coverage—the motion provided. "It's always nice and warm from the ovens." *You know: just like your personality, Captain.*

He shoved the notepad and pen at her and then turned at the end of the corridor. She juggled the items and scrambled again to catch up with him.

She blew a lock of hair out of her face. "Where are we going? I thought I was supposed to be showing *you* this place." She had already started to adopt his bad mood. "And what are these for?"

"I want you to write down all the details you know

about every area of the compound we inspect."

"But I could just talk about them, once we get there."

"I doubt I can pretend to listen for that long."

She narrowed her eyes at the back of his hooded head. *I wonder how hard it would be to jab this pen between his shoulder blades? Especially if I get a running start…*

"You'll also take notes on every modification I'll have to make, to bring things up to par," he went on as she squinted one eye and aimed the pen's tip at his spine. "That includes reinforcing walls, adding artillery, and repairing damage that has been left to sit. I need this facility secured while we're here."

"Well, repairs are going to make a long list." The same troublesome lock of hair tickled her cheek, and she used the ballpoint to fling it back. "This place has been falling apart for years. It was built back in the seventeen hundreds, when a nutty nobleman from Amsterdam decided to come up here and throw his money at it. And people have been struggling to keep it up ever since."

He turned his head to her but maintained his brisk pace. "So you know the history. I need that as well."

She wrinkled her nose. "What do you need that for?"

He kept his gaze steadily on her. "Because its history can reveal its weaknesses. And because I don't need to explain myself to you."

She pressed her lips together. *Sheesh, touchy.*

"All I know," she said and took a deep breath, "is that North Holland was still part of the Dutch Republic back then, when this fort was first constructed." She started to feel winded from trying to keep up with his lengthy strides. What was the freaking hurry? "We're only a few kilometers from the North Sea, which is what made the nobleman paranoid that this area wasn't well defended. Nobody else was doing anything about it, so I guess it kept him up at night. Anyway…"

She paused and forced herself to slow down. If he wanted her along on this grand tour, he'd have to wait for her.

"Fort Van Doorn never saw any action, but it made a

great tourist attraction later on." She gritted her teeth as the captain tramped on without her. "Then after the government shut it down to the public, it went to pot." She raised her voice so that it echoed down the hallway. "Till my parents and their friends started living here, of course." She stopped walking completely and put a hand on her hip to glare after him as he widened the distance between them. "There's more about the history on the big plaque outside the front gates. But you probably didn't notice it, since you were busy blasting your way through the back end!"

At last, near the end of the long passageway, he turned around. And the sight of him in that moment sent a chill down her back. He looked like some hellish phantom surrounded by cloth so black it swallowed the light coming through the gaps cut high into the stone wall beside him. The shadows inside his hood were deep enough to erase even his eyes within the mask. Not one human feature left—like she was staring into nothingness. It was only when he spoke that she freed the breath locked in her lungs.

"I haven't seen the armory yet," he said tersely. "What condition is it in?"

She flexed her fingers around the large notepad that she'd been clutching in a near death grip. She swallowed and approached him. "We, uh…we don't exactly have anything worthwhile in it." She hated the tremulous sound of her voice as she stumbled over her words. "You've probably guessed that we're not equipped for battle. We just use it for storage."

He waited for her to reach him before he said, "I gathered. First note: convert and stock the armory."

She stared at him as he paused. It was a relief to see his eyes again instead of that empty darkness. His gaze dropped to the notepad.

"Oh, right." She clicked the ballpoint pen to scribble at the top of the first page. "Load up with lots of dangerous doohickeys. Got it."

He held his head back. There was no interpreting the

expression in his eyes. Was he beginning to find her amusing, or was he only perplexed as he tried to categorize her? He turned away before she could decide and resumed his pace. But this time, she noted with gratitude, he took smaller strides.

"So," she began as they made their way down a new corridor, "black's your favorite color, huh?"

"It suits me."

Certainly suits your mood.

"What do people call you, when they don't call you Captain Evans?" she ventured.

"Sir."

She let out a short breath through her nose. Evidently this personal guide gig was not going to get very "personal."

After that, although she pointed him down the right path, his inclination seemed to be to get a feel for the layout himself, like he was memorizing every turn until he knew the compound intuitively. Compared to the number of soldiers, there were only a few of the residents around. Most stayed hidden, but the reason for that was obvious: the captain and his men scared the crap out of them. She, herself, should have been more wary of these invaders, like Cornie had admonished. But in all honesty, it was kind of exhilarating. Not that she endorsed their violent approach to things, but she certainly couldn't deny its peculiar appeal.

These men were all so different from anyone she had met before. Their presence at the fort, as they imposed a new order on the compound, was like something she had only read in stories. Her own life wasn't exactly adventurous, unless she counted cruising the government-restricted internet in the new Café 't Vogeltje that opened in town. And that was only in order to have her defective padded-for-discretion bra delivered to a local store for purchase. So these guys presented a fascinating incongruity to her more humble existence.

But, again, why were they really here? If they were like most marauders she'd heard of, they would have cleaned the residents out by now and left the compound a wreck. The captain's "army" seemed diverse enough that he must have crossed the continent to recruit them all, creating his own European Union, since the real one had been disbanded years ago. But so many isolationist countries were still struggling to protect themselves in the wake of China's economic collapse that closed borders were no joke. Getting through national boundaries could only be done with a high degree of secrecy and skill. Why would he go to such trouble? Why not simply pick one country where he could play pirate?

She tapped the pen against the notepad. *Unless that's what he's doing now. And we're going to be his permanent secret base.*

"What are your duties in the kitchen?" The captain's gruff voice hauled her mind back from where it had drifted.

"A lot of cleaning. A lot of serving." She clicked the ballpoint in and out as she walked. "But my biggest job is taking care of the fruit trees and other plants in the garden."

"All the fresh food you grow is contained only inside the fort, in the area where my men and I came in?"

She coughed lightly. "Yep." He'd said that last part like they had politely rung the doorbell and joined the residents for brunch.

"Are you the only gardener? That's a lot of work for one person." His tone was doubtful.

She lifted her chin and hugged the notepad to her chest. "There are others who help, but I'm the best at it. I can make things take root, even in places they don't necessarily belong. I can coax just about anything to grow for me." She paused and twirled the pen around her fingers. "I'm told I have a tender touch."

"Care to prove it?"

She fell back a step. *What is that supposed to—?*

"Take me there." He faced forward once more. "I want a closer look."

She squeezed the ballpoint in her fist. *He enjoyed that.*

Well, it's the last one he gets.

No doubt he'd try again, though. Because this show-and-tell torture session was just getting underway.

CHAPTER SEVEN

VANESSA

When Vanessa and the captain reached the vast garden, there were a number of the captain's men trying to reattach the rear gates. All of them struggled under the weight of the old iron-banded wooden doors.

She squinted up at him. "I have to ask: what was the point of blowing off our gates if you were just going to have to put them back on?"

He didn't turn his head, so she could not see within the robe's hood. He cleared his throat. "I have my reasons."

She choked back a laugh. There was no mistaking the defensive tone to his voice. *Wow. He didn't think it all the way through!*

Had she discovered a chink in his armor? Captain "Look-at-Me!" Evans: given to grandiose acts of intimidation without foresight.

"So," she said casually as she drew a curly doodle in the margin of the notepad, "you do this all the time, huh? Blow things up, I mean."

He held his fists beside him as he walked. "I do what's necessary. And a show of force can be very effective."

"What happens when you want to take over a campground? Do you rip people's tent flaps off, wave them around, and then sew them back on?"

He turned his head and his bright green eyes went through her like a pike.

She flinched back. "I–I'm just saying, you could have knocked and pointed your guns at us. It would have had the same result."

He looked away and jerked the top of his hood even farther forward. "It would take too long to explain the strategy to you."

How about summing it up as: "Oops"?

Silence fell between them. She had apparently hit a nerve. Maybe the captain was good at leading his men and organizing an occupation, but he had an irrational side. She glanced over his robed figure.

Wonder if this Cloaked Crusader look had been a knee-jerk notion, too.

Maybe she should keep her distance, after all. Because what would she do if he got an irrational impulse about her?

Morgan's voice called out something in the distance, which distracted her from that last thought. The Englishman walked slowly behind the men who were fitting the gates into the stone archway. He seemed to be delivering directions as to which way to shift the doors. He stopped and stood off to the side, hands clasped behind him. The lieutenant—like the captain—was evidently keen on long-sleeved black clothing, although she could see that the back of his trim-fit vest today was a satiny dark green. Morgan turned his head over his shoulder and his eyes instantly found her. She caught her breath and looked away. The last time he had focused that intently on her, he'd been about to frisk her.

And, honestly, she'd been about to return the favor.

She followed the captain into the orchard as he wandered toward one of the trees. "We have a nice variety: Elstar, red prince, golden delicious, and so on. There's a local distillery in town—Distilleerderij Tuinstra—that buys a lot of our apples to make their brandy, so that's a plus. And to help with pollination and ensure a better crop, there's our trusty old crabapple tree." She pretended to look down at her notes. *You and that one have a lot in common!*

"What kind is this?" He plucked a greenish-yellow apple near his head and turned it to examine the dark-red blush on its side.

She tucked the notepad under her arm and took the large rough-skinned fruit from him. "A Belle de Boskoop." She gave it an appreciative sniff and smiled as the sharp woody smell filled her nose. "The variety has been around forever and, I'm proud to say, is uniquely Dutch." She handed it back to him. "They're my favorite. I could eat these all day."

She paused. Actually, she had done that many times when she was a youngster. And a teenager…and last week. She winced. Her Havana rabbit friend wasn't the only one with a bottomless-pit reputation.

The captain regarded the apple for a moment and then held it to his nose.

He's missing out. I doubt he can smell anything through that goofy mask.

"You'd asked about our two greenhouses over there." She waved the notepad off to the left. "We can grow peppers, tomatoes, and other veggies out of season. That's also where we keep the few citrus trees and the peach and apricot trees. Pretty tough commodities to come by these days." She pulled the notepad in front of her again and started adding to the elaborate doodle in the margin. "Do you have any favorite garden goodies?" She snuck a look at him. "If you want anything special, I might have something to offer."

He did not appear to be listening as he stared down at the apple and turned it again in his hand. "Asparagus," he mumbled.

She stopped the pen in mid-doodle. "Oh?"

He continued to stare at the apple. "It used to grow wild where I lived as a boy."

She lowered the notepad and strolled closer to him. His voice was smooth for a change, like the rough edges had been sanded off by whatever memory he now worked on.

"My mother used to—" When he looked up, his eyes flicked away. He dropped the apple into the grass. "We still have a lot of ground to cover. Let's get humping."

She stared at him. "Let's, uh…what?"

"Move it."

She wrinkled her brow as he strode away from her and bent down to grab the apple he'd discarded. She shook her head as she polished it against her hip. *Unbelievable. He pulled the chain mail back over that soft underbelly so fast, it made a sonic boom.* She took a bite of the Boskoop and shoved it in her skirt pocket before jogging to catch up with him.

The morning marched well into the afternoon as he put her on a more structured course through the compound. He left no part of the place unexplored, with the exception of the propane-heated showers. No surprise there, since he and his men had obviously taken advantage of the facilities already. There had been no plumbing at the time of the fort's original construction, of course, but drainage holes had been hand-bored into one section of stone flooring. Per the tourist sign posted on the wall inside, the military personnel would simply use buckets of water to wash themselves. It wasn't until her parents and the other refugees arrived and installed pipes and shower-heads that a formal bathing area was created. Because if there was one thing scientists were sticklers about, it was cleanliness.

According to the brochures she'd read as a child, the overall layout of Fort Van Doorn—inconsistent with others in the Netherlands, thanks to the nobleman's ineptitude with architectural design—did have elements borrowed from the star-shaped forts popular in the fifteenth and sixteenth centuries. There were triangular areas protruding from several places around the multi-sided structure, as well as a canal—long since drained and filled in with earth—that zigzagged around the spiky edges.

And while the majority of hallways and rooms were

clustered within the east and south sides of the building, what really made the whole structure feel lopsided was the grand dining hall that her parents had helped commission as a frivolous add-on. It rose far above the battlements and actually could have provided a great vantage point for any lookouts, were the roof not so steeply angled to achieve its gothic effect. The fort's founder, with his eccentric tastes, would have been thrilled.

She took the captain up on the ramparts that formed the angular circumference and pointed out some of the features outside the compound: the cluster of woods that curved from the east to the north behind the fort, the small brick smokehouse that Cornelis had built himself for his meat-curing projects, the tiny cemetery in the distance—

She couldn't stop her voice from fading as her eyes settled on the faint outlines of her parents' gravestones. She was glad she hadn't rented space for them in the town's crumbling cemetery, but having them nearby didn't make it any easier to visit the site.

She shook off the encroaching memories and turned instead to show the captain one of the old windmills, once used to grind grain. It sat out on the lower level of a diamond-shaped double bastion on the fort's west side, where the walls surrounding it had long ago fallen away to leave it open and unprotected. But its broad, tattered blades continued to turn lazily in the wind, like an old gray worker who insisted on keeping at it and refused to admit that he could no longer perform the role he used to. However, there still remained the one viable windmill on the east side that had been kept in better condition and supplied the compound's water by pumping it from deep within the earth in the only spot with no saltwater intrusion.

Vanessa held the notepad to her chest and spread her other hand toward the mill. "Although this example was meant to provide Fort Van Doorn with a source of fresh water," she informed the captain in a sing-song voice, "windmills in Holland were historically built to siphon water away from low-lying land beneath sea level. Often, a mechanism known as an Archimedes' screw was used to lift water up over nearby dikes." She cupped her hand and raised it dramatically. "This practice allowed the Dutch to reclaim land for farming." She leaned against the corroded cannon behind her and gestured at the landscape with a formal sweep of her arm. "The remains of a drainage mill are still visible on the horizon directly in front of you." She shaded her eyes with her hand and slowly twisted her body at the waist. "See if you can spot the historic structure. Did you find it?" She gave an exuberant thumbs-up. "Good job! Be sure to mark it on your Fort Adventure Map!"

The captain stared at her like she had lost her mind.

Wilting under his gaze, she pushed herself off the cannon and tapped her pen against the plaque bolted to the parapet. "I have it memorized by now," she explained with a sheepish shrug. "And…that's how it sounds in my head."

He turned to look down at it. The Dutch, German, and English translations were hardly visible any longer, even under the bright summer sun, but the diagrams of a windmill's internal workings could still be seen on the weathered sign. As a kid, she would clamber up inside the giant structures to pore through stacks of sundry American magazines and comic books her mother had collected as a child. She would voraciously absorb each vintage periodical, enjoying the strange slang and colorful idioms as much as any Mark Twain novel. Happy to be left to herself, she would stretch out across the worn, dusty boards inside the cap of the grain windmill in particular, soothed by the wooden creaking noises the old gears made.

"You'll have to get used to all the plaques everywhere," she said, clicking the ballpoint in and out as the captain delivered his usual *I-am-not-amused* look. "This was a tourist attraction, like I said. I don't know if you noticed, but there's a sign next to your room that says Commanding Officer's Quarters. Which I guess…is appropriate." She trailed off and gave him a tentative smile.

In lieu of a comment, he glided along the bulwark walkway again, which forced her to trot after him.

"And—and there are signs for the barracks that were divided up into smaller rooms by the early residents. The kitchen is still the kitchen. My room was always its own living quarters, though, and it has a sign—"

Nope. She stuck the pen between her teeth and chomped down on it.

At her abrupt silence, the captain stopped and looked at her. "Well?" he asked blandly. "What does it say?"

She swallowed and let the pen fall from her mouth as a flush crept up her throat. "Uh, yeah, that." She clicked the ballpoint in and out slowly. "As I understand, the Dutch doesn't translate into English very well. But...it says...Officer's Pleasure."

He straightened, and his eyes almost glowed brighter within the hood.

"Back when this fort was manned," she went on hesitantly, "the highest ranking officer—the one who commanded the fort—would often keep a...girl handy. So that she could, you know—" She rolled her hand in the air.

Don't say it. Don't say it.

"Satisfy his needs," she blurted.

Damn it.

"She'd live here in the fort, in my room. And—and he'd come to her whenever he wanted her." She swallowed again. "The nights can get very cold here, as you'll soon find out, so I'm sure she kept him very...warm."

Shut up, shut up, shut up, Vanessa!

She stopped, the flush now raging across her cheeks like a fever. The captain looked at her wordlessly, and his gaze seemed to penetrate her like a slow-turning screw. A rush of relief left her lightheaded when he finally pivoted and began walking again. She took a breath and hurried after him.

"By the way," she said as she drew up beside him, "thank you for letting me keep my room. I know you've only done that for your officers, so I appreciate getting the privacy. Besides, I don't make a very good roommate. People say I talk too much and that they can't hear themselves...think..."

Her words dwindled when he turned his head to her and gave her what looked like a smirk behind the mask. "Now who would ever say that?"

Oh, so now he's Captain Comedian.

"Anyway," she said as she repressed the urge to kick him, "thanks."

"Tell me about the town south of here."

Okay, moving on.

"Well, due to all the provincial sanctions, Achterwaartsstad is more or less stuck with older technology, including the basics, like power. Lots of fuel- and wood-burning going on when the town's electric grid is offline. And not a lot has been done to modernize the village. But the atmosphere is quaint and not so different from a lot of traditional towns in North Holland. We do like the historic look around here."

"What about weapons? I assume the government has confiscated all of them, as other countries have done?"

She nodded. "And law enforcement isn't allowed to keep them either. Here in the Netherlands, the only other use is for hunting, and even that's not permitted now. We don't have guns for self-defense, like...Americans." She peered at him to see if she had guessed his origin correctly, but his eyes—sharp and steady—would not cooperate. Getting information out of him was proving to be a preposterous task.

But before she could heave an aggravated sigh, a gunshot rang out.

CHAPTER EIGHT

VANESSA

The captain ran for the nearest set of stairs that descended from the ramparts into the center of the compound. Vanessa—her heart beating hard—followed, but he was far ahead of her by the time she reached the bottom step. There was a raucous scuffle taking place near the back of the garden, where two men grappled with each other. Her eyes fell on a gun in the grass near them. Both brawlers were trying to keep the other from reaching it. A crowd of onlookers had already gathered as the two men went at it. Vanessa drew up beside the captain, who'd stopped a few meters away.

As the head honcho now, why isn't he intervening?

As soon as she finished the thought, Morgan's tall, commanding figure appeared. He thrust himself into the fray and shoved the two men apart. Then he gave an extra push to the antagonist who tried to stand his ground. That brawler turned out to be Cornelis.

The other man—obviously one of the captain's—bounced on the balls of his feet, practically foaming at the mouth. "Go ahead, ya fuckin' knacker, try it again! I'll batter ya till ya shit your teeth out!" He pulled back his fist and advanced on Cornelis.

"That's enough, Liam!" Morgan slapped a hand to the young soldier's chest to restrain him. "Collect your weapon."

Liam's breathing was jerky as he glared at Cornelis through bangs that were rust-tinted black. Anna, one of the other residents, stood near the scene. She hovered closer to Liam as he bent and scooped his gun from the grass.

Cornelis glanced at Morgan before nodding in Liam's direction. "Tell this smeerlap to leave the women alone." His voice was as steely as the color of his hair in the harsh sunlight. "They're not here for his amusement."

Anna stepped forward and tightened her hands into fists. "Cornelis," she hissed. "Stop it."

Vanessa squinted at her. Cornie was just being his typical over-protective self, but the other residents usually didn't mind it.

Morgan turned to Liam. "Private, did you instigate this altercation?"

"For feck's sake, Lieutenant, this langer came after *me*!" Liam jammed his gun into the holster at his side and threw a hand out at Cornelis. "Then he grabbed my Browning and tried to put one up my fuckin' arse." He had a lively and lilting accent, which would have been more charming were he in a better mood.

Morgan said nothing, but stood with his arms folded.

"I'm tellin' ya, he ain't the full shilling!" Liam insisted, the pitch of his voice rising higher.

Morgan spoke sternly. "This is not the first occasion on which you have disregarded our process. We do not fraternize whilst initially structuring our occupation."

"Well, look at her. She's a total ride." Liam pointed at Anna, who tossed back her long, brown hair and did not hide the smug smile that darted across her lips. "A pretty girl like that knows her own mind. She didn't have any trouble giving me direction. And she ain't the only one." Liam looked straight at Cornelis. "Seems to me, they don't have much to fuckin' choose from round here."

At that, Cornelis bolted forward, and Liam sprang to meet him. Morgan again pushed them apart, but this time he sent Cornelis sprawling.

With a shout, a male resident charged up behind Morgan and leapt onto his back. Vanessa gasped and shrank down. Morgan reached over his shoulders and seized the attacker. He bent with a twist and flipped the man forward. The resident thudded to the ground on his back, and Morgan stood over him with his feet spread.

Confusion followed as Liam pounced on Cornelis, while off to the side another male resident barreled at Morgan. But Morgan stepped out of the assailant's head-on rush, put a boot against him, and shoved the man so that he stumbled to his hands and knees. In the space of the next second, Morgan had pulled both his gun and his knife and held them out to the sides. The sinister-looking blade was pointed into the throat of Morgan's first attacker, who had lumbered to his feet. The muzzle of the gun was pointed at Cornelis's chest.

"I advise we call an end to this spectacle," Morgan said evenly. When Cornelis glowered at him, Morgan raised the gun to Cornelis's forehead. "Agreed?"

At last Cornelis gave a hesitant nod. The other male resident yielded and took a step back.

Morgan lowered his arms and replaced both his weapons in one fluid motion. His voice cracked the hush of the garden. "As you were! *All* of you!"

The incident had brought forth every person in the compound, but at Morgan's command, they began to disperse, muttering to each other as they dawdled back to their tasks.

Vanessa froze. She turned to look at her hand clutching the captain's arm and then lifted her face. His eyes studied her as she leaned against him, and she became all at once very aware of the feel of his bicep under her fingers. His flesh beneath the shirtsleeve did not seem smooth, but it nonetheless bulged with the familiar hard curves of a masculine body kept in excellent shape. She let go and clamped the notepad against her chest as she stepped back. But he continued to watch her with that same animal attentiveness he'd shown yesterday, when those bright eyes—the irises almost neon-green in the darkness of the robe's hood—had been those of a crouching creature about to spring.

"Well, now, aren't you a fine thing?"

The voice made her jump and nearly drop the notepad.

Liam stood with his arms crossed as he scanned her. Then he looked at the captain. "Hey, Cap. I see you ain't foosterin' about, in gettin' a feel for the place."

"And I see you're making friends wherever you go, as usual," the captain replied curtly.

Liam's attitude immediately soured. "Aw now, Cap, every one of these lads is keen for a scrap with us, but I amn't a fuckin' punchbag. Though *you*, on the other hand"—he turned to Vanessa again—"would be worth a slap in the mouth." He rested his hands on his waist and stepped closer, giving her a wink. "Mind if I have a private tour, when you're done here with our captain?"

Before she could roll her eyes in response, the captain's voice broke in like a fist through glass. "Get back to your post, Private. Start these antics again, and I'll put your Irish ass in a sling. Understood?"

Liam's mouth hung open for a second as his bangs drooped into his hazel eyes. He straightened to give the captain a formal salute. "Sorry, Cap. Loud and clear." Then Liam ran a hand through his hair and glanced once more at Vanessa before he hustled off.

"I could have handled that myself, you know," she said, nodding after Liam.

"He's my responsibility."

"Then maybe you should have been a little harder on him. I don't think a slap on the wrist is going to get through to a guy like that."

The captain narrowed his eyes at her, and she, herself, got the urge to salute and apologize.

His voice was as sharp as his gaze. "Maybe when you get a gold oak leaf on your shoulder, then I'll give a shit what you have to say about disciplining my men."

She gave a limp shrug. "Look, I know that most of you guys are used to wallowing in testosterone, but there should be a line, right? And you're their leader, so they listen to you. I mean, is that how *you* get a date? You beat your chest and carry a girl off caveman style? If that's your best tactic, no wonder you're grumpy and alone."

He stood even straighter and gazed down at her. She closed her mouth and fingered the bottom edges of the notepad's paper.

…and thank you for that verbal face-plant, Vanessa.

The gap between them smoked with tension, thickening the air until she thought she might choke.

"Take me to the areas that need the most repairs," he said, seconds before her lungs quit.

She hugged the notepad harder, then turned away and took a full breath. The sun cast the captain's shadow far out in front of her as she led him across the grass. "I have to warn you," she said, "I think you're in over your head. We have a whole slew of problems Caretaker Dijkstra never bothered to fix. Like the huge hole in the east wall that I—"

—tried to escape through last night, before you made me your personal lackey.

"—think is a health hazard."

He brushed close against her as they walked, and she dared to glance at him. Did he do that on purpose? They continued on with their sides nearly touching—the same kind of proximity as two sweethearts holding hands after a lovers' tiff. Or like two people testing the waters. His bicep brushed her shoulder again, and an unexpected tingle flittered through her stomach.

Stop enjoying it. This is weird enough without your imagination kicking in.

She showed him the worst of the dilapidated areas around the compound that were on the verge of collapse. Other sections were not exactly broken, just bizarre features that Fort Van Doorn's creator thought would make the fortifications more fearsome. There were stone rain spouts shaped like screaming sea eagles, curly wooden spikes—most long since rotted away but others now petrified stumps—bristling out from the walls, and bug-eyed gargoyles strategically placed along the parapets so boiling oil and refuse could be dumped through the snarling mouths onto enemies below. But even confronted with such an eclectic mix of oddities, the captain's eyes moved in an experienced analytical fashion, seeming to catalog every detail.

At last, he told her to start a new page and then rattled off an exhausting list of items that she scribbled under the heading "Contingency Supplies." But as she was trying to remember how to spell "antiseptic"—now that her brain had begun to zone out—the captain turned away and stuck his hands inside his hood. She got halfway through "water purification tablets" when she paused to watch him wrestle with something in the back of his cowl.

She waited. And waited. Then sighed. "Here, let me help—"

He pulled back when she reached for the sides of his hood. "I'm fine."

He fumbled a minute longer with what must have been the pins that held the back of the mask together.

"Look, if you would let me—"

"No." By the tone of his voice, he must have been blushing under that mask…though that was hard to believe.

She lifted the notepad and noisily flipped over a page to continue the supplies list. "And more safety pins," she called out, writing the words with exaggerated care, and then added an exclamation point with a theatrical swish.

The captain finished fiddling with his mask, readjusted his hood, and glared at her.

She steeled herself. *Here it comes.*

"What time do you eat dinner?" he demanded.

Well, that was nothing close to what she'd expected.

"Around eighteen hundred."

"Then I expect you to bring my meal at eighteen thirty."

She gave an inward groan. She had fancied settling down with a Jane Austen book while she ate. "Any kind of food you don't like?" she asked.

"I'll let you know when you bring my dinner."

And with that, he snatched the notepad and left. Vanessa stared after him, feeling like she'd been shoved toward the chasm of a precipice to teeter at the edge.

Tonight. Alone again in his bedroom. Considering the in-depth tour she'd just given him of the compound...

Maybe there's only one thing left for him to explore.

CHAPTER NINE

VANESSA

Vanessa knocked lightly on the door.

The captain's deep voice came from a distance behind it. "What is it?"

"Room service." Her own supper sat like a block of wood in her stomach, since she'd been too uptight to eat more slowly.

She glanced over her shoulder at Morgan, who leaned back on the rear legs of his chair with his feet propped on the wooden table that had appeared there sometime during the day. He held an English-translated copy of the *Noordster Courant* in one hand and seemed to be studying it. Why on earth the little town of Achterwaartsstad still bothered to crank out a newspaper that could have been easily accessed in digital form, she couldn't say. But for whatever reason, they insisted on reverting to many of their outdated ways.

The oil lamp mounted to the stone wall behind him made a soft hissing sound as its fat flame chewed on the greasy wick. Vanessa shifted her feet and rested the serving tray against her belly to support the weight of the wine pitcher. She turned her head over her shoulder again.

Morgan raised his eyes just above the top of the paper to look at her.

She nibbled on her bottom lip for a second. "You do

know that's chock-full of government propaganda without any real news, right?"

Morgan used one finger to fold a corner of the paper toward himself, and his mouth—neatly framed by his raven-black goatee—lifted at the corner. "Quite."

She waited for more, but he merely returned her gaze. The lantern's flame hissed again and crouched low, the wavering light deepening the color of his eyes to the dusky hue of an overcast sky. Like a hovering storm about to trap her in a downpour.

The door opened and Vanessa jumped, rattling the metal lid against the dinner plate on the tray. The captain's usual outfit made him appear as a man-shaped inkblot against the warmly lit room beyond as he ushered her in.

While he closed the door, she set the tray on his desk and removed the metal cover from his plate. "Voila! Your hodgepodge dinner is served."

The smell of baked brown bread blended with the sharp lemony aroma of hollandaise sauce. Rhetta had done her best to provide an assortment of meats, sides, and condiments to accommodate the captain's unknown tastes. He walked over and stared down at the chipped clay dish. The varied portions of food sent their steam up into his hood as he took the fork and poked it into a hunk of chicken. He turned and held it in front of her face.

She pressed her lips together. *Great. All that sparkling charm and trust issues too.*

Finally, she took a bite. Then lifted a hand to start clawing at her throat—ready to foam at the mouth and fall on the floor to put on a good show—but felt his stare harden as his lips became a stern line within the opening of his mask. So instead, she swallowed and held her arms out to the sides to show that she was not about to writhe in the throes of death. He picked up a piece of ham and popped it into his mouth.

She let her arms flop back down. "Oh, so, pork gets a pass?"

"I'll gamble that if the kitchen poisons one thing, they'll poison it all." He chewed while he picked up another bit of the ham. "Also"—he tossed the other piece in his mouth—"I don't like chicken."

"There goes tomorrow night's menu," she grumbled, but then softened her tone as she nodded toward his plate. "I found some asparagus for you, by the way. It's out of a can, but…I thought you might like it."

He stopped chewing and looked at her.

"Ya know, because…because you said you remember having it as a kid," she prompted him. "You said something about your mother…where you grew up—"

He scooped up the piece of brown bread and dropped the cover onto his plate with a clang. "Have you created the diagrams of the compound I asked for?"

Now hear this: the iceberg is showing no signs of melting. Not one dribble.

"I haven't had a chance, since I had to catch up on my work in the garden and the kitchen," she informed him with a frown. "Most of my day was tied up playing Little Dutch Docent."

"No excuses. You had an assignment. My orders supersede your other duties." He shoved half the bread in his mouth and discarded the rest onto the dented plate cover.

"Oh. Well." She paused. "I suppose I'll…get right on it."

Before you pull that stick out of your ass and beat me with it.

He seized the napkin from beside his plate and briskly wiped off his gloved fingers.

She sighed quietly. *At least this is turning into just another "Gab with Grumpy" session. No ulterior motive so far.*

She crossed her arms and sauntered away from him, looking around at the sparsely filled room. She felt small as she stood in the middle of the warped wooden floor. He'd had his men move out practically every stick of furniture. He'd left the double bed, but had turned it ninety degrees, so that it was pushed lengthwise against the back wall. The desk remained as well. By comparison to the previous eyeball-numbing extravagance of Caretaker Dijkstra's far-from-humble abode, the desk was surprisingly plain: stark lines, squared corners, straight-legged, not a clawed foot nor a knobby carving to be had. No wonder Captain Cold Fish liked it. It did have a warmth to it, though, as it was hewn from a honey-brown wood that soaked up the lamplight's glow.

And lastly, he'd kept the old cherrywood armoire painted with tendrils of ivy she'd admired that morning. He'd positioned the armoire squarely in front of the window, which defeated the purpose of *having* a window. All the gilded trinkets had been swept off the fireplace mantel, with the exception of a modestly decorative silver clock topped by a leaping stag. The only new "embellishments" the captain had introduced to the now spartan quarters were the holsters he usually wore. He had hung them both on the wall pegs behind his desk, two different guns secured in the black leather.

"Well, you sure know how to take a room from one extreme to the other," she remarked.

His eyes were set far back in the gloom of the hood, as if he'd deliberately pulled the garment forward to obscure his masked features further. It reminded her of earlier, when he had turned to her in the hallway—his face consumed by shadow. He'd looked inhuman. Was that all on purpose? His preference for intimidation rather than interaction? It had to be the reason for the druid-like garb. And how old was he? From his voice and mannerisms, he seemed perhaps six or eight years her senior.

I wish he'd drop this whole Man of Mystery act and take the stupid mask off.

"I've been reviewing the notes you took." He poured some red wine from the pitcher. "They're incomplete."

She opened her mouth to retort but stopped when he casually extended his glass toward her. She put her hands on her hips. "I poured that wine from the bottle myself."

He continued to hold forth the glass, his eyes glowing catlike within the hood.

With a sigh, she ambled back to him. She took a large sip and swished the wine around. She swallowed it dramatically and set the glass on his desk. "Satisfied?"

"For now."

"Well, getting me drunk on the first date won't get you anywhere." She cringed as soon as the wisecrack came out.

He took a gulp of wine, and his gaze seemed to press down on her. She knew next to nothing about this man. As it was, his reserved behavior seemed strained, as if he were barely withholding his darker impulses. She should watch her step, like Cornelis had said. Like any sane-minded individual would, in her circumstances.

"You can scratch 'attention to detail' off your skills list." The captain picked up the notepad in his other hand and tilted it toward her. "You have no trouble running your mouth, but you do a piss-poor job of listening. Several items are missing that I expressly told you to include."

She had to bite the inside of her cheek. *Careful, Vanessa.*

"Well, sometimes you threw me a bunch of terms I'd never heard of," she said.

"Such as?"

She twirled her hand in the air. "Such as fifty thousand caliber something-or-others and antiperson...whatevers."

"Mines. Antipersonnel mines." He took another drink and set his glass down firmly. "Next time, I'll draw pictures."

The last threads of her restraint unraveled. *Okay, there's a difference between being careful and being a doormat.*

"Well, burying a bunch of mines is a half-baked idea. We do have cows and other animals that wander around the fields here. And if you're not crazy about chicken now, just wait till one explodes all over you."

He walked around to the back of his desk. "I've made updates in the margins, but you can rewrite the notes tomorrow." He said it as if he were doing her a grudging favor. "And make them more legible this time."

"Because I have nothing else to do," she said under her breath.

He dropped the notepad into a drawer and fixed her in

a stare. "Care to say that a little louder?"

She gave up the passive-aggressive approach. "Well, come on. Who ever heard of a pirate needing a stenographer? No one ever spun any daring tales about Blackbeard and his trusty secretary—"

"Keep pushing your luck, and I'll find someone to take your place. And you'll be confined to quarters with a bag of rations for the duration of our stay here. Now"—he walked toward her slowly—"are you ready to drop the wiseass attitude?"

She rolled her tongue behind her teeth and squashed the comeback that sprang forth.

He turned to the dinner dish on his desk and picked up the bread crust he'd left on the cover. "I'm only going to say this once: insubordination doesn't fly with me. I don't accept it from my men, and I'm sure as hell not going to accept it from you."

"Which would make sense if I'd *volunteered* to be part of your admin staff." Comeback unsquashed!

"I'm in command, whether that suits you or not." He stuffed the crust into his mouth and took his time chewing it. "So you can either follow my orders or have all privileges revoked."

"Privileges? You mean I'm already enjoying some?"

"Watch your step," he warned.

She threw out her arms. "Or what? Seriously, what's the worst you're going to do to me if I quit asking how high, whenever you tell me to jump? None of us wanted you to barge into our home, so we don't have to do what you say. You're not *our* leader. You're not our caretaker. Nobody else will say it to your face, but it's true. You've been nothing but a…a big bully. I've only been doing all this stuff for you, because—" She halted and snapped her mouth shut.

The air around him seemed to hum with angry energy. "Because what?"

She eased her shoulders down and crossed her arms loosely. "Because I want to see if maybe you're more than that." She glanced at him from the corners of her eyes. "If you're *better* than that."

The silence in the room grew heavy. But the energy around him had changed. When she met his gaze again, the look in his eyes was something like…bewilderment. But then the usual gruffness returned.

"You give a lot of leeway to strangers," he said in a low voice. "That's a very dangerous attitude when you don't know what they're capable of. You may regret that."

She was hit with a painful twinge in her chest that cut her breath short.

I do.

A vision began to play: the smiling man from her youth, when he put his hands on his knees and bent over her, asking where her parents were. He wanted his money. He wanted them to pay. He smiled so wide that his mouth seemed full of too many teeth…

She steadied her chin, though she couldn't do the same for her voice. "My parents taught me to look past the surface. People aren't always what they seem. Even those who act like they're so tough. I don't think most human beings want to hurt anyone."

Some do. Some like to dump people in a gutter with their throats cut open.

An even sharper twinge stilled her breath.

Cornelis had pulled her away before she could reach their bodies, before she could see them for herself. Then Rhetta had been the one to identify their corpses at the morgue. The cook had not wanted their twelve-year-old daughter to witness the grisly sight. But Vanessa had pictured the scene of the assassination in so many different ways over the years that being shielded from it never lessened the horror.

"Anyway," she said, getting a grip on her thoughts, "they made me understand a lot about people, so I can make my own decisions about them." She paused. "And sometimes live with the mistakes. They knew I'd always deal with the world in my own way. That means I can survive anywhere out there."

"And yet, you're still here."

She bristled. "I'm here because this is my home. And it's important to me. But I'm not afraid to leave. In fact, I was *trying* to leave, long before you showed up. I can't sit around here until something happens that will change my life."

She folded her arms, and they stared at each other. Her face flushed.

"No, the irony is not lost on me," she told him. "I just mean that there's a destiny out there for me, where I'll start my own life. And where I'm supposed to be with—with someone who—who appreciates—"

Crap. Why am I telling him all this?

"Besides, I may get voted out of the compound soon anyway," she went on. "I've never won any popularity contests around here, but judging by the pissy looks I got today for showing you around, I think I fell down the ladder a few rungs."

His gaze grew sharp. "Why? Has someone said something to you? Or done anything?"

She paused. He actually sounded a little irate.

Since when does he care about how I'm treated?

She lifted one shoulder in a feeble shrug. "The other residents being annoyed with me is the status quo."

He said nothing, but there was something going on behind those starkly green eyes. Concern? No, that couldn't be it.

Could it?

"Why does it matter to you?" she asked slowly.

He stood straighter and hesitated. Then he tugged on the cuff of each of his black gloves. "Because nothing should happen at this compound that I don't know about."

She pressed her lips together and uncrossed her arms. So that was it. His unreasonable fixation on control.

"Nothing you don't know about, huh?" she popped off. "This coming from the man wearing his food."

His voice cracked like a whip. "What?"

She walked up to him and made herself meet his glare.

"Based on your eating habits, I should have brought a bib, not a napkin." She batted at the front of his robe, where a cluster of brown bread crumbs clung to the fabric. "Just look at how filthy this—"

His eyes flared and he seized her wrist. But instead of pushing her away, he pulled her against him. "What are you doing?" He sounded more startled than angry.

She took a deep breath, waiting for her pulse to quit freaking out. "Making human contact?"

He brought his masked face close to hers. "Don't." He released her.

She drifted backward and cradled her right wrist in her hand. A warmth lingered on her skin from the firm pressure of his gloved fingers. It was the first time he had deliberately touched her. And though he could have snapped her wrist with minimal effort, the way he had squeezed it had not been threatening. It had been anticipatory. Like he had been thinking of doing something audacious. Something that would test the limits of what she would allow him to do.

And what would *you allow, Vanessa?*

"That's enough," she muttered, rubbing her wrist.

The captain squinted at her and flexed his left hand beside him.

"That's enough…of that dirty robe," she said louder and motioned at the full length of him. "Take it off."

"Excuse me?"

Her ears grew hot, but hopefully he couldn't see them under her hair. She tugged a few locks in front of them for good measure. "You heard me, Captain. Strip. I can tell that thing is getting stiffer by the minute. Let me handle it, and I'll give it what it needs." She halted when he tilted his head, and she mentally kicked herself. "I mean y-your robe. It needs a trip to the laundry." She put her hands behind her to keep from spastically clutching them together where he could see the nervous habit.

The captain squared his shoulders, and she was sure he was doing his best to glower at her. But the way he started to tap his fingertips against the desk betrayed his discomfort. And the most surprising part: he was seriously thinking about it.

Stop the presses! Iceberg is showing signs of melting after all!

He took a few slow steps away from his desk, and she sidled around him to back up against it. Finally, just when she thought she had cut off the circulation to her arms by hunching her shoulders too hard, the captain grabbed two handfuls of his heavy robe and dragged it up over himself.

He smoothed his mask against his face and ran his left hand down the back of his head, as if worriedly checking to make sure the pins had not been dislodged. As she'd suspected, every centimeter of cloth covering him was black: Jeans and belt. Knee-high leather boots. Leather gloves. Long-sleeved shirt with the collar turned up to overlap the part of his mask that extended down his neck. But although there was still something off about the flesh around his eyes and mouth, what could be so unusual about the rest of him that warranted such painstaking concealment?

Because the rest of him—much easier to distinguish without the robe in the way—looked very fine from where she stood.

The way the muscles along his arms stretched the fabric of his sleeves was the same way his immense chest pulled his shirt taut. Though she had not caught any glimpses of his daily exercise routine yet, his solid soldier's body was obviously built by long years of discipline. It made her want to glide her hands down his sides and along his belt to where it pressed snugly against the flat expanse of his abdomen. And now she knew how he was able to cover so much ground when she tried to keep up with his swift strides. It was clear that his strong, defined legs made that powerful gait possible. Her eyes flitted across his tight-fitting jeans and stalled on the front of them. Yes, indeed. This man had been hiding some very impressive dimensions beneath all that cloth.

The captain weighed the robe in one hand, still seeming thoughtful. Finally, he held the garment out to her. He cleared his throat. "Light starch in the collar."

She stared at him. *Did he just crack a joke?*

A smile pulled at her mouth as she cautiously accepted it into her arms. "I'll make a note of it."

"I want you back here tomorrow. Make sure the laundry staff has it ready for me so you can bring it with you." He paused. "If anyone has a problem with that, tell them you're acting under my direct orders, and you have no choice about it. And if they still give you shit, you let me know."

Unexpectedly, a wave of heat rolled over her skin at his words, and she hugged the black bundle to herself. "Will do."

"Be here in the morning at the same time. And when I say *same* time, I mean *on* time. Understood?"

"Yes, sir. Crack of dawn it is, sir."

She saw the frost form in his eyes and she winced. *Okay, so maybe I* am *a smart-ass.*

He stepped forward slowly and towered over her, close enough that the robe bunched against her was the only thing separating them. "And tomorrow you may want to do a better job of covering those." His eyes skipped down to her legs. "They're a little too tempting."

She felt her cheeks begin to catch fire again. Who exactly was she tempting? His men…or him?

She squeezed the bundle in her arms to quell the quiver in her stomach. Without the robe, he had an alluring musky fragrance—like freshly tilled soil and dark fruitwood. She hadn't been near enough to notice it before, and it began to infuse the very air between them. She swayed toward him as the close masculine aura of him seemed to envelop her, invade her. She breathed in deeply and then lifted her eyes to his.

"Something else on your mind?" His voice was silky this time, inviting.

You have no idea.

Her eyes popped open wider. "No, I-I should get going. I'll make sure that—ow!" She caught herself as she stumbled back against his desk. She squinted one eye as she rubbed her rear end. "Sorry. Maybe you should start padding this thing, huh?" She gave a jittery laugh and turned to drift backward toward the door. But then she stopped. "Oh, uh…can I go?"

"Unless you'd rather stay."

She sank her fingers into the robe and massaged the thick cloth. She glanced at the bed.

He's testing me. I know he's testing me.

But the way his gaze roamed over her as he flexed his left hand beside him made her lungs tighten.

She pulled herself together and grabbed for the door handle behind her. "Rain check."

He angled his head as soon as she said it.

Rain check? What the hell, Vanessa?

But she swore his mask shifted upward at the corner of his mouth. "Dismissed," he said quietly.

She nodded and quickly opened the door. But before she backed out, she let her eyes dart over him. It was a shame he was going to cover all that up again.

She closed the door but stood motionless in front of it for a second. When she turned, Morgan was watching her above his paper, his legs still crossed upon the table. His gaze fell onto the black robe bundled in her arms. His forehead creased, and he lowered the *Noordster Courant* to his lap.

She plucked at the heavy material and shrugged. "I've been promoted to valet."

Morgan's eyes again swept across the robe. "A rare honor." But then he followed the deadpan delivery with a much gentler tone. "You've made quite the impression. Most never cross his threshold, let alone linger beyond it."

She wormed her fingers into the folds of the robe. "Guess I'm just special."

He rested his gaze on hers. "Indeed you are."

His voice had turned dulcet—that English accent laying every syllable on a satin pillow—and her limbs started to go slack. But she nudged herself and squeezed the bundle of fabric in her arms before it could slip through them.

"I, uh, need to get this to the laundry staff," she said.

"They're probably about to knock off for the night."

"Then please"—he inclined his head so that the lamp-light glinted off his cropped midnight hair—"do not let me keep you."

"I don't mind if you keep me," she said, but then clenched the bundled cloth with a start. "That is…later, you can keep me all you want. I mean, next time you can—when I'm not—Goodnight."

She turned and hurried down the dimly lit corridor, eager to turn the corner so she could bury her face in the robe and scream.

CHAPTER TEN

VANESSA

Vanessa rolled her eyes at the small three-legged alarm clock squatting on her mantel. Its tarnished square case was dimpled with dents—the scars of having been thrown from its spot each morning over the course of many years.

Bet Captain Clock-Watcher can't wait to give me another verbal spanking.

She stuck each arm into her short-sleeved white blouse and shrugged it onto her shoulders as she leaned down to yank on the heel strap of her sandal. She was running late again and could not possibly make it by zero seven hundred—much less six forty-five—on the dot.

She glanced at the robe laid neatly across her bed. The heavy garment presented a stark contrast to all the pleasing pastels in her room, like a black shadow spreading over a field of purple heather and buttercups. At least she had that ready to go, though Neve and Margo had not been happy about the last-minute washing assignment, right when they were finishing their shifts in the laundry room. But luckily they were two of her few friends in the compound and did not blame *her* for the tardy drop-off…though they did have some choice words about her request to add more fabric softener to freshen it up. Regardless, she would entreat Rhetta to share her homemade boerenmeis-jes so that she could get back into the young laundresses' good graces. The cook's spiced, brandied apricots could win anyone over, and were often Vanessa's secret weapon when begging for favors.

She gathered her hair behind her, tugging the trapped ends out from under her bra straps, and met her mother's steady gaze coming from the wall over the fireplace. She smiled at the framed sketch and idly pulled a lock of hair over her shoulder to weave her fingers through it.

Her father had been a wonderful artist. He'd lovingly captured the gentle curves of her mother's face in a set of wispy pencil strokes as she'd sat cross-legged under the Belle de Boskoop—a much smaller tree at the time— trying to hold a giggling, wriggling six-year-old Vanessa in her lap. They had just moved into the old fort with their small band of refugee friends, and though Vanessa should have been troubled by the confusion and displacement, her mom had made everything seem perfectly normal. Like they all belonged there.

Vanessa stopped twisting her hair and glanced around. She'd been so excited when her parents had let her have her own room a few years later, with a grown-up's double bed. And it hadn't taken long for her father to install bookshelves on every wall and fill them with classics from his own collection. Whenever she wasn't playing in the garden or helping Rhetta in the kitchen with whatever delicious thing needed stirring at the time, Vanessa would be spread out on the mauve upholstered bench beneath her wide-open windows to read in the sunlight. Or, in the evenings, she'd lounge on the plush blue rug in front of her little fireplace, with all her favorite Douglas Adams books fanned out around her, and read a few chapters from each one. Now, every shelf sagged under the weight of the novels she'd continued to pile on top of each other throughout the years. No doubt about it: there would come a night when she'd be jolted awake by the sound of splintering wood and be buried in an avalanche of Hemingway and Kafka.

She bent over to pull up her dark-blue skirt. This time, she'd made sure the garment would fall modestly past her knees. But just as she started to shimmy her way into it, the door to her room burst open. She turned with a yelp as the captain barged in, followed by Morgan. She grabbed the front of her blouse closed with one hand while she wrenched up the skirt to cover her lacy pink panties.

"You should consider locking your door," the captain said tactlessly as she whirled away to face the fireplace again.

She threw a smoldering look over her shoulder as she jerked on the skirt zipper. "You should try knocking."

"You should've been ready by now."

She jammed the buttons into the holes of her shirt and spun around. "And you should kiss my—"

She stopped when her friend Marien from the kitchen staff walked in to set two plates of food on Vanessa's small wooden table. With a glance at Vanessa, the auburn-haired cooking assistant backed away and hurried out.

"Since you're finicky about breakfast," the captain said tartly, "I ordered the kitchen to make something. Yesterday, I had to listen to your stomach growling between all the sarcastic comments. Obviously, it puts you in a bad mood when you miss a meal."

She stared at him. *He* was calling *her* cranky?

The captain spotted his robe on her bed and swiped a hand across it. He pulled it onto himself, and his body visibly relaxed as soon as the cloth settled over him. But his voice was as wiry as ever. "A completed assignment. There's hope for you yet."

She looked at Morgan and gestured toward the captain. "Really? Is that how he always says thank you?"

Morgan bent his head, obviously hiding the smile that swept across his mouth.

She turned to the captain. "Why are you in my room?" She nearly stamped her foot. "I was supposed to come to *you*."

"It's clear I can't rely on your punctuality, so I didn't have much choice."

She formed her hands into fists. Then both officers

moved their gazes to her chest. She ground her teeth. *Men.*

She put her fists on her hips. "Aren't you afraid having breakfast will throw us off schedule?"

"Only if you keep standing there bitching." The captain seated himself at the table while Morgan left the room and closed the door behind him. He glanced at his watch. "We have ten minutes."

She dropped herself into the opposite chair. "You honestly think I can enjoy myself in the space of ten lousy minutes?"

"That's up to you. I can make it a pleasant ten minutes or your worst ten minutes."

"I can tell you which one it feels like so far."

She crossed her arms. Again, his gaze lowered to her chest.

He does that one more time, and I'm going to dump this plate on his lap.

But she felt a flutter in her stomach. Having the brooding masked captain in her bedroom without an easy exit was not the way she had pictured her morning going. As he bit off a piece of sausage and chewed the ossenworst slowly, his sharp eyes never left hers, and her stomach became one giant flutter. But when he glanced at her breasts yet again, she flattened her palms on the table.

"What is so fascinating about my—?"

He pointed the sausage at her chest. She looked down. In her haste, she had missed a button, so that her shirt gaped open in front and put a large portion of her pink bra on display. Her hand shot up to cover the hole.

"Excuse me for a moment," she said tightly.

She twisted around in her chair and did up every last button until there was not a millimeter of cleavage in sight. When she turned back, she stared at the small bowl of buttermilk porridge on her plate, evaluating whether it was deep enough to hide her face in. The captain rested his forearms on the table and dug his fork into his uitsmijter. Rhetta usually only made the open-faced fried-egg-and-ham sandwich for weekend brunches—and hangovers—but she had apparently tried to anticipate the captain's hearty appetite.

Vanessa picked up her spoon and scraped at the edges of porridge that had already cooled against the inside of the bowl. The quiet of her room—normally something she welcomed—made her squirm. She glanced at the door and strained her ears for any indication that Morgan had not completely abandoned her to the captain, but she couldn't hear anything beyond her own heartbeat.

She dipped her spoon into the karnemelkse pap. "So…why does Morgan follow you around everywhere?"

"He doesn't." As he lifted the fork to his mouth again, she glimpsed bare flesh at his wrist, where the black shirt cuff pulled away from the bottom of his glove. There was something wrong about the skin's texture. Then his wrist vanished back into his sleeve, and she dropped her eyes to her plate.

"Well, he never seems far behind." She piled more porridge on top of the spoonful she'd already taken but not eaten. "Is he your bodyguard or something?"

The captain paused, and his eyes glowed within the hood. "Do I look like I need a bodyguard?"

She glanced over his weird disguise. *You look like you need a therapist.*

"Then why do you keep him outside your room at night?"

He stared at her wordlessly. She scowled at the appel-stroop-drizzled slice of bread on her plate. She might as well resign herself to the fact that he was going to make every discussion as delightful as a bikini wax.

But he surprised her by finally answering. "When we first take over a facility, I can't always watch my back while I'm running things. And at night, in the dark, someone usually gets up the nerve to try and slit my throat. So yes, the lieutenant acts as a guard, but he's also my second-in-command."

He did not pronounce it as *lef*-tenant, like everyone else did. Again: American? In any case, that explained why the others all followed Morgan's orders as if they were the captain's. But one bit of information had caught her attention in an unsettling way.

She sprinkled a few almonds into her bowl and asked hesitantly, "How many *facilities* have you done this to?"

He rested a gloved hand against his plate and turned the slice of Maasdam cheese between his fingers as he watched her closely. "More than you'd like to know."

The words had a chilling effect. She put her spoon back into the bowl to warm the porridge she had let go cold on the utensil again and opted to change the subject. "What's my assignment today?"

But he evidently picked up on her tone of voice. "You're getting off easy, compared with your peers."

"What, so no one else gets to play 'Guess How Ticked Off I Am Today'?"

"A game you're decidedly losing." His words were edged with ice.

A tremor of discomfort made her twitch back in her seat. "I'm not that important around here, so I don't know why you're putting me through this."

"I can make it much harder for you, if you'd like."

"I bet you say that to all the girls," she mumbled.

With that, her face practically burst into flames, and she sank down in her chair. An intensity entered his eyes. It was both disturbing and magnetic, like standing too close to a fast-flowing river. All at once, she felt as trapped as if he were pressing her up against a wall, and the image of his hand wrapping carefully around her throat made her shiver.

"That mouth of yours loves being open, doesn't it?" His words came to her as if purred into her ear. "I may have to find something to put in it, if you can't keep it under control."

She took an involuntary breath as he seemed to back away. She touched her fingers to her throat and swallowed.

"Now"—he stabbed his fork into another piece of ossenworst—"I want to know every detail about all the people living in this compound."

Shake it off. Don't let him get to you.

She slouched forward and stirred her porridge. "That sounds exciting."

"I need you to focus." He threw a slice of cheese in his mouth to chew it along with the sausage, then pushed his dish aside. "Let's get started."

She straightened and glanced down at her untasted meal. "But that wasn't even ten minutes!"

"Close enough."

With a glare, she let her spoon clatter into the bowl before he pulled her plate away.

"I want every resident name inventoried," he said. "And I want to know who works hard and who's dead weight. Who might have a fighting background? Who has specialized skills or knowledge? Who's disgruntled and needs to be monitored? Who has the most blah-blah-blahs? And blah-dee-blah-blippity-blooh…"

She placed an elbow on the table and set her cheek in her hand as she continued tuning out his laundry list.

"…blah-ditty-blah, and that includes you."

She'd almost reduced his voice to white noise, when those last words made her sit up. "Me? Why me?"

He pushed back the hood of his robe, and that same intensity lit his eyes. "Because I want to know you inside and out."

She gripped her knees under the table. *He's doing that on purpose. Stop reacting.*

"Start the list." He reached behind himself and into the robe. "Who's been here the longest, besides you?"

She made herself quit digging her nails into her knees as she took a breath. "Well, there's Herman—"

She stopped when he pulled the dreaded notepad out from some hidden pocket and slapped it down on the table, like the world's most half-assed magic trick.

Ta-dah. Now watch all my free time disappear.

Her shoulders slumped, and she took the ballpoint pen that he also inexplicably produced. She flipped through the pages to find a clean one. "Herman is our building maintenance man who's supposed to make sure broken things get fixed," she said as she jotted down his name. "And you can see for yourself how good he is at that. He's been here since I was about fourteen. As for his special skills: I'd say napping while standing."

"Disgruntled?"

"Only when he has to fix something. Which is…pretty much all the time."

She could have sworn the remark made his eyes crease a bit. Maybe he did have a sense of humor after all.

"Next."

Or not.

"Rhetta." Vanessa decorated the older woman's name with a cursive look on the paper. "She came here about a year or so after we did. She's our head cook—our hands-down fantastic head cook, in case you haven't noticed." Vanessa's voice trailed off, and the pen slowed in her hand as she stared down at the words she had written. "She's been like a mother to me." She shook herself. "Anyway, there's Cornelis—"

My ex-boyfriend with eyes the color of a cool sapphire sky and a body that still makes my lady parts tingle.

She cleared her throat and stared hard at the notepad as she skipped to the next line. "There's also Pieter, who's kind of like a personnel director, since he deals with the residents' complaints. And Steffen, who helps me in the garden—"

"Fine. Make note of them. Now what about the ones who arrived in the last few years? The ones who haven't been integrated into the community very long." The captain paused and drummed his fingers on the table. "They're less predictable."

"First one to show up was the rabbit," she said straight-faced. "But I can't put his name down, because I never came up with one."

"It's Tim."

The immediate reply took her off guard, spoiling her sarcasm. "What?"

"Next."

Her mouth worked silently for a few seconds before

reengaging. "Oka-a-a-y…There's our brewer, Sven, but he stinks at what he does." She shook her head as she scribbled. "Every beer he makes tastes like he strained it through his socks." She put down the pen to meet his eyes. "And I mean while he's still wearing them."

"Fair warning, then."

He seemed to relax marginally. At least now he was letting her experiment with how much levity she could shoehorn into this monotonous chore.

What other boundaries will he let me push?

"Speaking of names…" She started a small flower-shaped doodle in the margin. "I think it's only right that we record an entry about the commanding officer of the fort now, don't you? What was your full name again?"

He drummed his fingers once on the table, and his eyes never shifted from hers.

"Oh, right: Leonard. Leo Evans." She made as if to write it down, but paused. "Or was it Gustav?"

He leaned back in his chair and crossed his arms.

"Ivan? No…Denny." She cocked her head. "Elmo?"

"Finished?"

She sighed. "Evidently."

"Good. Get back on track."

Worth a shot.

"Our brewer Sven: He grew up in the town and moved in here maybe three years ago. He spends—well, before you guys got here, he *used* to spend half his time here and half in town—"

"Stop. He hasn't been living here full-time?"

"I think he stayed with friends a lot."

What does it matter?

"So he has a relationship with the townspeople," the captain said. "He's positioned to agree with either their agendas or the compound's."

She held her pen suspended above the pad, not sure what kind of notes she was meant to make about this.

"Circle his name," he said.

She did, but the contemplative silence that overcame him was a little unnerving. Like he was calculating a next move. She hesitated for a second and then glanced down at the notepad again. The creation of this "list" was beginning to tweak her conscience.

"There was the caretaker, of course," she resumed when he signaled her to continue, "but we all know how that ended." She drew a frowny face next to Dijkstra's name. "Although he's probably gone crying to Mayor Visser, since he always bragged that they were such good buddies."

"Is that so?"

She stopped adding big teardrops to the sad face and glanced up. "Yeah, but he was a blowhard, so he used to say a lot of things."

The captain seemed to grow thoughtful once more, and she decided to keep going. Something about the vibe he now gave off was even more disconcerting.

"So, uh, Marien works in the kitchen with me. You saw her a second ago. She's an assistant cook about my age and, unfortunately for all of us, she's not exactly setting the culinary world on fire. Though she did once set her own apron on fire—"

There was a knock on the door, which instantly made the thought *You couldn't manage that earlier?* fly through her head as Morgan stepped in.

"Sir, Frank and Mabayoje have made a discovery which you'll want to see," the lieutenant informed him.

But the lack of further explanation did not seem to irk the captain. Had *she* delivered such an arcane message, he probably would have steamed and screeched like a human teakettle!

The captain pushed back his chair and stood. She rose to her feet and started to follow.

"Stay here," he ordered her. "I need you to finish the list. And be thorough about it. Don't omit any details, I want them all. You also owe me yesterday's notes, rewritten."

"But—" she started to say as he motioned to Morgan to bring the plates of now-cold food, which made her protest louder. "Hey!"

"And where are my diagrams of the compound?"

"In the same place as my imaginary art degree," she said as she woefully watched her porridge being whisked away.

"I asked you to draw them up for me. Twice. Why haven't you done so?"

"Listen, I told you I'm not good at that sort of thing, unless you want everything to look like a five-year-old did it."

"I want them in my hands today. I have business near the kitchen this evening, after your dinner shift is over, so I'll expect you to be there with what I've asked for."

She flapped the notepad toward him. "But what about—?"

He and Morgan turned and walked out of her room.

She gripped the ballpoint pen so hard she could hear the plastic crack. She ran to the door, shoved it closed, and stared at it. Then she hurled the notepad at it. The papers fluttered wildly as the pad fell to the floor with a smack. She took a deep breath, and one of her blouse buttons popped open just as her stomach let out a long rumbling growl. She almost screamed.

Today had already reached new levels of *suck*.

CHAPTER ELEVEN

ETHAN

Drips of water echoed throughout the network of tunnels, sounding like the deep, muddy bowels of one of the old Pennsylvania coal mines Ethan used to tour as a boy. He rolled his shoulders, this time glad for his robe, since the tunnels had proven to be on the wintry side.

He felt a prick of irritation. Vanessa should have told him about these underground passageways during his inspection. The compound was already bigger than it looked, and now these created even more of a containment headache. Especially if they were in as poor condition as the rest of the old fort and were riddled with breaches from the outside. It would only take one resident to slip down here and navigate their way to an opening at the surface, where they could make it past his patrols and gather reinforcements. He didn't need that interruption to his timetable right now. Regardless, he should have noticed the entrance to the tunnels himself, as he rarely missed such details. But he'd been distracted. If she just hadn't been wearing that damn short skirt—

"Captain?"

Ethan turned his head to Morgan. "What?"

Morgan held up his lantern with the wick burning high and raised his eyebrows toward the colossal machine that filled the underground chamber off the main passageway.

"Oh…yes." Ethan glanced from Mabayoje to Frank as they stood on either side of the giant generator. There were two more just like it housed in the domed chambers next to this one. "Do we think we can get them running?"

"Unknown." Morgan lowered the lantern and frowned as he brushed at a drip that fell on his sleeve. "We need to bring Nicolo down, to provide his estimation, but I'm uncertain as to his experience with this manner of machine." Morgan rested his palm on the pommel of his Fairbairn-Sykes knife at his left side. "If it lacks wheels and a drivetrain, he typically shows little interest."

"Don't be fooled." Ethan smoothed the neck of his mask. "He's not happy unless he's got grease on his hands, no matter the contraption."

Morgan smiled and let out a breath through his nose. Even that small sound whispered down the length of the musty corridor.

Ethan turned to Mabayoje, who stood next to the center generator leisurely chewing his gum. "Do all three of these look to be in the same condition?"

The Nigerian lieutenant nodded. "Beeni, Oga." He knocked on the rounded side, which broke the quiet of the tunnels like a muffled gong. "All the same model, apparently." Mabayoje rubbed a finger absently up and down the scars of the three-lined tribal marks on his right cheek that mirrored the long vertical ones on his left. "And all installed at the same time."

His accent sounded much like Morgan's in its formal style. But since he spoke both English and Yoruba fluently, Lieutenant Okusanya—like most of the men— could switch to his native vernacular so deftly that it kept Ethan from bragging about the mediocre language skills he'd picked up while stationed in Germany.

Ethan passed by Frank, who stood inside the domed chamber, opposite Mabayoje. "I'm guessing these aren't steam-powered." Ethan scratched his chin through the mask as he examined the rusty bolted seams of the metal beast. "No boilers nearby."

"They may have been removed," Morgan suggested.

"Maybe. Or there were wind turbines." Ethan pointed up to where, in the back of the chamber, a stout round pipe brushed the ceiling. But it was too dark to tell if it bored through the brick or not. "Could have been attached to a windmill."

"Ooto ni, but it would take more than one to run all three of these," Mabayoje remarked.

Frank's handheld lamp swayed with a squeak as he crossed his arms and leaned against the wall. "Do you know where they came from, Captain, sir?" The Russian sergeant rolled his *r*'s with the same tongue-defying ease as Angus with his Scottish burr.

Ethan nodded slowly. "According to the Dutch girl—"

Morgan cleared his throat lightly. "Miss Brouwer."

Ethan squinted at him. "I know her name, Lieutenant."

Morgan inclined his head but did not lose his smug smile. Ethan turned back to his other officers. "According to her, this compound was a historic site open to the public, so most likely the tourist board had these installed."

"There are a great number of electrical outlets about the fort." Morgan kicked at a loose stone in the floor to dig it up from a puddle. "Archaic devices that are more rust than metal."

"I'll take it, if it means we can have real lights while we're here."

"And internet," Frank muttered with a heavy frown.

Ethan smiled to himself. The big sergeant had become hooked on streaming daytime serial dramas during their last few occupations. The language barriers evidently posed no problems, when most every plot point could be gleaned from the number of times characters slapped one another or slept with one another.

"Well, let's see what Nic says." Ethan looked at Mabayoje. "Radio him, and tell him to put on his electrician's hat."

"Beeni, Oga," Mabayoje said with a nod as he plucked the walkie-talkie off his belt and turned away.

Ethan looked between Frank and Morgan. "Make this a priority. No telling if these tunnels were even here when the original fort was constructed. Lots of brick instead of stone, so judging by the switch in materials, they were probably dug out later. Which means we may be sitting on a cave-in waiting to happen." He focused on Frank. "Sergeant, start looking for signs of stress, where anything has crumbled or there are too many cracks, and make a note. There might be some residents with structural engineering knowledge, so we can figure out how bad off we are and if we'll be risking any injury while we're here. I'll have a list of names soon."

If she bothers to finish it.

"Morgan, find Angus and have him bring some men down here to map out the rest of this underground maze. I want to know how far it goes and what else may be in it that we can use. Also make sure there are no passages to the outside. We need to lock this place up tight."

He heard a "yes, sir" from both of them before he turned and made his way back through the corridor leading to the stairs.

Morgan drew up beside him as he exited the tunnels. "Far be it from me to suggest this," Morgan began, "but you seem rather preoccupied. Couldn't have anything to do with a certain set of pink lace lingerie, now, could it?"

Ethan gave his friend a sideways look. "A nice way to start the day, I'll admit. I noticed *you* didn't avert your eyes like an English gentleman should."

Morgan showed a small smile. "She is quite well-endowed for such a slender girl. Better men than I could not have disregarded the sight."

Ethan gave a grunt of agreement. Vanessa's fumbling attempt to cover herself had done little to hide the way she'd nicely filled out that bra. Too bad he hadn't shown up even earlier.

Morgan tossed a glance his way. "At the least, however, you could have seen your way clear to let the girl eat."

"Hunger is motivational, and I need her to do what I asked. Besides, she works in a kitchen, I'm sure she'll be fine."

"I would keep an eye on your dinner plate then, in case any mysterious foods appear on it," Morgan said as they turned down the next hallway. "Hell hath no fury like a woman unfed."

"In her case, that might be true. But she's harmless."

Morgan raised an eyebrow. "In my experience, a beautiful girl is the least harmless of all."

The lieutenant gave him a casual salute and split off to make his way toward the armory, where Angus was no doubt already deep into cataloging the miscellaneous ammunition and equipment the army had picked up on their way into the Netherlands.

Ethan pushed back his hood and ran a hand down the front of his robe. Even through his glove, the laundered material somehow felt softer and more plush. He glanced around as he walked before pinching the front of the robe to lift the fabric to his nose. He breathed in through the mask. The thick material was permeated with a fragrance that was instantly enjoyable, like traces of a woman's perfume on his bedsheets the next morning. But this was better, more enticing. It was the smell of spring, like the allure of fresh grass and lush berries. Something Vanessa herself could have coaxed from her garden and captured in the cloth.

He ran his hand down his chest again as he made his way toward the bright end of the stone passageway. He would rather have had *her* scent on his clothes, though. She probably smelled as sweet as one of her apples. But last night, after the touch of her tits when he'd pulled her against him, her scent had been the last thing on his mind. The sudden solid contact had sent a vibration down the length of him that made his entire body tense under the robe. And he was sure she could sense the full salute he had failed to control.

As the perimeter of the garden came into view, a resident girl with long brown hair turned the corner of an adjoining hallway to walk toward him. And fast on her heels came Liam. The girl held her head high with a blatant smirk on her face. She was the one who had been at the center of the squabble between Liam and the young gray-haired resident the day before.

Liam adjusted his rifle behind his shoulder and skirted around the girl to walk backward in front of her. "Come now, Anna, hear me out." His Irish lilt poured over his words like syrup. "A fine young wan like yourself must be starvin' for some good craic, what with being cooped up in this pile of rocks. I've got a few…entertainment options we can try later. Where'd ya say your room is again?"

The young soldier's typical attempts to charm the clothes off any willing female were in full swing, despite Ethan's most recent warning.

Liam turned to walk beside Anna. But when he saw the captain, he stopped short and gave Ethan a stiff salute. "Cap! Mornin', sir."

Ethan returned the salute. "Donegan. You'd better be off duty."

"Yes, sir," Liam answered promptly, his back straight as Ethan approached. "Just, uh…taking care of something before my next shift, sir."

Ethan paused in front of Liam and lowered his voice. "What have I told you about not making pussy a priority? We don't need more problems."

Liam's hand sank from his brow. "Sure, Cap, but I wasn't—that is, I just—"

"I know you don't compromise your loyalty to this outfit, Private, and I've been cutting the men slack because we've all had a shit time of it these past years." Ethan leaned back and shook his head. "But my lenience only goes so—"

Liam's eyebrows lifted slowly, and both shoulders slumped as he stared off into the distance. Ethan glanced in the direction of Anna, whom Liam watched disappear into the gloom the same way Vanessa had longingly watched her porridge being carried away that morning.

Ethan turned back to the young Irishman. With a sigh, he nodded over his shoulder. "Go on."

A grin spread across Liam's face, and he saluted Ethan with a broad sweep of his arm. Ethan started forward again as Liam sidestepped his way down the hall. Not long after, Anna let out a soft giggle that echoed through the passageway.

Ethan emerged from the end of the dim hallway and raised his hood to shield his eyes from the sunlight that flooded the garden. He glanced around. He half expected to see Vanessa out among her plants instead of finishing the assignment he'd given her back in her room. But she was nowhere in sight. Finally, she was learning how to follow orders. Ensuring she and the others fell into line would make things easier while his army dug into this place for the few months they needed it.

He turned out of the perimeter corridor to cross the grass, headed for the opposite side where the stairs led to the battlements overlooking the east field. As Nicolo had reluctantly admitted to him, the security shield drone was DOA, so they would need to procure a new one from whatever local black-market merchants they could find. In the meantime, intruder detection would have to be implemented the old-fashioned way. Once he reached higher ground, he could better evaluate the feasibility of burying their last few blast mines in an arc around the eastern stretch of land. Angus still owed him a report on the number and condition of the remaining explosives. The biosensors on those Slovakian ones were not known to improve with age.

As for other zones of concern, Frank had already arranged for a squad to guard the outer fringes of the forest that surrounded the back field to the north. The clusters of trees provided easy concealment for any enemies intent on observing the fort or planning an attack. The patrols mitigated the vulnerability further by zigzagging their way through the dense copses to root out anyone hidden within.

But the extra manpower measures still did not put him

at ease. He wanted a technological warning system that, for once, didn't fucking crap out every time it was turned on. Arms dealers could typically accommodate that kind of request. And Morgan had reserved his last two communication rings for the sole purpose of setting up discreet channels with such underground vendors, who were often found in abundance near the more remote towns of Europe. But this was *very* remote, so Morgan would likely tap out the data on both prepaid crings before he could persuade a black-market dealer to make the trek. And plus, without a dealer to refill the crings, that rendered them little more than junk jewelry.

As Ethan approached the orchard, the door to one of the two greenhouses opened, and an old male resident emerged. He didn't remember the man's name, but judging by the sack of potting soil he carried over his shoulder, he must have been one of the others who helped Vanessa in the garden. Ethan mounted the stairs that led to the east-side ramparts and returned the salute of a passing sentry as he crossed the stone walkway. He leaned on his hands on the parapet wall and let his eyes wander.

The surrounding land was flat, like most of the country. From what history he remembered—reinforced by Vanessa's eighth-grade-level plaques around the site—the previous generations of Dutch had fought an ongoing battle to claim the land back from the sea in order to live there. But Fort Van Doorn sat on one of the few low-rolling hills in the area, near the coastal side of North Holland, and so provided a better view of the scattered patchwork of grassy ground and strings of trees that stretched away into the distance.

He strained his eyes briefly toward the horizon. Was that a tree or the remains of a drainage windmill?

Number sixteen on the Fort Adventure Map.

He'd looked up that one, after his tour with Vanessa yesterday. Only forty-nine to go before he won his ticket. A smile escaped across his lips, and he shook his head. He grabbed a handful of the robe and held it against his mask again to inhale slowly. He could get used to that scent.

Probably the same fragrance that suffused her pillow. And all her sheets. And it probably perfumed whatever skimpy little nightie she wore to bed…

He buried his nose against the cloth and breathed in deeper.

Not to mention those lacy, delicate, pink—

"Ursäkta, Captain Evans," a male voice said shyly.

Ethan dropped the robe and turned with a start. Edvard stood close enough that Ethan had to tilt his head back to look up at the Swede, whose hair in the bright sunlight was the color of a redwood tree. Appropriate, considering he was about as big as one.

"I mean to say, excuse, sir, and god morgon," Edvard said as he stiffened his spine and held his hand to his brow in a formal salute.

Ethan swept his right hand up to return the salute. "Morning, Private Trogen."

The soldier lowered his arm, but stayed at attention, as if he were waiting for inspection. "I am sorry to bother you, Captain." His brow wrinkled as his light-blue eyes dropped to the front of Ethan's robe. "I waited for you to stop smelling your clothes, but you were smelling them for a long time. I did not know how much longer you would smell them."

"I wasn't sm—" He flattened his shoulders and tugged at the mask where his neck started to overheat. "What is it, Private?"

Edvard tucked his thumbs into his fists beside him. It was a quirk he often showed when nervous, like he was wishing himself good luck, since that was the typical Swedish gesture for it. "I want to ask something."

"Well?"

"Can we help buy more food for all the people here?" The bulky Swede tightened his fists around his thumbs so that his knuckles whitened. "The old kitchen lady needs help, and the pretty garden girl said we are like"—he squinted hard at his feet, and then his round face brightened—"like big talking food vacuums."

Ethan almost felt the steam swirl out from under his

mask. "She did, did she?"

"Jaja!"

"Well, we don't have the funds to support an entire community. They'll have to figure it out."

Edvard's tree-trunk-size chest sank. "Oh." Then his eyes widened, like a child watching fireworks for the first time. "I will use my allowance!"

Ethan angled his head. "You want to spend your own money?"

"Jajamensan! You said we can use our allowance for how we want. I will buy food."

Edvard's mere size and serious gaze were enough to make any opposition shit themselves, but he often sabotaged it with the broad, boyish grin that easily spread across his face. Edvard gave the captain that same grin now.

Ethan pushed back his hood and scratched the cloth at the nape of his neck. "Well, I won't stand in your way, Private. Do what you need to."

Edvard's grin stretched even wider. "Thank you, Captain!"

Ethan turned his head toward the movement in his peripheral vision. Darshan approached with the quiet fluid motion of an apparition, seeming to float along the battlement walkway. The slender but muscular Sikh was dressed in his usual neatly pressed tan shirt and pants, always as if fresh from the dry cleaners, and his serene manner often fooled anyone who'd never seen him in combat.

The Indian soldier drifted to a stop and held his hand to his brow in a salute. "Excuse me, Captain. I do not mean to interrupt."

"Yes, what is it, Private Singh-Khalani?"

"I bring the report from Sergeant Maxwell." Each of Darshan's turbans was meticulously wrapped every day, and their color varied with his mood. Today the neat, tight fabric of his pagri was dark green and was adorned in the center with a small military pin depicting a lion, the symbol of his former Sikh regiment.

Ethan nodded. "The mines?"

"Functional," Darshan said as he rested a hand absently on his kirpan—the short, curved-tip dagger sheathed on his thick cloth belt. "But the biosensors are old and may not tell between human and animal."

"Great," Ethan grumbled. "Exploding chickens everywhere."

Both Darshan and Edvard cocked their heads and glanced at each other.

Ethan waved them off. "How many do we have left?"

"Seven, sir."

Ethan grimaced. "That's it? What the hell did we do with all the others?"

Darshan lifted both coal-colored eyebrows. "Blew things up, sir."

In his mind, Ethan could almost hear Vanessa giggling, pleased at her own snarky observation from yesterday about his usual tactics. He reached in his robe to adjust the strap of his SIG Sauer's shoulder holster. "Well, it's all we've got right now, so let's use them. But make sure those mine detectors on the sentries' belts are all working, so no one takes a wrong step."

Any strangers wandering through this remote area were up to no good and deserved to get their asses blown off. But a protected perimeter was not worth sending his own soldiers to an accidental grave.

"Tell Benny to get a couple of men together so he can oversee the placement of those mines in the east field," Ethan said. "He can read the land better than any of us."

Benoît was downright fucking clairvoyant when it came to predicting the right spots—even hidden ones— where an enemy might tread. And Luxembourg's finest explosive ordnance technician also had a hand so steady that he could disarm a bomb the size of a quarter. Damn lucky, considering that when they first met, that Belgian "prisoner pacification" device planted at the base of Ethan's skull had been about to blow a hole through his brain stem.

Darshan inclined his head. "Yes, Captain, I shall do so

right away."

"I will help!" Edvard blurted, like he'd been dying for the chance to raise his hand. "I will help Benny the Boom Man! I can do better this time!"

Darshan raised his eyebrows again and exchanged a look with Ethan. Although Edvard was an enthusiastic volunteer for any task, no one counted on him to do it gracefully. And after the last instance of watching the giant Swede cheerfully stomp on the dirt each time he buried a blast mine, none of the men could handle the pucker factor anymore.

"I think you ought to sit this one out, Private," Ethan told him.

Edvard's face became that of a kindergartner who'd had his ice cream cone slapped away.

"I'll have something much more important for you to do," Ethan added then. *Once I think of it.*

Edvard took an excited breath and saluted. "Ja, Captain!"

Darshan stroked his full, somewhat wild beard and shared a smile with Ethan.

"Dismissed," Ethan said to both of them and pivoted back to the parapet wall as they went on their way.

It would be good to get a little more protection around them. But something about this place still made him feel exposed. And unprepared. The Ukrainians had not given up their vendetta against him in two years, so they sure as shit were not done with him now. And they seemed to have an endless supply of runners who would not hesitate to sacrifice themselves, or each other, in their pursuit of him. He had been careful to keep a separate map in which he traced back the apparent route each runner had taken, based on where the runners found him and what area the Ukrainians—"Ukes," as most immigrants had nicknamed themselves back in his hometown— had most likely originated from in order to stay in his army's wake. But it did him little good. The runners still caught up. And they still threw out a beacon that their horde of vengeful survivors could follow.

His men had tried several times to wrest the triggering mechanism from each runner, but the unexpected appearance of the Uke always ensured their failure to do so. The runner would push the button and switch the signal on the tracking device embedded somewhere inside the Uke's body to show he'd located his target. All the while, the grinning bastard would taunt Ethan in the heavy Russian accent that characterized the former little community in that region of Ukraine:

"You cannot burn us! You cannot kill us! We will bury you screaming beneath the bodies of your men!"

The words echoed through Ethan's head and made a flash of heat ravage his gnarled flesh.

Like hell you will.

In fact, maybe he'd leave the next runner's body where it lay, with a message carved into its chest: coordinates for a meeting place and an invitation to do their worst. Because he was tired of the chase. Tired of having his decisions made for him, thanks to this forced evasion. Tired of tolerating a body that kept his past deeds constantly in the forefront by reminding him of the mistakes he had made. Hands, arms, torso, face—all formed from twisted meat that still felt raw, as if the flames were never far from his flesh. A goddamn fucking freak. Something that would make anyone run.

Especially her.

Ethan looked over his shoulder. Down below, the thin-haired male resident he'd spied earlier stood under Vanessa's Belle de Boskoop with a ladder propped against the tree. The old Dutchman carefully scaled the rungs with a basket on one arm until he could reach the largest apples ready to be picked.

Ethan ran a gloved hand across the chest of his robe— its fresh spring scent reaching him faintly—and turned back to stare at the bleak line of the horizon.

CHAPTER TWELVE

VANESSA

"Come, child. Are you all right?"

Vanessa lifted her face from where her forehead had been pressed against the paper on the kitchen table.

A hand rested on her shoulder. "Why are you still here, mijn meiske?"

She yawned and looked up into Rhetta's face, which was lined like pale marble and bracketed by shoulder-length hair that still showed hints of brown behind the gray. Beyond Rhetta, daylight had been replaced by moonless night within the small glassless windows cut high into the half-meter-thick stone wall.

"Sorry." Vanessa slapped her cheeks twice and blew out a breath. "Didn't mean to become part of the furniture."

"You've been at this for hours, mijn liefje," the matronly cook scolded her gently. "I do not care what that captain thinks. You are not his servant. These bloodthirsty intruders have taken over our lives and will not tell us why they're here. We do not owe them anything."

Vanessa sighed. That was basically what she'd already told the captain, but to little effect. He still bossed her around, and she still ended up caving to him. He was just so good at *commanding*. But more than that, it seemed like the only way to find out more about him and his mission was to keep him happy and do his stupid busywork. Ever since the army showed up, it had boiled down to: we're in charge now, so sit down and shut your piehole. So how long was this supposed to last? Was this their new life now? What if the soldiers decided to make this a *permanent* military base? She didn't love the idea of strapping on a pair of army boots every morning and being forced to run laps around the compound.

Vanessa looked up when Rhetta squeezed her shoulder again. "I'm almost done. I just need to remember the name of that new guy who does the…thing with the…things…"

Her voice faded as she struggled to shake off her stupor and get those last few people noted in the list of fifty-three residents. Even her own parents had never given her this much homework in one day. When her mom had not been trying to teach Vanessa chemistry, she had drilled her in various biology lessons, like the stages of—What was it? Mitosis? An animal cell goes through the stages of prophase, prometaphase…um, something else, followed by something else. Crap. No wonder she'd had no interest in entering the field of science, like her mother. Vanessa was no dummy, but her brain did not work that way. Ask her to quote a few lines from a Charles Dickens novel, though, and she was all over it.

She looked up when Rhetta slid the pen and notepad out of her hands and set them on a table nearby. Vanessa tried to reach for them, but the cook held up a finger.

"You've done enough for today, especially after all the extra work here in the kitchen, thanks to our"—Rhetta frowned and worked her tongue as if to dig out something wedged between her teeth—"population explosion." She shook her head. "Ze zitten als haringen in een ton!"

Vanessa put a hand on her stomach when it growled. Maybe it, too, was remembering the unceremonious way the soldiers had all fallen upon Rhetta's boterkoek like a plague of locusts that night. Vanessa had not even gotten one bite of the butter cake. And her tummy had been holding a grudge ever since.

Rhetta sighed, the wrinkles across her forehead doubling, and stared at her feet.

Vanessa squinted at her. *Uh-oh. Something's up.*

Sure enough, Rhetta wiped her hands on the dish towel she clutched and sat down on the bench beside her. "Why are you doing these things for Captain Evans?"

Vanessa shrugged. "Because he asked me to."

Rhetta's lips made a slim line. Vanessa immediately felt like a student in a classroom who, when asked what two plus two was, had proudly yelled, "Potato!"

"Why does the captain need to know these things about us?" Rhetta tried again. "What purpose can it serve?"

"Because he's a control freak and annoyingly detail-oriented. Believe me, the man has a fetish for paperwork. I don't think he's going to *do* anything with the information."

Rhetta was quiet for a moment. Then: "Do you remember the stories I have told you about my great-grandparents in the Second World War, when the Nazis occupied Nederland?"

Vanessa nodded. *Where exactly is this going?*

"My great grandmother saw many terrible things, especially while her husband helped the Dutch resistance." Rhetta's eyes studied Vanessa's face. "And some of the things she saw were her own neighbors—young mothers like her—working with their enemies, giving them information. Aiding the Duitsers in their cruelty and betraying our Jewish friends. The women even gave their own bodies to the German soldiers. Anything to make themselves safe."

The cook paused then, and a sudden coldness pinched the skin along Vanessa's arms.

"Rhetta, I'm not betraying anyone," Vanessa said slowly. "I'm not a—a collaborator trying to make myself comfortable by—by trading any favors."

Rhetta patted Vanessa's knee. "I know that. But the other residents do not understand you, as some of us do, and they will not think the same. They are frightened of these strangers." The cook gave one brisk nod. "As you should be."

"I-I am," she said, but then it was her turn to pause. That had not sounded very convincing.

"You *will* be afraid," Rhetta said, "if something happens and it is because you let him involve you. He is not an honest man, and I do not want you to learn another hard lesson, mijn kleine meid."

Vanessa dropped her gaze from Rhetta's and plucked at the skirt fabric on her thigh.

"Do not be so quick to help him," Rhetta told her. "No good can come from his being here."

Again, that stubborn internal voice drove her to defend him. "But he hasn't done anything to any of us, really. I think he's spoiled and used to getting his way just by wagging his gun at people. None of these guys seem like they mean us harm, even if they did violently invade us and…drive out Caretaker Dijkstra with a death threat and…move right in with no regard for our…"

Okay, now I hear it.

She shook her head and took a breath. "But they still haven't hurt us. So I don't see why we…"

Her voice trailed off as Rhetta straightened and gripped the dish towel in her lap. "You always refuse to see. It will have to be the captain himself who shows you who he is. Hij gaat door de mand vallen."

Vanessa winced. The meaning of that old saying was not usually wrong: at some point, a person will invariably reveal their true colors. Especially if they have something to hide.

Rhetta sighed and glanced at the other papers on the table. "If you must finish, then at least leave this all for the morning. But perhaps you will understand me after a night's sleep and you can stop this nonsense."

Vanessa tried not to meet the cook's gaze. "I ought to wrap it up, before I get any rest."

"Je loopt op je tandvlees! You should not be wearing yourself down like this."

"I know." She sighed and bent her arm against the

table to lean her chin into her palm. "He's very insistent, though."

"Because I give orders for a reason."

Vanessa sat up. Rhetta's face blanched, and she rose from her seat.

The captain stood on the threshold.

As always, his tall, imposing figure almost filled the doorway, and his black attire looked even darker than the sliver of sky sitting beyond his right shoulder.

Rhetta's face was drawn, but—in true motherly fashion—she made a point of giving Vanessa a rub on the back before she returned to the cooking area. With everyone else gone for the night, the only other sound in the kitchen became the soft clink of flatware as Rhetta quietly put away the last of the dishes.

"Hey there," Vanessa said lightly, though it felt like every ligament had locked her joints in place.

The captain strolled toward her, and she sat up straighter. He picked up the notepad from the other table.

"See?" she said as he flipped through it. "All done…for the most part."

He looked up from the notepad. He pushed back his hood with a hand, and she felt frozen in place by those cold, bright eyes as he peered at her through the mask.

"For the most part." He dropped the pad in front of her, making her jump. "I asked for a completed list."

"Well, I got yesterday's notes rewritten, at least," she offered.

He said nothing.

She fought the urge to grab the notepad, rip every sheet out of it, and fling them at him.

He directed his gaze to the pile of sketches pushed to the side. He rounded the table's corner to look more closely. With a knuckle, he nudged the pencil to roll off the large topmost sheet and then lifted the paper.

She immediately glanced away and rubbed a finger behind her ear. "Those are the, uh, diagrams of the compound."

"Not what I was looking for." He set the sheet down

and picked up the next one. "Did you draw them with your feet?"

She clenched her fists under the table. "Excuse me, but I already told you they'd be bad."

"They're terrible."

She shrugged. "Yeah, well…"

Again, she restrained herself from acting out her rip-and-fling fantasy.

He shuffled through the pages until he came to the last one. He examined the sketch for a moment and then raised his head.

His eyes fixed her in a glower.

She bit her lip and looked down. She knew right away what he had been studying about the drawing.

"Funny." He said the word without amusement.

"It was a…last-minute addition." She showed him a faltering smile.

Rip. Fling! Rip. Fling!

He did not comment but gathered all the large papers and rolled them up together. He watched her as he knocked the end of the tube against his gloved palm. "I won't be needing you tomorrow."

She almost laughed at the unexpected furlough. *What? No Breakfast with the Boss? But how will I possibly survive the morning without all the awkward silences and please-kill-me-now chores to look forward to?*

He picked up the notepad and walked toward the door. She stared at his back as he stopped and turned his head to address her over his shoulder. "But I still expect you to finish the list."

Of course. Captain Clerk, the Paperwork Pirate, strikes again.

Then he stepped out into the one-sided hallway that formed the western perimeter of the garden, and his black-garbed form became an inky shadow merging with the others in the corridor.

Vanessa sat for a moment. *Okay. I'm off the hook for a while.*

Still, she didn't move. The careful click of clay dishes

being stacked came from the back of the kitchen.

Then why does it feel like I'm being punished?

She continued to stare through the doorway, where his dark shape had gradually disappeared.

And why am I upset about it?

She shouldn't be. She should be relieved. Exultant, even. But again, if she had no excuse to be around him, then she might miss it: that one vulnerable moment. Because the more bits of information she could pry from him, the more he seemed right on the verge of being human.

And what will I see, when he finally lets his guard down?

CHAPTER THIRTEEN

ETHAN

Ethan reclined in his chair that night, his robe discarded on the bed, and rested the back of his masked head in one hand while he held the last sketch Vanessa had made.

His eyes moved over the paper again, taking in the jagged outline of the compound, as if shown from the air like in one of the old tourist postcards he'd seen. He looked at all the extra elements she'd included. Not only had she drawn the fort itself and shown the greenhouses and the trees in the orchard—though the trees were more like electrocuted octopuses—she had also drawn several stick figures everywhere. A few of them wore oversize hats, while others stood with stiff triangles that covered their lower halves, arms stuck straight out to the sides. It was no great work of art, just as she had warned him.

But what made him stare closer was the scene portrayed outside of the compound, where there was a badly drawn figure wearing what appeared to be a robe.

The blobby shape around the stick man was dark, the pencil shading so aggressive that it looked as if the graphite point had almost punctured the paper. The figure waved a gun in one hand and pointed angrily at a group of stick people in front of it. But there was something about the depiction that suggested the figure was motioning in an overly bossy fashion, rather than with true hostility.

And there had evidently been a speech bubble above the robed stick man throwing his tantrum, but it had been erased so hard that only the merest pencil depressions remained.

He opened his hand to let the sketch float down and settle on the desk in front of him. He drummed his fingers twice on the wooden surface. And then, with a shake of his head, he chuckled.

CHAPTER FOURTEEN

VANESSA

Vanessa wrenched the apple from the branch when the captain's dark-robed figure came into view. He strode along the corridor at the perimeter of the garden. Beside him was a short, wiry man in grubby coveralls with an oily rag hanging out of a back pocket. The captain turned his head to his animated companion, who could not stop gesturing like a mentally unstable music conductor. The captain's eyes swept over her briefly as he walked, but he never slowed his pace or acknowledged her.

Oh, so now I don't even warrant the usual scowl?

It should not have miffed her. Being dismissive and inconsiderate was his modus operandi. A breeze passed over her as it made its way through the fluttering leaves, and she inhaled deeply when it pushed her hair behind her shoulders.

Fine. She wouldn't give him a second thought. Why should she let Captain Crotchety ruin her morning?

She yanked another apple off the tree and sent the branch swaying wildly.

In fact, I wouldn't hang out with him now, even if he came begging me on his knees.

She threw the fruit into her basket.

Hope he has fun playing with himself instead of with me!

She paused, about to grab the next apple.

Wait, no. I mean—

"Hey, Nessy!" a man's voice hailed her from behind.

She turned.

Thomas leaned his stomach against the other side of the orchard wall and laid his forearms across the top. "Figures I'd find you 'ere, pickin' away."

The handle of a crossbow poked up behind his right shoulder. What happened to the curvy-looking bow he had used when the army first arrived? He must have had a few such weapons that he alternated between. These guys sure loved having a variety of ways to kill things.

" 'Ow's ya gettin' on?" he asked with a smile that was as lopsided as his haircut.

She nodded toward the greenhouses. "Ask me that later, when I catch another one of you soldiers with his hands all over my tomatoes. That's when I turn into a blond ball of fury."

Thomas laughed. "I dies at you, ducky! You has a right fine sense o' humor. That's why I likes talkin' to you." Then he called out toward the ground near the tree trunk. "Ay b'y, Tim!"

She had to smile. The rabbit—who had kept her company while she worked and who had not hesitated to score himself two free apples—stopped munching on his chunk of fruit. He sat up, obviously trying to decide if the young soldier had something better to offer.

Thomas cocked his head. "He sure is a big bundle o' fluff."

"Trust me, that's not all fluff." She dropped another apple into her basket.

Thomas tilted his head the other way. "Why's 'is ear look so funny?"

She glanced at Tim, whose right ear stuck out from his other to make a big backward L. "I think it looks…unique."

Thomas squinted. "Why's 'is tail so stumpy?"

Vanessa stretched to twist off an apple above her. "Because there was a fox who was almost faster than he was."

"Why's 'is—?"

"Because it just is." Vanessa dropped the basket down against her side and put a fist on her hip. "Don't be rude. He's still a very handsome boy."

Tim stopped chewing and looked up at them both, his single front tooth hanging out in simpleton style.

"If you says so," Thomas mumbled.

"*Anyway*"—Vanessa set the apple firmly in her basket—"what are *you* doing?"

Thomas grinned and rubbed a hand in his hair, which was an untidy dusky blond mop, as usual. "Oh, I's just oat an' aboat."

She stared at him. "You're out in a boat?"

He furrowed his brow. "Me nerves, why does people keeps askin' me that? No: *oat* and *aboat*."

She raised an eyebrow slowly. "Doing what with a boot?"

He rolled his eyes. "O–u–t and a–b–o–u–t."

"Ah! Got it. Must be your accent."

He frowned. "What accent?"

She buried her smile under an equally heavy frown. "Sorry, it's my ears, then." She turned back to the tree. "So what are you *supposed* to be doing?"

He sighed as if conceding he had been caught. "Helpin' Angus itemize the remaining ammo an' firearms. But what odds 'bout that! Who wants to spend their time doin' long, boring lists and maths, wha'? Makes me head hurt."

"Tell me about it." She twisted an apple off a branch and threw it into her basket.

He came around through the nearby gap in the wall. Spooked by the movement, Tim hopped away, leaving his fruity snack half-eaten in the grass.

"Why's it's mostly you who does all these chores out the garden? I means, I sees some old fella's trippin' round, but he's got to be's fair useless."

She shook her head with a small smile. She'd gotten used to Thomas's fast way of talking so that she could now separate his words into understandable speech. But regardless, any eavesdropping grammar teacher would have an absolute meltdown.

"That 'old fella' is Steffen," she said, "but don't blow him off. He goes from sunup to sundown. And there are others who help me sometimes, too. But I, sir, am the Mistress of Mulch." She gave a quick curtsy. "And I don't trust many people not to totally hose up all my hard work."

He crossed his arms and leaned back against the stone wall. "Sweet moldy Moses, we's got a real ballbuster here."

"That's right. No one touches my peaches without my say-so."

Thomas chuckled and shook his head. "Pretty an' some saucy. You's some nice piece. All other girls we comes across blends together after a time."

"Speaking of that"—she placed another apple in her basket—"what's with the captain's all-male army? I mean, the Netherlands stopped letting women in the military a few years ago, but I thought other places were different."

He cocked his head at her. "Other places is worse, me love. We don't has any she-soldiers 'cause there ain't that many anymore. The laws've been that way for ages most everywheres. But just be glad your government's let you live a halfway normal life. Lots o' places makes their women…" He hesitated at that and scratched the side of his nose as his eyes darted away. "Well, let's just say I seen worse jobs than pickin' apples all day."

She shifted the basket to her other arm as an eerie sensation like scrabbling ants spread across her shoulders. She had heard rumors about certain areas—camps—in Belgium and in northern Germany, even France. Now she was sure that she did not want more details.

Instead she asked, "Why do you guys roam from place to place like this?"

He looked at her as if she had asked why he always walked on his feet instead of his hands. "To live."

"What does that mean?"

"We stops movin' when we has to. We get what's we need, and then we're off."

"And you like being nomads?"

Sure, she had been ready to strike out on her own, far away from the compound. But there was a purpose to that. An eventual destination where she'd settle down with someone special. A place free from old memories. She could not imagine never having a home.

"It ain't so bad." But there was a slight strain in Thomas's voice as he said it. "After doin' it 'bout sixteen times in four years, b'y, it gets to be easier."

She kept her jaw tight to prevent it from hanging open. *Sixteen?*

Her insides felt drafty, like someone had left a door open for a cold breeze to gust through.

And the captain will blow right through us, too. He'll move on when we're no longer useful to him.

She slowly pulled down another branch. "How did you end up falling in with a bunch of marauders like this?"

He squinted with a frown. "It ain't like that. We'ms helpin' people." But then the lines on his forehead smoothed out. "Well…we *helped* people."

"You mean you guys didn't always just muscle your way in and eat everything in sight?"

His frown flipped up. "You's sure rotted 'bout them tomatoes, eh?"

"My greenhouses are a sacred space," she grumbled, twisting off another apple. "But seriously, how did you join this gang?"

Thomas lifted a foot and placed it back against the wall. "Cap found me. In a bar." He leaned to the side and wiggled his eyebrows, as if to say "of course." She already knew his reputation as a drinker, from jokes she had overheard from the men.

"In Newfoundland?"

"In Wales. That's where the cap's originally from. But it was just a stopover for 'im at the time, 'cause his mudder moved 'im to the States when he was a kid. He's really only half Welsh, but you'll never hears 'im admit it."

That explained the captain's behavior. The Dutch

appreciated candor, but they still had manners! She had always heard that Americans could be downright rude in both speech and attitude, so he must have acquired their ways. And no doubt that being in charge for years, ordering people around, only exacerbated that.

She shook her head and pulled another bright red apple off the tree. "Were you stationed in the UK?" she asked before she sank her teeth into the fruit.

Thomas hesitated, and a strange look passed over his face. "I was out o' the army by then."

She stopped chewing. *Okay, something's not right about that.*

She finished her bite and swallowed. "Why?"

He glanced away and rubbed a hand in his hair. "Discharged."

She set the apple aside, in a corner of the basket. His briefly worded reaction was disconcerting, as it seemed so uncharacteristic. But then, most of the captain's men didn't like to talk as plainly as she preferred. She often had to dance with them around a topic in an exasperating tango of cryptic remarks and insinuations.

"Anyways, probably it's just as well, I says." He took a breath and reaffixed his lighthearted smile. "Got in too many scraps with the other guys. They'd always start teasin' me 'bout bein' a 'goofy Newfie,' like a bunch o' chucklehead scuts. You's on nish ice when you makes them jokes round me, b'y." He slipped a thumb behind the strap that crossed his chest diagonally and adjusted the crossbow on his back. "Not so bad bein' mucked off to a Canadian Forces base in Ontario for all them years, though. Me mudder was a mainlander, bless 'er, so I was used to their weird way o' talkin'. But one fella I was stationed with…Lard tunderin' Jesus, he was stunned as me arse, and he had more lip on 'im than a coal bucket, so's I got an earful o' stupid every time he opens his jaws! Whole thing made me miss the island somethin' fierce."

Her eyes jumped to the handle behind his shoulder. "Did the Canadian Army teach you about bows?"

"Nah, that was all me. The army taught me firearms.

I's best at long range, so I does a little snipin' for the cap." He tossed a fluff of dirty blond off his forehead with a flick of his head. "I'll shows you me Barrett M82, if you likes. It's best kind! Shoots fifty-caliber BMG, recoil-operated, pick off hostiles at near eighteen-hundred meters, it can."

She stared at him. "I don't know what any of that means."

He pointed his hand at her in the shape of a gun. "It shoots big-ass bullets a long ways away."

"Then why bother with the bow? It can't be as efficient."

Thomas reached behind him, grabbed the handle of the crossbow, and rocked it over his shoulder before pulling the trigger. Vanessa hopped back as the bolt shot past her face and thunked into the tree trunk. It had speared the apple she'd been about to pick. Eyes wide, she turned to him.

"Almost the sound it makes when it goes through a man's head," Thomas said, and smiled at her. But his brown eyes did not smile. Instead, for one fleeting second, they misted over.

A twitch of discomfort rippled along her shoulders. *Now I think I know why he was discharged.*

She slowed her breathing to force her heart rate down. "I guess you have an expert hand."

"I practices." He slid the crossbow back behind his shoulder. "Keeps me focused."

A distant *clunk, clunk, clunk* made her gaze leap to the corridor across the way.

Soldiers and compound residents had been walking around the expansive garden throughout the day, and yet they made little sound compared to what was approaching. There was no mistaking the now-familiar tread of that mechanized anomaly.

Clunk. Whirrrr. Clunk. Whirrrr. Clunk.

Sure enough, Sergeant Maxwell—his long braid swinging against his back—marched doggedly down the one-sided passageway near the kitchen. He seemed a prickly sort at times, usually frowning when he was clearly on the trail of some task. And, like Captain Ahab thumping across the wooden planks of the *Pequod*'s deck on his whalebone peg leg, so too did the trouser-wearing Scotsman tramp noisily along the stone corridor on his metallic prosthetic, eyeballing his surroundings like he was looking for something to harpoon. And she had a good idea about whom he was hunting.

"Look out, Moby Dick," Vanessa said to Thomas and set her basket down to amble toward him. "Not a good day to be a white whale."

Thomas squinted at her. "You gone warped? What's that you's—?" But when he turned to look over his shoulder, he let out a curse and dropped into a crouch behind the wall.

Angus swiveled his head in their direction. As soon as he spotted her, the sergeant headed straight for her.

"He's coming this way," she sang quietly in falsetto.

Thomas turned onto his back against the stone and pulled his knees into himself.

Angus maneuvered around the fenced vegetable beds as he made his way to her, his mechanical foot kicking up bits of turf in his path. He stopped next to the wall.

"Well, all right there, lassie," he said in a friendly voice that contradicted his stern-browed expression. "Have ye, by chance, seen a gallus wild-haired laddie by the name of Thomas anywhere about?"

He pronounced "about" similar to the way Thomas did. But otherwise, his accent was so thick, she almost didn't understand the question.

"Thomas?" she said with a slight squint.

"I've got need of him, but he's as skitie as a fish when I try to grab him," he went on. "Have ye laid eyes on the boy?"

She repressed the urge to look down when Thomas grabbed the top of her foot and jiggled it.

She stared at Angus. "Nope."

Angus scratched his head under the woolen cap and puffed out his cheeks, which made his beard bristle around his face like a brown thistle. Then his eyes settled on the apple pinned to the tree by the crossbow bolt. His brow furrowed, and he transferred his gaze back to her.

She discreetly shook Thomas's hand off her foot. "Oh! That. Um, that's a…a traditional Dutch…apple kebab." She shrugged. "I missed breakfast."

Angus peered closer at her. She smiled innocently.

A whining, clicking noise started from somewhere near the ground, and Angus looked down. "Ach, ye doaty piece o' shite," he grumbled and seemed to kick at something.

Vanessa peeked over the wall as he bashed his foot against the shin of his trousers covering the mechanical leg, which bent at the knee with a squealing of gears.

"Sorry, lassie," he said, and knocked on his artificial thigh with his thick knuckles. "She gets a wee bit carnaptious."

"Sounds like it," Vanessa agreed, though not entirely sure what she was agreeing with.

The Scotsman tugged at his beard. "Well, I'm off, then. I dinnae ken about that Tommy," he said with a grimace. "He's a right wee nickum!"

Then he groused something to himself that in no way resembled the English language and wandered away.

She let out a breath and knelt in the grass beside Thomas.

"Thanks for coverin'," the young soldier said. "He sure is some crooked today!" He canted his head at her. "You's a good kid, Nessy."

"What was that last thing he said? I couldn't make out a word."

"Beats me. Frank's the only one who can understands 'im most o' the time. It's all that tongue-rollin' they has in common."

"And what's with that old sword of his? The one he was carrying the first day you guys were here?"

Thomas stretched his legs out to cross his ankles. "He only pulls out Kenzie or his kilt when we has to go into a real fight. I guess he channels dead Scottish clansmen or somethin'." He leaned his head back against the wall and grinned. "I likes to be reminding 'im 'ow I read once that them Maxwells is just a 'family,' not a real clan. And that makes 'im some vexed! B'y, he blusters! But he bleeds his tartan, true enough, and he's one tough Scot. Didn't even faze 'im, I hears, when that Buffalo bit off his leg."

Vanessa's mouth popped open. "What?"

"Yeah, b'y." Thomas nodded and blew the hair out of his eyes. "He was savin' one man in his squad that got trapped under it, and when that Buffalo started rollin' again, it squat his leg into pulp."

"Wait," she said slowly, "we're not talking about a big hairy beast, are we?"

"A beast, yeah, but a heavy armored one. An MRAP called a Buffalo. Mine Resistant Ambush Protected vehicles. A bunch o' armies uses 'em."

"I'm learning a whole new vocabulary," Vanessa mumbled. It was hard enough just trying to keep up with all the different languages, without memorizing their military jargon too.

She picked at a blade of grass. *He seems in the mood to talk, so let's see how far we can take this.*

She pushed an apple with her finger and watched it roll off the top of the heap in her basket. "What's the captain's story? Why does he disguise himself like he's the Phantom of the Opera? What happened to him?"

Thomas grew quiet.

"If you wants to know 'bout Captain Evans, then you should ask Morgan," he said at last. "The cap is closest to 'im. They wents through a lot together, 'fore they made this army." He poked the patch sewn onto his chest: the same back-to-back red dragon and golden lion design that all the men wore. "They seen more shit-storms than any of us, when it was just the two of 'em. Anyways, it's not me place to talk 'bout 'im. In fact, he don't even likes us soldiers talkin' as much to you and them other residents as we does."

She sighed. *Great. Dead end.*

"I don't see what the big deal is." She ripped off a clump of grass blades and tossed it at the wall. "I'm just tired of guessing about him."

Thomas watched her tear off another handful of grass. After a glance to the side, he lowered his voice. "The cap ain't above mistakes, but he believes he made a bloody great one a couple years back. None of us really blames 'im for killin' them Ukes who killed the b'ys. But he got caughts by surprise when we was pullin' out, and the arse fell outta 'er right bad."

Finally! Making headway!

"Pulling out of where? And what are 'Ukes'? Did they do something to him? Mutilate him?"

Thomas paused. "Do yourself a favor and drop it, eh?"

She sat back on her heels. Judging by the frustration in Thomas's voice, he would not be any more forthcoming. It was obvious he had great respect for the captain and was not willing to commit what felt like a betrayal of trust. Evidently, the captain had a character that inspired men to follow him. And protect him.

If only I could get under all that emotional armor and find out for myself what kind of man he really is.

Vanessa stood and walked over to the tree. She waggled the crossbow bolt out of the trunk and handed it to Thomas when he approached her. He slid the apple backward off the shaft and wiped the bolt against his pant leg.

"I guess I'd better get these to the kitchen." She bent down to heft the basket onto her arm. "Good luck with your hide-and-seek game." She took the apple from his hand and traded it for one from her basket. "And maybe, for a change, you can try eating one of these *without* holes."

But instead of holding it, Thomas tossed the apple in the air and let it land on the point of the crossbow bolt in his fist. He shrugged. "This ways is easier."

She scrunched her face at him and shook her head. "I give up."

He showed her a Cheshire Cat grin and took an exaggerated bite of the apple as she left the orchard.

CHAPTER FIFTEEN

ETHAN

Ethan was careful to walk slowly alongside Nicolo, though the diminutive Italian's excitable nature made him a veritable yo-yo, winding himself up and shooting out in front of the captain's longer strides. Earlier, when Ethan had ordered a few soldiers to remove the metal casings of the generators, Nic had been happy to poke around inside. But now, thanks to that exercise, Ethan had been listening to the mechanic's rant about the condition of the machines for a good five minutes.

The whole of Nic's harangue, however, faded into a background buzz as soon as Ethan spotted Vanessa in the orchard. With his hood raised to screen his gaze, he let his eyes travel down her legs, which were tantalizingly bare again in another one of her summer-length skirts. She obviously didn't mind the attention she drew, though it was a bad idea to dangle herself in front of his men like that. And a worse idea to do it on a daily basis. He wouldn't let anyone touch her, of course—he'd promptly fuck up any man who did—but he couldn't keep them from looking. Hell, *he* couldn't keep from looking.

As he passed the orchard, he nodded when Nicolo made a grand gesture with his arms and rattled off a series of observations like a mini machine gun. But the only thing holding Ethan's interest was the way the wind lifted

Vanessa's hair off her shoulders, as if gliding its fingers through those long golden locks. Something he would have liked to do himself.

He followed Nicolo out the front gates and surveyed the now-familiar landscape. Though most of North Holland was flat, there were rare areas that rose up enough to provide a favorable vantage point. The compound had been built squarely upon one such grassy hill, so that the fort could sit up higher than both the town to the south and the western area extending to the North Sea, should an invasion approach from either side. His eyes bounded over the large yellowed plaque bolted to the wall a few meters from the entrance. It confirmed that this location was chosen by the eccentric Dutch nobleman for that very reason, though historians often argued that the structure should have been built closer to the water.

Ethan winced. *Jesus, I can almost quote from the damn thing, like her.*

He glanced over the fleet of vehicles that Nicolo and his team maintained with fierce dedication. Several of his men, moving between the military Land Rover trucks, saluted him as he walked by. He patted a hand on the scuffed camo surface of the well-loved Boxer MRAV when he reached it. The massive eight-wheeled armored transport was currently converted to its personnel carrier design with removable seats against the inside walls. Ethan walked across the Boxer's rear entry ramp that was lowered to the ground, sending the rattle of heavy metal hinges echoing around the empty interior.

He'd had the men line up all six vehicles with their backs to the compound so as to fan out around the sharply angled walls like a phalanx. He wanted them placed in such a way that the sight would reinforce the unassailable nature of his new base and give pause to anyone from the nearby town who thought to encroach upon them.

"Sure, Capitano, I can fix your generators," the short mechanic said as he rolled his hand in the air beside him, "but that is if I had the right tools, the right equipment, the materials to build new turbines to make them work, and many months to do it." The Italian glanced back at Ethan. "But what is the point, eh? We would be packing up by the time we turned the lights on."

"So what you're telling me is that it's a lost cause," Ethan said wryly.

Why the hell had he wasted his time listening to all this shit, then?

Nicolo shook his head ruefully as he stopped beside one of the three tan-colored Land Rover Wolfs. He hung his hand from the truck's hard-top roof above him, which only made him appear even more stunted, like a child dangling from a set of monkey bars. "I'm telling you, you should forget them. You would be better off buying a new generator to run this place."

Ethan pushed back his hood and scratched the back of his head through the mask. "That's out. We don't have the coin for something like that right now. We need to devote it all to munitions. And supplies."

"And petrol." The mechanic gave the vehicle a few tugs. "This one here, she is running on fumes. Lieutenant Winchester said we will send out teams to find the Ucraini, but we would not make it far."

Ethan rubbed his chin with the back of his left hand and then rested his palm on the grip of his H&K. "We have to prioritize." He brushed a thumb over the P8's hammer. "Keeping tabs on the Ukes is our top concern."

As it always did, the message flashed through his head upon the mentioning:

You cannot burn us. You cannot kill us. We will bury you screaming beneath the bodies of your men.

The mechanic let go of the Wolf and spread his hands out to the sides. "There you go, Capitano! Save the money and buy more candles!"

Ethan nodded distractedly.

Nicolo pulled the greasy rag from his back pocket and began to walk down the row of trucks. But he called back over his shoulder, "Tell Frank he will miss his daytime soap operas, eh?" The Italian laughed heartily and nodded at his chief assistant, Angelo, who grinned back and nodded his head of puffy curls as he wiped down the windshield of one of the two black Land Rover Snatches.

Ethan sighed. No use sparing any more thoughts on the decrepit generators, then. It was tempting to scrape up enough money to install a temporary fuel-fed one, but the only way to do that would be to knock over a bank. He glanced down the road to Achterwaartsstad.

I doubt these people have two nickels to their names. Most of the town's wealth is probably sitting under Mayor Visser's floorboards.

And robbing a government financial branch would undoubtedly put the crosshairs onto his army long before he was ready to leave. As with other countries in which he'd had to resort to such thieving tactics, Ethan would have to wait until they were almost to the border, before they could risk replenishing their coffers. And at that point, they would be well on their way out of Dodge.

Lucky that one of the results of international isolationism had turned out to be apathy. Ever since the European Union had been dissolved years ago, the European Central Bank no longer oversaw its monetary policy. However, most of the countries formerly part of the eurozone were too lazy and too cheap to bother printing different money. National identity gave way to convenience, and the former national central banks continued to issue the same currency as before. So his cash—stolen or not—was good everywhere the euro was. In most cases the lack of ECB regulation made for wild fluctuations in the price of goods and services within each country. The Dutch central bank was now completely under the thumb of the Netherlands government, but the regime leaders had somehow managed to maintain a fairly stable economy, in spite of the ruling authority's many vices. That stability was one reason he had come here.

Well, fuck it. A lot of good it did him right now. Though having electricity would have improved things substantially, it was still, at its core, a luxury. What he needed to concentrate on now was maintaining control of the compound and its people.

Again his mind flashed him the image of Vanessa under her Belle de Boskoop tree as the wind blew her hair and lifted her skirt higher against her thighs. Ethan jerked his hood up over his head.

Unfortunately, concentration and control were fast becoming his two biggest problems.

CHAPTER SIXTEEN

VANESSA

He's like a big moody moth!

Vanessa had seen the captain only from a distance all day as he flew from one team of soldiers to the next. Whenever she'd tried to catch him to discuss her belated "people list" assignment, he would already be on his way, his robe flapping behind him as he bore himself swiftly to the next landing spot down the line. And once more, she'd just missed him. She crossed her arms and blew out a loud breath as he floated off into a dark hallway and disappeared.

Well, he would have to pay attention to her, once she finished that dumb list and shoved it in his growly, scowly masked face. And never mind what Rhetta had said about it. Vanessa had done nothing wrong by jotting down a few names. The captain had not asked her for anything else, so she suspected her days as his personal assistant were at an end anyway. No harm done. She just wanted to get this one last thing over with.

She had little opportunity to work on the remaining resident names except in spurts, since she was constantly intercepted by people in the kitchen or in the garden. Or even on her way to the freakin' toilet! She finally barricaded herself in one of the stalls and used her knees as a desk. Holding up the pieces of paper in the dim light, she imagined the captain's frown at all the squiggly wording. Someone flushed the toilet next to her. Yep. That would probably be his reaction too.

But once she was done with sweeping floors, fertilizing plants, and everything else for the day, she grabbed a plate of gevulde koeken that Rhetta had baked for dessert that evening and parked herself at one of the kitchen tables to note the remainder of the residents' details. After a while, when her nose touched the sheet of paper as she squinted to see, she glanced at the lamp beside her. Its wick was a thin wedge of flame. But it gave enough light by which to finish the final sentence on the page. She scooped up the last buttery cookie and shoved the entire thing in her mouth. Wiping the smears of almond paste from her lips with the back of a hand, she brushed the crumbs off the scribbled list and dotted the period so hard that the pen tip stuck into the wood beneath the paper.

It was completely dark outside, and no one roamed the halls except for a patrolling soldier now and again. The men still made all the residents nervous; everyone shut themselves in during the evening and left the compound to the captain's army. The captain was probably done for the night as well, so she would not even get the satisfaction of handing him the list personally.

So much for making sure he can't ignore me.

As she navigated the hallways, her footsteps sounded like they pounded against the stone floor, so hushed was everything. Morgan—at his sentry station as usual—glanced up the moment she rounded the corner to start down the corridor to the captain's room. She approached him hesitantly.

"I'm delivering the rest of the list I promised him," she explained. "I know it's late, so I'll stick it in the door and he can get it tomorrow."

Morgan looked wordlessly at her over his copy of the *Noordster Courant.* Then he lifted a hand toward the captain's room, silently inviting her to proceed.

When she reached the door, she glanced at the plaque on the wall that read Commanding Officer's Quarters.

Who knew that sign would ever actually mean something again? But it was doubtful that Fort Van Doorn's original architect had ever anticipated his creation being manned by a renegade army!

She looked down at the pages she held. The long light-blue sheets were decorated with whimsical pictures of wooden spoons, carrots, and sprigs of rosemary down the sides with the words "Food for Thought" printed merrily at the top. Somehow it did not convey the gravity of indexing people's lives, but it was all she could get her hands on.

She folded the pages carefully and tried to slip them into the doorjamb. They would not fit. She tried to force them farther up the frame. But they still refused to slide in. She worked her way down the door, ramming the pages against the crack. She glanced back at Morgan as he lowered the newspaper to his lap and watched her. Cheeks burning, she kept at it. The papers became more and more mashed up until they turned into an unrecognizable lump.

At last, she knelt on the floor to cram them under the door instead, but they were so crumpled that they would not budge between the wood and stone. She gritted her teeth and shoved harder. She felt Morgan's stare on her back.

Come on, come on, please, please, please…

She wedged a corner of the wadded papers under the door and grunted as she beat on them with the heel of her hand. Her face on fire, she was one second away from screaming and pitching the balled-up mess down the length of the hallway.

Then the door opened with a jerk, and she fell forward.

She righted herself and stared up at the captain as he loomed over her. He was not wearing his robe. Only his black jeans, knee-high boots, and long-sleeved shirt. And his shoulders drooped slightly, like he'd been pulled out of a nap.

She sat back on her legs, the clump of papers clutched in her hands. "I-I finished the list."

His eyes behind the mask moved over her. "Why didn't you just give it to Morgan?"

He looked at his second-in-command, but Morgan only shrugged. When he directed his attention again to her, she gaped up at him like a two-year-old with a finger up her nose. Finally, he turned and leaned his back against the wooden frame.

He rested his hand on the door. "Come in."

She hid the ugly wad of papers behind her and climbed to her feet. He had created just enough space between himself and the door to let her squeeze by. As she ducked under his arm, her hip brushed against his thigh, and the touch of that solid flesh beneath his jeans all at once made her want to dally there. But she shook off the urge and went in to stand in the middle of the room as the captain closed the door.

She tried to flatten the sheets of paper against her stomach and work out the wrinkles with her palms. He walked over while she sawed them back and forth on the front of her thigh, like she was polishing a coffee urn with a dish towel. Finally, she held them out to him. He looked down at the limp papers.

She lowered her hand. "You want me to rewrite them on the notepad, don't you?"

"That won't be necessary," he said in a surprisingly mild voice as he took the pages from her. "They're fine."

She stared as he went to lay them on his desk. And she was still speechless when he turned to lean on it and face her. He watched her expectantly. She tugged on the pinky of her right hand, not sure what to do with herself now that her mission was concluded. She glanced at his bed, where he'd thrown his robe in a heap the way someone kicks off their shoes after a long work shift.

"So-o-o"—she rocked forward on her toes—"how was your day?"

"Nonproductive."

She waited. *Okay, not going to explain that.*

"That's too bad," she said, shifting her feet. "Well, I did my usual stuff. And that, of course." She gestured vaguely at the desk behind him. "I also gave Thomas a hiding place from Angus, so it might be my fault if your list of guns isn't up-to-date."

Why am I babbling like this?

He said nothing. Considering the very late hour and the singular purpose of her visit, why was he continuing to let her bother him?

I think he's made a pastime out of seeing me squirm.

But that did not stop her mouth from amusing itself. "Thomas is quick on his feet, but I think the sergeant caught him anyway. I heard what I'm pretty sure was a bunch of angry Gaelic echoing down the halls."

At that, she thought she saw a smile tug at the corner of his mouth beneath the black mask.

But then it was gone when he asked, "Why didn't you tell me about the tunnels?"

"The tunnels," she repeated.

Crap. That's why he's being nice. He's saving it up, so he can blow his lid and lecture me about my shortcomings as a tour guide.

"I forgot all about them," she confessed. "No one goes down there anymore if they can help it. I mean, with the way the rest of the compound is held together with duct tape, who wants to tempt fate? And for me, they're such a maze that I'd never see the light of day again. Rhetta used to have to come rescue me whenever I got lost down there as a kid. I'm surprised you didn't notice the entrance to them near the showers. There used to be a second entrance on the other side of the compound, but that was bricked over years ago."

Again, silence.

She bit her lip and twisted her fingers together. She hurried forward to his desk. "But I screwed up. I should have remembered to show them to you." She picked up the omnipresent notepad and flipped to a clean page. "I'll try to sketch them out, though it won't be very accurate." She snatched the pencil nearby and started to draw a careful line.

His hand covered hers and stopped it against the paper.

"It's all right," he said quietly. "My men are already working on it. We should have a good idea about them tomorrow."

He stood so close that the heat of his body flowed over her. And the soft black leather of his glove felt enticingly good on her skin. Plus, because he had ditched the robe, that delicious musky fragrance he naturally exuded made her lean the slightest bit closer to him so she could inhale it deeper. The room felt very warm, like a bath filling with water.

"How long since the generators worked?"

As he removed his hand from hers, she realized she had been gazing up at him with her mouth halfway open. "Oh, uh…they haven't functioned since I was probably ten." She made herself drop the pencil and move back from him. "There used to be these giant windmills that made them operate, but those were destroyed by a big storm. Only the two windmills I showed you survived. Then, with the electricity gone and ankle-deep flooding in the halls, a lot of the residents gave up and left. My parents and several others toughed it out, though."

"Where are your parents now?"

He did not ask the question in his normal interrogating way. He sounded interested.

"They died when I was twelve—" She stopped as her throat hitched.

Stop doing that. They didn't die. No one "dies" like that.

"They were…murdered when I was twelve." She blinked hard against the sting in her eyes. She had not talked to anyone about the memory in a very long time. "Killed in a back alley of Achterwaartsstad. I'm sure it was a man sent by the government. When my mom and the others decided to flee, then the military-controlled labs didn't see them as people anymore. They were loose ends." She pinched the pencil where it lay on the desk and began to turn it like a dial. "The assassin had probably been looking for them ever since they went on the run, and finally tracked them to the compound. They weren't there when he showed up. But I was." She turned the pencil faster as she stared at it. "I didn't know who he was. He said they owed him a lot of money. It was a lie. But I was mad at my parents because they made me stay behind, grounded for something stupid I did that I don't even remember now. So I told him. I *told* him where they were. I was glad that *they* were in trouble. I thought it served them right for punishing me." Her voice creaked like an old weathered rope twisting tighter. "I'll never forget the way he smiled at me. I'll never forget his face. He had a sharp nose and pointed beard—like one of those devil masks you think of for Halloween. And his eyes were cold."

She stopped the pencil against the desk and watched it blur for a second before she let go of it.

"I should have seen what he was. But I was too blinded by my own temper. And I didn't believe that anyone could actually commit—" She shook her head. "The police never even went after him. The same useless constable is running things today. And he's a degenerate, only interested in serving himself. Even though that devil man who killed—" She gritted her teeth. "I overheard Rhetta once, talking about what she'd seen that day. She'd said that the way he did it…it looked like he'd *enjoyed* it."

She paused again as this time her throat closed off completely. It still hurt so much. And her imagination still clung to the horrific images invented by her twelve-year-old brain. Cornelis, only fourteen at the time, had caught her before she'd run into the alley. He'd held her back, hugged her so hard that the sound of his frantic heartbeat had filled her ear. He'd kept her from the crime scene, but it still felt like she'd seen it in detail…

Her parents' bodies crumpled over each other, their limbs splayed at odd angles. Her mother's golden hair stained with the grime of the street. Her father's lifeless mouth twisted open as he'd watched his wife butchered in front of him. Two human beings dumped together on the wet cobblestones like they were garbage.

She took a breath as the images dissolved. "Rhetta's the closest I have to family anymore. She took care of me.

I don't know what I would have done, otherwise."

"What were your parents like?"

She turned her face up to him. His voice was gentle. Comforting.

"They were very kind," she answered. "And very, *very* patient."

At that, he actually did smile just a bit, which made the warm-bathwater feeling rise up over her shoulders.

"My dad was an accomplished musician, in his own right. He knew a lot of instruments." She absently rolled the pencil back and forth under her palm, making a light rumbling sound against the desk. "I remember when he used to play the piano, when we still lived in our old house. My favorite song was 'Moonlight Sonata,' so he'd always play it for me when I sat next to him. He was quiet and thoughtful and forever with a book in front of him."

She sent the pencil rolling across the desk to bump the captain's hand as he leaned back against the edge and watched her.

"My mother was part English, so I'm named after my grandmother. And Mom was not only really smart, but playful. She'd tie purple feathers to Dad's violin bow, because she said it made Bach sound less fuddy-duddy. She made him laugh even when he didn't feel like it. And she could talk for hours. I used to fall asleep in her lap, with her voice still in my ears." Vanessa shrugged, unable to keep from smiling. "She always said she and my father were made for each other, because he was so serious and she was his funny bone." Vanessa picked at the fabric of her skirt and then met the captain's gaze. "I miss them all the time. They're buried in the little cemetery we created in the back field—that one I pointed out to you—but there are so many days when I can't even bring myself to visit their graves."

He listened earnestly, his eyes never leaving hers. But his demeanor seemed charged with an impulse he was barely repressing, and it made her move nearer.

"Were you close to your parents?" she asked. "You seem like you're used to being on your own."

He hesitated, but his voice stayed even. "My home life was not like yours."

She let her shoulders slump. So that was all she was going to get? Not exactly a fair trade.

He pushed himself off the desk. "This army is my family now."

He surprised her with the admission. Was he actually opening up to her?

"But it sounds like you have some happy memories," she said. "You spoke fondly about your mom."

"Because she was a good woman. An unselfish woman." His eyes—normally so bright and critical—darted away as they lost their sharpness. "She deserved better than what she had. Better than what she endured, for my sake."

Her stomach twinged. What had *he* gone through as a kid?

The captain grew silent once more and backed away, the motion so much like what he appeared to do when wearing his robe. But the dark garment was currently discarded beyond his reach.

Vanessa followed and drew close to him. "I'm sure that whatever she went through, it was worth it to her. She obviously loved you. I'm sure she would have done anything for you." When the captain glanced at the robe piled at the foot of his bed, she glided both hands up his arm and wrapped her fingers around it. "*You* deserved that. And you deserve something good in your life now, too."

He gazed at her, and her heart beat faster. His bicep flexed slowly against her palms as he curled his left hand into a fist and then relaxed it beside him. She shivered when his voice rumbled through her.

"You don't know what I deserve."

It wasn't said with menace. Or with anger. He sounded...sad.

She squeezed his arm as her voice emerged tentatively. "I do know that you don't have to be alone."

His eyes gleamed within the black mask, the reflection of the nearby oil lamp setting a steady flame within their glowing green halos. It was a flame that looked ready to consume her.

She released him and pulled away. "Well, anyway, I suppose I-I'm prying again." She twirled her hair around her fingers. "And you've listened to me long enough. I tend to be an open book, but you can just put your bookmark in me for now. I mean, *a* bookmark, not your—uh—*anyway...*" With a hasty shrug, she stumbled backward.

He jerked forward and circled an arm around her waist an instant before she collided with his desk. They stared at each other as she clutched the front of his shirt and pressed against him. Now the room was no longer a warm bath. It was a full-blown steamy shower.

"Thanks." She swallowed down the bubble in her throat. "I guess I should be careful."

She tried not to gasp as he tightened his arm around her.

"Yes, you should." His hard, heated frame spread its fire through her flesh until her body started to melt against his. The virile scent of him wrapped around her as he hunched his shoulders forward. He seemed about to envelop her.

She licked her lips and swallowed again. "Well, we should get some rest." Her voice was faint. "I'm sure we're both tired."

At that, he held her even closer, and something very solid shifted against her belly, pulsing between them. "We should be in bed," he murmured in agreement.

Every single hot primal juice within her seemed to rush down and collect between her legs. She struggled to slow her breathing as she squeezed her thighs together. In the low light, his eyes glimmered like pools of absinthe, with the same effect as if she'd drunk a glass of it. But she forced herself to peel her body away from his. She reached for the desk's edge behind her for support. She tried to clear her throat, but it came out as a whimper.

What is wrong with you? Get ahold of yourself!

She gripped the wooden edge till her nails dug in.

"Will you want me again tomorrow?"

His gaze traveled over her face. "Yes."

"Do you have anything in mind for us to do?"

He seemed to study her every breath. "I'll think of something."

The softly spoken words made her core tremble. Her palms were damp as she backed away from him toward the door. "I'm off kitchen duty in the morning, so you'll have me all to yourself." She rubbed a hand down the front of her skirt. "When do you want me to come?"

His eyes seemed to blaze brighter within the mask. "Whenever you're ready for me."

Her limbs turned as weak as if the bones had fallen right out of them. "Okay. Sex forty—I mean, six forty-five tomorrow. Also known as zero seven hundred. We'll stick to that." She grasped the handle of the door behind her and spun away. "Goodnight."

She closed the door behind her and leaned her head back against it.

Morgan's eyes were leveled at her over the top of the newspaper he held. Legs crossed upon the table, he flexed the toes of his boots forward. "You made out successfully, I take it?"

She stared at him. "No, we did not! Not at all! What makes you think that?"

The lieutenant lifted an eyebrow and set the paper in his lap.

"Oh." She wiped her hands on her skirt. "Yeah, it was—it was fine. I mean, he was fine. That is, he didn't yell at me."

Morgan shook his head slightly as he folded the newspaper and tossed it on the stack in front of him.

She shut her eyes. *Pull yourself together, Vanessa.*

She took a breath and nodded at the papers. "You certainly have enough to read."

"I am a student of sensationalism, and your journalists have provided me ample material." The Englishman nudged the stack with his bootheel and then sighed. "Though one does risk a sudden onset of narcolepsy during the perusal."

She rolled her eyes toward the door as she pushed away from it. "And I'm sure it's no barrel of laughs watching out for Captain Cantankerous all the time, either."

"Ah, I see that he has already swayed you with his effervescent disposition."

She couldn't help a smile. Morgan's dry sense of humor was cute, the more he let it show. "Well, he's back to being *your* problem now," she informed him. "I'm off to bed. Goodnight, Lieutenant."

He eased his legs off the table and stood slowly. "Please, no need for formalities." His storm-colored eyes seized upon hers, and his voice held the soothing energy of a gentle rainfall. " 'Morgan' will do fine."

"All right," she said as a new heat crept up her throat. "Then no more 'Miss Brouwer' for you."

"I am humbled." He inclined his head with a gradual smile. "My Lady, Vanessa."

The gentle rain drummed harder in her ears, making her dizzy, and she began to sidle past his desk. "Goodnight."

His gaze followed her as she backed down the hall. "Sleep well."

She held her breath and turned away. *Not likely.*

What was it about mysterious men that got her juices flowing? The captain and his second-in-command were like stone bookends on a bedroom mantelpiece. Perfect counterparts that kept all their stories contained. But not as cold and stoic when a fire was stoked on the hearth underneath. Something had definitely lit it for the captain tonight.

A tingle zigzagged down her back as the sound of his deep voice reverberated through her mind. Ordinarily, the subtle lyrical rhythm of his speech lent even his brusquely spoken words a pleasing cadence. Tonight, though, he had been anything but abrasive. Tonight he'd been accessible. Tonight he'd been…

Desirable.

She had shaved off a thin layer from that invisible armor of his. And she was getting closer and closer to real flesh. The true essence of him. She rubbed her elbows against a chill. And she did not imagine what was going on back there. He had been as turned on as she. She bunched the sides of her skirt in her fists as she walked. Even now she could feel his arm squeezing around her, his gaze stroking her naked shoulders. He'd slid his fingers down to her hip to grip her there, while he'd maneuvered the front of himself against her, watching her, pulling her closer where she could feel so much more of his very noticeable, very impressive—

She slapped a hand to the wall next to her and clenched her thighs as all the muscles in her core seemed to spasm at once. She shut her eyes and beat a fistful of skirt against her leg before taking a deep breath.

Okay, unless I do something about this right now, sleep will officially be off the table.

It had been way too long since she'd had a really good reason to use her imagination. But tonight, she'd probably need to use it three or four times before it was enough to get some rest.

She wanted to be clearheaded and ready for whatever he had in store for her in the morning. Because when it came to Captain Concrete, there was no telling what would light the fire under his mantel tomorrow.

CHAPTER SEVENTEEN

ETHAN

"We have some housecleaning to do." Ethan handed the clipboard to Morgan as they walked along the trail of yellow squares cast by the early morning sunlight through the rough-cut windows of the stone corridor.

Morgan flipped a page of the notepad clamped to the board. "I suppose it comes as no surprise that there are a great many unhappy citizens under our roof."

"And outside our walls. But we're not here to make friends. We're here for the resources. And I don't want any lurking threats. Have the potential agitators relocated, where they can't interfere."

Morgan tapped his thumb against one of the names next to which the captain had placed a bloodred mark. "I see Caretaker Dijkstra did not earn his freedom for long."

"As we know, most men—even that little shit—won't let go of their power so easily," Ethan said tersely. "I want him out of the way before he can make trouble. It appears he may have the ear of the mayor, who sounds like he wouldn't be above a little bloodshed. We don't need that extra complication while we're settling in."

"And if he's already engaged the mayor for help?"

"Then we'll put Frank on the job." Ethan tugged on the bottom of each glove. "At that point, we'd have to silence any hostiles before they show up at our door, and that'll need to be done quietly. We don't want to draw more attention than necessary."

"The sergeant does, indeed, have a special affinity for such matters," Morgan remarked.

"No shit."

Ethan remembered the last time he had seen the burly Russian use the garrote wire he kept coiled at his belt. When in Frank's hands, the weapon could turn an act of strangulation into one of decapitation, which never failed to impress.

"By the by," Morgan said as he raised the list again and flipped a page. "Who, pray tell, is Sven, the brewer who strains beer through his socks?"

Ethan suppressed a smile at Vanessa's deadpan quip from the prior morning. "Just another expendable."

"I would say so, for any injustice against a pint," Morgan muttered as he turned the corner in unison with Ethan.

"That reminds me, I have another assignment for you." Ethan smoothed his mask down his throat with a hand. "Meet me up on the eastern battlements this evening. I need help killing off a bottle of Old Forester."

"A double funeral with your liver, no doubt." Morgan let the pages fall back into place on the clipboard. "Why you insist upon carting around that carcinogen, I'll never fathom."

"Relax," Ethan drawled, "it won't do any damage to those pretty-boy abs you're so proud of."

"This particular temple takes discipline." Morgan knocked a fist against his ribs. "Unlike you, I prefer to perfect my body, not pickle it."

"Oh, please. You know you love the stuff, you Limey bastard."

"I will admit I've developed a certain tolerance of the spirit, in moderation," Morgan said in his typical droll tone. "Though bourbon is the boor to its betters. Gin is the liquor of His Majesty, whose palate is above reproach."

"Fucking spare me," Ethan grumbled. "I'd rather

smash my last bottle of booze over my skull than listen to you extol the virtues of the latest ruling prick."

"A sovereign to whom the Welsh still bow."

"The Welsh don't bow."

"Caused only by an exaggerated sense of self-importance."

Ethan looked at him sharply. "Bwyta fy gachu."

"Really?" Morgan flipped a page on the notepad to scan through it. "I believe you'd already informed me earlier this morning that I should eat your shit. Lack of imagination is apparently a persistent Welsh trait."

Ethan snatched the clipboard away from him. "Twll din pob Sais!"

"All of us arseholes, indeed." Morgan grabbed the clipboard back. "My countrymen should be sainted for having to endure your people's gibberish. I understand your babble only because you have yet to recall more than five phrases in our nearly five years' acquaintance."

"At least the Welsh are proud of our heritage, and we don't try to pretend we're more posh than we are, eh, Chessie?" Ethan smiled when Morgan's face darkened like a solar eclipse. "What'd you call your gang of teenage lowlifes again? Rusty Knockers or Royal Cocksuckers or some shit?"

With a flash of white teeth, Morgan banished the shadow from his features. "Better to ask the Welsh female population. They seldom forgot the name when eagerly seeking out our 'low-life' affection."

Ethan gave him a hard stare as they walked. "You know, you're one high-and-mighty remark away from losing your Old Forester privileges."

Morgan ran a hand down the front of his burgundy-hued vest. "The Signature 100 variety?"

"What else?"

"Then I shall clear my diary accordingly."

"Good call." Ethan took a sharp breath and reached around to massage his lower back. Morgan furrowed his forehead at him, but Ethan waved him off. "Woke up with some stiffness. Probably from adjusting that goddamn bed against the wall again last night."

Morgan tipped his head with a smirk. "Signs of your advanced age. You will be reaching a milestone next January."

Ethan straightened briskly, despite the pain. "Thirty years is not a milestone. Talk to me if I survive another twenty."

"Before which you'll have taken the proud command of a wheelchair."

Ethan jerked back the hood of his robe and glared at him. "You're only about four years behind me, you cocky fuck."

"And yet, I will not soon be gumming my meals," Morgan mumbled, ostensibly studying the list.

Ethan pivoted to stop in front of him. "Try saying that again, after I knock your teeth in." He shoved Morgan back a step.

Morgan's eyes flashed, and he dropped the clipboard to the stone floor with a clatter. "Oi! And how will you understand me without your hearing aid, ya knob?" He shoved Ethan in turn.

"Oh, you're a dead man, Lieutenant."

"I reckon you'll beat me to that, grandfather."

"Actually"—Ethan grabbed Morgan by the vest—"I'll just beat you, period."

Morgan gave a small smile. "Lookin' for a barney, eh? Right, then."

Morgan swung his fist, but Ethan swiveled full circle and managed to get an arm around the Englishman's neck from behind. Morgan dug his fingers into Ethan's wrist.

"Careful!" Morgan said through his teeth. "We wouldn't...want to...break a hip, now, would we?"

Ethan bent forward to force Morgan into a headlock. "Not before I break your neck."

Morgan gave a muffled chuckle with his face pressed against Ethan's side. "You forget...your opponent," Morgan grated. "The only victim will be...your massive ego!"

He punched his fist toward Ethan's groin. Ethan twisted out of reach just as Morgan wrapped a leg around Ethan's and pulled his foot out from under him.

Ethan caught himself and staggered back with a breathy laugh. "You cheating dickwad."

Morgan grinned and held his hands before him, feet spread. "Sticks and stones, my thick-headed Taffy."

Ethan lurched forward and grabbed for Morgan, who ducked aside. But Ethan caught him by the shoulder and tried to land a jab to his stomach. Morgan deflected Ethan's fist, flipped around behind him, and dragged him back by his robe until they both slammed into the stone wall.

Morgan let out a growling cackle, wrapping an arm around Ethan's neck this time, and started to climb onto his back. But Ethan ground a bootheel onto Morgan's foot to keep him in place and then rocked forward. With a grim smile, Ethan started a backward headbutt, when a voice said, "Well now, if ye lads are done muckin' about..."

They froze in mid-fight and stared.

Angus stood regarding them with crossed arms. The Scotsman raised his eyebrows, his beard billowing out in a dark cloud around his face. With a *clink-clink-clink*, he tapped the toe of his robotic foot against the floor like an impatient schoolmarm.

Morgan slid off Ethan's back, and they both cleared their throats.

"What is it, Sergeant Maxwell?" Ethan jerked his hood up, while Morgan straightened his vest and leaned down to scoop up the fallen clipboard.

Angus shook his head with a half-hidden smile as he combed his fingers down one side of his beard and then reached into the pocket of his olive-drab trousers. "I have the report and map fer the tunnels, Captain."

"Good." Ethan snatched the folded papers from Angus and handed them to Morgan. "And the repairs to the compound?"

Angus grimaced and scratched the nape of his neck, where his long, tight braid began. "That wanker of a caretaker has left a right mess. It'd be like paintin' the Forth Bridge! A ne'erending pain in the arse. We dinnae have time to fix it all."

Ethan began walking, and the two officers fell into step beside him. "Well, narrow it down to the must-have's." Ethan glanced at Morgan, who was thumbing through the tunnel notes against the clipboard. "Lieutenant, get some of the residents onto a repair detail. I saw a few in the list with handyman skills. And then—"

A blur of blond came tumbling around the corner and collided with Angus.

The sergeant caught Vanessa's arms as she bounced back from him. "Easy there, lassie," he said with a chuckle.

"Sorry!" She put a hand to her chest and then bent down to pull one slipper back on. "Sorry, I was—"

"See to it," Ethan said to Morgan. "I want the repairs started by the time I get back this afternoon."

Morgan put two fingers to his brow in an informal salute, but then his eyes wandered over the girl. He inclined his head. "Vanessa."

She blushed brighter. "Hi, Morgan."

The skin tightened across Ethan's shoulders as he glanced between them. First-name basis? When did that start?

But as Morgan turned and went on his way, Angus leaned in. "I must say, yer bonnie Dutchie is lookin' especially tidy, Captain." The Scotsman spoke from the side of his mouth. "Does she ken this isnae a date?"

Ethan clenched his jaw. "Dismissed, Sergeant."

Angus nodded and turned to follow Morgan.

Vanessa, still catching her breath, flinched backward when Ethan focused his eyes on her. "Let me guess. You lost your watch."

She pursed her lips. "I don't have a watch."

"Shocking."

He brushed past her and rounded the corner. She hurried up to him as he walked.

"I see Morgan is in charge of the notepad today," she

said, and he could hear the prelude to a sarcastic comment. "He must have really done something to tick you off." And there it was.

He looked at her as she walked beside him. She had pulled part of her hair back and had secured it with a glittery dark-blue clip in the shape of a butterfly. The effect was appealing. It afforded him a better view of her bare neck and shoulders in the ruffled blue peasant top. Not to mention, an unobstructed vantage point over those nicely rounded breasts. He would have put his mouth all over them last night if she'd given him an invitation. The feel of her—warm and soft against him—had jump-started old urges, despite his body belonging in a Dali painting.

He had always enjoyed a good game of flirtation, back when he and Morgan used to frequent the seedier bars of Germany at night, where there was always a chance to wet both his whistle and his wick. These days, he could resist the chase. But last night, still fuzzy after dozing off at his desk, his resolve had been at its weakest. And the tantalizing feminine essence of her had been at its strongest. Those lovely eyes had revealed every ounce of delight and surprise and indignation. And the way those long legs had pressed against him had presented so many possibilities. Her lips seemed always on the edge of a sultry smile…and would have looked even better on the tip of his—

"Did I miss something?"

Startled, he turned his head. "What?"

She shrugged. "You're smiling. I can't imagine that happens very often."

He straightened as he walked. "I was…strategizing."

Nice save, jagoff.

"Oh," she said. "Well, it must have been an in-depth strategy. You were thinking pretty hard."

Harder than you know.

He reached into his hood to rub the back of his neck. She fidgeted with a lock of hair. He suppressed a sigh as his body started to relax. Under control again. Situation contained.

She swung her arms beside her. "So what kind of

things would you like to do with me today?"

He gritted his teeth as the denim seams of his crotch swelled and pinched him again. "We're going to town." He swung into the next corridor.

She matched his pace and squinted up at him. "Why?"

"I'd like to see it for myself. I want to know more about their capabilities. My men's reports are thorough, but a direct reconnaissance can be very valuable."

"Well, I think you're going to be disappointed. Or relieved. There's no one there that can stand up to you."

Her skirt—long and flowing today—blew against him from a draft that slipped through the passageway. Ethan glanced down at the white gauzy material as it laid itself gently upon the thick black fabric of his robe. He started to brush a hand over the delicate material, to trap it there between his glove and thigh so he could feel the movement of her body tugging it as she walked. But when he caught sight of her gazing up at him—her eyes brightening as the hallway gloom gave way to the sunlight ahead—he drew away and pulled his hood farther forward.

When they emerged through the front gates, Nicolo looked up from where he had been busying himself with something under the raised hood of one of the armored black Land Rovers. He finished whatever he had been tweaking and then jumped up to catch the truck's hood and slam it closed. The mechanic had already folded down the heavy mesh screen from the windshield in preparation for the captain's trip, as well as removed the side-mounted grenade launchers he had rigged up a while back. Good, no need to overdo it yet. The mere bulk of the ancient battle-ready Snatch itself, when the townspeople saw it, would be intimidating enough.

Nicolo walked over as he wiped his hands on a grease-stained red cloth. "She's ready, Capitano." The Italian stuffed the rag into his back pocket. "But watch the third gear, it keeps popping out."

Ethan gave him a nod. "Thanks, Nic." He stepped aside to let Vanessa climb up into the vehicle.

She stared at Nicolo, who was a few centimeters

shorter than she. He grinned as he tipped his grimy cap at her and then tossed Ethan a wink. She returned his smile before noticing Ethan waiting for her.

"He's a spritely little guy, isn't he?" she said to Ethan in a whisper. She put her foot on the doorframe to haul herself up and plopped herself onto the seat. She paused. "Not that I'm an expert, but isn't this on the wrong side?" She indicated the steering wheel in front of her.

"It's UK-made, meant to drive on the left side of the road over there. But all you need to worry about is putting your ass in the other seat." He made a shooing motion with his hand. "Move it."

She pressed her lips together at him petulantly—a mannerism he was coming to enjoy—and then laboriously crawled over the center console to the passenger side. She caught her long skirt on the stick shift and threw Ethan an extra scowl as she yanked to free herself.

Ethan stepped up into the truck and looked at her as they both settled in. "Have you ever been in a vehicle before?"

"When I was little, but I don't remember much," she admitted. "My parents and the others all had to stow away in big trucks to get here. I've seen vehicles pass through this area over the years, though. Usually because someone got themselves lost." She glanced in the direction of the remote town they were about to investigate. "Really lost."

"Well, then. Time to pop your cherry."

"Excuse me?"

He smiled to himself and wiggled the shifter to see if it was in neutral. "Enjoy the ride." He stomped one foot on the brake and twisted the key to bring the engine to life.

Vanessa grabbed the sides of her seat as Ethan pressed the clutch to the floor with his other foot and knocked the stick shift into first gear. He feathered the clutch initially as he gave it some gas, but then purposely released it faster than he normally would have. The vehicle lurched forward with a roar. Vanessa squeaked at the sudden movement and gripped the seat. Ethan smiled to himself again.

It was a fairly rocky ride down the road to Achterwaartsstad, but not a bad way to go, since the way it made Vanessa bounce on the seat near him was very easy on the eyes. He draped his right wrist over the top of the wheel where the hard rubber had worn down into a perfect cradle to accommodate his yearslong habit.

"So why am I along on this outing, anyway?" Vanessa's hands clutched the sides of the seat again as another bump jounced the Land Rover.

"In case I need to ask questions. I don't speak Dutch."

"Join the club."

He turned his head to her with a frown. "You barely have an accent, but I thought you could at least speak your native tongue."

"Boy, are you in for a letdown." This time she grabbed the door handle strap as the vehicle jolted again. "I mean, I used to know it as a child, and I can still remember simple stuff. But you should have seen me prattling away at five years old. It was 'koekje' this and 'mooie bloem' that and 'Mama, kijk naar de eekhoorn!' I was very talkative back then."

"How times have changed," he remarked dryly.

"But now most of it's gone, probably because my parents decided to switch to English exclusively, once I started to use it. I can understand a little Dutch when I hear it, but most people around here know both, so it's not an issue. I don't think you'll need me for much."

He tapped his fingers against the stick shift. He could relate. He'd spent his formative years speaking Welsh, due to his mother's influence, but lost that ability after their move west across the pond. And now only fragments remained. Regardless, what the fuck was he supposed to do with her now? Why even bring her along? He ought to turn around and drop her back at the compound.

Her body bounced in his peripheral vision as he swerved around a pothole.

Probably not worth backtracking. Might as well keep an eye on her.

"How can you see through these...grate thingies?"

She pushed her face near the passenger window to examine the metal mesh screen.

"You get used to it."

She looked around at the stark, battered interior. "All the stuff you guys have seems kind of old." She wrinkled her nose at him. "I mean, it's 2066. There's got to be more modern equipment out there."

"New technology costs more money than we're willing to spend. And your pockets have to be especially deep if you want it scrubbed clean." He leaned forward over the steering wheel to peer at the sky when a shadow moved over the Land Rover's hood. But it wasn't the right shape for a bird. He tapped his fingers against the stick shift knob.

"Scrubbed?" Vanessa repeated.

He glanced at her. "Every government controls all weapons production. They can embed heat-resistant circuits in the makeup of the materials themselves. Those weapons can be tracked anywhere they go. Older tech means no numbers, no trackers. Same goes for vehicles."

"Well, why do you need all these guns and big, tough machinery anyway? It can't take all that much to subdue a bunch of unarmed civilians like us. It's like you guys are constantly ready for war."

"We are."

"Oh."

She went quiet, which made him glance over at her again. She was probably imagining what exactly a war would be like. Another jarring bump rocked her on her seat.

With any luck, she'd never have to find out.

CHAPTER EIGHTEEN

ETHAN

After about seven more kilometers, past the long stretches of trees that lined both sides of the dirt road, the town appeared. It was composed of mostly one- and two-story buildings, all fashioned of either stone or brick. From a distance, it looked like a place frozen in time. As the Land Rover neared the fringes of Achterwaartsstad, horse-drawn carts rolled past neatly maintained sidewalks. Building entrances were overhung by window boxes burdened with purple and yellow flowers—dahlias, if he'd heard Vanessa correctly when she had identified them during their tour of the compound's garden.

Most of the wagons' drivers, as well as the people milling around the streets, turned and stared at the black armored vehicle as it approached. And their faces seemed to reflect a shared worry. Good.

He pulled up beside one of the outermost buildings of the town and shifted into first gear before turning off the engine. He opened the door, hopped down, and slammed it shut. Vanessa opened hers, but then there was silence. He bent to look under the Land Rover. Her slippered feet were not there. He shook his head and walked around to the other side. Vanessa perched on the seat, clutching the leather strap of the door handle.

He folded his arms. "What's the problem?"

"It looks farther going down than it did going up." She dangled her legs and leaned forward to seemingly judge the distance to the ground. Then, poking her tongue against the corner of her mouth, she wrapped her arms around the back of the seat and twisted herself to slide off the cushion. For several agonizing seconds, she inched her way down like she was clinging to a cliff face.

"Holy shitballs," Ethan muttered and stepped forward. He grabbed her waist and swung her around to set her on her feet.

She stared up at him with her hands on his arms. The bright day made her emerald eyes sparkle, and her bare shoulders glowed in the warm sunlight. They looked just the right shape to rest his hands on, were he to kneel behind her as she bent onto all fours—

Stand the fuck down, Captain. We don't have time for this.

"Let's move." He pried his fingers from her waist and brushed past her.

The truck door closed with a rattle, and then her light footsteps hurried to catch up. He tried not to look at her as she walked beside him. The balance he kept between organizing the compound and fighting a growing attraction to her was disorienting. He needed to get his shit together.

And not think about what she'd look like with her hair spread over my pillow if I ripped out that cutesy butterfly clip and put her on her back...

He picked up his pace. "Get the lead out of your ass. We're burning daylight."

"Get the lead—!" She blew out a loud breath. "Well, you're not going to be able to see the town very well if you're galloping through it!"

She drew next to him again, and her arm pressed briefly against his side. The accidental touch made his mind spring to the image of her head tilted back on his pillow as he propped himself over her and curled his fingers into the long tresses fanning out to either side of her. He clenched his teeth and walked faster.

"Fine." Her voice popped like water on a hot griddle

behind him.

He could almost hear her crossing her arms with that sulky expression she whipped out whenever he gave her an order.

Let her pout. Whatever it takes to keep her quiet so I can focus.

Ethan's eyes swept over the buildings around them to take in the strange assortment of styles that seemed to range from old Dutch architecture to more modern. Certain buildings, if they were taller than two stories, were narrow in width, with either curved or stepped gables. But those were few within the small village, even toward the more commercial center. Most structures were shorter with simple angled roofs over a second-floor attic. Many of the houses were painted a dark green or a navy blue and were so similar that probably only the occupants could tell them apart.

There were picturesque canals throughout the town. As he and Vanessa crossed over small white-painted drawbridges, they looked down at the myriad houseboats docked along the banks. The damp grassy smell of the channels' earthen slopes mingled with an occasional waft of fishiness as small vessels cut serenely through the dark water on their way to other parts of the village. And there were innumerable bicycles tied to trees and railings, in addition to the ones being peddled down the streets by every manner of person in every manner of dress.

At one point, Ethan had to throw an arm around Vanessa's waist to pull her out of the path of a man speeding up behind them. She clutched his robe as the cyclist darted past, and she gave him a searching look identical to the one last night when he'd held her. Like she was waiting for him to do more. He drew away swiftly, the nearness of her threatening to make him respond in a way he had been resisting since the start of their journey. Hell, since he'd seen her step forward to save the caretaker's skin on day one.

The people of Achterwaartsstad were an odd medley. Many of them wore more contemporary styles of brightly colored clothing, but several still dressed as if the decades had never passed. A number of women wore long dresses with peplums and even sported the traditional peaked lace hat, like he'd seen in picture books as a boy. Many others wore the wooden shoes apparently prevalent in old Holland, though they couldn't truly be that comfortable, since most of the village residents resorted to regular lace-up shoes or boots. Overall, the contrasting fashions made for a curious sight as the townsfolk mixed together into one shifting crowd throughout the brown-and-gray cobbled streets. All of them, though, stared at the captain and Vanessa. Because as strange as he found them, he and the girl probably made a much more bizarre-looking pair.

And the longer the villagers watched them and whispered to each other, the more his muscles twisted like steel cable feeding a winch.

They should have all been instilled with a sense of fear and awe, so that they would continue to leave him and his men to their task at the compound. They also should have been intimidated enough to accommodate his demands, should he need to make any. That was standing operating procedure, and it was SOP for a reason: because it always worked for him. But instead, these yokels seemed fascinated. He was not a serious threat for them to hide from, but a hulking black creature for them to gawk at.

A familiar heat began to rise and spread out across his flesh until his face felt like it was combusting under the cursed cloth mask.

Goddamn it. Goddamn them. Staring at me like I just crawled out of a fucking circus cage. I could level this whole fucking village if I wanted to.

Vanessa touched his arm. And then slid her hand down to hold his. The fire blazing through his thoughts guttered out, like something had sucked all the oxygen from it. He turned his head to her. She gazed up at him, her brow wrinkled. With a hesitant smile, she put her other hand on his arm and squeezed it against her as they walked.

In that instant, everything around him was blotted out,

like a sudden fog rolling in. None of the shapes or people or sounds that faded into that gray veil had any importance. Only he and she were left in the light. A light that seemed to emanate from her alone. She squeezed his arm once more and then withdrew her hands to walk wordlessly beside him. He faced forward. He followed no conscious route then. He simply wandered, his own footsteps muffled as the world seemed suspended in a calming stillness.

But all the noises popped back into place when they turned onto a busier street, and he pulled his hood forward.

Good way to get your ass handed to you, Evans. Stay frosty, damn it. You're here to observe, so get your head in the game.

He pushed the shoulders of his sleeveless robe closer to his neck and committed himself to absorbing every detail he could about the rest of Achterwaartsstad and its inhabitants. If he was going to potentially guard against the town or use the town for his own purposes, then he needed to *know* the town. Know their weaknesses, their hostilities, their depravities. And see if this Mayor Visser of theirs was capable of organizing them against the compound. He trusted his men's evaluation of the little village and its people, but he was the one responsible for every soldier's life. And there was no substitute for a firsthand appraisal. Not in this world.

A small boxy shadow appeared on the sidewalk and drifted alongside him, but it disappeared just before he tugged back his hood to look up. Something about the shape was familiar. He strained his ears to detect anything unusual outside of the town noises around them, but nothing stood out. He fixed his gaze on a squat building and then shifted his eyes to study one of the men's faces passing nearby.

"What is it you're looking for?" Vanessa asked.

"Opposition." He ducked down a side street and entered an area evidently used by the locals as an open-air market. "And opportunity."

She approached a vendor's booth and trailed her hand

along a shelf of jeweled trinket boxes. "How much of each have you seen so far?" The merchant behind the wooden counter gave her a suspicious glare, and she pulled her hand back.

He yanked his left glove on tighter. "Mostly opposition."

Vanessa's gaze moved to the P6 holstered under his right arm. She probably wondered why he carried both his weapons with him everywhere. She wouldn't understand how many times that behavior had saved his life.

"Does that mean you're not going to let any of us come into town yet?" she asked. "Supplies are getting pretty sparse. And all our poor bicycles are rusting away from neglect."

"Some of you will be allowed back, with an escort."

Her voice turned shy. "Are you *my* escort, then?"

He glanced down at her. She twined a lock of hair around her fingers as she looked up at him. She caressed it as gently as she'd touched his hand only a moment ago, and he slowed his pace beside her. He began to open his mouth. But instead of answering, he moved away from her to cross the road.

He approached a solitary stand set back from the others and scanned a collection of colored leather wallets that were neatly arranged across a board laid atop the vendor's wooden cart. The merchant's back—broad and covered by a ratty brown sack of a shirt—was turned to Ethan. But after the man seesawed his shoulders with a crackling sound and pivoted, Ethan tensed. The hulking merchant's wide pitted face creased like an accordion when he frowned, but his close-set dark eyes did not waver from Ethan's gaze. There was a jagged notch on the man's jaw, healed but mangled. Like someone had clawed off part of his flesh in a desperate act of self-defense.

This one is dangerous.

The thought was instantaneous, since he was long accustomed to picking up on signs that told him when someone was looking for a fight. Or an excuse for worse.

He held the man's eyes, making it plain that the fucker

was welcome to try something. Whenever Ethan entered a town, he made sure his strong-arm reputation spread, because it never failed to draw out those who sought the prestige of hammering him to a pulp. It showed him which enemies to pick off first. And this ogre looked like he was next in the ring.

But when a large wallet set in an intricately carved wooden stand caught Ethan's attention, he halted. It was dyed a deep burgundy color with slight puckering across the surface. He ran a gloved finger over it. He had seen material like this years ago in Serbia, when the atrocities against its people were reaching their height, and he knew instantly what he was looking at. There were two dozen more of the same, stacked carefully around the rest of the cart's display. Ethan swallowed back the acidic taste in his mouth.

These were not made from animal skin.

When he lifted his eyes, the merchant leaned forward and set his beefy hands on the board. His fingernails were dark crescents packed with dirt. Or dried blood. The black-haired merchant started a slow grin that made Ethan instinctively reach for the gun at his hip. But he turned as someone drew up next to him.

Vanessa rested her hands on the board and moved her gaze across the contents of the booth. When Ethan glanced at the merchant, the man was dragging his eyes over her. An odd purring seemed to rumble through the merchant's thick chest, and he rubbed the line of stubble on his chin the same way he might have forced his meaty fingertips along her soft curves. At that, the damaged skin across Ethan's scalp prickled, and he started to curl his left hand around the grip of his H&K.

Oblivious to either of the men, Vanessa smiled and reached for the burgundy wallet that was prominently on display. Ethan let go of his gun and snatched her wrist. Her mouth fell open but then she promptly closed it with a scowl.

"Let's go," he said before she could take a breath to bitch at him, and he pulled her away.

He took her elbow firmly and kept her close while she stumbled along beside him. "What is your problem?" she demanded as she threw a look back at the leather merchant. "I was thinking about getting one of those for Cornelis."

"He won't want that kind," Ethan muttered, that bitter tang revisiting the back of his tongue. But then he paused and turned a frown on her. "Besides, why would you buy him anything?"

"Because he's a friend," she said with another scowl. "Ever heard of those?"

Ethan squinted. "How close a friend are we talking?"

Vanessa hesitated. "Does it matter?"

His stomach twinged as if touched by a lit match. "Evidently matters to you."

She crossed her arms and tucked them tight against herself, mumbling something under her breath. He glanced back. Even across the widening distance, the vendor still stalked them with his eyes.

"Look," Ethan said gruffly, "from now on, stay next to me and away from men like that merchant. I don't trust him."

She rolled her eyes. "You really do see everyone as an enemy."

"That's because everyone is an enemy until they prove otherwise."

"So what am I?"

He sighed. "A pain in my ass."

She gave him a sour look, then smiled at something up ahead. He furrowed his brow at the way she lit up.

"Come on!" she said, making a grab for his hand.

He pulled out of reach. "What are you—?"

But she had already skipped away from him toward a booth squeezed between one vendor hawking copper-bottom pans and one selling amateur still lifes. The awning, more elegantly fashioned than those that flanked it, advertised Sieraden en Parfum. Vanessa was already pulling the tops off different small vials by the time he reached her.

She gave one of them a sniff. "Heaven in a bottle," she said happily. She sprayed the perfume on her wrist.

Ethan folded his arms. "What did I just say about staying close to—?"

"What do you think?"

Ethan stood unmoving as she thrust her arm up to him. "I think we're off track," he told her flatly.

She frowned and waved her arm at him more insistently. Finally, he took a step forward and put his nose near her proffered wrist. He kept his voice toneless. "Heavenly."

"Oka-a-a-y…" She tiptoed her fingers over the stoppers of the crystal bottles as she searched for another sample.

There was also a variety of jeweled rings and bracelets displayed next to the collection of perfume bottles, but most of the baubles were horrendous. Ethan glanced up. The female merchant stared at him, and her heavily wrinkled face showed that she wasn't sure what to make of this scene before her: a vivacious girl bubbling over as she wasted the merchant's wares, while her ominous hooded companion brooded next to her. The woman looked down when the captain narrowed his eyes at her.

Vanessa brushed back her hair from one shoulder and sprayed a new fragrance on herself. "What about this one?" She tilted her head and presented her neck to him.

He hesitated. "It's fine."

"How do you know? You're way over there." She stepped closer and strained on her toes to extend her throat toward him. "Sniff me."

Against his better judgment, he pushed back his hood to lean down to her. He held his nose near her neck and breathed in through the mask. It was a sweet but sharp perfume, like peppermint. But when her hair brushed against his cheek, he turned his face to take a deeper breath, because this time he had caught *her* scent beneath the candy-like fragrance. Something natural and rich, like warm butter. Or gingerbread. And under that—he dipped his head closer—dewy flesh, like fresh melon. He closed his eyes, his lips millimeters from grazing her skin.

"Well, Captain?"

He pulled back to stare at her. He adjusted his mask with a tug. "It's fine."

Fuck. Fuck. Fuck. This is getting out of hand.

"That's all? You seemed to like it." A smile sauntered past her lips. "Well, back it goes, then." And she returned the tester to its place on the green velvet.

"Are we done here?"

She shrugged. "Sure. I know you're dying to get back to tromping around and glaring at people—"

"This isn't the only thing I have to do today." He pushed by her and headed farther down the street.

"If you're so busy, then why are you window-shopping through the market?" she asked as she caught up with him.

"I'm not browsing," he said curtly.

He glanced down at her. And invariably, at her breasts. God, the way those things couldn't help but vie with each other for room against that low, snug neckline…

He bit his tongue and looked away. "I'm ascertaining the extent of their supplies and how much we can obtain from them without having to search outside the area."

"So that you can take those things from them?"

He detected the tone of disapproval in her voice and felt a pinch of irritation. "Don't make assumptions. We'll trade or buy, if we're able. We took over the compound out of necessity. We're not complete barbarians." Almost unconsciously, he glanced again at her chest as she adjusted the neckline where it rested off her shoulders. "Why don't you wear any jewelry? Don't girls like that sort of thing?"

"Sure they do. But rubies and pearls are a little out of reach for most of us." She quirked one corner of her mouth as she gazed at the ground. "But maybe someday." Her voice was soft, with a wistful tone to it.

He rolled his shoulders uncomfortably. "Didn't your parents ever buy you anything nice?"

"They could never afford it. And things in the compound haven't changed since then." She met his eyes and shrugged. "You see us. We grow everything. Anything else we need we can get here in the town, if we sell enough of what we grow or bake. Just like with my apples that the Tuinstra Distillery purchases for their brandewijn: if we have a good harvest, then we can get by. But that doesn't leave a lot for luxuries. And when Caretaker Dijkstra was running things, he'd use up any surplus on a set of diamond-encrusted bathrobes for himself, so all his simpering girlfriends could drape themselves over his lap like he was a sultan. These days I'm actually happy if I have enough supplies for my monthly—" Her jaw hung open a moment and then she looked away.

Amazing how she never saw where her sentences were going when she started them. Her mouth had embarrassed her more times than he could count since he'd met her. She coughed lightly and pretended to be very interested in a display of rakes and shovels at a nearby vendor's booth.

Over the next few hours, they made their way around the city, poking into every street and every alley. He mentally recorded the people and other images around him and mapped out every turn. It was not a large, sprawling town by any means, and so would have taken a casual tourist only an hour or so to explore, but he wanted it memorized. That knowledge could become very useful to him if there came a time when he needed it.

Vanessa talked to him as they went, and honestly, her idle chatter wasn't so bad. Her range of topics seemed endless, though, and it was a wonder she didn't pass out from lack of air. But the bright and genuine smile on her pretty face held his attention, even if most of the opinions she spouted did not. Overall, in spite of trying to keep his focus purely on his surroundings, he enjoyed himself. Shit, that was an almost foreign feeling now. He glanced at her and then shook his head. He should never have brought her.

The time passed swiftly, and the afternoon came upon them sooner than expected. He should have been able to keep track, considering how many times she would make a loud comment about how tasty the foods looked in various store windows. She complained when they passed a bakery that it was a shame how *some* people came to a new country and never bothered to sample the local fare. It was a point she brought up three more times as they passed a booth selling raw herring, one marketing puffy pancake-like edibles called poffertjes, and then a cheese shop. At that, he finally capitulated. As he had quickly learned since his arrival, her nagging stomach could defeat the patience of a sphinx.

After he reviewed the cheese shop's selection and picked up one green plastic-wrapped ball, he flipped a wad of euro bills at the clerk behind the counter and then escorted Vanessa back out into the street.

"Here." He tossed the cheese at her. "Now, let's keep moving."

She stared at the wrapped Gouda in her hands. "This is your idea of a meal?" She put a fist on her hip. "And what am I supposed to do after I get the wrapper off? Chew through the wax?"

"If you know what's good for you, you will."

She put the fist holding the Gouda on her other hip. "Well, what's *not* good for me is plugging me up with four hundred grams of cheese! You do know that never ends well, right?"

"I'm not here to babysit." He tugged on the cuff of each glove. "You wanted food, you have food."

"I wanted *us* to have food." She followed him as he started walking again. "You know, *together*? Like real humans do."

He turned on her. "Why? Why is it so damn important to you that we do anything together? I only brought you along because I thought you'd be useful, which was a supreme error in judgment. I'm in charge of thirty-four battle-hardened men. We don't spend time 'getting to know' the people we have to subdue. This is a routine resupply and reassess scenario for us. And I have to make sure we succeed and move on with our mission. So excuse the *fuck* out of me if I don't have time to play tea party with you." He yanked his hood back up over his head and pivoted to make his way up the road.

When she fell into step beside him, she was looking down at the Gouda and turning it in her hands. He could hear the plastic crinkle softly even amid all the sounds around them. They walked in silence. Although he continued to scan the buildings they passed, ignoring the more timid people who slinked back into their homes when they saw him, he could not perform his survey with the same level of concentration. Maybe he had been too harsh. But damn it, she knew how to push his buttons.

"Is it true that you've taken over sixteen facilities before ours?" Her voice was quiet.

He regarded her closely. Someone had been talking to her.

"Yes." No point in contesting it.

"So we're just one more stop on the road."

He glanced at her again. Why did she sound upset about it? She should have been glad to be rid of him.

She dropped her arms and swung the cheese beside her. "When are you leaving?"

He squinted at a small redheaded child who ran down the sidewalk. "I haven't decided yet. It depends on how fast we can set up exchanges with the nearest arms dealers and scope out the surrounding territories."

"I guess you have a lot of enemies to worry about."

"I do."

"Have you killed many of them?"

"Enough."

"Are you going to kill anyone here?"

He almost stopped walking, but instead rubbed his eyes through the cloth mask. "If I have to."

God, just quit asking fucking questions.

As if she had heard his thought, she said nothing more as she walked beside him. He pushed away the conflicting sentiments that nipped at him and was glad for her silence. Because one more word out of her mouth, and he might tell her exactly how he was beginning to feel toward this entire endeavor. Choosing North Holland had been a mistake.

One of several I've made.

He shook off the thought and surveyed the streets. There were a few large delivery trucks that wended their way through the town now and again. These people did have a way to bring outside goods into the town. That would prove beneficial. And, as already predicted, he never once saw a gunsmith shop or any other establishment that sold firearms. There were plenty of stores peddling knives and axes, but any such implements were geared toward farm life.

A loud gaggle of teenagers laughed and talked while they bounded along the sidewalk toward him. As they neared, they didn't seem deterred by his imposing presence but rather ignored it altogether. Ethan shook his head and put an arm out to Vanessa to shield her as they bustled around him, caught up in their raucous conversation…but his hand touched empty air.

Ethan jerked to look beside him, but Vanessa was gone. What in the ever-loving fuck? He whirled to stare after the teenagers who were already well past him, but she wasn't anywhere in sight. His entire body went cold. He backtracked along the sidewalk and pushed by the bubbling group of young townsfolk who paused only marginally to give him a puzzled look. Sweat started to dampen his clothes, the robe seeming to weigh heavier and heavier as he wrenched back his hood and swiveled his head to search one way and then the other.

How could he have lost track of her? How could he have possibly not noticed her slipping away? Goddamn distractions. He always lost his focus around her.

He swept his gaze down side streets as he passed them, and though there were several blond pedestrians ambling along, none of them were Vanessa. The icy tingle of panic raced through him as he spun and headed in a new direction. He started to cross the street, fixated on a spot where he'd seen the flash of a blue blouse, and he nearly collided with a string of cyclists streaking by. When he reached the other side, he wove through clusters of wandering townspeople, peering around them for any sign of her. He gritted his teeth and jogged ahead, elbowing his way past startled pedestrians. He tossed a glance down one avenue and then another and another. Nothing. Until he caught sight of a broad-backed figure at the opening to an alley across the street.

A shabby brown shirt spanned the bulky shoulders, which the man seesawed stiffly when he bent forward over something. The figure made a sudden movement and pivoted to reveal his profile. Ethan stopped dead. It was the leather merchant. And he was gripping Vanessa's wrist high in the air so that she was on her tiptoes—face pale and mouth stretched open—while the merchant ran his big grubby hand down her arm. Examining her.

Every color in Ethan's vision went vivid as a wave of fire roared through his gut. He shot forward into the street and shoved himself off the back of a rickety wagon that hurtled by. His clenched jaw sent spasms of pain down his neck, and his heart hammered as he barreled straight toward the merchant, who had pulled Vanessa farther back into the alley. He lunged at the man and seized a fistful of his shirt to haul him back. The merchant stumbled and jerked to face him, Vanessa's wrist still clamped in his brawny fingers.

"Get the fuck away from her," Ethan ordered with a throaty growl.

But the merchant did not let go. He only smiled with a sinister glint in his eye. "I am not done with her yet."

Vanessa turned to Ethan, her chin trembling. "He says I stole one of his wallets."

Ethan met the man's glare. "He knows damn well you didn't. He's looking for an excuse." Ethan narrowed his eyes as the merchant grinned. "Except now, he's looking at a fuckload of trouble. Let her go."

"Krijg de tering," the man spat, and straightened. He was bigger than he had first appeared behind his makeshift vendor's booth. "I have heard of you, mierenneuker, and you do not frighten me, like you do these other sheep in town."

Ethan took a slow step toward him. "Good. Then you won't run before I put you in your place." Ethan nodded slowly toward Vanessa, never taking his eyes off the merchant. "Let her go. Now."

The merchant eyed Ethan and then opened his hand one finger at a time. Vanessa pulled her arm away and cradled it against her belly as she backed toward Ethan. She leaned down to grab the green ball of Gouda from the street where it had been dropped and stood off to Ethan's right.

The merchant seesawed his shoulders with the sound of cracking wood and pointed a thick index finger at Ethan's masked face. "Maybe you have my wallet, hoerenjong," he sneered. "You will pay for it. Three hundred euros."

Ethan cocked his head. "You sure you want to stick with that bullshit story?"

The man grinned wider, and the mangled flesh around the notch in his jaw twitched. "If you will not pay, then give me what was stolen."

The big dumb fuck wasn't budging. Time to make him regret it.

Ethan spoke in a calm, even voice. "I don't have your wallet. Because if I did, I would have shoved it up your ass by now."

The merchant closed his pudgy hands into fists and bumped his knuckles together. He shifted his glare briefly to Vanessa. "Your little *slet* is nice quality. I was going to let her make up for my wallet." A nasty smile slipped across his lips, and he slid his chin forward. "But you are worth more than her. People will pay more for you, Captain. And after you are gone, she will be a fun project for me. I will work on her slowly, so she can feel how good I am. My favorite raw materials"—he cupped his hand in the air and wriggled his fingers—"are the pretty parts between her thighs."

At that, everything pulsed around Ethan, like a sonic blast rippling the air. His stomach twisted with a swell of true rage.

He extended his arm across Vanessa and moved her behind him, saying in an icy voice, "Touch her again, and they'll have to bury you in pieces."

Ethan could feel Vanessa press close to him and bunch the back of his robe in her hands, her body rigid. The three of them were alone in the alley as people continually passed by on either end.

But the few town citizens who glanced in this direction were about to get an eyeful.

CHAPTER NINETEEN

ETHAN

Ethan waited just until the man's eyes flashed.

Okay, Evans. Cleared hot!

The leather merchant reached behind himself to grab something, but Ethan landed a punch to the ogre's stomach. The man bowed over and dropped the curved knife he had pulled.

The merchant may have exceeded Ethan's height, but he was no match for Ethan's speed. He seized the man's head and rammed a knee up into his face. The ogre staggered backward, pinwheeling his arms. Blood streamed from his nose. Ethan swept up the knife and held it before him as his opponent recovered and charged at him. He braced for the attack while Vanessa retreated far back against the alley wall.

The merchant, his face fixed in a snarl, managed to avoid the swipe of the knife blade. He sank his brawny fingers into the front of Ethan's robe to wrench him around. Unbalanced, Ethan lost his footing, and the sharp weapon flew from his grasp. But he righted himself and thrust his arms up between the merchant's. He knocked the man's arms outward and followed with an upward jab to the merchant's already-broken nose with the heel of his hand.

The ogre yelled and clutched his face before blundering forward. Half-blinded by his own blood, he clawed at the captain, but Ethan had already dodged him. He hauled his robe up over himself to discard it on the street, freeing himself to advance on the merchant, who spat out a glob of red mucus and swung a fist around as soon as the captain was within range.

The blow glanced off Ethan's cheekbone hard enough to make everything flash white for an instant, but he nonetheless caught the ogre's fist and pried it open. He bent the man's hand far back against his wrist as he twisted the attacker's arm. He jammed an elbow into the merchant's ribs, hearing a muffled crack before the man doubled over and fell to a knee. Ethan delivered a vicious kick to the man's wounded side, to spread the damage. Breathing heavily, he grabbed a handful of the merchant's greasy black hair and wrenched the ogre's head back to look at him.

"I know your kind." Ethan gave him a virulent shake. "These streets are your hunting grounds, where you take your trophies. And everyone who runs this shithole turns a blind eye, don't they?" He heaved a knee into the man's chest and sent him into a fit of choking coughs. "Well, I'm not one of your victims, asshole. You really thought you could take me down? And then profit off my corpse, you sick fuck?"

Incredibly, the merchant smiled, his teeth coated in red. "I would rather have *her* flesh." His eyes slid past Ethan to where Vanessa was standing. "I would use it over and over with pleasure while it is warm." He gave a garbled laugh. "And then take it from her while it turns cold."

A bolt of hatred shot through Ethan, and he looked back over his shoulder. Vanessa hovered against the alley wall. Though her eyes were wide as she watched them, he was sure she could not make out their words.

Ethan slugged the merchant and toppled him onto his back on the cobblestone pavement. Several citizens, as expected, were clustered at both ends of the alley. They stared and jabbered to each other as Ethan reached across his chest with his left hand and pulled the SIG from its holster. Placing a boot on the merchant's throat, he bent down, forced the muzzle into the man's mouth, and angled it upward.

"I'm going to pull this trigger," Ethan told him in a low guttural voice. "And that tiny pea in your skull is going to explode. Or"—he leveled the barrel—"maybe I'll just make you a fucking cripple."

The man's hurried breath fogged the metal surface of the gun, and he stared up at Ethan with the first real sign of fear. It was immensely gratifying.

"You'd better hope like hell my aim is off and that bullet goes past your spinal cord. You might even survive if you don't choke on your own blood first." Ethan showed him a tight smile and leaned closer. "But I wouldn't bet on it."

"Captain, please."

He tensed at the sound of Vanessa's voice behind him but deliberately did not look at her. He twisted the barrel between the man's teeth to drive it deeper.

Then he felt her hand on his shoulder. "I think you made your point."

Ethan's back went rigid, and he gritted his teeth. Though his mind yelled the words, he managed to speak quietly and evenly. "Stand away."

She removed her hand, but he could tell she had not stepped back.

"He's not armed now." There was a hesitant but firm tone to her voice. "Do you have to sink that low?"

Anger and disbelief flared through him. If he had not already been using every ounce of restraint he had, he would have turned the gun on *her* instead.

"Stand away," he repeated slowly.

She paused. "No."

Ethan closed his eyes for a moment, and his finger tightened on the trigger. The ridge of his cheekbone began to throb with the tingle of hot needles where the merchant had smashed against it. When he again looked down, there was a growing smugness in the man's eyes.

Ethan's finger squeezed tighter. Tension crackled down his arms and legs like free-flowing electricity, and he could practically feel his scarred skin burning with it.

Ethan jerked the gun barrel from the man's mouth and rose to his full height. The merchant, his face a bloody mess, wiped a hand across his mouth and pushed himself backward to lumber to his feet. With a growl, Ethan bent down, grabbed the fallen knife, and plunged it into the merchant's left shoulder. The man howled and clutched at the wound. Ethan seized the ogre's middle finger and snapped it in half. The man roared again before cradling his crooked finger, and Ethan shoved him back against the alley wall. He holstered his gun as he stepped up to the merchant, who was breathing raggedly.

Ethan raked his glare over the man's face. "When I see you again, we will finish this."

The merchant stared at him, eyes like two hot coals while blood leaked from his impaled shoulder. Then a corner of his mouth stretched upward. The man slowed his breathing, pushed himself off the wall, and—with his broken-fingered hand—jerked the knife out. With one last glare at Ethan, he turned to swagger down the alley. The people at the end parted for him as he approached, but it was the captain they all glanced at with fear.

Ethan gazed at the ground and flexed his gloved fists as he listened to the spectators ride out on a wave of loud mumbling. He raised his head and looked directly at Vanessa as she stood clasping the ball of Gouda to her chest. Without a word, he turned and picked his robe off the ground and pulled it back over himself.

Then he walked down the alley away from her.

CHAPTER TWENTY

ETHAN

"You did the right thing," he heard Vanessa say when she caught up to him. "I know he was asking for it, but putting someone six feet under can't always be the solution, right?"

He raised his hood and tugged it forward but did not answer.

She cleared her throat, and her voice became lighter. "I guess he really takes his craft seriously, though. He wasn't going to let that wallet thing go. Just think if someone steals a whole handbag from him—"

Ethan stopped and turned to her, barely able to breathe.

"You think this is funny?" A molten mass of rage churned in his gut, and he wanted nothing so much as to shake her senseless. "Do you have any fucking idea what a man like that is capable of? Do you know what he would have done to you?" He stepped toward her. Every muscle felt fused together like melted clumps of iron. "Why the fuck were you anywhere near him, when you were supposed to be with me?"

"You were s-so preoccupied with looking around," Vanessa said, "and...and I only wanted to see something in one of the store windows. But then he was just *there*, and he started saying all this stuff and pulling me after him—"

"He was following you." Ethan pointed over her shoulder. "He was waiting for an opportunity, and you gave it to him. That knife wasn't meant for me."

"But why would he want to hurt me?" she asked in a trembling voice.

"Because that's his nature. And if he'd managed to put that knife in my gut, then he could have taken his time with you. He wouldn't have killed you right away. He would have dragged you into one of these buildings, where the bastard would have raped you until you screamed yourself hoarse. And then he would have left your body there, after he—"

He cut himself short as the images reared up at once: Vanessa lying tied up on some filthy floor…the burly merchant squatting, naked, next to her with his knife…the blade flashing as he methodically began to flay her soft skin from her beaten, crumpled form.

Ethan shut his eyes and said through his teeth, "For Christ's sake, your own parents were murdered by an animal like him, someone doing it because they got off on it."

Her face paled. "That was different."

"No, it wasn't, goddamn it. Wake the fuck up." The words poured out, a lava flow of fury. "Evil stares you in the face, and somehow you don't even see it. It preys on everything around it, *corrupts* everything around it. And it'll swallow you fucking whole, once it finds you. That shit, just now"—he thumped a hand against his chest—"that should have been about *me*. It should have been *my* problem. But you were something easy to feed on. You gave him something to chase, which means I had less control of the situation. And then you stopped me from doing what was necessary. Right now, his brains should be covering the street, and then *no one* would fuck with me after that." Stinging sweat ran down his body under his clothes, and the robe weighed on him like a leaden shroud. "Do not get in my way again." He held a gloved index finger up to her face. "Do you understand me?"

Her eyes were wide, but after another pause, she nodded.

He pivoted and resumed his pace, not bothering to see if she followed or not. His senses simmered as he glared at the ground. How could she not see reality? How had she escaped being brutalized years ago, considering the toxic life the world's collective depravity had created and her importunate blindness to it all? No one was safe from it, not even her, tucked away in a crumbling building buried in the countryside. He felt a stab of disquiet, and he could not help but glance at her.

She walked with her head bowed, and her thumbs smoothed the green plastic of the Gouda.

Why couldn't she understand that there was danger in places that seemed safe? Her moral compass had become more than merely irksome; it was out of place in this world. And yet, she had convinced herself that she could thrive outside of her shallow microcosm. She thought she could leave the compound, her home, and venture into new territory without consequence. She wouldn't make it a day before someone found her body stuffed in a trash compactor.

Another jab of unease made him push the thought aside. He sighed, his ire beginning to recede, consumed like a last sheet of paper thrown onto the fire.

"Is there anything else you want, before we leave town?" he asked in a controlled voice.

She lifted her face to him. He felt a twinge at the wavering look in her eyes. She shook her head and bowed it once more.

This is not my fault. I won't feel guilty. He knocked his fist against his thigh as he walked, another twinge making his right temple twitch. *She needs to see things for what they are. Someone has to be the one to show her.*

They continued on and finally emerged from the alley.

"I shouldn't have left you," Vanessa spoke up in a timid voice. "I know you only wanted to keep me safe. Thank you."

His stride slowed, and he turned his head to her.

"I-I didn't expect it to get so ugly back there," she said. "I thought he was only trying to swindle me. But the way he smiled at me when he grabbed me…I should have known." She swallowed. "I tried to look past the surface, like my parents taught me, but I guess some people are exactly what they seem to be."

He began to unclench his jaw, letting his fingers uncurl beside him, and watched her turn the Gouda in her hands.

"I still don't believe killing him would have been right," she went on, "but I understand you've lived a different life. I don't always agree with you, but I suppose I shouldn't have—" She shook her head and turned the Gouda faster. "I'm sorry. I'm not used to someone like you. I don't know how to act sometimes, when I'm with you. You make me feel confused about things that I never even questioned before." She peeked at him again. "And you make me feel other…things, too."

He was taken off guard by the confession and so had no ready response. But, as usual, she filled the gap.

"I wish you would wear the robe less often. It obviously gets in your way when you have to act fast. And your physique is impressive, so you ought to let it breathe a little anyway." She hesitated, and her eyes darted away from his. "I like seeing more of you, like that." She gripped the Gouda and rubbed her thumbs over it. "I-I can't stop thinking about what you must be like under all those clothes—I mean, what you're like when you're not hiding from the world."

Her voice faded, and she had that look on her face like she was ordering herself to stop talking. He, on the other hand, was at a loss for words.

How the hell could she be attracted to him? No woman would make such an admission, considering the condition that lay beneath all the layers he wore. His appearance was equal only to his deeds. And those had been vile and many. Wherever his army went, he expected people to fear him. Despise him. And if Vanessa realized that what he had almost done to the merchant was one of the mildest sentences he had doled out over the years, she would never look at him the same way.

The Ukrainians had been the worst of his victims. They were his constant shadows, demons of his own making, and he'd prepared their punishment with the calculated care of a wronged father. All the male conspirators who tried to flee had been caught and hung upside-down within the community's main hall. He had stood before them—cold, calm…vengeful. He'd locked his glare in turn with each man's as their faces purpled with pooled blood. Then he had nodded at Frank to loop the wire around the door handle. The Ukrainian men's eyes had widened as they'd bent their heads up to stare at the thin metal line that was attached to each of the white phosphorus grenades strapped to their ankles.

At last, he had turned and followed his soldiers out. Without glancing back, he had wrenched the door shut to seal off the makeshift kill room, which pulled the pins on the grenades and released the volatile substance. And he'd known, without seeing, what the results would be. He had witnessed the effects before. The white phosphorus had ignited upon exposure to the air and had flowed in fiery sheets down the Ukes' chain-wrapped bodies, eating deep into their flesh until it reached bone. He and his men had vacated the area as soon as the garlicky smell of the chemical curled out from under the door. Ethan reserved such incendiary weapons for those he wanted to execute slowly, excruciatingly, for crimes they had committed against his men. This retribution was for the lives they had taken ruthlessly from his ranks, from his family. They'd murdered his men with cold-blooded precision. And so the goddamned Ukes had deserved every scream that was torn from their twisting, burning bodies. That's what he'd told himself at the time.

But now, a familiar shame crept over him as his mind plodded through those scenes. Were those the actions of a decent man? A sane man?

A buzzing sound—at first indistinguishable from the noises of nearby townspeople and the whir of passing bicycle wheels—grew louder behind him. Ethan turned his head over his shoulder as he walked. A dark object under the roofline of a distant building zipped out of sight into one of the alleys.

Ethan faced forward. Something about this trip to Achterwaartsstad had seemed off from the get-go, like he and Vanessa had not been alone since leaving the compound. He had a suspicion as to what was going on, but now was not the time to act. Best to wait this one out. He'd made the mistake of reacting rashly on too many occasions. That was what had led him here, where he had to hide from a band of hostiles who had every intention of winding his intestines around a flagpole and carrying it as a gory keepsake.

Because I destroyed them. Their people. Their home.

A dense ball of fire began in the pit of his stomach and rolled up into his chest as he clenched his jaw. But just when he started to close his hand into a fist again, Vanessa's fingers slid gently into his palm and wrapped around it. He turned his face to her. She gazed up at him, and the expanding heat behind his ribs dwindled to a hesitant flame. It burned low and flickered at the way she squeezed his hand and held it against herself as she walked. But this time, unlike before, she did not let go. Instead, she leaned close, almost cuddling against him as she watched the cobblestones beneath her feet.

What if her affection *was* real? Maybe her desire for him was actually…genuine.

Experimentally, he extended his index finger from around her hand and stroked it across her hip. When she looked at him, her eyes seemed to flash with pleasure, and she squeezed his hand tighter. The flame inside him blazed higher, and warmth flowed through his every fiber.

You can't have her. She'll never understand the things you've done.

At that, a blanket of ice encased him and turned the fire in his chest to cold ash. It was a suffocating truth that snuffed out every bright thing that tried to survive it.

She was drawn to him. But she did not know him.

And I'll be damned if I ever let her see what I am.

CHAPTER TWENTY-ONE

ETHAN

It was late afternoon by the time they returned to the compound, and though the walk around the city—and the unexpected skirmish—had not taxed him physically, Ethan felt drained from the thoughts that kept circling in his head. His only distraction had been the same mysterious shadow that passed over the hood of the Land Rover on their drive back. After seeing it on the way to town, he had dismissed it as a bird, maybe a hawk. But this time he knew better.

When they pulled up to the fort, Nicolo was hanging off the Boxer as he inspected one of the four tires on the left side. He looked up as Ethan parked. The short mechanic jumped down to meet them.

"Hey, welcome back, Capitano!" Nicolo called out good-naturedly and then pushed his hat back from his brow. He stuffed his hands into his pockets and glanced over at Vanessa, who had managed to slither down awkwardly from her side of the vehicle. He smiled up at the captain. "So? How was the Snatch? Did you take good care of her?"

Vanessa's mouth fell open as she came to a stop nearby.

Ethan tugged on the cuff of each glove. "Naturally. She was sweet. I think she likes the way I handle the stick.

I could tell as soon as I got inside of her."

If it were possible, Vanessa's mouth opened even wider.

Nicolo grinned. "Ah, yes, she can make a man very happy. You have only to turn her on!" He glanced at Vanessa and acknowledged her with a wink. "I think I'll take her out later and give her a good ride."

"Only off-duty, Corporal," Ethan reminded him. "I need the MRAV tuned first."

The Italian held up his hands, splotched with oil stains. "Of course, Capitano! After work, the Snatch is for fun. I will play with her when I can enjoy her, eh?" And then he chuckled, nodding again at Vanessa, and walked back to the armored Boxer MRAV.

Ethan started forward but stopped when she did not follow.

Her face reddened as she pointed after the mechanic. "What was that all about?"

He cocked his head at her. "What was what all about?"

"You know exactly! I can't believe how rude you guys—I mean, talking about me and about my—!" Her cheeks flushed crimson. "And especially after what just happened in town! You have terrible timing *and* a terrible sense of humor, if you think it was okay making all that up about us just now. I know I may dress a little…casually, but I've got news for you, Captain Craphead: I'm *not* a hussy. And—and even if we'd *done* anything, you can't decide to pass me around like a cigarette. I don't know how it was with girls back in the United States, but here, we don't tolerate guys being jerks. And your—your behavior is unacceptable. And you owe me an apology."

He waited until she folded her arms and blew out a loud breath. Then he calmly stepped past her and leaned against the bull bar enclosing the grille of the Land Rover. He pounded the side of the vehicle once with his palm. "Snatch."

She opened her mouth but then let it hang for a second. Her arms slowly came undone. "Oh. Th-the car. That's what the name—that's what…Oh."

He pushed himself off the Land Rover and walked in the direction of the front gates again. "Don't forget your cheese."

She looked back at the truck, probably picturing herself clambering in and out of it again. "No, I-I think I'll leave it for Nicolo."

"Good. At least he'll appreciate it."

But then he stopped and looked over his shoulder to survey the area with narrowed eyes. A soft buzzing sound grew steadily louder from somewhere behind the Land Rover.

"I didn't say I didn't appreciate it," she grumbled as she drifted toward him.

There was movement near the line of trees that grew on the gradual slant of the hillside. Ethan drew his H&K and cocked the hammer.

Vanessa eyed the weapon as he held it beside him. "Okay, okay, I'll go back and get the freakin' cheese!"

A dark boxy object peeked out through the branches of one of the distant trees and bobbed in the air as it seemed to adjust its position. Ethan aimed his gun and pulled the trigger, making Vanessa clap her hands to her ears. The gunshot shattered the calm as the thing jerked, wobbled, and crashed to the ground.

Nicolo and his assistant Angelo ran from behind the Boxer MRAV, while a few other soldiers—their rifles out—sprinted through the front gates. They all followed Ethan as he holstered his pistol and made his way over to the sputtering object in the grass. The captain stared down at the device as it let out a harsh clacking sound, and he kicked one of its broken propellers. A drone. That confirmed his hunch.

Thomas's shout came from a distance. "Ay! What's after 'appenin' now?"

"Yeah, what's goin' on, Cap?" Liam's voice rang out beside Thomas's. "We under attack?"

Ethan looked up at the front battlement, where Liam

and Thomas both leaned over the wall gripping their rifles. Ethan cupped a hand beside his mouth. "Stand down!"

He turned back to the drone, which rattled and gave off a shower of sparks. He nodded at Nicolo. The mechanic squatted and used a greasy rag to grab one side of the small aircraft's frame. Nicolo hefted the device and pointed at the underside.

"Capitano, the drone is not very good, but the camera…" The Italian rubbed together the fingers of his other hand. "She is very pricey."

"That so?" Ethan mumbled. "One guess as to who would have the cash for toys like that."

Achterwaartsstad's honorable Mayor Visser evidently has more money than brains, if he thinks he can fucking spy on me.

"See if you can fix it," Ethan ordered the mechanic. "Maybe we can modify it to replace our perimeter drone."

Nicolo nodded and handed the aircraft to Angelo, whose prominent Roman nose wrinkled as the thing jittered at him.

"Sì, Capitano." Nicolo rose and wiped his hands on the rag. "But what about the camera, eh? It is no use if we cannot control the video feed."

"Actually, it's got one last use." Ethan pivoted to Angelo and reached under the drone. The young mechanic held the aircraft firmly while Ethan twisted the camera off the frame and stretched the attached wires as he pulled it toward himself. He glared into the lens. "Nice try, Mr. Mayor. Next time you want to know what I'm doing, have the balls to face me."

Then he ripped the camera from its wires and slapped it into Nicolo's hand. "Sell this. Keep the rest."

Nicolo chuckled and shoved the camera in his pocket.

Ethan walked toward the front of the compound, where Vanessa stood next to the Snatch.

She fell into step beside him as he neared the entrance. "What happened? What was that?"

"An unwelcome visitor. But I think I got my message across."

When he glanced down at her as she followed him into the compound, she pulled part of her hair over her shoulder to twist it around her fingers. The faint light in the hallway highlighted the deep golden hue of her tresses and gave her hair a luminescence of its own.

I bet if I wrapped it around my fingers in the middle of the night, it'd feel just like silk.

He smoothed his mask against his face as he fought to think of something else. Anything else. "I assume you have duties in the kitchen this afternoon?"

She avoided his eyes. "We're a little understaffed for the number of people living here now. So the work piles up. I'll probably be up to my elbows in dirty dishwater most of the night."

He was quiet a moment. "I'll see about having more resources allocated to the kitchen by the end of the week. You won't be so overwhelmed then."

She looked up at him. "Thank you."

She sounded mollified by his gesture, and she walked closer beside him. He gave her a sidelong look, for he'd half expected her to reach for his hand again, like she did in town. And he couldn't deny the sinking feeling when she didn't.

He set his jaw firmly. *Get it together, dickhead.*

They continued in silence as they made their way toward the kitchen. They passed a few residents talking in the halls. Many were people who performed the same community job roles, judging by their matching work apparel. Others were couples seeming to steal a few moments of private conversation as they huddled close. But every small cluster of residents abruptly dispersed when the captain looked their way.

That's more like it. I'm in charge, and I'm not your fucking friend.

But instead of the satisfaction that typically accompanied that thought, there was a flash of melancholy. Why the hell did he feel that?

Involuntarily, he glanced again at Vanessa. She met his eyes and gave him a faint smile.

Shit. I need to get the fuck away from all of this.

He quickened his pace and turned to go on the path to the armory, leaving her to walk the rest of the way alone.

But she called to him before he had gone far. "So, tomorrow again?"

He paused, his back still to her, and closed his eyes. He rubbed the cloth-covered nape of his neck within the hood. "We both have enough things to keep us busy without these daily…briefings. We'll give it a rest for a while."

He took a step to resume his course, but her voice—soft and airy—stopped him again.

"I don't mind, really. And I'll be more than on time. Zero six forty, in fact."

For fuck's sake, she actually sounds hopeful.

Though he struggled against the urge, he did not turn around. His voice was as rough as he could make it. "No. You'll hear from me if I need you."

Silence met his words.

Don't look. She wants you to look.

Finally, she spoke. "I see. Okay, then. Sorry for wasting your time." The injured tone beneath her bitter response was impossible to miss.

The same hollow sensation as back in town, after the merchant's attack, tweaked his stomach. Her slippers swished against the stone walkway as she left.

He balled his hands into fists and strode forward once more. *Stay in formation. Don't let her get to you.*

He was not here at her whim, and he was not here to entertain her. He had much more work ahead of him if he was to pull this compound together to resemble a functioning base, however transient. And he had executioners on his trail that would eventually catch up, so he did not need to worry about the emotional state of one headstrong girl.

He paused. He was breathing in a faint but pleasurable fragrance that made him inhale deeper the more agitated he grew. He must have brushed Vanessa's neck with his nose back at the perfume stand, infusing the fabric of his mask with her candied scent. He ground his teeth and walked faster.

She was bad news. She'd already served her purpose. She had strictly been another source of strategic information and not someone he had to impress or appease. She was a nuisance, pestering him and defying him at every turn. There were countless times when he knew she was about to roll her eyes or pop off a smart remark. He didn't need that shit right now. Not while he was surrounded by enemies.

But the most frustrating part?

He hadn't met an enemy yet who weakened him like she could.

CHAPTER TWENTY-TWO

ETHAN

Ethan stared down upon the eastern field beyond the parapet ledge, where Liam and Thomas were just about to blow themselves to kingdom come.

Mabayoje monitored them as they buried the last few antipersonnel mines in the army's possession. Benoît—Benny—oversaw the operation and directed Liam and Thomas where to place the bombs. Benny didn't like others touching his tools of the trade, so the lanky young Luxembourgian shadowed them closely while gripping the hair at either side of his head.

Sweat streamed down Liam's and Thomas's faces and darkened the fronts of their olive-drab T-shirts as each private gingerly carried one of the devices. Liam tiptoed toward a pre-dug hole. He held his mine far out in front of himself with one hand, while he covered his crotch protectively with the other. Thomas walked contorted and hunched over, skimming his own mine across the grass toward a nearby hole.

It would be a wonder if they made it through the rest of the early evening without vaporizing each other.

Ethan shook his head and grunted as his left cheek-bone throbbed again. He lifted his glass and held the coldest part of it against his mask where the flesh beneath it twinged. But he sat up when there was movement off to the side.

"About damn time." Ethan held a glass tumbler toward Morgan as the lieutenant strolled along the battlement walkway. "I'm not making a second trip to the kitchen's ice house just because you're dragging your ass."

Morgan accepted the glass from Ethan and, with a finger held to the cubes, tilted it to drain the excess water. "I would be better able to accommodate your social schedule, were I not constantly carrying out your slightest whim," Morgan told him dryly as he seated himself upon the parapet wall and held out his tumbler.

"Sorry if my *orders* interfered with your afternoon tea," Ethan said as he poured Morgan some of the Old Forester. "I know how that gets your knickers in a knot."

"You also know that I never partake of the stuff," Morgan said with a frown.

"The only Englishman to shame his crumpet-munching, pinky-waving heritage."

"Better an offender to the Crown than a sheep-shagging enthusiast of Welsh lineage."

Ethan raised his glass along with Morgan for a casual toast. "Fuck you."

Morgan let out a chuckle and brought the glass to his lips.

"Speaking of supposed whims…" Ethan nodded down at the eastern field. "You don't think that's a reasonable precaution?"

Morgan swallowed and glanced at the moving figures below. "I think it is an appropriate response, but perhaps an unnecessary one. We will soon be in a position to address our perimeter with more modern—and reliable—means."

Ethan sniffed the Kentucky bourbon and relished the aromas of maple syrup and butterscotch. He adjusted the mouth hole in his mask and swallowed a sip. He paused to enjoy the burn on the back of his throat before the alcohol worked its way warmly to his stomach. "You managed to snag the attention of an arms dealer, then? How did you accomplish that small miracle?"

"Sophisticated charm." Morgan eased a thigh up onto the battlement ledge and leaned back against the stone block jutting up behind him. "Something you have yet to appreciate."

"Only because you have yet to develop it," Ethan mimicked in Morgan's tight-ass tone. "Just because you memorized the *Oxford Dictionary* doesn't mean anyone's impressed."

"Sod off, ya berk" Morgan grumbled as he rotated a shoulder and tilted his drink up.

"Careful, Lieutenant, your Cockney's showing, innit?" Ethan drawled. "And I know how hard you try to guard that little secret, Chessie, ol' boy."

Morgan leveled his gaze at Ethan. "I disclosed that childish nickname in confidence. I would prefer you let it perish alongside your sense of civility." Then added under his breath, "And I was never Cockney; merely Cockney-adjacent."

Ethan grunted a laugh. "And a juvenile delinquent. But take it easy, jailbird, I won't tarnish your image. Just nice to be reminded I'm not the only scumbag around here."

Morgan shot him a glare, but Ethan only smirked and took another sip, his tongue again catching the familiar notes of caramel and old oak within the liquor, with a touch of apple to round it out. God, this shit was good.

"All right, what dirtballs did we dig up this time?" Ethan asked, shifting back to business.

"Willing ones." Morgan set his tumbler down on the parapet ledge in front of his knee. "Our remote location has yielded few candidates."

He lifted his right hand and tapped the band on his ring finger. A spray of blue light fanned out above the cring, projected by the clear crystal set in the communicator. A list of dealer names and locations—generated by the black-market code programmed into the cring—solidified in the air. Morgan began to scroll through them with a swipe of his left index finger. "The only ones receptive to a face-to-face meeting are these." He stopped the rolling list on one line that was highlighted red.

Ethan rested his bourbon on his leg as he leaned forward and squinted at the glowing text. "Never heard of them."

"Hardly surprising." Morgan tapped the band again, and the ghostly projection disappeared. "From my conversation with them, they are newly established, headquartered in Romania."

"Romania? They're a long way from home."

"Perhaps not by choice."

"Their rates?"

"Less than ideal, but they are agreeable to trade. In reviewing Angus's latest inventory records, we may have adequate leverage in obtaining the things we lack. Add to that, they apparently have a market in this area for more rare weapons."

"Fine, we'll trade off whatever existing reserves we need to." Ethan swallowed another mouthful of Old Forester and rattled the nubs of ice in his glass. "Make sure Raphaël's briefed before the negotiations. He'll take over from me following the initial rendezvous, as usual, so he can use that French finesse of his to get the price down. In the meantime, collect all the harder-to-find ammo and the guns we're having trouble scrounging up cartridges for."

Morgan rocked his glass side-to-side on his thigh as he seemed to check off a list in his head. "That would include the Glock 20s and their 10mm rounds, our Daewoo K5s, the rest of the Parabellum ammo—"

"Some of the men won't like it, but we all have to make sacrifices. If these dealers are interested in scarce commodities, then let's use whatever advantage that gives us."

There were shouts down below, and Ethan and Morgan both turned their heads to the eastern field.

Mabayoje waved his arms and charged toward the three privates, who all threw down their collapsible trench shovels and dove together into one spot.

Liam surfaced from the group first, with Tim held high in the air by the scruff of his neck. The rabbit had evidently wandered out to inspect one of the freshly laid mines, probably hoping for something edible, since all the men had taken to sneaking him food from their plates every day.

Benny staggered back, his fists frozen out to either side of his head, where no doubt he'd actually pulled out clumps of his hair. Mabayoje came to a lurching halt beside him. Liam and Thomas argued loudly as Tim huddled into a black-and-white ball against Liam's chest.

"But best we forgo the acquisition of more blast mines," Morgan said flatly.

Ethan gave a snort. "Just as well. We're sorely strapped for cash. Short of selling one of the Land Rovers, we don't have much buying power." Ethan downed the last of his bourbon and paused to unscrew the bottle's cap. "A temporary setback. We'll be filling our pockets again in another month."

Morgan stopped the glass halfway to his mouth. "One month? That is not our standard practice."

"This place may give us plenty of cover for now, but the drawbacks are wearing us thin." The remembered feel of Vanessa's waist between his hands as she pressed against him beside the Land Rover made him tighten his grip on his glass. "You know we need to stay on the move." Ethan poured another shot of bourbon and twisted the cap back on roughly. "The Ukrainians may have gone dark, but they're still out there. And we can't get sloppy."

"They may have at last given up their pursuit."

"Do you believe that?"

For answer, Morgan dropped his gaze to his glass, where he ran a fingertip around the rim.

Ethan grunted. "That's what I thought. So we keep relocating until they finally lose our scent, even if that means we only spend one more month here."

Both men looked to the side when Liam trudged through the rear gates and into the fort garden with Tim in his arms. When he reached the orchard, he set Tim in the grass and shook his finger at the bunny. Tim perked his one good ear forward, as if listening patiently to the reprimand, but soon started nibbling on a stray wildflower. The near-death experience was obviously a distant memory in the face of his never-ebbing appetite.

Ethan shook his head. "That rabbit must have nine lives."

"Providence favors fools, children, and…peckish herbivores, apparently." Morgan lifted his glass but then paused and lowered it to his lap.

Ethan followed his friend's gaze.

Vanessa had appeared through the kitchen doorway on the west side of the garden and was walking toward them with an open book in one hand. She was still wearing her work apron, so she must have been on a break. And, naturally, she had chosen to spend it with her nose stuck between the pages of a novel.

She wandered into the orchard, and, with her eyes still glued to the words in front of her, reached out with her free hand to pluck a low-hanging apple from her Belle de Boskoop tree as she passed it. She took a bite and used a thumb to turn the page as she ambled along the orchard wall. Tim paused on his mouthful of late summer grass and sat up on his hindquarters when she neared him. She raised her face to say something to the animal and then looked up at the battlements. When she saw Morgan, she grinned and gave him a shy wave with her apple. Morgan lifted his glass toward her and bowed his head.

Ethan narrowed his eyes at the lieutenant, but then sat up straighter as Vanessa turned toward him. But when she met his gaze, she squinted and took a sharp bite of the apple. Then she deliberately opened the book in front of her face and glared at it as she walked.

Ethan's shoulders tensed, and he took a gulp of his bourbon. *Go ahead. Pitch a fit, little girl. You're wasting your time if you think I care.*

But the cold reception made the liquor sour in his stomach. There had certainly been no hint of chill in the feel of her the night before, in his room, with her sugary gingerbread scent rubbing into his clothing.

Forget it. I'm glad to keep my distance. And her bratty little attitude doesn't bother me.

She was so fucking self-righteous. Back in Achterwaartsstad, she'd interfered where she shouldn't. It would never have been a problem if she'd followed his lead. But…before that, when the townspeople had watched him like he was a walking sideshow, her small hand had reached for his, held it, offered him that simple gesture of concern, of kindness. A show of warmth meant only for him. But no longer.

Fine. Let her toy with me all she wants. It doesn't bother me.

Vanessa leaned back against the corridor wall in front of the kitchen. She peeked at Ethan over the top of her book but then raised it even higher.

Morgan chuckled. "She seems to have a less than favorable opinion of you."

"It doesn't bother me, goddamn it!"

Morgan, eyebrows raised, held his drink motionless before his mouth.

Ethan forced himself to take an extended breath and then sipped from his glass, wincing at another sharp pain in his swollen cheek. "Why does everything have to be about her and what *she* thinks and feels?" he muttered.

Morgan peered at him. "I was not aware that everything *was* about her."

Ethan unscrewed the cap of the Old Forester and carelessly poured Morgan another shot so that it sloshed over the rim. "She gets in the way. She doesn't understand how things work."

Morgan frowned at the bronze-colored liquor sliding down the sides of his tumbler. "I don't follow."

"She doesn't know how to live in the real world. And that gets in my way. I do what's necessary, *when* it's necessary."

Morgan put a restraining hand against the bottle as Ethan shoved the mouth to the Englishman's glass again. "And I gather such a necessity has arisen, to inspire this tirade?"

"She can't keep being naïve. There are consequences

to thinking everyone is—is like her!" He pushed past Morgan's hand and tipped more bourbon into his friend's glass before slamming the lid onto the Old Forester.

Morgan frowned harder as he held his dripping glass away from himself. "Really, mate, what the bloody hell are you on about?"

Ethan tapped an index finger against his glass and glanced at Morgan. "We may need to stay on our toes in the next day or so."

His friend's voice was cautious. "Why?"

"There was an incident in town today. Some sleazy fuck tried to jump us, and I had to beat him down."

Morgan straightened abruptly. "And what of Vanessa? Was she hurt?"

Ethan regarded him closely. *That's a hell of a strong reaction.*

"No. I made sure that didn't happen. But he was look-ing for a prize. Something for his collection." Ethan paused and took a quick sip. "You remember Serbia?"

Morgan's knuckles turned white around his glass. "A skinner? I trust you showed him the error of his ways?"

"I showed him how easy he bleeds."

"Good."

"But she kept me from doing more."

Morgan listened silently, rubbing a fingertip across the rim of his glass.

"I had my gun in the bastard's mouth," Ethan went on. "I was one second from ending it." He gritted his teeth. "She stopped me."

"If you believed she was wrong," Morgan said quietly, "then why did you stop?"

Ethan stared at him. Then he lifted the glass to his lips and took a hurried drink before looking away. "I don't know."

"Come now, Ethan, don't be thick." Morgan shifted against the stone block behind him. "She is a creature of compassion, of principle. She has never witnessed the open violence that comes so easily to us. With a single trigger pull, you would have condemned one person to a justified death, but the other to a moral contamination." Morgan pointed his finger at Ethan from around his glass. "You chose not to risk the latter."

"I did it because she refused to listen," Ethan said sharply as Morgan took a drink. "She didn't understand."

"No, she did not." Morgan held his gaze steadily. "And for that you should be grateful."

The lieutenant glanced over at Vanessa. Her brow was wrinkled as she concentrated on the novel and nibbled at the core of her Belle.

Morgan ran a hand down his goatee before giving Ethan a half smile. "Her steadfast beliefs are exasperating at times, on the occasions I've had the pleasure of her company…"

Ethan's jaw clenched. *The pleasure of her company. Why is he enjoying the pleasure of her company?*

Startled by the flash of jealousy, Ethan took a swallow of bourbon.

Morgan continued, "But it is because I mourn my own losses. I cannot reclaim what I once was: innocence before experience. We have seen too much to live comfortably in her world. But we should take care in trying to force her to live in ours."

Again, Morgan looked down at Vanessa.

And again, Ethan took a rushed gulp of bourbon.

"She is special," Morgan murmured. "She is what we have always fought to preserve. Grounded in unspoiled idealism. Can we fault her for her illusions?"

Ethan sharpened his stare. "If it jeopardizes our goals."

"Perhaps our goals jeopardize our *needs*."

"Jesus Christ! Is this the kind of bullshit you think about when you do all that meditation hoopla?"

Morgan's voice turned wry. "A calm center would serve you well, were you to treat the attempt with more than mere disdain."

"Ti'n llawn cachu! You've been trying to sell me on it since we met." Ethan swallowed another mouthful. "No one takes it seriously but you."

"I believe Darshan would take exception to that."

"He does it because he's spiritual," Ethan said in annoyance. "You do it because you're a douche."

Morgan gave him a fittingly British two-finger salute. "Get stuffed." But then he took a slow, thoughtful sip, and his eyes moved once again to Vanessa where she lazed in the corridor outside the kitchen.

Ethan set his drink down hard on the stone ledge, nearly chipping the bottom of the glass. "Whatever she is—innocent, naïve, insane—I don't give a shit. She's a distraction."

Morgan swirled his liquor, the last slivers of ice clinking softly within the glass. "Less a distraction, more a fascination."

Another flare of jealousy burned through him. *Goddamn it, what the fuck is wrong with me?*

Ethan threw back the rest of his bourbon in one gulp and set his glass on his thigh. "Well, I'm ordering you to stay away from her."

Morgan did not answer at first, but his face settled into that all-too-familiar stoic mask. "At the risk of insubordination, may I ask why?"

Sharp pain pinched Ethan's cheek as he grimaced under the mask. "Because we're not here to make friends. She's off-limits. Understood?"

"Hardly."

"Are you *trying* to get your ass whooped, Lieutenant?"

"I'm merely curious about the irrationality."

"I'm not being irrational!"

When Morgan stared wordlessly at him, Ethan jerked on the chin of his mask. Then he held his arms out to the sides, nearly losing the grip on his glass.

"Fine, you know what? You do whatever the fuck you want. Go get chummy with all these civilians." He set his tumbler on the ledge and unscrewed the bottle. "But when it comes time for us to pull out, you sure as shit better be ready. That means no ties. No sentimental bullshit. We leave, without compromise."

Morgan sat up straighter against the stone block as Ethan poured another two fingers into his own glass. "I assure you, Captain, I know our path and what is required to stay upon it. I will not allow distractions."

But at that, his eyes wandered down to where Vanessa now sat cross-legged against the corridor wall. And Ethan could have sworn his friend's expression softened, his disciplined veneer slipping.

Ethan took a tight-lipped sip of his Old Forester. *Yeah. That's what I said, too.*

CHAPTER TWENTY-THREE

ETHAN

Ethan stood in front of the compound entrance with his arms folded and watched the vehicle make its way up the dusty road.

Frank, who had first spotted the car and sent word to the captain, stood next to him. The huge Russkie glowered at the dingy white vehicle, waiting with a team of six soldiers gathered close by. Ethan knew, without looking, that several of his men were already lined up along the battlement walls, their rifles ready. Nicolo and Angelo were perched on the hood of the Boxer MRAV. Both mechanics leaned their elbows on their knees as if merely spectators, though the 9mm Berettas tucked into the back of their belts made it clear they had no intention of staying out of the way.

The morning sun shone warmly on all of them. Good thing he'd decided to leave his robe behind…even though it was becoming more obvious as to why he had ultimately chosen to abandon the heavy garment. He turned Vanessa's words over in his head:

I wish you would wear the robe less often…Your physique is impressive…

Ethan reached up and jerked on the chin of his mask, stretching his jaw against the rough fabric. *Focus, damn it. Don't let her take credit.*

Getting the robe off was only practical. Freedom of movement.

Her voice again, this time with a sultry tone: *I like seeing more of you…*

He jerked on the mask again. *Damn it.*

He glanced to the side when someone drew up next to him. Morgan did not even look at him but kept his eyes fixed on the white car as it closed the distance to the compound. Mabayoje and Angus appeared on Morgan's other side. Good. All his officers were in place now. Ethan returned his attention to the arriving vehicle as it stopped.

Clouds of pale dust rose to coat the already dirty windows. All four doors of the battered Opel swung open, so that now he could distinguish the blue logo of the town's police department on its sides.

He uncrossed his arms, the muscles across his body tightening like they always did when he was about to beat the shit out of someone. Thomas damn well better have Vanessa safeguarded somewhere deep in the compound, away from all this, as Ethan had instructed. She didn't need to see him in his element again.

Two men climbed out of the Opel. The driver seemed to be the only one wearing anything that resembled a uniform. The other was a tall, gangly older man who had occupied the front passenger seat and who wore a neatly pressed suit. But the next to exit the car was a familiar hostile.

Caretaker Dijkstra clambered out of the back seat, as skinny and stiff as ever—like a Popsicle stick wearing a tunic. Only this time, he was also dressed in what looked like a long gold-embroidered green bathrobe, the entire ensemble held together by a sequined belt. He tripped once on the robe's bedazzled hemline before he skittered forward to hover behind the gray-suited stranger. But then Ethan's body went rigid as a fourth man emerged from the back seat.

Known hostile number two.

The burly leather merchant strolled forward. Limping slightly, he came to stand beside the driver of the vehicle.

A large white bandage was taped prominently over the swollen bridge of the merchant's nose and there was an obvious bulge under the left shoulder of his shirt where someone must have dressed the knife wound Ethan had given him.

He should have ignored Vanessa's pleas for his life and put that dagger through the bastard's heart instead. She hadn't recognized the merchant's wares spread obscenely across his cart. She didn't know what human skin looked like when it was tanned and treated, like the hide of a common white-tailed deer. One of Achterwaartsstad's homeless had probably given their life for a pair of gloves that neatly matched those wallets.

The merchant seesawed his hulking shoulders and glared at Ethan as he wiped his right index finger under his nose, the gauze-covered splint on his middle finger making the motion clumsy.

Ethan felt Morgan shift. His second-in-command was no doubt resting a hand on his Glock 17.

The man in the suit stopped a few meters away and made a huffing noise as he smoothed his tie. The man's eyes swept twice over the mask covering Ethan's face, making it plain that the unusual sight unnerved him.

"I am Mr. Alpers, one of Mayor Visser's chief advisors and representatives," the man announced.

His voice shook almost as badly as his hands, which were unbuttoning and rebuttoning the bottom of his dust-gray suit jacket.

"We have come to press charges against all of you here, who have unrightfully taken over this building. You will be evicted at once and made to leave this province after we exact proper fines. In addition, we have come to take one of you into custody, who yesterday perpetrated a heinous act of violence against one of our upstanding citizens." The man indicated the leather merchant with a swipe of his arm. "Mr. Reust is one of our most reputable vendors and was attacked in our streets."

The merchant's lips drew up, exposing the same crooked teeth that Ethan had recently tried to punch through the back of his skull.

That encounter in the city alley had been no accident. It had been obvious from the moment they'd locked glares that the merchant would come after him. Ethan was constantly prepared for such confrontations, as they had become routine for him whenever he occupied new territory. But he had not been prepared to feel rage. To feel possessive. And all of that had been his own fault.

Because he'd brought Vanessa with him.

He had not had that kind of distraction before, when facing an opponent. He had never been compromised by any motivation outside of defeating an enemy for the sake of survival. But she had a way of making him abandon his logic when she was near him, of evoking some primal need to protect her at all costs. Even now, every nerve ending sizzled as he recalled the way the merchant's eyes had probed her—greedy and sadistic, as if he'd already tied her down and wormed himself onto her naked, bruised body. And then to see him actually putting his fucking paws on her...

Morgan grabbed Ethan by the elbow, stopping him when he unconsciously started moving toward the merchant. The lieutenant shook his head, and Ethan unfisted his hands.

"Mr. Reust accuses you, Mr. Evans, of this crime," the well-dressed man went on firmly, seeming to have gathered confidence from the silence that met his speech. "It was done in the presence of several witnesses. We know you believe you can enforce your own set of laws within the walls of the compound, but we will not tolerate—"

"*My* compound." Ethan kept his voice deceptively serene. The mayor's representative paused with his mouth open. "And my rank is 'captain.' Use it."

Mr. Alpers made a louder huffing noise than before, and his fingers began to unbutton and rebutton his jacket again.

Dijkstra pushed past Mr. Alpers and jabbed his finger at Ethan. "The compound is not yours! It is *not!*" he declared in his shrill, whining voice. "Burgemeester Visser recognizes only me as the rightful caretaker! I have told him how you—"

"Kop houden!" Mr. Alpers stepped forward and seized Dijkstra's sleeve, glaring so hard it shriveled his face. "Laat mij dit regelen!"

Dijkstra adjusted the belt on his robe with a jerk, which bounced the hundreds of sequin reflections dotting the ground.

Mr. Alpers swiveled back to Ethan. "As for your recent conduct, we will neither tolerate nor exonerate such behavior. Therefore, we have come to arrest—"

"Then you've wasted a trip."

Off to the side, both Nicolo and Angelo straightened and slid off the Boxer's hood. Morgan had already drawn his pistol and stood with it held at his side. The movements of all Ethan's men were not lost on Mr. Alpers or the others accompanying him.

Ethan gave an upward nod to indicate the driver standing behind the mayor's advisor. "This your constable?"

Mr. Alpers stiffened his back and tugged briskly on his suit vest. "Yes. Our hoofdagent—senior constable—of the Achterwaartsstad regiokorps politie."

The mustached driver sauntered forward. He was almost as tall as the captain and tried to emphasize that point by standing much closer than was necessary. He was a walking dump truck of a man with a broad forehead who—just like the leather merchant—looked about as sharp as a bowl of shit.

Ethan eyed the officer in his faded navy-blue shirt that sported two yellow bands across the chest, complete with four dark-gold bars on his shoulders to designate his rank. The constable overshadowed the others within the small retinue like a beady-eyed bouncer, but the bully image was diminished by the short sword at his side. There was a long scar that ran halfway around the constable's neck. He had probably inflicted that injury upon himself to exaggerate his tough-guy look.

And this was the man Vanessa said had taken no interest in finding her parents' killer.

Ethan flexed his left hand.

That alone was worth snapping the asshole's neck.

Ethan looked back at Mr. Alpers. "I don't have time for this."

Behind him, there came a chorus of safeties disengaging and gun hammers being cocked. He could sense that all his men had leveled their muzzles at the entourage.

Mr. Alpers blanched and took a step back. But the constable held his ground. Ethan slowly rotated his head like a tank turret and shot a glare straight into the man's eyes. He reached across his chest, pulled the SIG from its holster, and fully extended his left arm to aim the gun at the officer's forehead. The constable's eyes widened, though he immediately tried to hide the look of unease that crossed his face.

Ethan cocked the spurred hammer with his thumb. "Ready to try your sword skills?"

The corner of the constable's mouth twitched, and he pressed his lips together. The response was one Ethan had seen a hundred times: a precursor to retreat.

The constable's face reddened until his mustache looked like it would melt into the skin. Then he backed away.

Ethan eased the hammer back into place and was about to return the gun to its holster when the leather merchant lurched forward. It took only the barest movement of Ethan's index finger to make his soldiers hold their fire.

The merchant seized him by the shirt, but in a blur of motion, Ethan had already passed the SIG to his right hand and had his H&K drawn before the man knew what was happening. Ethan shoved both guns at opposing angles against the merchant's heart and spoke through his teeth.

"Now we're finished."

He pulled the triggers.

The double shots were loud but muffled. Red spray

misted the face of Mr. Alpers beyond. The caretaker jumped backward, his feet tangling in his bathrobe, and stared.

The merchant's eyes—frozen wide—glazed over. He dropped to his knees and fell to the ground face-first like a bag of dumbbells.

Ethan raised his head and looked at the constable, who clutched the handle of his sword and panted, a hand covering his cheek. He pulled his fingers away, and there was an oozing gash where one of the bullets had grazed his face as it had exited the back of the merchant's body.

Ethan slid his P8 into the holster at his hip and passed the SIG back into his left hand. He looked directly at Mr. Alpers. "Anything else?"

Mr. Alpers looked like he may have soiled himself. "Mr. Evans—" He wiped a trembling hand over his face—smearing the red speckles down his cheeks—and then swallowed. "I mean, Captain Evans..." His eyes fastened to the gun that now lay loosely on Ethan's palm. "You must understand, we—we cannot let this pass. Especially now that you have—have committed—" His eyes fell to the merchant's mountainous cadaver, where its blood pushed through the dirt in snakelike rivulets. "There will be a reckoning!"

Ethan turned away and started walking. "Put it on my tab."

Mr. Alpers huffed loudly, like he'd gone into an asthmatic attack.

But then a warbling cry went up behind Ethan, and he pivoted to see Dijkstra stumbling around the body of the merchant. The caretaker's swanky bathrobe was stained with spatter so that the gold thread borders shone with a carmine dye.

Dijkstra fell on the constable's arm, shouting, "Godverdomme! Ben je gek?" His eyes were wild as he pointed at Ethan. "Why do you not arrest him? He took my property! And he is a killer! He threatened to kill me, when he first came!" He yanked the constable's sword from its scabbard, causing the constable to start forward in surprise as Dijkstra tottered toward Ethan. "I will not stand for this!"

Ethan glanced over at Frank, but the sergeant had already unhooked the loop of wire at his hip and had started to uncoil it.

"I am the caretaker here!" Dijkstra wailed as he slashed the air in front of him. "I am their leader! I am—"

The sword spasmed out of Dijkstra's hand as Frank appeared behind him, and the caretaker jerked backward like a dog reaching the end of his leash. He clawed at his throat, where a metal wire had appeared across his Adam's apple.

"No one's here to save your ass this time," Ethan said as he approached the caretaker. "I warned you what would happen if you didn't keep your fucking mouth shut."

Ethan glanced at Mr. Alpers. The older man flinched and moved behind the glowering constable, whose cheek was wet with a sheen of blood from his new wound.

Ethan turned back to Dijkstra, who trembled against Frank so that rows of silver dots danced across his chalky face from the tiny gemstones lining his tunic collar.

"I was almost going to let it slide, but I made you a promise," Ethan said. "And I keep my promises."

Dijkstra squirmed, his voice squeezing from his throat. "You are a—a monster!"

Frank tightened the wire around Dijkstra's neck, making the caretaker's eyes bug from his sockets as he sputtered.

Ethan rammed the SIG's muzzle into Dijkstra's gut. "Yes. I am."

Frank whipped the wire off Dijkstra's throat and stepped aside. Ethan pulled the trigger.

Dijkstra jolted against the pistol barrel and sank to his knees on the ground. He bowed his head to look at himself. A patch of scarlet began to blossom across the middle of his pale green robe. He made a choking sound and sat back hard on his heels to lift his wide, glassy gaze up to Ethan.

"Now"—Ethan dropped his gun into his shoulder holster and swept his eyes across the constable and Mr. Alpers—"get the fuck off my base."

Ethan turned and pushed through his soldiers to reenter the compound.

He glanced at Morgan, who had materialized at his side. "Stay with the men and ensure our visitors make a full withdrawal. And tell the constable to take his dead cronies with him."

"We should anticipate retaliation."

"Agreed. It won't come from the outside, since Visser doesn't want government goons sniffing around his little kingdom. But I think he's just stupid enough to try something on his own. As soon as this little welcoming committee is gone, I want our perimeter doubled."

Morgan nodded and dropped back to rejoin the other officers.

Ethan would have to pull Nicolo aside and prioritize the repair of the mayor's captured drone. They needed to get it up and running ASAP. If the mechanic could get their laser perimeter shield integrated and operational with the aircraft, it would take a shit ton of burden off his men. The sprawling size of Fort Van Doorn already strained their defenses as it was.

He reached up and tugged at the chin of his mask to readjust it.

Hopefully, this tumbledown stack of stones wouldn't become their tomb.

CHAPTER TWENTY-FOUR

VANESSA

"Hold your breath," he said against her ear, "and focus on the center. Then let go."

Vanessa made herself perfectly still, pulled the string back until it bit into her fingers, and released.

Thomas straightened beside her. They both stared at the arrow lying flat on the ground a few meters away.

"Hmm," he said. "Well, that sucked harder than befores."

She lowered the bow. "I'm a beginner! This doesn't come naturally to me, you know."

"I has to agree, there ain't nothin' natural 'bout that." Thomas lifted his arm toward the arrow as if he couldn't believe what he was seeing. "Oh me nerves, ducky. I thought after this many tries, you's would at least get in spittin' distance."

She swung the bow by its string to gesture toward the round straw target. "Oh, and I'm sure you did so great on your first lesson."

Eyebrows raised, he nodded. "Yeah, I was good. But you—" He blinked twice. "It's like you handed your bow to a blind man and then scared the Jesus out of 'im." He rubbed a hand in his scruffy dishwater-blond hair. "I guess you can'ts teach this in one mornin', eh?" He tilted his head at her. "Is you sure you don't wear glasses?"

"Okay, we're done." She shoved the bow at him.

He snagged the weapon before it fell to the ground and then caught her arm to keep her from leaving. "Come on, Nessy, me ol' trout. Sure, you shoots like you's in the middle of a fit. Sure, I squandered an hour o' me life I'll never get back. And so what if your bow is where archery itself goes to die?" He threw his arms out to the sides. "That's no reason to give up!"

She let out a tired growl. "One more try. But if I'm way off again, I quit. This was your idea, remember?"

He nodded with a smile and nocked another arrow for her on the recurve bow. As he handed it to her, Morgan's voice broke in.

"Mind if I borrow your pupil?" The question, though made to sound casual by that elegant English accent, was accompanied by a strangely meaningful glance toward Vanessa.

"Ay b'y, go ahead. I ain't doin' any good here anyways." Thomas grinned and then stuck his tongue out at Vanessa after she pushed his shoulder.

Morgan took her elbow, and she looked up at him as they walked back to the old Dutch fort from the rear grounds. As usual, he was wearing mostly black, similar to the way the captain always did, but the color of his vest today was a royal blue crisscrossed by gold threads. He certainly had a better sense of style than his robed commander.

"What's going on?" she asked, now a little worried by the lieutenant's grave demeanor.

"The captain feels it advisable that you not leave the compound, so he requests that you remain within its walls."

She raised an eyebrow at him. "Requests?"

Morgan gave her a sidelong look, but his jet-black goatee lifted at the corner.

"He hasn't even talked to me in over a week," she said. "Why should he care?"

The pit of her stomach turned cold, like she'd swallowed an ice cube.

He doesn't. Captain Control Freak only cares about making sure nothing messes up his mission. Whatever it is.

At least he had quickly supplied the kitchen with more workers to help her out, though she wasn't sure how thrilled those residents had been to be reassigned from their other chores. But that didn't mean he really gave a crap. It just meant that he was good at keeping his promises.

Morgan rested his palm against the small of her back as they neared the fort gates, and she felt a pleasant flush at the warmth of his hand. It was surely how a gentleman would act when escorting a lady through the English countryside.

The captain probably would have dragged her into the compound by her hair.

"So how long am I under house arrest?" she asked as they passed through the giant old doors—one of them still hopelessly wonky from when Mabayoje had blown it off its hinges.

"Until the captain deems it safe." Morgan frowned while his eyes swept the expansive garden alertly, as if examining it for the first time. "There's trouble afoot."

"And you're supposed to keep me out of his way, is that it?" She canted her head at him as his gaze settled on her face. She sighed when he didn't answer. "What sort of trouble?"

"Nothing I need divulge at the moment." They reached the one-sided corridor near the kitchen, and Morgan removed his hand from her back. "Suffice it to say that we're being cautious."

Her stomach sank at losing his touch, but she squared her shoulders.

"No, Morgan, that doesn't suffice." She crossed her arms. "Why does everything have to be a secret? Why can't you just tell me, like I'm an adult? I just turned twenty-two, not ten."

He regarded her for a moment before tossing a glance up to the ramparts. He drifted closer, and his voice grew soft.

"Please, m'lady. This is not a matter of paranoia." His gaze was steady but tender. "I, too, am concerned. And I will not have your safety compromised."

As he hovered near, a faint scent—like citrus and leather—began to tickle her nose, along with deeper, richer tones of spice. It was the kind of fragrance that made a girl bury her face in a man's shirt, after he'd left it on her bed.

"Will you indulge me?" Morgan asked and cupped her elbow.

She swallowed, holding her breath, and finally nodded.

Morgan's shoulders relaxed, and he squeezed her arm gently. He backed away, the alluring scent of him ebbing like a sea tide. As he turned to walk through the stone corridor nearby, her eyes traced the outline of his tall, lean-muscled figure. She nibbled on her bottom lip. She was accustomed to his close-to-the-vest manner, but there was a different edge to it this time.

She listened to the fading cadence of his brisk boot-falls for another few seconds and then looked up at the ramparts. There were several men with large assault rifles patrolling, which was still difficult to get used to.

But ever since the day after she and the captain had made their eventful trip to town, the captain had doubled the number of guards around the compound. And regardless of how much he'd previously pissed her off with his dismissive attitude, she had still panicked when she'd heard he had been attacked right outside their front door. And by people sent by the mayor, no less! She'd been busy exploring some very old parts of the tunnels with Thomas at the time, to test out some new maps Angus had made, but she'd heard later through the rumor mill that someone had gotten shot.

She twisted her hands together and gnawed harder on her bottom lip. And now, judging by Morgan's behavior, Captain Evans was in the shadow of a new danger.

"I think they are all in a hurry to kill something."

Vanessa jumped at Rhetta's voice and put a hand on her chest as her heart leapt against her rib cage. The older woman stood next to her and wiped her hands on a dishcloth, frowning up at the men who moved slowly along the ramparts.

Vanessa nodded and put her hands on her hips. "I pity the squirrel who wanders too far from his tree. Easy target practice, now that the boys have their shiny new guns and grenades."

Not long after her trip into town with him, the captain had succeeded in setting up relations with the closest arms dealer he could find, which was not all that close from what she had overheard. Curious to see what "arms dealers" looked like, she had peeked out the back gates when they had arrived to negotiate in the north field behind the compound. They were, indeed, a brutish lot, not very trustworthy in appearance. But maybe that went along with selling on the black market. The captain—his masked visage half-hidden in his hood to employ his usual intimidation tactics—had stood before them in all his *I'm-not-to-be-screwed-with* glory. She could tell by his posture that he had already decided to let his men blow away the dangerous-looking visitors if he didn't like what he heard.

"You and many others are making them too comfortable here," Rhetta said, waving away Vanessa's thoughts like a cloud of gnats. "But they are our wardens, and we are in danger. Some of our men have disappeared, and I have seen the soldiers' vehicles leave late in the night, carrying something." She glanced then at Vanessa, her mouth a firm line.

A coldness flashed across Vanessa's skin, and she rubbed her arms. She shook her head to herself. No. That didn't prove anything. The soldiers were probably doing some kind of night reconnaissance, not…carting dead bodies around.

"They should never have come here." Rhetta's voice turned brittle. "One of these days, we may do something about it, and Captain Evans and his boeven would do well to leave."

Two soldiers were approaching them in the passageway.

Vanessa took Rhetta's arm and pulled her back toward the kitchen. "I don't think it's a good idea to say things like that," she said after the men walked past.

Rhetta stared at Vanessa. "I refuse to live like this, where I cannot breathe in my own home." She patted back the wisps of gray hair at her temple. "They have taken advantage of us long enough."

Vanessa's voice dropped to a whisper. "Look, we need to be more careful right now."

"Uit de doeken ermee, girl! Why should we?"

"Well, because…there's trouble afoot."

"Bah!" Rhetta flipped the towel at her. "They *are* the trouble, meiske. But for now, I've greater things to worry about. Like fixing the cracks in the brick ovens and getting their mortar repointed, as well. But maybe that would drive these animals out, if they've no bread to eat!" Rhetta sniffed loudly and reentered the kitchen.

Vanessa glanced up at the northeast parapet, where the heavily muscled Frank leaned against the wall, dressed in his faded green-and-brown camouflage pants with an olive-hued jacket. A lit cigar hung from one corner of the Russian's mouth. He watched her as he puffed out grayish clouds that curled up through his thick black mustache and made a halo around his shaven head. She could almost smell the stinky sweetness of the cigar smoke as he repeatedly flipped the lid of a metal lighter open and closed with a thumb.

Crap. How long has he been there? I wonder if he can read lips.

But then he lifted a hand in what was outwardly a friendly gesture. She waved back, forcing herself to smile, and spun around to make her way up the corridor toward the grand dining hall. Maybe she could sneak in a reread of "Bartleby, the Scrivener" before her kitchen shift started…if she could get her mind off the mysterious threat everyone seemed to be so uptight about now.

"Hiya, missy, how's she cuttin'?"

She gasped when Liam pressed against her side as she walked. *Damn it, why do people keep trying to scare the bejesus out of me?*

"Hi, Liam." She turned to the person who had drawn up on her other side. "Hey, Miguel."

"Good morning, Vanessa," the young Argentinian responded with a warm smile that crinkled his dark-brown eyes.

Miguel was lean and the same height as she, with black hair that he liked to slick back only enough to keep it under control. He created a noticeable contrast to Liam's almost hyper theatrics.

She slowed her pace as they moved down the hallway together. "What are you guys up to?"

Liam laid his arm across her shoulders and leaned in. "We're mitchin' off. Cap hasn't caught us yet, so keep it quiet."

Miguel shook his head. "Che boludo! You are a child, like Thomas." He picked up the Irishman's wrist between his thumb and forefinger and tossed his arm off Vanessa. "We are between shifts," he told her, "and we will be next on grounds patrol."

"Does the captain honestly think there are people lurking in the woods, ready to jump out and attack us?" Vanessa asked. "Everyone from the town is too afraid to come near you guys."

Miguel shrugged. "The captain is very careful, bombón. He does not like surprises."

"Especially when a surprise might blow his clackers off," Liam added.

Vanessa puckered her face, but Miguel simply rolled his eyes.

"By the way, about that garden of yours"—Liam combed a hand through his rust-tinted black hair and snuck an arm across her shoulders again—"I noticed there's a special plot marked Liam's Delight." He winked. "You know, darlin', if you're tryin' to get me down on my knees to play in the dirt with you, we're gonna need a bigger bed."

Vanessa scrunched her face again and gave Liam a shove, making him stumble as they walked. "That bed is where I'd planted the seed potatoes," she said. "We're getting a pretty good harvest this year. I thought you'd be honored."

Liam's expression turned indignant, like she'd just told him he smelled like old cabbage. "Really now, do you think all the Irish are cravin' potatoes every minute? Jaysus, Vanessa, what do you take me for, a real Paddy?"

She stared at him. "But you like potatoes."

He grabbed the top of his head with both hands and let out a loud sigh. "Yeah, but that's not the feckin' point, is it?" He dropped his arms and threw a hand out toward Miguel as they meandered along the garden's perimeter. "You think it's normal for him to go around munchin' on burritos and tacos all day?"

Miguel frowned at him. "What continent do you think I am from, bobo? Everything is 'Mexican' to you."

"Well, it's close enough, ain't it?"

"Yes..." Miguel stroked his chin as if in thought. "Just as you and Lieutenant Winchester both come from the UK, no?"

Liam's eyebrows shot up but then plunged into a glare. "You can fuck right off, Cardozo, ya bollox!"

Miguel laughed and shook his finger at Liam. "One day I will teach you where Argentina is on a map, pelotudo."

Vanessa giggled. The soldiers never lost a chance to insult each other in every language. She was fairly confident she now knew how to say "asshole" thirty different ways.

"But I would not turn down the thing I do miss from my country..." Miguel paused, seeming pensive for a moment. "Cordero patagónico."

Liam leaned forward past Vanessa to squint at Miguel. "What in the hell is that?"

"A whole lamb, stretched out and barbecued on a big metal frame in front of the fire." Miguel smiled and crossed his arms as he walked. "Mi abuelo from Patagonia used to hold such meals at his house when I was young, and we would eat very well."

"Ya see?" Liam said triumphantly, turning back to Vanessa. "His people eat dead things off a fence. That ain't normal at all!"

Miguel smiled and shook his head.

Liam nudged Vanessa distractedly in the ribs with an elbow. "Well, I can't keep hanging round with you lot. It's a cracker of a day, and I've still got five minutes on my break."

He split off from them and semi-skipped his way through the garden. Evidently, he had spotted Anna in the distance, since he was making a beeline right for her. She seemed to be loitering in the corridor adjacent to them, casting glances in their direction. The young Irishman slowed to a leisurely strut as he neared her, and Anna tossed her long chestnut-colored hair off her shoulders with a smile.

Miguel uncrossed his arms with a smirk in Liam's direction. "I do not think five minutes will be enough." He held up a hand to Vanessa in farewell and backed away.

"Oh, you'd be surprised," she mumbled.

If the captain would give her the time of day lately, there was plenty she could show *him* in five minutes.

CHAPTER TWENTY-FIVE

VANESSA

"Maybe I can't do anything about the strawberries you just massacred, but you're not touching my radish plants."

Vanessa finished wrapping the wire around the last section of fencing to close the gap that had clearly been forced wider by a small, furry face sometime late that afternoon.

She sat back on her heels and dropped her hands into her lap to look at Tim beside her. The rabbit took one hop closer, and his scraggly puff of a tail stuck straight out as he stretched toward the repaired section. Then he put a paw on her knee and wriggled his nose up at her, his big brown eyes blinking—which did nothing to diminish the pirate-look of that black patch of fur over his left one.

She tapped a fingertip on his head between his ears. "You bring this on yourself, you know."

Tim's nose stopped wriggling. Then he sneezed with a shake of his head—as if to say, "Fine, be that way!"—and twisted away to scratch behind his floppy ebony ear with a hind leg.

Vanessa laughed lightly, but then paused when goose bumps pricked the nape of her neck. She glanced behind her. Morgan, who was sitting up on one of the rear rampart walls, looked away as soon as she met his eyes. He'd been watching her a lot lately, like when she'd be serving meals in the kitchen or chatting with Neve and Margo in the hallway outside the laundry room. But he never had time for a conversation when she approached him, as the captain seemed to keep him busy with one assignment or another.

She chewed her bottom lip for a second. Well, he appeared to be enjoying some downtime now. Good chance to get to know him better. He was as mysterious as the captain, but at least seemed to invite her company—*unlike* Captain Cold Shoulder. And frankly, the way the Englishman cast his eyes over her sent her senses pleasantly reeling, so his attention was more than welcome whenever she could get it.

Something tugged on her clothing, and she looked down. Tim sat huddled in the grass with one of her apron strings in his mouth, his furry cheeks quivering as he munched on the end of it.

"Seriously?" she drawled. "You have *got* to be part billy goat!"

She snatched the cotton canvas string away, and he pricked his good ear forward with that single-toothed bumpkin stare.

She climbed to her feet and dusted herself off as she started walking toward the closest set of stairs up to the ramparts.

Morgan sat near one of the old cannon, gazing out at the back field and copses of black poplars in the distance. As usual, he looked so well put together, like a magazine cover for gentlemen of leisure: one foot was up on the ledge, while he leaned against a block of stone jutting up from the parapet. He rested an arm over his knee to dangle a green flip-top bottle of beer in his hand. The sun was already inching its way toward the horizon. Its late orange rays stretched over him but seemed unable to break through the midnight black of his hair. Those short, layered locks only swallowed the light, like they were made of night itself.

"So this is what you do for fun, when you're not guarding the captain." She leaned against the block of stone across from him. "You guard everything else."

Morgan smiled. "Though it appears you have the security of the garden well in hand."

She laughed and glanced down toward the radish bed. "It's a twenty-four-hour job with Tim around."

Morgan shook his head and lifted the Grolsch bottle to his mouth. "A fellow of infinite appetite."

Vanessa gazed at him and leisurely twirled a lock of hair around her fingers. *That accent should automatically come with a glass of wine, not a beer.*

When his eyes jumped back to her, she shook herself and fidgeted with her apron strings, one of which was now frayed at the tip.

"I see you've steered clear of Sven's brews." She nodded at the bottle in his hand as she sat down on the other side of the cannon whose crusted mouth yawned over the wall. "I swear he goes to De Haarloze Hond in town because he can't drink his own swill. Twelve of the people here have a close acquaintance with the privy, thanks to his last batch."

Morgan tossed her another small smile, and a giddy heat flushed through her. *I love making him do that.*

But she paused. "I wonder if the captain let Sven finally move to Achterwaartsstad after all. He seems to have just…disappeared."

Morgan's eyes, their blue-gray depths looking stormier than usual, held hers for a moment. Then he rested his arm back over his knee and returned to surveying the grounds at the fringe of the compound.

She rubbed her arms with a shiver. *Well, that was a weird conversation killer. What was that all about?*

"So-o-o…has trouble come knocking yet?" she asked instead.

But then she had a passing image of the handwritten note wrapped around the arrow Thomas had sent over the battlements that first day when the captain's army had arrived. Could there be another gang out there? Maybe those "Ukes" Thomas had mentioned? If so, she didn't want to meet any men fearsome enough to have the captain on the run.

Knock, knock!

She rubbed her arms again.

Morgan lowered his leg to rest his thigh upon the parapet ledge and knitted his eyebrows. "I did not mean to alarm you this morning. We are military men. And as such, we anticipate threats, however implausible. But we will let no harm come to you or the others."

"I believe you. But I am worried about something happening to *you*."

Morgan's eyebrows lifted slightly. "I...see." Then his voice turned gentle as his eyes moved over her face. "You need not fear for us. We are accustomed to peril. And we will not make our enemies your enemies."

She started to pick at a flake of black paint that was peeling off the cannon. "I don't see how you can avoid it. Unless you...really are going to move on."

Morgan opened his mouth and then hesitated. "The captain is considering our options."

"I'll bet he is." She pressed her lips together and scraped harder at the knobby metal surface. "Not that he'd tell me what's going through his head, since His Excellency no longer deigns to acknowledge my presence."

A pang in her chest made her rip off a paint chip and crumble it between her fingers. She stood abruptly and began to untie the garden apron from around her waist. "He's so...so...impossible sometimes!"

"Sometimes?" Morgan swung the bottle up and took another swig as he watched her pull off the apron and throw it down over the cannon. He swallowed and leaned his head back against the stone. "Rest assured, it is a chronic condition."

She came around the cannon's four-wheeled wooden carriage to plop herself onto the parapet ledge near him. "Then why have you stayed with him for so many years?"

She drew her feet up onto the wall. Now that the weather had turned chillier with September fading away, she wore her long moss-green skirt, and it felt good to hug her knees to warm them under the woolen fabric. "I mean, you've been around him since long before you put this 'army' together, right?"

Morgan leveled his gaze at her. "Thomas is quite loquacious, I see."

The words that came out of the Englishman were few, but he apparently loved to stuff them with syllables.

She squeezed her legs between her arms. "Well, I think the least I'm owed is a little intel about the people I'm now sharing a roof with."

The look Morgan gave her was hard to interpret, but he seemed to be suppressing a smile. "*Intel*, is it? We may yet enlist you as one of our own."

"Oh no." She held up a finger. "You will never catch me wearing camo. Or pants, for that matter."

Morgan's smile escaped his control, and his eyes dropped to where her ankles showed beneath her hemline. "A refusal that will delight many, I've no doubt."

She hugged her knees harder as a blush suddenly swept across her chest like wildfire. She cleared her throat.

"About Captain Evans…" She smoothed a wrinkle in her skirt. "Thomas mentioned he's Welsh."

"Extremely," Morgan grumbled, but there was a joking tone to the word. "He possesses all the defining characteristics of his kind: an unreasonable temper and a fondness for muttering insults in a language he's otherwise forgotten."

She set her chin on top of her knees. "Is that why you two became friends? Because you both felt a connection to the UK?"

Morgan gave a sharp laugh. "God, no. The Welsh hate the English."

"Then why do you two get along so well?"

"Too bloody daft to know better, I suppose." He raised the bottle and took a long swig. "His mother was his Welsh half. She was a petite woman with culinary expertise and a lovely voice, as the captain tells it." He lifted an eyebrow. "Appropriate for a people given to an obsession with leeks and bursting into song at every opportunity."

She twirled a lock of hair around her finger. *Singing? Well, well. Maybe there's a poetic soul buried beneath that moody exterior, after all.*

"But he inherits his height from his father's Cossack side—once native-born Ukrainians—though he'll never admit to being other than a pure-blooded Celt."

She smiled at that. Cossack, huh? She could imagine the captain as he stood up in the stirrups of a charging horse, his robe billowing out behind him as he aimed a long lance at an oncoming battalion.

"Unfortunately, his relationship with his father has never been…harmonious," Morgan added. "Hence the reason he took his mother's maiden name when he was young and claims only her heritage."

"Bad blood between father and son," she mumbled. "That's never good."

But it explains some things.

Morgan glanced to the side, as if he had noticed a suspicious movement within the meadow below.

Her stomach tightened, and she lowered her legs to lean toward him on the ledge. "What is it?"

Is it here already? The mystery threat?

The countryside around them was drenched in ruddy orange from the quickly sinking sun. But no sign of anything that shouldn't be there.

"I don't see any—"—she turned her face back to him—"thing…"

Morgan, who had sat forward, moved his eyes downward to where her hand rested upon his knee. The casual contact seemed to vibrate the air between them. Morgan lifted his eyes to hers.

Does he feel that too?

She pulled her hand away, and her fingers went immediately to fiddle with the buttons at her cleavage. She swallowed dryly. "So, uh, how did you and the captain get together?"

Morgan said nothing at first but finally leaned back against the stone block.

"I encountered him whilst we were both stationed in

continental Europe," he answered quietly, seeming to study her. "Germany, to be exact, when he was a captain in the United States Army." He tapped a finger absently against the Grolsch bottle and then lifted the beer to his mouth. "Three years following our meeting, we were discharged," he mumbled before downing the rest of it.

She picked at a spot on her skirt where the wool had started to pill. "What about you? Where were you discharged from?"

Morgan's face began to look half-shadowed as the sun sat lazily on the horizon, its feeble rays glinting off the golden threads in his royal-blue vest.

She tilted her head at him when he didn't answer. "Is it a secret?"

He ran a hand down his mustache and goatee and then bent to set the empty bottle on the stone walkway next to the wall. "Actually, yes."

That startled her. "So…not even a hint?"

He seemed to think about it as he reached up and dug a finger into the collar of his black shirt. He poked down a loop of brown leather cord that stuck up against his neck. A necklace? How had she never noticed it before? But then, how could she? He obviously kept it hidden for a reason.

"I was a lieutenant in the British Army," Morgan said at last and rested a forearm on the holstered gun at his side.

"That doesn't seem so unusual."

"As part of the SAS."

She shook her head with a frown.

"Special Air Service," Morgan clarified. "UK special forces."

Vanessa raised her eyebrows. *Wow. A sexy badass.*

"Special forces," she echoed. "Does that mean you went into enemy territory and did covert stuff?"

"Yes," he said, and a subtle smile began on his lips, "covert *stuff,* to be sure."

"Is that where *that* came from?" Her eyes wandered to the dagger at his left hip. The narrow blade had to be almost eighteen centimeters in length, with a black ribbed handle. "Some kind of commando knife?"

Morgan glanced down at the leather-sheathed weapon and then gave a single nod. "It is called a Fairbairn-Sykes, and it has extended my life on more than one occasion."

"And let me guess: no asking for details. More hush-hush spy stuff."

Morgan inclined his head in affirmation. "My own mother was not aware of my service until years later." He propped his foot up on the ledge once more. "Identities are guarded and one's membership undisclosed but to a select few."

"The captain being one?"

"Yes, well…" Morgan began a slow smile as he rocked his forearm upon his gun. "Our initial introduction prevented all customary secrecy. Especially as I very nearly killed him." Morgan looked at her with a smirk. "A misunderstanding, of course."

Whoa. That takes their English-Welsh rivalry to a whole new level!

"But even now, my background is seldom revealed," he said as he glanced off to the side and scanned the trees bordering the back field.

"So then, why tell me?"

He returned his gaze to her. "Because I recognize integrity when I see it." He interlocked his hands around his raised knee as his voice softened. "And because I imagine there is very little that I could deny you."

A tingle danced up her legs beneath the long skirt. *Same here.*

"Did your…service ever bring you over to this part of Europe before? You seem at home here."

"Adaptability is the nomad's creed."

"So is subjugation for convenience, I guess," she said and then had to keep from slapping a hand over her own mouth.

Morgan fell silent.

Terrific. Good job bringing every conversation to a screeching halt, Vanessa.

Morgan straightened off the stone block and lowered

his foot from the parapet wall. But when he spoke, his voice was calm. "The facilities we commandeer are typically unoccupied." He placed a hand on the pommel of his knife. "Medical buildings, abandoned warehouses, empty estates. Our intention is not to wield power. We are concerned only with existing."

"By leeching off others, when there's no empty building handy? How do you justify that?"

Damn it, Vanessa! Does everything have to be a debate?

Morgan's fingers began to rub along the ribbed handle of the Fairbairn-Sykes, but his voice never modulated. "It is a necessity of our present nature. Modern man's regression to a mode of pure instinct is not a proud position, but it is inescapable. We survive and control, or we are victims."

She leaned back against the cannon and folded her arms. "So the victims in your path don't matter, as long as you get what you need."

Morgan paused at that.

Ding-ding-ding! You win, Vanessa! You're officially pissing him off!

She cringed and tucked her arms tighter.

Morgan set his elbow on his knee and leaned toward her. "Our preliminary actions were never designed to be predatory. The original purpose of assembling this army was to aid people against their government oppressors."

But his eyes dropped away momentarily. Maybe part of him was acknowledging who, in reality, had become the oppressors. And how maybe their fledgling code of might-for-right had warped into a selfish mantra of survivalism.

"You could change, you know," she began carefully, smoothing a hand across her apron where it lay over the cannon beside her. "Why don't you go back to your original mission?"

Morgan lowered his thigh from the wall and pivoted to lean back against it. "There is no return to the past." His voice was low, hesitant. "We are not the same men."

"Then take a new direction. Find a new purpose." She

picked at the buttons of her shirt. "You could settle down. Stay in one place. With all your different backgrounds and training, you could—"

"Become upstanding members of the working class?" Morgan finished blandly. "We are fugitives, each of us ostracized in one way or another by countries to whom we once pledged unflinching fealty." He opened his arms out to the sides. "And would you now have us pretend our way into society? Risk entrapment, so that we are pressed into service as soldiers for some new dictatorship?" The logical tone to his voice became tinged with feeling. "Our army may have transformed into other than what we were—and yes, sacrificed many of our social virtues in the process—but we have never condoned nor supported a broken system. And we will not start now."

"But…but you can't know that's what will happen." She couldn't control the pleading sound in her voice, but she pushed on anyway. "If you don't try to change, then you never will. You can't just keep running all the time and treating people like…like we're all temporary. Eventually, you have to belong somewhere."

"We do not belong *anywhere*." The lingering light from the sun, which had slipped beneath the skyline, cast his face in a fiery mask. "Truly, Vanessa, I envy you your ignorance." He shook his head. "Most of us will never know a life in which we are not outsiders."

"Lieutenant Winchester!" a voice called out. Both of them turned as a sandy-haired soldier—he had to be barely eighteen years old—came running toward them along the rampart walkway. "Lieutenant, sir! Sorry to bother you on your evening off—"

But he skidded to a stop as soon as he saw Vanessa.

"Oh!" He smiled and pinched the front of his brown beret, to tip it in greeting. "G-good evening, Miss Brouwer," he said, his cheeks lighting up a bright red.

Wow, what a beautiful way he rolled his r's. Her surname had never sounded so elegant!

"Hi," she said as he stood and gazed at her. "It's Jakub, right?"

He smiled wider and nodded quickly, the blush spreading to his ears. "Yes, Miss! Jakub Kijek!"

He tugged on his beret again, which bore a fabric emblem of an eagle wearing a crown with its wings spread upward. Now, which country's army did this symbol represent?

"Private, I assume you're here on business," Morgan said in a brisk tone that jolted the young soldier out of staring at Vanessa.

"Yes! Sorry, Porucznik—I mean, Lieutenant!" Jakub wiped a hand across his forehead. It was clear that he had sprinted here to deliver his message. "We have caught one of the residents trying to escape. He was at the front gates, getting ready to run."

"The main entrance? Poor choice for a clandestine departure."

Jakub's expression turned blank. "Sir?"

"Why is my presence required?" Morgan asked.

"Sergeant Maxwell sent for you."

Morgan gave Vanessa a wordless look before he motioned for Jakub to lead the way.

As they left, Vanessa slipped down off the wall and placed a hand on her apron upon the cannon. She scratched her nails back and forth on the tough fabric. Should she be nosy? She pressed her lips together. Absolutely. These were her people, after all.

Walking quickly but quietly in their wake, she trailed them through the compound halls until they reached the front entrance, where Angus's stocky profile hovered in the open gateway. She ducked into an alcove as the Scotsman turned his head to Morgan. She leaned farther out until she could distinguish their words. She could also discern the faces of Pieter and one of the young men of the compound named Abel, who was only about seventeen.

"…and this wee numpty claims ye had told him he could go into town alone fer supplies. He tried to convince the lads here to let him pass." The burly sergeant nodded his head toward the blond teenager. "I thought ye might want to handle this one yourself, Lieutenant, since the wee slater seems to think he's a personal mukker of yers."

Morgan absently fingered the handle of his dagger as he regarded the two residents. Then he took a slow step toward Abel.

"I trust you now comprehend how inadvisable it is to contrive such fiction when its veracity is easily dispelled," the lieutenant stated firmly.

By how the color drained from the young resident's face, he had understood the Englishman's long-winded way of saying, "Bad idea, dipwad."

Abel twisted the strap of a satchel between his hands as it swung in front of him. "I thought—I mean, I was—" He scrambled for words. "My mother is sick…in the town, and I wanted to—"

"Bah! Haud yer wheesht!" Angus made a gesture as if to smack the boy's head. "The lieutenant disnae want to hear ye haverin' on!"

Abel's eyes grew even bigger. "But I—no, really! I was—"

Vanessa looked at Pieter when he sighed loudly.

"Don't dig yourself deeper, boy," the older resident advised Abel in a tired voice.

Pieter was right. That lie would soon be found out. Abel's mother had passed away three years ago, so it was just he and his father at the compound now. His mother's death, though, was what had also driven Abel's interest in becoming a doctor one day. And it was why Vanessa often found him camped out on one of the parapet walls with a medical book in his lap.

Morgan took the bag from Abel and pulled open the zipper to rummage inside. He extracted wadded clothing, bottled water, and containers of food. He dropped it all to the floor. He then withdrew a stack of magazines and displayed them to the young Dutchman. There were nude women in various poses on the covers.

"I see you were planning on reading to your dear old ailing mum from this collection of fine literature," Morgan said in a deadpan voice.

Obvious even in the dim light, Abel flushed furiously. His straw-colored bangs fell forward as he stared at his feet.

Vanessa shook her head. *Well, at least they're related to anatomy. Every medical student has to start somewhere, I guess.*

Morgan shoved the magazines back in the bag and pitched it at Abel, who caught it awkwardly.

Angus's braid swung against his back as he jerked a thumb toward Pieter. "This other gomeril expects we should believe he's helpin' us."

"Oh?" Morgan turned to Pieter, whose short dark hair gave him a spiky silhouette.

"I was stopping him," the resident said.

"Why?"

Pieter leaned his head back and, despite the murky light, she could see that his features had hardened. "I thought it better that he sleep here and be unhappy than rest in a grave due to one of your bullets."

He was not nearly as confrontational as other long-time residents like Cornelis, but was just as determined to be everyone's guardian.

Morgan held Pieter's gaze for a moment and then signaled the two front guards without looking at them. "Escort these gentlemen to their quarters and confine them," Morgan ordered. "I shall decide what penalty to impose in the morning."

At that, the guards started toward the two residents.

But Abel, his face panicked, threw his satchel at Angus.

With a startled-sounding grunt, the Scotsman batted it away as Abel took off through the front gates.

Morgan lunged to grab him but missed. Growling "Bollocks!" under his breath, he charged after the Dutch teenager, followed by the two sentries.

Abel already had a good head start, but Morgan held an arm in the air as he ran and yelled up at the ramparts over his shoulder. "Hold your fire!"

Vanessa jogged forward as Morgan and the others gave

chase, but a hand grasped her elbow to hold her back. She looked at Pieter, who shook his head. He stepped over the threshold and began to walk out toward the road.

Angus, his hand hovering over his gun, watched Pieter's unhurried exit for a moment before he tugged his beard. His mechanical leg whirred and clicked as he stepped out as well.

Morgan and the two sentries finally halted in the distance. The lieutenant turned back toward the compound, his eyebrows lowered, and motioned curtly to the soldiers to follow him.

"Sergeant," Morgan said as the Scotsman came out to meet them, "pull together a team. We'll send them out to retrieve our wayward youth before he gets any further."

"Lieutenant." Pieter stopped Morgan before the Englishman could move past him. "I know where he is going and where he most likely will hide. I can fetch him."

"Very well," Morgan said and then addressed the two front guards. "Go with him and ensure that—"

"No," Pieter said, and Morgan squinted at him. "It would be better if a friend brings him home. Your men will only frighten him more."

Morgan stood motionless, his breathing deep but controlled even after the hard pursuit, and seemed to consider it.

"Lieutenant, ye are nae serious about goin' along with this?" Angus demanded gruffly.

Morgan rested a forearm on the grip of his holstered gun and took a step toward Pieter. He fixed the spiky-haired resident in a serious gaze. "And I have your word that you shall return?"

Pieter, his voice equally solemn, nodded. "You have it."

"He's pure sleekit, this one!" Angus shook his head. "Lieutenant, ye cannae trust—"

But Morgan held up a hand to silence him.

"You have until morning," Morgan informed Pieter. "Should you betray us, we will find you. And it will not go well for you."

"I understand."

Angus's mouth dropped open again, but he snapped it shut when Morgan directed a look at him. The Scotsman visibly ground his teeth, making his beard writhe like a bramble full of finches trying to take flight, but he kept all further commentary to himself.

The Englishman turned and headed toward Vanessa. The two sentries raised their eyebrows at each other, but then took up their posts on either side of the front gate. Pieter started down the road toward Achterwaartsstad.

Vanessa stepped out of the way as Morgan reentered the compound, but she touched his arm. "Why did you do that?" she asked. "Why take the chance?"

Morgan gazed at her for a moment.

"You may believe we have lost our purpose, but do not assume we have lost our humanity." The depths of his eyes churned like darkening clouds in the tenuous light. "Once we let rot that final seed of faith in others, then we shall truly grow into the villains people think us."

With that, he walked away, and his figure blended with the shadows of the hall.

CHAPTER TWENTY-SIX

ETHAN

"I said I wanted all this shit moved out of here!"

Ethan kicked over an empty vegetable oil canister. The sound of it rolling away echoed down the tunnel. The three soldiers behind Angus exchanged looks wordlessly.

Angus stepped forward, and his metallic foot clunked down toe-to-toe with Ethan's.

"Captain, the lads have worked on this night and day till they're knackered." The Scotsman matched Ethan's irritated tone. "But there's a shiteload of rubbish down here. We shouldnae have bricked over the other three tunnel exits to the outside of the fort. It left us only one in the back to haul it all out."

Ethan jerked back his hood. "Sergeant Maxwell, when your team mapped out these tunnels, you told me there was not much to move."

Angus nodded brusquely so that the lamplight sparked off the crest badge on his red-and-green patterned cap. "Aye, sir, yer right about that. But nobody counted on findin' hidden rooms that had been sealed off. We didnae ken they were there, till they fell open like a whore's kirtle."

Fucking excuses, everywhere he turned today.

All available storage spaces should have been cleared

out by now and filled with the guns, ammunition, fuel, and supplies they had brought in during the last few days. It had been two weeks since their first meeting with the arms dealers, and so far the supply line had proven adequate. But something about the dealers still gnawed at him. They were a little *too* accommodating, as if they did not take much care in vetting their clients. As long as the money was real, they took it. That usually made such men untrustworthy. And that unease was just one of the things pissing him off today.

Ethan pointed a gloved finger at Angus's face. "Get it done."

The sergeant closed his mouth firmly with a glare of his own. The joints of his prosthetic leg complained with a metallic pop as he straightened and gave Ethan an abrupt salute.

Ethan spun around and left the tunnels. As he headed toward his quarters to retrieve the papers he wanted, musings about Vanessa plagued him the whole way. That was nothing new. He couldn't seem to go one fucking hour without some thought of her popping up. Even keeping his distance from her did no good. The more he avoided her, the more distracted he became. She had tried to approach him several times, but he deliberately dodged her, aiming to drive her away with his silence. And then he would spot her in the orchard or the kitchen, and he would be helpless against the barrage of graphic reveries.

When she was bent over a table to clear it, he saw himself behind her with his lips on her neck while he pulled down her panties from under her skirt. When she would kneel by a vegetable bed tying young plants to garden stakes, he would watch those nimble fingers in a trance, imagining them on the button of his jeans, then his zipper, then his...

Ethan yanked on his hood to pull it farther forward. *Not fucking helping.*

After he had scooped up all the papers and notepads off his desk, he made his way through the halls. The few men left behind from that morning's reconnaissance mission, as well as many residents, quickly stepped out of his way as he approached. Evidently, they had all heard about his mood. Even Morgan—normally unbothered by Ethan's temper—had seemed withdrawn and preoccupied during the daily officers' briefing, as if infected with the same brooding frame of mind.

When he reached the great double doors leading into the dining hall, he pushed one side open and stepped through.

The huge building, made from an almost rose-colored stone that contrasted with the rest of the compound, had been constructed as a splendid addition to the otherwise drab fort. For a scientific people, the original residents had dramatically romantic tastes, as they'd chosen to design the dining hall with a Renaissance flair.

Tall leaded windows spanned the side of the room opposite the double doors, beyond which a pastoral courtyard could be seen. The area had been walled off, he guessed, to preserve the undisturbed tranquility of it so that it was merely a backdrop against which diners could daydream. Admittedly, it did have a soothing effect.

Two candle-laden chandeliers hung on long sturdy chains from the vaulted ceiling, the height of which made the hall stand up behind the walls of the fort as a glaring inconsistency. A large empty fireplace that could have allowed five of his men to stand in it bulged out from the wall to his right. Its tall stone chimney stretched up to the ceiling and disappeared. No telling where the original residents had dug up the funds to complete such a palatial undertaking as the hall, but considering the creative solutions they had developed for other aspects of the compound, their resourcefulness should not have come as a surprise.

A few tapestries depicting medieval forest scenes hung on the walls to lend the cold stone some formality and to help dampen the noise. Beneath the long oaken table, a rectangular blue rug patterned with leafy swirls cushioned the captain's boots as he pulled out a chair and dropped all of his papers to scatter across the polished wood surface.

He dragged his robe off, tossed it over the back of the chair next to him, and then settled himself in.

Finally, a place where he could concentrate without interruption. The residents did not use the dining hall on a regular basis, as most of them gathered for their meals in the casual setting of Rhetta's kitchen.

First, he would look over the tunnel maps again, to mark where the miscellaneous goods he had acquired should be stored and organized. Then he would cross-reference the plans with the list of residents. Time for a refresher on which people had been there the longest and therefore might know the layout of the tunnels well enough to assist his men in carting off the remaining clutter without getting lost.

But the more pressing motive: re-review the resident names with greater scrutiny, in light of some recent indications of unrest in Achterwaartsstad. He did not need anyone in the compound, who might yet have ties to the town, burying a knife in his back. It was bad enough knowing that fate was constantly trying to catch up with him.

You cannot burn us. You cannot kill us. We will bury you screaming beneath the bodies of your men.

Ethan breathed out slowly and set an elbow on the table. He leaned his face into his hand and rubbed his eyes through the holes in the fabric mask. Then he spread all of the papers and yellow notepads out in front of him. He picked up the tunnel maps, but his gaze fell on the sheet beneath them. It was the sketch Vanessa had made of an aerial view of the compound, which looked like a crude copy of one of the postcards left over from the tourist materials he'd seen when he first arrived. But in this version, outside the old fort's walls, Ethan himself was represented in stick-figure form.

He stared at the drawing.

The exaggerated movements of the robed figure were frozen in the middle of his long and fitful speech. The erased speech bubble was still just visible above the stick man's head.

He had not meant to bring that one with him, but he had never bothered to separate it from the rest.

There's no escaping her, is there?

The rear door creaked open on the left side of the fireplace. As he looked over, Vanessa entered. He almost groaned aloud.

Fuck.

She stopped when she saw him. And it may have been his imagination, but he could have sworn her eyes traveled over him in an admiring way as she noted the absence of his robe. In spite of himself, he sat up straighter and squared his shoulders.

"I didn't know anyone would be in here," she said. He stared at her until she added, "I'm not leaving."

He sighed inwardly and turned back to the papers in front of him.

She made her way through the room, her slippered steps creating scarcely a sound in the echoing hall.

She extracted one of the elaborately carved chairs across from him, perched herself primly on the red velvet seat, and set down the hardback book she had brought with her. She wore a long royal-blue skirt with white lace filigree running up either side. It was very fetching paired with her simple long-sleeved white shirt, which was unbuttoned at her cleavage down to the point where it made him wish it was undone one step lower. He swatted the thought away and moved his eyes instead to the cover of her book: *The Brothers Karamazov.*

When he looked back up at her, she shrugged one shoulder.

"Dostoevsky. I've never read this one of his. It's supposed to explore a lot of deep human issues, though: what it means to be a good person and what morality is, how much control you really have over your own actions—"

"I know what it's about," he said flatly.

He bowed his head to sort through the maps again. She was trying to needle him. And he almost succeeded in ignoring it. Almost.

"Very heavy subject for someone so...carefree," he

remarked. "I expected a poetry book."

"Oh sure, because poems aren't serious, right? They're just about people pining and whining—"

"They are," he said dryly.

She pressed her lips together for a second but then shrugged. "Okay, so maybe *some* of them. That's why I stick to the C. S. Lewises of the world. No time for navel-gazing when you're fighting witches on the other side of a magic closet." She ruffled one corner of the book's pages with her finger and angled her head so that her hair slid forward. She peeked at him from behind the blond curtain. "So…does this mean the silent treatment is over?"

"I would have sent for you if I needed you." He shoved the top page he was examining behind the others. "There was no 'treatment' because I had already told you how this relationship would be."

"Well, at least now you're admitting we're in a relationship." Her smile withered when he sharpened his stare. She sat forward and nudged the book in front of her to fidget with the bottom of the ragged cover. "I mean, I thought we were connecting, that's all. Why can't we just talk, instead of you always cutting me off at the knees?"

He tried to dismiss the dejected tone in her voice, but the sound of it pricked his stomach nonetheless. He set down the papers and, with a sweep of his arm, he pushed all of them aside. "All right, then let's talk: why aren't you tending to your duties in the kitchen, or weeding the garden, or doing something more productive than interfering with *my* work?"

"I have the morning off," she shot back with a frown. "Not all of us are tethered to the grindstone like you."

"Then why don't you go read somewhere else?"

"Because I like it here." She pulled the book toward herself on the table. "This is my place to be alone, because no one else uses it." Then she added in a grumble, "Until now."

"Your bedroom is just as good. Don't make me lock you in it."

She hesitated. "You would do that?"

"In a heartbeat."

"For the whole day?"

"And all night."

He stopped. The very words exiting his mouth had drawn up the image of her curled under the covers, her breathing soft and slow as she nuzzled deeper into her pillow. And the words branded into the worn tourist plaque posted outside her quarters beckoned his imagination: Officer's Pleasure.

Vanessa blew out a breath and slouched in her chair. She opened the book and propped it up on the table in front of her so he could not see her face.

He jerked one of the papers off the pile to his left and glared at it. The page might as well have been blank, for as much as he could concentrate. He set his elbows on the table and hunched forward, making himself read. It was a compilation of notes Vanessa had written about the day-to-day activities of the compound: kitchen supplies inventorying, tending of the water windmill, prepping meats for curing in the smokehouse—

Locked in her bedroom all night…She probably sleeps in some little baby-doll nightie. A blue one with ruffles.

He stared harder at the empty words on the page.

But maybe not. Maybe she sleeps in the nude.

Somewhere, some lucky bastard probably already knew the answer to that. An overnight guest who had gotten to glide his fingers down her body under the sheets as she slept. And wedge his hand gently between her thighs. Ethan winced and discreetly adjusted himself beneath the table. He picked up his pen and started to trace the tip down the bulleted list of resident chores.

She had probably woken up as she'd felt the man ease his palm across her supple lips, massaging her there. With a drowsy, sultry look, she would have grasped his arms to pull him nearer. And held her mouth close to his with a gasp as he slipped his fingers up into her. Her breathing deepened when he started stroking her warm, wet insides. Steadily, insistently, he built her toward a release that would wash over his hand until he could make his way down to put his tongue in its place.

Ethan dug an angry black gash into the margin of the paper beside the trivial description Vanessa had scribbled about pest fumigation.

The silence dragged on. His thoughts seethed as she sat across from him and leisurely turned a page every so often. He snatched another sheet and stared at the scraggly blocks of writing that seemed to fade in and out of his vision.

He brought his fist down on the table. "How much longer are you going to be here?"

She licked a fingertip and turned another page. "Until your head explodes, I guess."

"If you *know* that you're pissing me off, then you ought to have the sense to walk your ass back out that door."

She looked at him and blinked innocently. "But I haven't even finished the translator's introduction."

He threw himself forward, pulled the book from her hands, and slammed it closed on the table. "Guess what? You're done."

She pressed her lips together at him for a moment. "Being a total grouch isn't going to make me leave."

"Then for the love of fuck, tell me what will."

"Say your first name and I'll go."

"Somehow, I doubt that." His face burned beneath the cloth mask as his aggravation grew. "And why is it so damn important to you?"

She put her hands on her hips and sat up straight. "Why do *you* feel like you have to hide it? Your own men won't even tell me. Do you truly think it threatens your authority if people find out that you're human?" She squinted. "Unless it really is something like Beauregard or Melvin. Then I'd get why you want to keep it to yourself."

Goddamn it, she was not going to let this go. As much as he tried to keep her at arm's length—hell, a kilometer's length would have been better—that stubborn look on her face said that she would keep asking him every time she saw him. She obviously knew how to wear a man down.

He sighed gruffly. *Fuck it.*

"Ethan."

"Your full name is Ethan Evans?" she asked slowly, arching one eyebrow. She considered it and then nodded, as if she had reached a decision. "I'll call you 'Double E' for short."

"No, you won't."

"We'll see," she mused. Then her voice turned sly. "Do you have a middle name?"

"Edmund."

"Seriously?"

"No."

She leaned back with a pout. "Do you *have* a middle name?"

He deliberately did not look at her as he felt the ache of an old scar, much deeper than the ones marring his body. "Yes. My father's." *The arrogant asshole.*

"Well? What is—"

"Not open for discussion."

She hesitated as he held her eyes. But then she shrugged. "Well, I like the name Ethan Evans by itself." She circled a finger on the book's cover, and a smile started on her lips. "Very lyrical. Feels nice on the tongue."

He shifted in his seat. "It's what the Welsh are known for."

"Being lyrical or…the tongue part?"

His groin tightened at the tentative, teasing glimmer in her eyes.

Fine. She wants to play?

He lowered his voice. "Take your pick."

Her smile faltered. And, as it so often did since that night she had delivered the list of names to him, his mind forced on him the image of her on her knees in his doorway, clutching the wad of papers with her head tilted up to him. The desire to stand over her and hold her face in his hands had almost overpowered him in that instant. It had taken the remainder of the early morning hours to stop imagining what her mouth would have felt like, had she let him slide himself into it. He had not had an erection that hard in years. And he'd almost forgotten the aching pleasure of it.

He glanced away as she twined a long lock of hair around one finger. He pulled the pile of papers in front of him and flipped through them, not searching for anything in particular. But when his hand touched the one sketch of the compound, he stopped. He withdrew it and laid it carefully on top of the stack. Vanessa sat forward slightly but then dropped her gaze.

"I noticed there seems to be one thing you omitted from your…diagram." He tapped a knuckle against the bottom of the drawing. "What was he saying?"

She rubbed a finger behind her ear, squinting and looking off to the side.

"You obviously redacted what this stick man was telling the others," he pressed her. "At one point, you felt it necessary to include this little detail, so I'd like to know what it was."

A blush spread across her neck like red dye dribbled into water. "Oh that. It's not important. I was tired and it just came out like…" She paused as she avoided his eyes. "I was tired."

Ethan said nothing.

Wait for it. Any minute now, that mouth of hers will take off on its own.

"I can't remember it verbatim," she finally blurted, "but it was something like: I'm in charge around here, and you better not make me mad, or I'll hold my breath till I get what I want, because I'm impossible to please. And I like to dress like I'm always at a funeral or joining a monastery, and I have no sense of humor, and look how tall I am, and—"

"Well," Ethan broke in and folded his hands in front of him. "He sounds like a real dick."

She shut her jaw and scraped a thumbnail back and forth across the frayed spine of her book.

That's right, smart-ass. Once again, your mouth is a shovel and you just can't stop digging.

After he let her squirm a bit longer, he gathered up all the sheets from the table. Nothing worthwhile was getting done here. But then she rose to her feet at the same time he did.

"Wait, please," she said as he turned to grab his robe. "Tell me what it takes."

Ethan eyed her as she wrung her hands. "What *what* takes?"

"What it takes to make you pay attention to me." She walked around the table as she spoke. "To make you stop treating me like an inconvenience and refusing to let your guard down. I want to know more about you."

"You know enough."

She stopped in front of him and took a breath. "I want more."

He dropped the papers onto the chair seat and folded his arms. "You have no leverage to make demands."

"Then give me some leverage," she persisted, holding her shoulders back. "Offer me a deal. What do you want in exchange for what I want?"

He tapped his fingers against his arm and cocked his head. "No trade. I've got a better idea. And it's the only offer on the table."

She bit her lip for a second but then lifted her chin. "Fine. What is it?"

He stepped closer. "We're going to make this physical. And I'm going to enjoy it."

Her mouth hung open for a second. "What?"

"You use your body to turn every man's head around here—"

"Hey!" She slapped her hands onto her hips. "Excuse me, but how dare—"

"So why don't you put that body to work and use it on me?" He bent down to her, arms still crossed. "Let's see how much you really want my attention."

She lowered her hands from her hips and licked her lips. "What do I have to do?"

"You'll only need one hand for it." He gave her the slightest smile and watched her breathing quicken.

"Shouldn't take long, if you're any good."

He advanced on her again, and she stumbled backward and trailed her fingers along the polished wood top as she retreated. When they reached the end of the table, he stopped.

He nodded down at the chair behind her. "Take a seat."

She fumbled for the chair pushed against the end of the table and plopped into it. She was squeezing her hands together as she gazed up at him, but the flush in her cheeks gave away a building excitement. For a moment, Ethan hovered over her. She licked her lips again—slower this time—and swallowed. Again arose the image of her from that night outside his bedroom. Kneeling in front of him, her face turned up to him in supplication as he cupped her cheek. The fantasy of feeling her open her mouth and take him into her throat. A fantasy that had been driving him crazy with its frequency.

Ethan quickly took the chair diagonal to hers and repositioned it beside the table. He sat facing her, trying to quell the sudden nervous clenching of his stomach.

She straightened, and her voice turned uncertain. "Now what?"

He met her eyes as the late morning light gleamed over them and brightened the emerald depths. "Now you try to get what you want." He set his right elbow on the table's corner and held his arm toward her. "I'll even use my weaker hand. I win, you leave me the hell alone from now on. That means no surprise visits, no casual chitchat, no complaining, and most of all no questions. Name your terms."

Her eyes widened. "Arm wrestling? How am I supposed to win at that?"

"Name your terms, or we're done here."

"But—"

Ethan pulled his elbow off the table and sat back.

"No, wait!" She jerked forward with her palms up. "I just mean…" She glanced from side to side, as if chasing a thought from one end of her brain to the other. "If I win, you have to tolerate me whenever I want to talk to you. That means surprise visits, chitchat, and lots of questions. You can't blow me off anymore, like you've been doing. Agreed?"

He set his elbow firmly on the table again and held out his hand. "Show me what you've got."

She pressed her lips together and then nodded. He waited while she unbuttoned one cuff of her shirt and rolled up the sleeve. She set her right elbow in front of her on the table's corner and started to reach for his hand.

But then she pulled hers back and lifted her chin. "I might be stronger than you think."

"Then, please"—he glanced over her face—"don't hold back."

She wiggled her fingers and pursed her lips. "Oh, you'll get what's coming to you, Double E."

He stared at her silently.

She sighed. "*Captain.*"

He accepted her palm when she rested it against his. But as he slowly wrapped his fingers around her hand, his leather glove started to absorb her body heat. He met her eyes, and the room tilted just a bit as the close contact unsteadied him, lulled him.

Shit. Something about this feels like a very bad idea now.

She leaned forward over the table. His gaze was pulled to the open front of her shirt, even though it was clear that was exactly what she'd intended.

Yep. A very fucking bad idea.

"Ethan Evans," she cooed, composing her face, "prepare for your beating."

He nearly acted on a familiar impulse, one in which he reached out and glided a finger along the top of her breasts and then down between them. He shoved the urge away and focused instead on her eyes. "Count it down."

She leaned back into her seat and, with a nervous movement, tucked a stray lock of hair behind her ear. "Okay, well, on one then." She cleared her throat and adjusted her elbow against the table. "Three...two...one."

Their hands gripped each other tightly. The tendons

on her arm stood out, her muscles visibly straining. She was obviously putting her best effort into it, but he applied only a portion of his strength. It was just enough to validate and prolong the match in order to humor her. Then he could move on with his day and be left in peace. He almost shook his head. Why the hell was she so insistent about getting close to him? She had to know this match was just a way to make her back off. She should have turned him down as soon as he'd proposed it. It was all going to end the same.

Vanessa's eyes were squeezed shut. After a minute, she pried them open partway. "You are giving this your full attention, right?" she asked in a raspy, suspicious voice.

His arm stiffened further as he gazed at her. "Of course."

Another half minute passed. The only sound in the great room was her breathing, which grew heavier. He let his eyes brush over her body, and his gaze touched every part of her. Her panting became more rhythmic as her arm trembled against his. He inched forward in his chair as the inner seams of his jeans began to compress and cut into him. His heart drummed a little harder as a warm tingling started to spread through his thighs.

She looked at him again and dragged in a short breath. "I can feel you weakening."

He tightened his grip as a surge of heat hit his chest. "You haven't begun to feel me."

She took a gulp of air and then gave an extra push on his arm. Her chair tipped to the side a few centimeters at the resistance she met. He watched her struggle against him, her arm shuddering as she breathed more rapidly. Perspiration glistened on her face and on the skin that showed through the unbuttoned placket of her shirt…skin that would have felt soft and moist, could he have touched it with his bare fingers. He fought back the vision of tearing that blouse open wider and groping each plump breast before he dipped his head and filled his mouth with them.

Vanessa held his gaze intently, as if she could see his

thoughts. As if she could see how, in his mind, he had caught one of her nipples between his teeth and was tracing the tip of it with his tongue. Without warning, Vanessa managed to lean his arm the slightest bit over, and she raised her eyebrows with a panting, open-mouthed smile. What the fuck? He edged himself closer and reasserted the pressure, erasing her progress. Her expression wilted, and she clenched her teeth.

She pushed against him, breathing faster as she defied him. He gripped her harder, fire swelling up through his thighs. Vanessa's body shook with ferocious exertion, and the noises she made echoed off the walls around them. His pulse pounded as he dug the fingers of his left hand into the chair arm. His mask clung damply to his face. He closed his eyes as her bare flesh rubbed his arm. He needed to end this, to relieve the explosive pressure behind it. This match was meaningless. A distraction.

Just take her.

He began to let go of his restraint, allowing his muscles to do what they were programmed to do against something that opposed him. He pulled her closer so that her breasts bulged toward him upon the table. He thrust his arm against hers, and she gasped. He wanted this. He wanted her to feel him win. Vanessa panted faster, her gaze held to his. He squeezed her hand, and her arm shuddered again. But she loosened her grip. She was giving in, letting him have this. The way she began to bend beneath him made his very flesh throb with a pleasure that trickled down into every flexing muscle.

But it was her small moan that took him off guard. It came to him—a simple helpless sound of surrender.

Suddenly, her hand clutched his so tightly, so desperately, that he instinctively responded in kind. The room around them vanished for an instant, and a dizzying hypersensitivity struck him. The wet gleam of her skin, her lips open, her body trembling—all of it overcoming him at once. He forced his eyes shut and gritted his teeth, his arm seizing up and locking with hers. He drew a sharp breath as Vanessa began to cry out.

The back of his hand hit the table.

He opened his eyes with a start. Vanessa, her breathing labored, stared at him with her jaw hanging slack. They both looked down at where she pressed his gloved hand against the satiny wood surface. It was another moment before either of them moved, but Vanessa was the first to pull away. She sank back in her chair, her chest still pumping like a bellows. She swallowed and slipped her fingers behind the buttons of her shirt. Neither of them said a word. The air was charged, hovering around them like static.

Ethan's heart began to slow at last, though there was no powering down the stiffness that now made it impossible to sit. He stood up and inched backward to where his robe lay. He dragged it off the chair and pulled it over himself. The sound of Vanessa's chair sliding back reached him as he bent and swept the papers and notepads into his hands. He stacked them together and then felt her hand on his back.

"I guess I win," she said faintly.

"I guess you do." He did not look at her, the groin of his jeans still unbearably tight.

"You'll keep your part of the bargain, won't you, Ethan?"

Ethan.

Somehow, it had a different sound to it, coming from her.

He turned to her. "Contrary to what you think, I am a man of my word. As pointless as your terms are, I'll honor them."

He started toward the doors, but she stepped in front of him to block his way. She ran her fingers down the front of his robe and gazed up at him. "Guess you shouldn't underestimate me, huh?"

"Congratulations." He pulled his hood up and peered at her from within the shadows of the cowl. "Apparently, you *are* stronger than I thought." And he was only getting weaker.

He brushed past her, pulled open one side of the double doors, and left.

CHAPTER TWENTY-SEVEN

VANESSA

Over the next several days, undoubtedly much to the captain's annoyance, Vanessa tried out her newly won prize of grabbing his attention whenever the mood struck her.

The afternoon following the match, she glimpsed him walking along the corridor toward the kitchen where she was working. When he saw her, he paused, and his eyes darted around him. Then he turned in a different direction. But she popped outside and ran to cut him off.

"So-o-o," she said as she stood squarely in the middle of the stone archway, "what do you think about silk scarves? Is that a look I can pull off, or should I start with fancy hats?"

The next morning, she waited until he emerged from an inspection of the armory and fell immediately into stride with him. As he balled his hands beside him and stared ahead, she demanded to know whether he would rather be reincarnated as a tricycle or a wheelbarrow and to provide convincing reasons for his choice.

On each occasion, though his observations were delivered with a greater dose of sarcasm than usual, he never once ignored her. He was, as he had said, a man of his word.

She was relentless throughout the morning and afternoon of a cloudy Thursday, savoring every chance to approach him. She managed to squeeze in more serious, probing questions when she caught him in a pensive mood or they were out of earshot of everyone else. His words would be sparing, but at least he'd answer. She had to be getting through to him on some level. It was obvious by the way that outer ice shield was melting off.

But the best moments were the ones that put his body language to the test.

When she talked, she would step closer and let some intimate part of herself press against him, to see what he would do. And every time—every single breathless time— his eyes within the black mask would flame like two green pilot lights igniting in the darkness. Then she would shift against him more deliberately. At that, the muscles in his arms would seem to contract in succession, like ripples sent along a chain, and those eyes would glow all the hotter.

If only he would act on it. Or at least say something. How many more chances did he need?

It had been a strange string of weeks trying to get to know him, of drilling deeper, but now she felt so much closer to hitting his true core. Because, beneath the obvious heat of his gaze, there was also a kind of yearning when he looked at her, especially when she pretended to ignore him. Getting under his clothes would have to be as much fun as getting under his skin had been so far. Whatever his hang-up was about his appearance, she could make him forget it. She needed to find the right trigger, the one touch or gesture that would remove the last brick from his emotional wall. He had abandoned his self-consciousness just fine, back in the dining hall that day, where those pilot-light eyes had nearly burned out of control.

The memory of his hand gliding onto hers and the strength of his grip—restrained but firm—made a slow heat prowl through her. Maybe he would apply that same steady pressure anywhere else he put his fingers on her. She had luxuriated in her own arousal as his eyes had moved over her body with a possessive appreciation, like he had no intention of letting her go, once the match was over. And she hadn't wanted him to. Because there were a few ways she could picture him using that lyrical Welsh tongue of his. But she should have known his inhibitions would come calling again, and she'd lose out on getting to strip away those last layers of his self-restraint.

She ambled through the one-sided corridor along the south perimeter of the garden, on the front side of the compound. She stopped to lean against one of the sand-colored columns.

It was already fairly dark, dinner long since passed so that the overcast day was being eaten away by the later evening hours. But she could still make out Ethan's dark-robed form where he stood on the north side of the garden. He was talking with Morgan, their heads close together as they pored over a large sheet of paper. The captain spread his gloved hand over the page as if describing something, while Morgan nodded. She rested her cheek against the cold stone pillar and shook her head with a smile.

Oooh, so serious! She glanced up at the ramparts, where the shadowy figures of several soldiers glided along the parapets. *And way too paranoid.*

Ethan had sent out two separate teams for some kind of extended reconnaissance mission. But they had already returned, evidently with nothing to show for it, since she had seen the dissatisfied stance of his body when they had delivered their reports. No one said as much, but the captain's army was running from something. That wasn't a stretch, considering they had probably made boatloads of enemies along the way. But the fact that they were coming up dry on producing evidence of a real boogey-man made their preparations seem like an overreaction. But then, maybe ex-soldiers never knew how to quit soldiering.

Regardless of the tension that clogged the compound, it was a beautiful evening.

She puckered her lips and exhaled. Still not quite cold

enough to see her breath. Nevertheless, mid-October was fast coming upon them, and they would be bundling up for November before they knew it. Most of the compound residents had already retired for the night. The remaining few wandered through the halls to their rooms, and so a peaceful quiet had settled over everything. Vanessa relaxed her shoulders and had started to draw a long breath when a coarse hand wrapped around her mouth from behind.

She clawed at the fingers that dug into her cheek, but then stiffened as the point of something sharp pressed against the nape of her neck.

"One scream, meisje, and I will stick this up through your pretty head," warned a man's voice with a thick Dutch accent.

He turned her onto her back against the wide column and angled her away from the openness of the archway. He turned his hand to keep it pressed over her mouth as he practically enveloped her with his bulky body, which smelled like cigarette smoke and mildewed cloth. Vanessa breathed jerkily through her nose and stared up into the black eyes of her captor. In the waning light, she could see the angry red line of a fresh scar on his cheek. Even amidst the fear clouding her mind, there was something familiar about him.

The man rammed her harder against the stone, and she nearly bit into his dirty palm from the shock of pain. He yanked his hand away and grabbed her arm.

He put the flat of the knife blade against her throat. "Where's Captain Evans?"

And then she froze. *It's him.*

The constable. The one she had begged to find her parents' killer. The man who had smirked at her—a twelve-year-old girl sobbing against Rhetta's shoulder— and told her that she was better off, that her parents were bad people. Traitors. And then the way he had eyed her young body as he had stroked his mustache and smiled. Pulling her aside, he had said he might work harder if she were to follow him alone into his musty, bottle-strewn office and show him how much she wanted his help. Rhetta had descended upon him like a mother hawk, and he'd left Vanessa alone for all the years since.

"Where is he, hoer?" The constable's voice was a hiss.

He's distracted. Nervous. He hasn't seen Ethan yet.

She swallowed and felt the edge of the knife graze the underside of her chin. Her heart began to beat like a bass drum.

"Gone," she said, keeping her jaw clenched. "He's—he's gone. Left yesterday. With a group of his men. On a m-mission."

"Do you think I am stupid, trutje? You're lying!"

A dribble of wetness—blood—snaked down her throat from where the cold blade dug in.

"Please," she said, blinking to clear her vision. "Please, he's gone."

He grabbed at his shoulder, where a little black box clung to the gray cloth. Keeping his dark eyes on her, he pressed a button on the device and whispered gruffly, "Val deze klootzakken nu aan! Nu!" Then the constable leaned his face closer and leered at her. "I remember you. Your name is Brouwer." He canted his head to push his gaze down across her body. "Pretty little meisje with dead parents." She gasped as he twisted her arm to draw her closer. He flashed his teeth at her, glistening sweat beading between the coarse hairs of his mustache. "Maybe I will keep you alive after we're done here."

Zip!

The constable's head jerked to the side. She stared into his eyes as he released her arm. He staggered backward. And then dropped to the stone floor in a heap.

Vanessa stared down at him, at the dark hole that had appeared in his left temple, and then turned to see the starburst of blood on the wall of the corridor. She looked dazedly up at the distant rear ramparts.

Thomas—his face eerily calm as he blended into the parapet wall like one of its shadows—swung his rifle muzzle away from her and fixed on a point farther to her left. There were running footsteps and then *bang!* followed by the same *zip!*

This time the sharp report from Thomas's gun registered through her stunned senses, and she whirled as another man collapsed in the corridor. She stared numbly at the gun in the stranger's hand. He'd been charging at her with it raised.

As if moving underwater, she looked into the garden. Both Ethan and Morgan had pulled their weapons and were running full tilt in her direction.

All at once, the entire compound exploded with noise.

She cringed at the raucous thunder of men's yells, boots pounding over stone and across grassy ground, rifle shots, handgun blasts, bullets ricocheting off stone and ripping through tree branches. All of it echoed off the fort walls and rended the air, forcing her to crouch down and cover her ears.

Damn it, Vanessa! Run! Run!

But her legs felt welded in place. Her heart hammered wildly as unfamiliar men of all shapes and sizes poured out of the corridors from the front side of the compound, all of them armed and screaming. Her fellow residents had started to emerge from various corners, confused by the clamor. Upon seeing the ensuing violence, they scrabbled in different directions. Many of them, she knew, were now locking themselves in their rooms.

While there she slumped, useless. Drowning within a rising bloodbath.

Soldiers came down off the ramparts, and others streamed into the garden from everywhere within the compound to meet the attack.

She searched the area on the northeast side for any sign of Ethan and Morgan. She bent down to scan the area around the trees obscuring the scene beyond. But she could only make out Angus and others grappling with a few of the intruders to pin them to the ground.

Frank was nearby. He fired his giant chromed gun in a horizontal arc around him, methodically felling bodies as he went. Mabayoje was behind him. The towering lieutenant punched out first one and then another of the attackers, their heads whipping back so brutally he must have broken their necks.

Then, there they were! Ethan and Morgan were near the northwest end in the back.

She clutched the stone pillar as two large men charged at them and lifted rifle butts against their shoulders. But Ethan and Morgan raised their weapons simultaneously and shot the attackers point-blank. They dropped the men at the same time, and then each turned in opposite directions to face the next assault. After putting down another assailant, the captain began to run toward her once more. But another man hurtled into his path and blocked him.

Move, Vanessa, damn you!

She staggered into the next archway to her right, farther away from where men had been hurtling in from the front of the compound. She looked again at where Ethan was. Her heart jumped into her throat when a man came up behind Ethan with startling speed. She screamed his name, though the sound was lost in the din of the battle.

Morgan stepped suddenly between the captain and the onrushing attacker. He slashed his dagger through the air and sliced open the man's throat in one ruthless motion that sent a spray of blood fanning out over the ground.

Ethan merely glanced over his shoulder and nodded at the Englishman. With that, he whipped his masked head to throw off his hood and shouted something at a group of nearby soldiers, though she could not distinguish his voice from all the other yelling.

A man ran by her, and she pressed back. She covered her mouth as her vision went momentarily black, and she sagged against the archway column behind her. When the world reeled back into focus, she leaned out to see Frank standing next to Ethan. The Russian sergeant's smooth head bent toward the captain as he listened to whatever Ethan was ordering him to do. Then Frank took off, and Ethan and Morgan advanced on a small knot of intruders scrambling toward the rear gates. But three more attackers closed in on them. Then nothing but blurred movement as she lost her line of sight.

No, no, no, no!

She blundered back down the corridor, desperate for a clearer view. Her limbs were stiff and uncooperative, and she scraped her shoulder along each of the hallway pillars as she went. Her fingers grasped at the rough stone beside her as if feeling her way in an alien place.

Ethan and Morgan were fighting off four men who had cornered them beside the rear gates. Vanessa pushed herself away from the arch and tottered forward. A huge man stepped in front of her. A knife gleamed in one hand, and a pistol smoked in the other. She halted, her heart wrenching into her throat. She hyperventilated as he loomed over her. His eyes were blazing, his face twisted by a crazed sneer.

Run! Run!

But instead, she cowered low. With a roar, he turned the knife to drive the blade down into her.

A thin loop of steel flashed in the air above him, glinting in the light of the rising moon. The man made a choked gurgling sound as a metal line formed across his throat. Then came the sickening sound of flesh and bone being severed by an ax stroke—like one of Cornelis's pigs at the butcher shop. The attacker's head lolled toward her.

And then it tumbled to the ground.

Her mouth stretched open so wide that the hinges of her jaw shot hot pins through her ears. Her lungs pumped as she panted down at the bloody-necked head at her feet. Only one of its eyes was open, but the bulging orb twitched and fixed its gaze on her.

The rest of the body toppled, and she stumbled back. She looked up at Frank, who was recoiling the wire he always kept at his belt. He showed no expression, his mustache anchored in place like a piece of black iron. He took one step and threw an arm around her waist. He hefted her against him and strode with her across the grassy ground, carrying her like a child would carry a kitten.

She did not question where he was taking her, her

mind dulled by the horrors she had witnessed in what must have been only a matter of minutes.

He burst into the kitchen. A single lamp lit the middle of the dining area. When the draft from Frank's entrance struck the flame, the shadows around them writhed and reached for her. Vanessa recoiled and shut her eyes, clasping Frank's arm as he held her. He went to the room that they used as a walk-in pantry and pulled open the door.

He set her down and placed one of his big palms on the side of her head.

"Stay in here, lapushka," he said as gently as that heavy Russian accent would allow. "We will come for you."

He shut the pantry door. She heard a lock being jammed onto the hasp, followed by the main kitchen door slamming closed. She could not have left if she'd wanted to.

Vanessa backed up in the pitch-black room. She flattened herself against the unseen shelving behind her and lowered herself to her knees. All the muscles in her back sang with pain as if turned on a crank, twisting until they snapped. She grasped her hands together in the dark and tried to steady them. Her entire body trembled uncontrollably, the aching in her head producing a grainy phantom light that pulsed against her eyes.

Muffled tones hummed through the heavy wood of the pantry door and the stone walls of the kitchen beyond. The shelves vibrated at a distant explosion, knocking over a mountain of cans. They bounced across the floor like metallic claps of thunder that made her jerk as each one struck. Footsteps rumbled by overhead. The smell of ancient dust and fresh gunpowder crept into her nostrils, making her eyes water.

Every sound was a hammer's blow. Every muted scream sent her imagination sprinting. Her stomach cramped hard, and she fell forward to prop herself on her hands, choking on a dry-heave. She sank to her side on the floor and curled her body, blind to everything around her—as if she were already dead and biding her time in a timeless void.

At last, the deep-voiced shouting and the crack of rifles seemed to dwindle like the dying drums of a departing cavalcade. The cacophony decayed into one or two random thuds and shots. Finally, all was hushed—the solemn stillness of a graveyard.

The sound of blood rushing in her ears soon took the silence's place. She coiled her arms around her knees, the stone floor as cold as a coffin against her shoulder, and fought to calm her pulse as her mind still raced through the images she had seen. Her neck was wet where her own blood was drying in a long, tacky streak.

The kitchen door whined. Slow footsteps crossed the floor.

Vanessa carefully rolled to her knees and rose, pulling herself up in the darkness by the edges of the shelves.

The lock on the outside of the pantry jiggled.

The footsteps moved away briefly and then returned. She jumped as the door quaked with a loud thump. The sound of the metal lock hitting the floor echoed in the empty kitchen, and the door was wrenched open.

Morgan's distinctive silhouette appeared against the dimly lit room.

Relief geysered through her like a hot spring un-capped, and she flung herself forward to wrap her arms around his neck.

He hesitated. And then slipped both arms around her in return.

His body was fevered and damp from the fighting, but he felt wonderful. She let out a grateful moan that became a whimper.

"Morgan." Her chin trembled upon his chest as she struggled against the tears she'd been too numb to shed.

But he turned his mouth into her hair, and she could feel his breath on her ear as he held her closer to him. "Nothing to fear, love. Safe as houses now."

After a moment, she pulled back from him, her heart still galloping. His usually stoic face was relaxed, softened by the glow of the flickering lamp nearby as he gave her a tender smile and spread his fingers against her back. She managed to take a full breath and nodded in acknowledgment.

Then she squeezed his arms with her hands. "Is Ethan okay?"

He paused, and his eyes ran a single circuit of her face before his goatee settled around a slight frown. He stepped back from her slowly. "Yes."

Her throat unclenched, the reaction creating a domino effect through the rest of her muscles. She smiled shakily and was about to ask further, but he had already pulled an unreadable mask over his features.

Leave the questions for later. I'll probably find out more than I want to know, soon enough.

He led her out of the kitchen, where the scene that confronted her nearly made her knees buckle.

CHAPTER TWENTY-EIGHT

VANESSA

All around her, in the light of a shrouded moon, it was a confusion of tangled bodies and torn-up turf. Weapons lay scattered amid hazy clouds of stone dust that still hung in the air. Soldiers darted up the various sets of stairs to resume their positions on the ramparts and scan the surrounding fields. A few residents dawdled timidly out from where they had been hiding. In the grass around the greenhouses, glass shards glittered in the feeble light of the evening, fallen from the walls of the colossal buildings where stray bullets had shattered many of the panes.

And blood, glistening in black streaks, seemed to cover everything—the hallways, the grass, even the soil of the many root vegetable beds. The leaves of her plants drooped with dark glimmering droplets that she knew would have been bright red in the daytime. Reflexively, she wiped hard at the dried line of blood running down her throat, newly disgusted by the very feel of it on her skin.

The captain walked among the dead—some forty bodies from what she could guess—kicking a few out of his way and looking over the extent of the carnage. Thomas sat on the orchard wall and casually rubbed the lens of his riflescope with the hem of his shirt after blowing on the glass a few times. Other men wandered through the grassy area. They picked up weapons along the way and nudged the fallen assailants to check for signs of life. Frank, along with Liam, walked into the garden from the front of the compound, the tall Russian holstering his gun.

The captain looked at Frank. "Did you get the stragglers?"

He nodded. "They should have run faster, after waking the wolves."

Ethan turned to Angus, well off to his right.

"Dinnae worry, the ones we caught are all dead and sent to hell," the Scotsman said in answer to the captain's gaze.

"Oga, e wo!" Mabayoje's voice broke in. "I believe you'll recognize this oyinbo well enough."

Everyone looked to see him dragging a heavy, bulky body forward. The lieutenant released the corpse to let it lie sprawled before the captain.

It was the constable. Vanessa's hand went to her throat and touched the small sticky cut made by the man's knife blade.

Ethan only then turned to Vanessa. But she could not see his eyes. The pale light in the garden complex failed to penetrate the black shadows within his hood.

Morgan touched her elbow gently before he moved forward to approach the captain.

Ethan leaned down to grab the gun from a body in front of him.

"They appear to all originate from the town," Morgan informed him, pausing to rest his hand on the pommel of his Fairbairn-Sykes. "Only one compound resident amongst them. However, he seemed uninvolved with the attackers. I, myself, saw him cut down by them."

Ethan was inspecting the weapon he had retrieved. He snapped his fingers at Raphaël nearby. The blond French soldier tossed him his assault rifle. The captain held a rifle in each hand and, to Vanessa's eyes, they looked identical. He returned the private's weapon to him and then showed the dead man's gun to Morgan.

"Looks like our munitions friends have been busy selling on both sides of the fence," Ethan remarked with displeasure.

She had to step closer to hear more clearly, since several of the soldiers and residents were talking quietly to one another as they milled through the halls and garden.

"Entrepreneurs overeager for profit," Morgan said grimly. "It was only a matter of time before they indulged their opportunistic nature."

"And apparently, they also offer lessons on how to handle their firearms," Ethan added and heaved the weapon onto the unmoving body.

"Are you okay, Ness?" a voice said gently into her ear as someone pressed against her from behind.

She turned to look at Cornelis but lost her voice when she saw him.

There were smears of blood on his neck and bare arms, much of it soaking his shirtsleeves, and he was clutching a long, curved butcher knife. It was one from his tool case. He had often used it in preparing and curing meats at the compound, before the captain had ordered all such larger implements removed. Evidently, Cornie had preempted the confiscation and hidden his best blades.

Acid roiled in her stomach at the thought of what he had used the knife for tonight.

"Forget about me." Vanessa placed her hand on his cheek. "What about you?"

His eyes mirrored the blue moonlight with a muted glow. "I'm fine."

"Why did you get involved?" she demanded. "You could have been hurt! Why would you do something so dangerous?"

The young Dutchman tilted his head at her, his normally springy silver curls matted with sweat. "Those may have been people from our own country, but they were here to attack all of us, not just the captain and his horde. Antonie is dead. They got him before he had a chance to defend himself."

"What? But why? Why would they—?"

"You know we've never been entirely popular with the town. But until tonight, they've left us alone." His gaze shot toward the captain. "Now we're a target, too."

Her lungs hitched at the thought of poor Antonie. The retired metalworker had always been sweet and soft-spoken. But his death was not due to Ethan.

"You know this was the constable's doing," she said as he shifted his focus back to her.

"And who provoked the constable?" He posed the question so harshly that she stepped back.

Someone placed a hand on Cornelis's shoulder. He turned to Pieter, whose stained clothes were in a similar state. Pieter was holding one of Cornelis's cleavers, which was caked with gore, and Vanessa's stomach heaved. Cornelis mumbled something to Pieter in Dutch—a trick many of the residents had adopted so the soldiers could not understand them—and then looked down at her.

"Stop trusting these men," he advised her in a tight voice. "They don't care who gets hurt."

He drifted away from her to follow Pieter.

Swallowing, she turned back to the scene in the garden as Mabayoje walked up to the captain and said something in his ear. Ethan paused and responded with a nod. He looked at Morgan and held two fingers out toward him, a gesture that Morgan acknowledged with a solemn nod of his own.

Ethan pushed the hood slowly back from his masked face. His eyes seemed to flicker like green fire beneath the moon's light, which now shone past the clouds.

Vanessa shrank back.

He appeared to loom even larger as his measured movements turned the mounting tension palpable. The captain shoved the constable's prone corpse aside with his boot and walked forward. A hush blanketed the entire compound as all eyes fixed on him.

"How did this happen?" he asked the assemblage of soldiers. His voice seemed to boom through the still night air. "Every one of you men is trained and lethal at what he does. Ever since we got here, we've worked to protect ourselves from any such attack. We've secured every weakness. And now this?"

The rage in his voice sent an icy shiver through her, sharper than the night's biting cold descending on them all.

He jerked forward. "How did this happen!"

Even the most seasoned-looking soldiers flinched.

Angus's prosthetic joints whined and clicked as he took a step and pointed with his gun toward the front of the compound.

"Captain, the only way the bawbags could have got in was through those tunnels." Though the Scotsman's voice was quiet, it carried clearly in the rigid silence. "They were comin' from over that way, but our front defenses were sound, and none o' them were breached. The only other hole these rats could get through would be from below."

The captain motioned for Thomas to come over.

When the Canadian stopped beside him, Ethan said, "Go check the rear tunnel door."

Thomas gave a quick nod, shouldered his rifle, and trotted toward the back gates.

"Collect all the weapons," Morgan called out to the gathered men, his voice rebounding off every wall, "and then remove the bodies to the back field and burn them."

"No!" Ethan barked as several men started forward. "Corporal Montanari!"

Nicolo elbowed his way to the front and stuck his pistol into the back of his waistband.

"Yes, Captain?" the short mechanic asked with a quick salute.

"Pop the seats out of the Boxer," Ethan ordered him. "I want every one of these bastards thrown into the MRAV and hauled down to the village." His gaze swept over all his men. "Dump them inside the town, where they'll be easy to find. Pile the bodies high, so that they never forget the sight. And put this piece of shit"—he kicked the leg of the lifeless constable—"on the top of the stack."

A myriad of "yes, sirs" echoed around the compound. Vanessa shivered again.

As the garden complex began to fill with sound once more—the men tending to the grisly work given them—Thomas bounded in through the back gates. He hurried over to the captain and leaned in to speak to him.

As soon as Thomas was done, Ethan held up a hand to those around him. "Who was watching over the rear entrance to the tunnels?"

The soldiers quieted down as one of them, who had returned to the battlement walls above, gradually raised his hand.

By the way the soldier licked his lips and seemed to pale, the look Ethan gave him must have been deadly.

A movement off to the side down the corridor caught her eye.

Rhetta approached her, wrapping a thick shawl around herself. "Vanessa! Vanessa, liefje, are you all—? God nog aan toe!" the cook exclaimed softly. She stood next to Vanessa and looked around with wide eyes at all the bodies on the garden ground. "Look what these butchers have done to those poor townsmen," she said bitterly. "I heard the terrible noises from my room. But I did not think there was such slaughter!"

Vanessa furrowed her brow. "How did you know that they're from the town?"

Rhetta pulled the shawl tighter around her shoulders. "W-well, where else would they c-come from?" Her eyes looked teary as the older woman turned back to the garden, where many of the bodies had already been lugged across the grass toward the back gates.

Vanessa's brow remained furrowed. *This doesn't feel right. She's hiding something.*

The rumble of an engine approaching broke her concentration. The army's big armored vehicle rolled up beyond the rear gates, which were thrown wide open. The brakes squeaked harshly as Nicolo's assistant Angelo brought the Boxer to a halt and then spun the wheel to begin backing the mammoth carrier toward the compound.

Rhetta's arm nudged against her as the cook made a spastic movement. When Vanessa turned, Rhetta was staring at something in front of her, her mouth a tremulous line.

Vanessa followed her gaze.

The captain stared at the cook from across the grassy space where men moved around him to clear away the corpses. And both his hands curled into fists beside him.

Vanessa's nerves iced over. She looked at the woman who had been like a mother to her.

Oh, Rhetta, no. How could you?

CHAPTER TWENTY-NINE

ETHAN

As soon as Ethan saw the old cook come into view, his vision went dark.

Fucking bitch.

The only way the townsmen could have made it into the heart of the compound through the tunnels was if they had been guided. It had to be someone who had been around for many years and knew the underground passages well enough. Someone who was not happy about his being there. And that person would have unlocked the door from the inside and brought in the army of attackers.

He narrowed his eyes as he fixed them on Rhetta, who stood beside Vanessa.

The woman realized he was looking at her. She dropped her gaze and started to back away. Ethan tightened his fists at his sides, his knuckles popping, and strode forward.

Vanessa, who had thrown an uncertain glance at Rhetta as the woman hurried toward the kitchen, now met his stare as he drew closer. "Ethan—?"

He moved past her, his glare focused on the departing cook.

He followed the woman to the kitchen and shoved the door open as it was closing. It banged back against the wall as he stepped over the threshold. Rhetta jerked her head to look behind her and shuffled deeper into the kitchen, but Ethan did not slow his pace. He nearly had her cornered in the cooking area when Vanessa ran around in front of him and grabbed a handful of his robe at his chest.

"Captain, please, no!"

Anger boiled through him, melting away any mercy she might have begged of him. "Get out of my way."

Vanessa's eyes scanned his frantically. "Rhetta didn't—she wasn't thinking, she wouldn't—Please! She probably didn't know they had guns. She probably only thought they would—"

Her voice faded as she seemed to struggle with what else she could say to convince him. Her eyes began to gleam in the dim light from the single lamp in the room, and she twisted her hand in the folds of his robe. "Ethan, please."

He held her eyes. The desperation welled in every soft feature of her face. Rhetta was all the family she had, the only remaining tie to her parents. And he was about to take that from her. He stood still as his chest squeezed tighter. But then the room seemed to shrink in on him and crush the last of his breath.

No. Not this time.

He seized her wrist and pried her fingers off him. He pushed past her.

Rhetta huddled in the shadows in front of the sink. He drew up to her in a rush and slapped his hands down on the sink's rim on either side of her. He could feel her trembling.

He gritted his teeth and shoved his mouth next to her ear. "You *killed* two of my men tonight. For that, I should fucking gut you right here."

She trembled harder.

"But I want you to suffer." His fingers gripped the metal sink rim. "I know you wish I had never come here. You think I'm an evil son of a bitch who would sooner break both of your goddamn legs than look at you. A man who tortures his victims as he murders them. A monster." Ethan's jaw clenched painfully. "Now I'm going to show you that you're right."

Rhetta made a small whimpering noise in her throat, which only made his hackles rise higher.

But he hesitated.

In some remote part of his mind, he had thought he would feel a gentle hand on his shoulder. A touch full of pleading and tentative defiance. A touch that would make him question himself, as it had that day in the alley. A touch from the only person who had ever stopped him from losing all control and indulging his animal instinct to attack.

He leaned back from Rhetta, whose eyes were squeezed shut as her lips moved in what sounded like a murmured Dutch prayer. He watched her for a moment and then turned his head over his shoulder.

Vanessa's attention was centered on him. One hand covered her mouth, and her chest rose and fell deeply as she supported herself against the table next to her.

Ethan straightened, and his hands fell away from the sink's rim. He stood stiffly, trickles of fire flowing down his limbs as he stared at Rhetta in silence. He turned his back to her. Glaring at the floor, he clenched and unclenched his left fist, the leather of his glove creaking in the quiet.

"You have one hour to drag your lying ass out of my compound." His gut burned as his last ember of disgust smoldered. "And you'd better hide in the deepest fucking hole you can find."

He jerked on the chin of his mask and then strode past Vanessa without looking at her.

CHAPTER THIRTY

VANESSA

Marien and Vanessa stood on either side of the long wooden food-prep table and stared down at the squashed amoeba-shaped cake between them. Marien lifted her head, smoke practically pouring from her ears. Much like the smoke from the oven only a few minutes before.

Vanessa held up her hands. "Don't look at *me*. I had nothing to do with this. There's a reason why they strictly give me water-boiling duty around here."

Ever since Rhetta had been expelled three weeks ago, Marien had volunteered to take over Rhetta's duties. Which also meant that for three weeks, the kitchen had become ground zero for exploding pastries, incinerated pork slavinken, and inedible "mystery" stews.

"How am I supposed to serve this?" Marien threw her arms up with her usual melodramatic flair. "It's the third bad boterkoek this week!"

Fourth. But who's counting?

"Hey, at least you got the Bundt hole right." Vanessa turned the burnt brown cake on its side and wiggled her finger through the middle.

Marien put her fists on her hips. "It's not supposed to have a hole!"

"Oh." Vanessa let the cake flop back down. "Well…maybe it tastes better than it looks."

Marien sighed and pushed her short auburn hair behind an ear. They each broke off a piece and put it in their mouths. They chewed for a few seconds.

And then paused in unison.

Vanessa spat the dense, tangy clump into her hand and ran with Marien to the sink.

"Okay, that is not supposed to have a fish flavor, right?" Vanessa shook the clingy lump off her fingers while Marien wiped at her tongue under the running water.

Vanessa handed her a towel and tried to smile. "Maybe the oven's broken."

Marien squinted. "How can a brick oven be broken?" She finished rubbing the towel on her mouth and looked thoroughly depressed.

Vanessa squeezed her arm and returned to the prep table.

"Onto the midden heap with you," she directed the cake as she raised it on her palm like a lopsided serving tray.

"Wait!" Marien cried and gave her tongue one more swipe with the towel. "I made a list for you. I need you to go to the commissary and get these ingredients for dinner."

She frantically patted the pockets of her apron and then started shuffling mixing bowls around on the countertop. She grabbed a piece of paper and shoved it at Vanessa.

Vanessa pinched the corner and shook off the coating of brown sugar. She peered closer. Most of it was in Dutch. "Uh, Marien, I don't think I can get—"

"You have to, Vanessa!" her friend said with a wild-eyed look and flailed her hands above her head. "I can't do everything!"

"No, no, I don't mind," Vanessa said quickly, "but you know I can't read—"

"I'm not done with that!" Marien suddenly yelled at one of the other kitchen helpers and careened toward the propane stove.

"But it's burned," the girl said as she held up the pan.

"It's called deglazing! I was deglazing!" Marien snatched the pan away, sloshing brown juices onto the floor. "What is wrong with all of you? Do I have to explain everything? I cannot work like this!"

Vanessa stuffed the list in her pocket and tiptoed backward. Time to exit stage left, before someone broke out the straitjacket and wrestled Marien to the ground.

As Vanessa turned with the cake balanced on one hand, she swiped the glass of thick kogel mogel she'd prepared a few minutes ago and rattled the spoon stuck into it. She'd looked up the Polish dessert in an old cookbook she'd found in the pantry, and even she could manage the recipe well enough: eggs and honey beaten together with some vanilla for extra flavor.

As she swept through the dining area, she used the lumpy cake to wave away the light haze of smoke still suspended in the air. She gave a cough as she glanced around.

She had never seen so many people look so listlessly at their lunches as she had since Rhetta was forced to leave. Actually, whenever *any* meal was distributed, an utter lack of enthusiasm came over the face of every diner, due completely to the dishes' dreadful contrast to Rhetta's cuisine.

The kitchen dining room was full of soldiers at this time of the afternoon, as the residents still kept their distance and staggered the timing of their meals. She knew almost all of the men by name now. It was not only from walking among them during mealtime, but also because she had doubled as their volunteer nurse, after several of them were wounded in the attack. She had patched them up, dispensed medicines from the compound's supplies—something Ethan had been good enough to supplement through his new connections—and had checked in on them periodically if they were laid-up in bed.

Now, the soldiers would all greet her while she worked by the vegetable beds or in the orchard. They had even started asking her if they could pick an apple from her trees or take a tomato from one of her greenhouses. And then they would give her a playful salute when she granted them permission to proceed. Thomas had probably spread the word about how to get in her good graces!

But after a week of bearing witness to Marien's crimes against cookery, Vanessa had taken pity on the soldiers. She had put together a basket of assorted fruits that she restocked every day and left it as a permanent fixture on a small table inside the kitchen door. It was likely one of the reasons why so many soldiers had volunteered to help with the repairs to the broken panes of her greenhouses after the attack: sheer gratitude for offering the men safer edible options than what might land on their plates!

Vanessa paused next to one table and set the cup of kogel mogel down with a flourish.

"Here you go, handsome." She winked. "I even sprinkled a little cinnamon on top."

Jakub gaped up at her, his sandy-colored bangs falling back from his forehead. "M–miss Brouwer!" he said as his cheeks turned cherry-red. "Ojej! You made this for—for me?" He pulled the dessert to his chest, like he was going to hug it. "Thank you! Thank you so much!"

Vanessa laughed and bumped her hip against his elbow. "Anything for one of my favorite guys."

At that, his smile went so wide it practically split his face.

As she continued through the eating area, most of the men lifted a hand in greeting. She smiled back at each of them and then met Angus as he stepped through the doorway. He had freed his dusky hair from its long braid so that it fluffed out to the sides in the same untamable way as his beard. So that's why he usually wrestled it into ponytail submission each day!

"Ah, feasgar math, bonnie Vanessa." The Scotsman tipped his woolen cap with the stag-adorned crest badge. "Goin' out fer a wee donder?"

"Uh, sure." She was clueless about what activity she had now ascribed to herself, but it seemed harmless enough. She glanced down at his side. "I see you're taking Kenzie for a walk."

He beamed proudly, a reaction she could always elicit at the mere mention of his beloved broadsword.

"Aye!" His mechanical knee squeaked as he leaned out his hip to pat the Sinclair's basket hilt behind the walkie-talkie on his belt. "She needs to breathe now and again. Thought I would poke at Mabayoje's straw dummies out back."

"Want to use this as a target?" she asked.

He stared down at the baked failure in her hands. "And what's that meant to be?"

"We thought we knew, when it first went into the oven." She jiggled it and sent a shower of crumbs to the floor. "Would you believe me if I told you it was a cake?"

He chuckled. "Nae, I widnae believe that, lassie. But maybe it tastes better than it—"

"Nope." Her tongue still felt laminated with the waxy flavor of raw flour.

"Aw, now, dinnae get yourself in a fankle." Angus smiled and lowered his voice as he nodded toward the back of the kitchen. "At least our Marien didnae poison it like she did the beef stew last night."

Vanessa grimaced. "True, she outdid herself."

Just then, Thomas appeared outside the doorway and started to squeeze his way past Angus.

The young Newfoundlander gave Vanessa a grin. "Whaddya at, treasure?" Then he ruffled Angus's hat against his head as he popped through into the kitchen.

The Scotsman huffed, readjusting his woolen cap. "That Tommy! I've a mind to skelp his head!" But the fondness in his voice was fatherly. "Well, now"—he squinted one eye down at the cake—"best go put that out of its misery."

She gave a firm nod. "We'll all be better for it."

Angus stepped aside and gave her a pat on the shoulder as she passed.

Raphaël was walking briskly along the corridor toward the kitchen, his face puckered up as always, like he was concentrating. He wore his usual wide-brimmed dark-blue beret with the yellow hunting horn insignia on the right side. The entire hat seemed way oversized, flopping comically to the left. But from what he'd told her, it was the traditional headgear of the Chasseurs Alpins—Alpine Hunters—which was some kind of special mountain infantry brigade of the French Army.

Darshan was at his side, somehow managing to move just as swiftly in spite of his sedate manner. The tall Sikh pressed his palms together in front of his chest as he neared, and the sun glinted off the steel bracelet on his right wrist.

"Good afternoon, Soniye." He bowed as he greeted her.

She waved him off bashfully. "Charmer."

Soniye, she'd found out, was the Punjabi word for "beautiful one."

But both soldiers slowed to a stop and stared down at the drooping cake in her hands.

Raphaël—swiping an index finger down each side of his thin mustache—puckered his face even harder and opened his mouth.

"Don't ask," she advised the Frenchman.

Darshan stroked his bushy beard. "Please warn us, Soniye." He glanced into the kitchen. "Is the fruit basket empty today?"

She smiled at the lively twinkle in the Indian soldier's mild expression. The navy-blue color of his carefully wrapped turban made his soft brown eyes seem all the more golden. She liked it better than the saffron-colored pagri he often wore.

"I just refilled it an hour ago," she assured him. "But I think Marien's catching on, so at least try to pretend you're here for the main course." She looked pointedly at Raphaël. "Can't *you* do something about that, Raph? You said your father was a chef. Don't you have some words of culinary advice you can pass on?"

Raphaël shook his head so that his giant beret flapped against his ear. "I am sorry, ma choupette. I do not know that any person can fix such a thing." He nodded toward a group of soldiers sitting inside. "I have even taught many of these tetes de citrouille to cook, but she...she, uh..." He snapped his fingers as his eyes searched the air above his head. At last, he sighed and shrugged. "It is best said: toute nourriture qu'elle touche devient de la merde de chien."

"Okay," Vanessa said, "I'm pretty sure you're saying 'forget it.' "

Raphaël's face finally unpuckered, and he smoothed his mustache with a chuckle.

"Well, good luck with lunch," she told them cheerfully as she backed out of the corridor and into the garden. "Whatever doesn't kill you makes you stronger, right?"

Darshan and Raphaël both paused with raised eyebrows.

Hey, based on Marien's recent history in the kitchen, it was not an unrealistic aphorism.

Vanessa made her way out to the large plastic compost bin in the garden, where Tim was sniffing his way along a line of weeds. He sat up when he saw her and wiggled his nose in her direction. She stepped on the pedal to pop open the bin lid and shook her head at him.

"Trust me, even *you* will never be *this* hungry," she informed the bunny as he swung his crooked ear toward her.

She jettisoned the cake into the open container and gave the confection a salute as the lid dropped closed. Then she pulled Marien's list from her pocket and headed for Commissary #2, where most of the cooking supplies were stored.

"Augurken," Vanessa mumbled. "Augurken, augurken..."

She squinted down at the word on the scrap of paper, as if staring at it harder would somehow magically translate the term. She gave up and folded the list in one hand while she pulled the pencil from her apron pocket and slid it behind her ear as she walked.

Hopefully, all the items Marien wanted—most of

which had been canned or otherwise packaged by Rhetta—were labeled. And more than that, they had better be tagged in both languages. The oats, syrup, and cheese wheels were spelled out in English on the list and were easy enough to identify on their own. But for anything described in Dutch that Marien had insisted be brought to the kitchen, Vanessa might have to take a wild guess. Ten euros said she would end up lugging back an unlabeled tub of shoe polish.

She suppressed a smirk. *Which would be a more palatable ingredient than anything Marien included in today's lunch!*

But at that thought, the dark cloud that had been floating at the fringes of her brain for the last three weeks began to form over her thoughts once more.

Where are you, Rhetta? I miss you.

The only place the cook could have traveled to easily was Achterwaartsstad. Her younger brother lived in The Hague, but Rhetta would not have wanted to impose, no matter the circumstances. Vanessa had searched for her every time she had gone to buy goods for the kitchen. Thomas—who had been assigned by the captain to escort her on her trips to town—encouraged the investigation, probably because Rhetta might have a toothsome handout they could sneak back to the compound with them. On her first "captain-sanctioned" foray into Achterwaartsstad, she had visited Cornelis's parents, to let them know that their son was all right. Cornie's safety was something that must have been worrying them sick, after suffering no news since the attack. But when she told them about Rhetta, Mr. and Mrs. Meijer promised to stay on the lookout for any sign of the cook.

It still gave her chills to remember the violent blaze in Ethan's eyes when he'd pushed past her in the kitchen. Like he was about to get blood on his hands. So Vanessa had not interfered with the banishment, as things could have gone far worse. She'd only dejectedly helped Rhetta pack.

She rounded the hallway corner and let out a squeak as she crashed into a solid wall of camouflage.

Mabayoje caught her by the elbows as her vision reeled for a second. He pushed her gently back, his jaw never pausing as he leisurely chewed his gum. She looked up between the tall Nigerian lieutenant and Frank, where they stood together at the intersection. They had evidently been in the middle of a conversation.

"Good afternoon, Ododo Mi," Mabayoje greeted her with a smile as he released her.

He'd been calling her that for a while now, but she only recently got up the courage to ask what it meant: My Flower. At least it was better than Garden Girl, which Edvard the Swede still insisted upon.

"Hi, Lieutenant."

Mabayoje nodded his head toward Frank. "Our apologies. We did not mean to be in your way."

Vanessa gave a quick laugh. "Well, you guys can't help it. You take up a lot of space."

Frank stood with his arms folded, the faint light glinting off his smoothly shaved head. But he let his thick black mustache twitch up at the corner in what she had come to recognize as a smile. He was the only other who matched Mabayoje in height, but the giant Russian sergeant practically filled the entrance to the hallway all by himself.

"I didn't mean to interrupt," she said, tugging the grocery list between her hands.

Mabayoje shook his head as he blew a big pink bubble and popped it. "I cannot imagine a more pleasant distraction than you. How are you today?" He held up a finger as if to correct himself. "Bawo ni?"

Vanessa paused and squinted one eye as she dug back in her memory from the past week. What was the response he had taught her in Yoruba?

She looked at him hesitantly. "Daadaa ni, e se-e."

"Aaah!" Mabayoje smiled widely and set his hands on his waist. "I am impressed at how well you've picked up my brief lessons!"

Relieved, Vanessa smiled in return. "E se-e o, Lieutenant, but I think you're being too nice. I can't even speak my own Dutch language right!"

Mabayoje let out an explosive laugh, grinning so that the three long vertical scars on each cheek wrinkled. When she'd once asked if he got those in battle, he'd told her they were tribal marks—called "ila"—from when he was a boy, to represent his father's clan. But because such marks were cut into the faces of infants, they had long ago been outlawed in his state in Nigeria.

His father, whose cheeks also bore such scars, had regretted not being able to give the same to his son. But young Mabayoje had been determined to honor his family's traditions and so had done it to himself in secret, using the ceremonial dagger his grandfather kept mounted on the wall. Mabayoje's parents had come home to find their seven-year-old son in the kitchen, rubbing his wounds with handfuls of pungent herbs that his mother often used when he would scrape a knee or elbow.

"What are you in pursuit of this afternoon, with such a serious look on your face?" Mabayoje inquired mildly in that accent so reminiscent of Morgan's.

Vanessa unfolded the list. "A bag of linzen, a jar of selderijzout, and five sticks of kaneel." She dropped her shoulders. "In other words, I have no idea."

He chuckled, grinding his gum. "You are a clever girl. I have no doubt you'll get what you're after."

Someone bumped her from behind, making her jump. When she turned to look, Morgan was gazing down at her as he stood close against her. He gave her the barest smile, which made her start to sink back into his warm, solid chest.

"I beg your pardon." He placed his hands on each of her shoulders and gently shifted her aside. "Blind corners appear to be a favorite feature of Fort Van Doorn's eccentric architect." His eyes captured hers for a second longer before he turned to Mabayoje. "Lieutenant, might I have a word?"

Mabayoje nodded. "Of course." He looked at Vanessa and tapped a finger against the six-pointed silver star insignia on one of his massive shoulders, right above the red dragon and gold lion blue patch on his sleeve. "Excuse me, but duty calls." Before he stepped forward to follow Morgan, though, he set his broad palm on top of her head. "Arina koore! That is: good luck on your quest, Ododo Mi." He gave her an affectionate pat and then walked away to join Morgan farther down the hallway.

She smiled bashfully up at Frank and held her list toward him. "I don't suppose you've picked up any Dutch since you've been here?"

He shook his head, the other side of his heavy mustache lifting so that his smile was almost discernible, even to someone who did not know him. Frank's walkie-talkie crackled to life, and he grabbed it off his belt. He spoke into the unit and released the button so that Angus's voice came through. But she could not for the life of her make out what he was saying. It was as if his Scottish burr suddenly congealed beyond the semblance of human speech whenever he and Frank spoke exclusively to one another. And Thomas had been right: lots and lots of *r* rolling going on between those two. She thought back to what Angus had told her the other day, when she had asked him about the Russian.

"Frank can't be his real name, right?"

Angus had shaken his head. "Nae, it's some godforsaken strange mince. He penned it fer me once on paper, in a mess o' capital letters and symbols, but I couldnae make head nor tail of them. So I made him Frank."

"You didn't give him a Scottish name?" she had ribbed him.

Angus had stared at her, in that likable cartoonish way of his. "Do ye think he looks like a Scot?"

"Not in the least," she had agreed with a giggle.

Vanessa glanced over to where Morgan and Mabayoje were still deep in discussion, their faces businesslike. The difference in stature between the two was not enough to be farcical, but Morgan would have had to work a little harder to throw a punch, if he'd needed to.

She smiled to herself. She always had to tilt her face up to Ethan when she stood near him. And the several centimeters in disparity suited her just fine. Because although the captain towered over her, he was still comfortably within kissing range. And Morgan—only a few centimeters shorter than Ethan—was even more so. Of course, in order to make it a fair comparison, she'd need to be pressed between the two of them. Maybe Ethan in front, Morgan in back. Then, after a few minutes of mutual over-the-clothes exploration, she'd only have to turn around for them to switch places.

Morgan looked at her then.

She wiped the dreamy smile off her face and quickly stared down at her list. Luckily, Frank finished up his indecipherable conversation with Angus so she could shake herself out of it.

"So tell me," she said as he clipped the walkie-talkie back onto his belt, "what is your actual given name? I'd like to call you by the real thing."

He crossed his arms again and bent his head forward to fix her in a solemn gaze.

"Are you sure you want to know?" he asked in his deep, rumbling voice.

"Lay it on me."

And then he said something that she could not have parroted back if her life depended on it. She must have been staring at him vacuously by the way he gave a small shake of his head. He reached toward her and pulled the pencil from behind her ear. He tugged the list out of her hands and turned it over to write on it against his palm. He handed it back to her when he was done.

She looked down at what he had printed:
Иннокентий

Um, okay.

"Wow, that's a…" She turned the paper upside down to make sure she hadn't held it wrong. "A very nice name."

He slid the pencil back behind her ear before resting his big hands on his waist. "It means 'innocent,' in my homeland."

"And are you?"

"Rarely."

She laughed. "I think I'll stick to Frank." But she quickly added, "Only because I'm used to it."

Again, Frank's mustache twitched. "I am all right with that, lapushka."

"Sergeant, you're with us," Morgan called out to Frank.

The Russian acknowledged him with an upward nod. He gave Vanessa a gentle pinch on the cheek and started away. But then Morgan paused as the other two were moving past him, and he said something to which they both responded with a nod and kept going. Morgan walked toward her, and he seemed hesitant as he clasped his hands behind him and stopped before her.

He cleared his throat. "I, ah, was wondering if you would care to accompany me for another stroll this evening?"

"Tonight? I thought you were on watch tonight."

"I have time in advance." At that, he scratched his beard with a finger and gave her a sideways glance. "Rather, I shall make time, if you are amenable."

"Oh! Well then...I'd like that." She reached out and tugged on the hem of his maroon vest. "This is kind of becoming our thing now, isn't it?"

He lifted his eyebrows slightly but then exhaled a short breath through his nose with a smile. "Yes, quite."

Morgan always sensed with uncanny accuracy when her cabin fever level crept too high, giving her a chance to escape the sometimes claustrophobic walls of the compound. But there was something different about his invitations lately. They'd become more informal, more...intimate. As she and he would make their way through the shadows at the edge of the back field, he'd talk about his hometown, she'd talk about her childhood. And whenever they were alone like that, his voice held the type of tone usually reserved for lovers late at night: quiet and relaxed, like the pillow-talk that followed a vigorous coupling.

She absently worked the paper between her hands as she stared off.

I wonder if that's how he really sounds, afterward.

"I look forward to our nightly ritual, then," Morgan said.

She jumped, ripping the list in half. "What? Oh! Yes." She crumpled the two pieces in her fists and held them behind her. "M-me too."

With an amused smile, Morgan placed his arms at his sides and gave her a modest bow. "M'lady."

A thrill zipped up her spine. The gesture came so naturally to him, like a knight taking leave of his damsel. Her voice was barely audible. "Bye."

Morgan smiled again as he backed away and then turned to follow Frank and Mabayoje.

Taking a deep breath, she spun around and tried to piece the two sides of the list together. But as the scribbled Dutch words became even more smudged and unreadable, she dropped her arms and stopped in the middle of the hallway.

"I give up," she grumbled and crammed the pieces into both apron pockets. "Marien gets whatever I grab."

She looked around. She wasn't anywhere near Commissary #2. Somehow, she'd ended up at the intersection leading to the captain's quarters. There was Morgan's sentry desk down at the end, right outside Ethan's door. Lately, whenever the captain was in his room, Morgan could always be found on duty, sticking to Ethan like his shadow. The Englishman evidently was unwilling to take any chances with his friend's life, in light of the attack. But maybe Ethan was in there by himself anyway, making plans for a counterattack.

She swallowed. It had taken her all of these weeks after the raid to stop feeling queasy at the memory. She'd had to help the next day when the residents were cleaning the gore off the stone walls and corridor floors. She had hosed down the plants in the vegetable patches, the acrid smell of blood making her gag. And she could not stop picturing the constable's leering face when Thomas's bullet had exploded through his skull. And the way the garden—*her* garden—had looked under the glare of the moonlight...all the bodies twisted and sprawled…the captain's men clutching arms that dripped red or limping from leg wounds…that horrible head that had rolled through the grass and stared up at her…

And yet the soldiers had all treated it with a sober familiarity that made her shudder. *How do you just get used to something like that? What kind of life makes you that way?*

She stared at the captain's door and slowly started down the hallway toward it. Well, this was not the kind of life the residents had made for themselves. And if there was more danger on the way, then they deserved to know about it. *She* deserved to know.

CHAPTER THIRTY-ONE

VANESSA

She floated to a stop in front of the captain's door. She knocked. Silence. She pushed down on the handle, and the door swung inward with a long groan.

Empty.

If he'd left it unlocked, then he must have planned to be back soon.

She entered carefully and wandered through the bands of weak sunlight flickering in around the cherrywood armoire in front of the window. She reached for the wardrobe handles, but then pulled back. Ethan wouldn't be too thrilled if he knew she was poking around in his stuff. She chewed her bottom lip. But then again, it didn't bother him one bit to charge into *her* personal space whenever he felt like it.

She threw open the old wardrobe doors. Swaying on their hangers were two long-sleeved black shirts. On the shelf below that, four black undershirts and another pair of black jeans.

She quirked her mouth. *Well, that certainly makes his decisions easier in the mornings!*

She pushed the doors closed and dawdled across the creaky warped floorboards to hover by his canopied bed. The cream-colored sheets were pulled tightly across the mattress, every corner flawlessly tucked and the wool blanket folded into a square against the footboard. She ran a hand over his pillow, which was centered precisely between the bedposts of the headboard, and created a wave of wrinkles upon the neat surface. She bent down and pressed her face deep into it and breathed in. Musky. Sexy.

It would be nice to wake up to that scent in the morning.

She drew back and brushed both hands across the pillow to smooth it out.

And then, of course, his desk: the infamous focal point for all his captain-y studies and strategies. She opened the drawers on the right, but each of them was empty. She moved to the other side, and within the lower left drawer a bottle rolled forward, sloshing its contents noisily. She picked it up and turned the label to read it: Old Forester Kentucky Straight Bourbon Whisky, 100 Proof.

She unscrewed the cap and took a sniff. *Not bad. Kind of sweet, like boozy fruit.*

She'd never had bourbon before. Jenever had been the only liquor she'd ever really tried. She screwed the cap back on and returned the bottle to its place. The middle drawer had only one item in it. She pinched the edge of the large black cloth and held it up. The light from the window showed through the three holes cut crudely into the cloth, in the exact places for two eyes and a mouth.

So he does have a spare. She wrinkled her nose. *And it's just as ridiculous as his other one.*

She shook her head and dropped it back where it was. But as soon as she opened the top drawer, two faces popped out and gazed up at her. She retrieved the old photo—probably printed from someone's mobile phone long ago—and examined the smiling slender woman, whose fawn-colored hair bounced freely about her shoulders, the sunny day highlighting its coppery tint. She was standing beside what looked like an ancient red-brick train station, like from the nostalgic paintings by American artists in some of Vanessa's childhood magazines. A young brown-haired boy—maybe seven or eight years old— stood on his tiptoes in front of the woman and held both her hands out to the sides with a wide grin.

But there was another picture in the drawer, lying facedown. She pulled it out. Written at the top was: *On leave in Austria.* She turned it over. And sucked in a breath.

Morgan stood next to another man in front of a tall, narrow clock tower of some kind, which was painted powder-blue and white with all sorts of statues, ornate curvy stone accents, and a cross at the very top. Morgan—sporting only a mustache instead of his full goatee—was in a camouflage jacket wearing a beige beret with a cap badge on the front that looked like a sword pointing down with…wings? Vanessa held the picture closer and squinted. Or were those flames? There was some kind of banner across it, but she couldn't make out the words.

He was smiling with his hands on his waist, while the man next to him—also dressed in a camo jacket, but with a patch in the center of his chest displaying two vertical bars—had one arm draped around Morgan's neck. The unknown man had short-cut hair the color of rich dark tobacco and was leaning on Morgan with a cocky grin. But the eyes of the stranger gave him away instantly: bright, piercing green.

Wow! So this was what Ethan looked like in real life.

Used to look like. Otherwise, why would he hide what a hunk he is?

She traced their faces with her finger. They probably had no trouble getting the ladies to queue up, back in the day. Being caught between those two gorgeous sets of eyes at the same time would make a girl need a defibrillator. Talk about a scrumptious man sandwich! After one last lingering inspection of the photo, she placed it with the other one and closed the drawer.

She bent toward the pile of papers stacked on the left side of the desk and pulled the top sheets off. They contained the complete list of residents she'd made for Ethan. She sorted through the pages. Some names—Marien, Steffen, and so on—had check marks beside them, while some—like Pieter and Cornelis—had question marks. But others had a thick line drawn straight through them. The caretaker was one of those. And so was Rhetta.

A leaden weight seemed to press down on her chest. Over the past weeks, the absence of some of the other residents had become more conspicuous, as well. They had been the obnoxious, lazy, or belligerent ones. At least, that's how she had categorized them in the list. She'd done it flippantly, with hardly more thought than she gave to pulling a bothersome weed from her flower beds.

Rhetta's voice echoed faintly through her mind: *If something happens…it is because you let him involve you…The captain himself will show you who he is…Hij gaat door de mand vallen…*

As the proverb said, the truth of Ethan's actions would be found out. And Vanessa would have played a part in it.

She tasted a sour tang at the back of her tongue, and she dropped the pages onto the pile. But as she stepped away from the desk, her eyes fell on the corner of a document sticking out from the stack. She clamped it between her thumb and index finger and slid it out carefully, making the tower of papers shift precariously toward her. She flattened it out on the desk with her palms. It was a map, and it covered the whole of Europe. There were several places circled in pencil. But all of those were far away from the Netherlands.

His exit plan.

The weight on her chest made her breathing even more shallow. He was leaving. It hadn't seemed real, hadn't been incarnated until that moment. But there it was, spread across a stained stretch of parchment where so many bruise-colored countries lay like ragged scraps grafted onto a sickly skin. Unmasked and ugly, like a truth only whispered about but finally revealed. He was probably getting ready to pull out before anything else happened to the compound. And he was probably going to do it soon.

She blinked hard, her nostrils stinging. She rubbed her fingertips back and forth along the edges of the document as she leaned over it. Also marring the map were several red dotted lines—hand-drawn and cutting across the countries like bloody incisions, each of them dated different months and years. Like he'd been keeping track of something. Or someone.

His enemies.

But there were no such trails leading anywhere near the Netherlands. She took a deep breath and scratched her nails against the honey-hued wood.

This isn't right. No one's coming for him. They would have been here by now, wouldn't they? He's running away for no reason. She tapped all her nails against the desk for a few seconds. *Someone needs to make him see that.*

She grabbed the map and started folding it as she pushed away and marched across the room. She pulled the door shut behind her and jammed the map into her pocket as her footsteps swished through the hallway.

CHAPTER THIRTY-TWO

ETHAN

Ethan drummed his fingers on the table and turned his head over his shoulder to glare into the cooking area again. *What the fuck takes so long about slopping food onto a mess tray?*

He pushed back his hood and drummed his fingers harder, sending ripples across the surface of the water in the glass beside him. Why was he even bothering? He had a lot of work to get back to, in his office. The lists of countries and off-the-grid places where he'd made allies, the recon reports he'd collected along the way, the records of suspected hideouts of the Ukes hunting him—they all needed to be examined in detail. No single direction was presenting itself yet as the ideal choice for evasion, but there was one certainty: he needed to leave North Holland, whatever the consequence. This was no longer a sanctuary; it was a threat to their survival. The men were starting to relax again, letting the bucolic ambience of the old fort lure them, domesticate them, which could only be a reflection on his overly lenient leadership. And he would not condemn them all to death because he, too, had grown gullible.

The kitchen buzzed with the mumbling of his soldiers. The men chatted and ribbed each other as they downed a quick meal prior to their respective shifts. Thankfully, all of them merely saluted him on their way past and did not try to engage him in their usual lighthearted banter. He was in no mood for it. There came the slam of metal against stone, and he looked up.

Vanessa stood in the doorway, her back turned to him, and she was grunting as she yanked on the bent handle of a small wagon.

Ethan stopped drumming his fingers. *Fan-fucking-tastic. I thought she was off this afternoon.*

Her skirt swayed across her thighs as she spread her feet and waggled the wagon handle up and down, making her kitchen apron flap against her knees. She did have longer garments for the chillier days, as he'd seen, so the airy knee-length skirt she wore was obviously deliberate. Which also meant it had his full attention. She gave one more heave, and the little blue trailer hopped the threshold and rolled forward as she backed into the dining area. But when a paper-wrapped package slid off the mountain of objects she was hauling, she dropped the handle with a clang and went to pick it up.

As she bent over—even though it took a concerted effort for him to do it—Ethan averted his gaze. But at the crowded table next to him, all the soldiers' heads snapped up. They stopped talking as they nudged each other and nodded toward her. Ethan rocked forward onto both forearms and narrowed his eyes at them. Immediately, the men's smiles faded. They bowed their heads and began picking at their plates.

"Kudos for your bravery." Vanessa stopped beside his table and put a hand on her hip. "This is Mystery Meatloaf day. Heavy on the *mystery*."

Ethan rose from his seat and tugged on the chin of his mask. "I'll take mine to go."

"Nonsense!" She twisted around to grab a jar of pickled beets that started to topple from the wagon's pile. "You'll get indigestion if you don't sit down and relax."

Relax? Every meal has given me five kinds of heartburn so far.

Ethan settled back onto the bench and pushed the

shoulders of his sleeveless robe closer to his neck. "Fine, but I don't have much time."

"Yes, I know: busy, busy." She rolled her eyes and waved the jar in the air. "I'll fix you a plate, and you can be on your way soon."

She jammed the beets back into the heap and jerked on the wagon. He turned his head to watch as a cardboard canister tipped over and poured a thick line of what looked like salt along the floor behind her.

He stared at his hands on the table. He'd heard she was looking for him earlier, but it was probably to start nagging him about Rhetta. She'd brought up the topic only once before, but he knew she couldn't stand to keep quiet much longer. She wouldn't back down whenever she wanted something. His temple twinged as Vanessa's words whispered through his head:

Rhetta's the closest I have to family anymore…

And he'd sent that family away. He'd punished someone for defending their home.

Ethan leaned forward and pressed his fingers to either side of the mask to massage his temples.

No. He'd punished someone for their actions, because it had cost three people their lives, one of them a resident. He was in the right. Whether the old cook had known what she was doing or not, she had endangered *everyone* by letting in those armed townsmen to perpetrate their attack on his soldiers. All he'd done was eliminate a weak link.

And made Vanessa feel like an orphan again.

He winced and rolled his shoulders.

"What *is* all this?" a girl's voice cried from the back of the kitchen. "Rice crackers…rubber bands…cloves? And what am I supposed to do with a pound of licorice, Vanessa? How can you think drop is the same as melasse?"

Ethan looked over his shoulder.

The acting head cook, Marien, was practically jumping up and down as she pointed at the wagon. Vanessa, meanwhile, was dumping vegetables onto a plate and—by the look on her face—was also dishing out her usual sarcasm. Ethan shook his head and knocked his knuckles distractedly on the table. After another minute, a platter was dropped in front of him so that soggy bits of food splattered onto the cuff of his shirtsleeve.

"Some people just don't know how to show a little gratitude," Vanessa said as she stepped over the bench and sat next to him. "How am I supposed to remember what poedersuiker is?"

"*This* is meatloaf?" he asked as he stared down at the misshapen brown slice.

Vanessa shrugged. "An avant-garde interpretation."

"Terrific."

"If you're looking for an alternative, vegetarians don't stand a chance around here either." She fixed him in a serious gaze. "Have you seen what Marien does to a turnip? It's immoral."

He sighed and picked up his fork. "I'll live."

"Is that so?" She leaned against him to poke at a mound of peas on the dish. "Let's see how confident you are after you taste the secret sauce."

He tried to inch away from her when she pressed her thigh along his. *Damn it, if she keeps doing that, next time I'm going to just grab whatever she puts against me.*

She shifted closer, and her breast rubbed his arm. He gripped his fork until his fingers cramped.

But before he could dig his utensil into the meal, she caught his wrist and used his napkin to wipe off the stray bits of food from his sleeve. "Honestly, I'm afraid we're just one bad quiche away from a riot breaking out." She dropped the napkin in front of her. "Nobody's happy about what the servers have been slinging from the kitchen. We tell people it's 'food,' but even *we* can't keep a straight face." Her voice turned hesitant as she ran a fingertip along the table's edge. "Of course, there is a way to fix that."

Here it comes.

"If you could just send someone to find wherever Rhetta—"

"Not a chance in hell." Ethan stabbed his fork into the burned crust of the "meatloaf."

Vanessa sat up. "But you can't blame her for—for just wanting things to return to the way they were. For just wanting her home back. She didn't truly know what those men had in mind, I'm sure of it! They probably told her they were only going to catch you off guard and scare you out. Overwhelm you with numbers—"

Ethan looked at her sharply. "I lost two good soldiers. Two men who were under my protection. They gave the last full measure, not for a battle we'd chosen, but for a spineless betrayal. They died because she was selfish." He swept up the water glass and took a tight sip before setting it down hard. "And because I couldn't see it coming."

She fell quiet. Then her hand appeared near his as she brushed a smashed pea off the table. "No one can change what happened," she said. "You shouldn't blame yourself for your men's deaths any more than you should blame Rhetta for just trying to protect her home. She's human. We all are. Our decisions don't always turn out the way we thought they would. But you have to see things through other people's eyes for a change." Her voice had softened to a murmur. "Give people a second chance, even if you think they were wrong. It's the least you can do for *yourself*, too."

When he turned his head, she was gazing up at him. The green of her eyes deepened to an even darker emerald as the sunlight coming through the kitchen's small glassless windows retreated.

He clenched his jaw and looked away. "Her punishment stands. Don't bring it up again." He stirred the mushy red cabbage on his plate, but had zero interest in trying it.

"I suppose it doesn't really matter," she finally said in a small voice. "You're planning to leave soon, anyway."

He glanced at her and then down at her hand. She had slipped it into her skirt pocket and was working her fingers around something hidden inside it.

"Why do you say that?" he asked.

Her hand moved faster in her pocket, and she shrugged. "Just a guess." She fidgeted a few seconds longer and then pulled her hand out and took a breath. "Look, I know some of the residents and your guys have butted heads, and you want to stay on the move and all that, but how do you know the next place won't be worse? At least if you stay here, it's the devil you know, right? Or the…crappy deviled eggs you know." She flicked her finger against the rubbery white egg half on his dish and sent it seesawing.

"No dice." Ethan stopped the egg with a jab of his fork. "We stay here, we risk everything."

Her voice was faint. "What does that mean?"

He wrapped his hand around his glass and watched the condensation trickle onto his glove. *That we'll start to feel…normal again.*

"You wouldn't understand," he said before he took a slow swallow of water.

"Of course not," she mumbled as she sat forward and propped her cheek on the palm of her hand. "You won't give me the chance."

He ignored her and scraped at the brown hunk on his plate until he managed to chip off a piece. Her eyes followed his movements as he finally got up the courage to lift the food to his mouth.

"So how did you come up with that contraption, anyway?" she asked.

"What are you talking about?" he said around his mouthful and then frowned. He prodded the food with his tongue. Did he just bite on something…bony?

"The mask." She half closed her eyes at him as she looked over it. "It's so makeshift." She reached out and tugged on it under his chin, making him swat her hand away. "I mean, it's basically a giant handkerchief you've wrapped around your noggin. Couldn't you find something better than a big napkin? Like maybe a ski mask?"

He forced himself to swallow the dry clump as a flush made its way up his neck under the mask. "This works fine."

"Don't you want ear holes?" She pushed a fingertip against the cloth above his earlobe. "I can't imagine it's very inspiring to your men, when you have to hold a big metal horn to the side of your head and yell, 'What's that you say, sonny?'"

"Jesus Christ, if only I *were* deaf right now," he muttered.

"Personally, I think it could use some serious modifications."

"I'll be sure to consult with you on the upgrade."

He speared a small turnip half with his fork but then shook it back off. Probably best to heed her warning about Marien's way with root vegetables. Vanessa shifted her chin onto the heel of her hand and gazed at him as he tried for a piece of broccoli instead. He raised the fork to his mouth.

"Does food ever get stuck in there or dribble down the front?" she went on loudly. "Because that would get annoying."

He slammed down his hand holding the fork and nearly tipped his plate over. She stared innocently at him, her head tilted on her palm.

"Annoying?" he grated. "You want *annoying*?"

"Oh, come on, Captain Crumb-Catcher. That druid dress alone is a morsel magnet. I'm surprised you don't feed the birds every time you step outside."

He pushed his words through gritted teeth. "Go ahead. Keep that mouth open and see where it gets you."

That mouth of yours loves being open…I may have to find something to put in it…

He gripped his fork tighter when his body automatically reacted beneath the table at the memory of that warning given long ago, on one of their first mornings together. He raised the hood of his robe back up and began randomly stabbing the food across his plate.

"Okay, that's it," she said as she stood. "I can't watch you torture yourself any longer."

Ethan missed the plate when she scooped up his lunch, inadvertently driving his fork into the tabletop. She stepped over the bench.

"You need to eat," she told him. "And I need some

help." She tossed his plate onto the table nearby and startled a couple of his men who were timidly pushing the food around on their dishes. "Come with me, Captain." She took off her apron and flung it down on the bench. "That's an order."

CHAPTER THIRTY-THREE

ETHAN

Ethan followed Vanessa through the garden as she sashayed along in front of him.

Stop staring at her ass.

He forced his gaze away and smoothed the mask at his neck. She bounded through the nearest gap in the orchard wall.

"Why am I out here?" he asked as she spun around to face him.

"I told you"—she disappeared as she ducked behind the wall and then popped back up with her wicker basket on one arm—"I need help, and you need lunch. If you help me harvest, I'll give you a treat, the best thing in my garden."

He stopped short. "Now I have to sing for my supper?"

At that, she smiled brightly. "Why not? I hear that's something the Welsh are also good at."

He sighed and pushed back his hood. "I'll give you five minutes," he said as he rounded the wall and followed her. "Then I have to get to the armory. Angus reported some missing guns."

"That sounds serious."

"It is."

She paused beneath a mature-looking tree and

stretched toward a branch to pluck one of its heavy red fruits. His gaze clung magnetically to the additional centimeters of leg she exposed by the action.

"How many guns are missing?" she asked as she moved to swipe at another apple high above her.

He pried his attention away from her fluttering skirt hem. "Enough to be a problem. Have you noticed anything unusual?"

"You mean outside of a bunch of foreign soldiers taking over an eighteenth-century fort in the middle of nowhere?" She gave him a teasing look over her shoulder. "Nope."

Smart-ass.

She hopped on the balls of her feet and made another grab for the same apple, just out of reach.

Time to start singing, or this could take all day.

He jerked on the bottoms of his gloves and walked up behind her, where he reached out and pulled the apple off its twig. She turned as he held it between them, and a tentative smile started upon her lips.

"My hero." Her fingers brushed slowly across his glove as she took the apple from him. "Thank you, Ethan."

There it was again. That different sound to his name, when she said it.

She continued to meet his gaze while she nestled the apple against the others in the basket. He looked closer, drawn by the way the sunlight glimmered within those green eyes, which were rich and deep like the reflective curves of a perfume bottle. He nudged himself and started to step back. But she had already slipped away to find another branch.

"In any case, regarding your guns..." She glanced at him. "Maybe if you were a little nicer to people around here, no one would be trying to steal from you."

He smoothed the mask at his neck as she added another apple to the assortment. "Then you know something."

She let out a puff of breath, which scattered the lock of hair that had fallen into her face. "I didn't say that. I said be nice."

He frowned. "I am nice."

She rolled her eyes. "Whatever you say, Captain Cranky."

"Captain Cr—" He stood taller and folded his arms. "I'm glad you take me so seriously."

She shrugged one shoulder. "*You* take yourself *too* seriously. You should lighten up."

"And I'll bet you have an opinion on how I should do that."

"Of course." She picked a lower-hanging apple near her head. "Show me 'Little Ethan.' "

He glanced down at himself involuntarily. "Excuse me?"

"I want to know all about him." She backed up and leaned against the tree. "You don't have to hide anything."

He pulled down on the front of his robe awkwardly. "I'm not hiding anything."

"Then prove it." She tossed the apple in the air and caught it. "Open up."

"Open—?"

"Where was Little Ethan born?"

Okay, so that's where this is headed.

"You've never heard of it." He ripped off a leaf near his head that kept flapping against him, which immediately drew a frown from Vanessa. "I thought I was here to help, not be interrogated."

She tossed the apple in the air again. "And I thought you were a man of your word."

"What does that have to do with—?" He squinted and refolded his arms. "I should never have proposed that damn arm-wrestling match."

She shrugged her other shoulder. "I won, fair and square."

Hardly fair.

He tilted his head back for a moment, let out a slow breath, and then straightened again. "Fine, let's get this over with." He gave the chin of his mask a tug. "Born in

Tredegar, in Wales. Lived there till I was eight."

"And then you moved to…?"

He twisted off an apple to his left. "Another place you've never heard of." He pitched it into her basket from half a meter away. "Tamaqua, Pennsylvania. In an old coal mining region of the northeastern United States. A town stuck in the middle of a bunch of coal patches."

She had been flipping her apple in the air as he talked but now paused with a blank look.

He hung his hand from a bough next to his head. "Patches were small villages built by the mining companies for their workers. Groups of cheap housing sprang up all over that area in the eighteen hundreds. Many of my mother's ancestors originally settled that part of PA. We had roots there."

Vanessa tossed her apple in the air once more. But when she caught it this time, she turned it carefully in her hand as her voice grew quiet. "Your dad moved there with you?

A painful spark—still fresh after all these years—sizzled up his spine. But he kept his voice even. "Yes."

"How did a Ukrainian Cossack and a Welsh girl ever get together in the first place?"

"How the hell did you—?" He stopped and stared harder at her. "Morgan."

She bit her lip and turned the apple in her hand. "He didn't say much."

"He said enough. And he knows better."

"To be fair, he was probably on his second beer when he told me."

Ethan shook his head. "He always was a fucking lightweight."

"Well, what's wrong with telling me yourself?"

"Because it doesn't matter." His back went rigid, and he let go of the branch. "My father took off years ago, before my mom passed."

"Where did he—?"

"Don't know and don't care."

Vanessa's eyes darted away. She wisely sensed the

warning in his voice.

"Is Pennsylvania where the asparagus grew wild?" she asked, staring at the apple stem as she flicked it with her fingertip. "That's where you got the taste for it, right?"

"Other kids wouldn't touch it. But my mom knew her way around a block of butter."

His muscles relaxed at the memory of his mother's slight frame hovering near the stove. She would always hum to herself while she cooked. But he could barely remember the words to any of those old Welsh melodies she had taught him as a boy. His stomach twisted. Before he'd joined the army to get the hell away from his father, he should have asked her to record some of those songs. The sound of her gentle voice would have been a comfort during the long nights of his deployments.

"Tamaqua." Vanessa rested her apple in the center of the basket. "That's an interesting name for a town."

"It's a Native American word."

"Meaning?"

He quirked his mouth. "Land of the Beaver."

She laughed. "I bet that was the punch line of every juvenile joke."

"You have no idea."

She threw him a shy smile as she fingered the scooped neckline of her gauzy white shirt, the purity of which only drew more attention to those sparkling eyes.

He cleared his throat and bent down a branch on his left to wrest another apple from it. "We used to have a few orchards in the area." He glanced around as he rolled the fruit against his palm. "The trees never looked as healthy as these, though. You do decent work."

She pushed herself off the trunk and approached him. "I told you I have a tender touch." She took the apple from his hand to drop it in her basket. Then she curled her fingers around a branch swaying gently beside her and stroked it. "I've taught myself a lot about these trees," she said in a musing voice. "It was a shame to see how neglected they were, once many of the original residents moved out in 2056. Someone had to care for them. And now I know them intimately." She leaned her head and stroked the thick bough again, spreading her fingers to trail them over its knobs and ridges. "I notice how the smell of the leaves changes from month to month in the summer. I can tell by the feel of the bark if they're getting enough water or if they've had too much." She rotated her palm gently around the branch. "I know what they need." She nodded to either side of her, to indicate their surroundings. "I know what all of them need."

He tore his eyes from her to glance around the garden, where various vegetable beds thrived in the midst of late fall, and flowers still burst with color as the hazy sunshine played across the panes of the greenhouses beyond. This was a fitting place for her: a little patch of paradise where she—a creature of light and warmth—could bring it life. Here, where she shone her brightest, it seemed no darkness could intrude.

Lowering his shoulders, he pulled his hood up and retreated far back into it.

She looked down to rearrange the fruit in her basket. "Have you ever tried to grow anything?"

"I'm a carnivore," he said gruffly. "I don't nurture. I hunt."

She put a fist on her hip. "Why do you have to make everything about being at the top of the food chain?"

"Because it's kept me alive."

She shifted her basket to the other arm. "There are more important things than just breathing."

"Not many."

He eyed her legs as she walked past him. *But I can think of one very good thing.*

"Well then, Mr. King of the Jungle," she said in an airy voice as she focused her attention on her Belle de Boskoop tree, "what do you like to hunt?"

"Anything I've never chased before."

She flipped her hair behind each shoulder with a hand. "Do you at least eat what you catch?"

He let his gaze travel the length of her. "Every bite."

She stared at him, and the rims of her ears turned dark

pink. She quickly pulled her hair forward again and patted it over each one, as if to cover them. "You—you must get pretty hungry."

"I have a huge appetite."

She took a deep breath as if startled and then seemed to hold it, which only made his eyes rest on the generous swell of her breasts. She slid her hand down a long golden tress against her shoulder and said in a soft voice, "I would imagine you're very hungry now." She set her basket in the grass and sauntered toward him. "And I think you've earned something to help satisfy that huge appetite of yours."

A jittery sensation tripped through his chest, and he pulled down on the front of his robe while his eyes dropped to her cleavage once more. "What's on the menu?"

She stopped in front of him. "Something you haven't tasted yet."

He hesitated as she eased herself even closer. The faint essence of gingerbread rose to meet him, and he breathed deeper to capture it.

"After all," she went on, "I promised to give you the best thing I have."

She reached up and plucked one of the greenish-yellow Belles. Her eyes locked with his. Then she sank her teeth into it with a gradual, steady crunch and took a bite. She used a wrist to wipe the juice from her lips and slowly offered the apple to him. She waited as he looked down at it.

He lifted his arm, and the side of his heavy black robe shifted and dragged against the delicate white fabric of her blouse as he accepted the rough-skinned fruit from her hand. He turned it so that his thumb teased across the crimson blush on its side. Then he met Vanessa's eyes— their depths glittering like revolving gems—and an impulsive craving lunged through his body that tightened every muscle. He held the apple to his mouth and took an aggressive, greedy bite next to hers.

The apple's sweet-tart flesh burst in his mouth and

flooded his tongue with juice. He chewed slowly, savoring the bite with unexpected relish. Something about it stoked a need, made him want more. He was about to take another bite when Vanessa rested her fingers on his gloved hand around the Belle.

"It was worth working for, wasn't it?" she asked.

Tingling heat spread through him as she pressed close. She drew the apple to her mouth and ran her lips across its skin…and along his finger. "Feel free to eat as much as you want, Captain."

She nipped the apple's flesh right where his mouth had been and held his gaze as she chewed. Then she drew away and bent down to swing the wicker basket onto her arm. She brushed her palm over the multicolored collection of apples. "Would you like more?"

God, yes.

"No." He held his apple behind him. "No, this is fine. I need to get to the armory now."

"Well, thank you for the help," she said as she walked backward and surveyed the branches above her. "I know how very busy you are."

He stood staring at her as she stretched on her toes to grab an overhead branch. Her gauzy shirt hiked up across her bare midriff, so slender and smooth. It was the kind of hourglass shape he could have easily encircled with both hands, were he to recline against his headboard and lift her onto his lap.

He pivoted and strode along the wall, pulling his hood as far forward as it would go. He raised his arm to hurl the apple away from himself into the grass—

But instead took a bigger, deeper bite of it as he walked.

CHAPTER THIRTY-FOUR

VANESSA

Down on her hands and knees, Vanessa arched her back with a sigh and spread her legs wider as she yielded her body to the steady back-and-forth motion.

She hadn't done this in a while, but it actually felt good.

She tightened her core, curled her fingers harder, and rocked faster, losing herself in the demanding rhythm.

Morgan's rich, resonant voice came from directly behind her. "Such enthusiasm for a filthy task, m'lady. You put my own stamina to shame."

She slowed and looked back over her shoulder.

"Please don't stop on my account." He gave her a small smile as his eyes meandered over her. "I believe you were nearly finished."

She wiped an arm across her damp brow. "I certainly hope so. It feels like I've been doing this all night." She sat back on her heels and threw the dirty scrub brush on the floor. "I'm definitely going to be sore in the morning."

Morgan, dressed in his usual long-sleeved black shirt and jeans, leaned against the countertop next to her with his boots crossed. But as she started to climb to her feet, he stepped smoothly toward her and offered his hand. She took it gratefully and let him help her up. She gazed at him for a moment, his fingers warm around hers, and her stomach fluttered when he smiled again.

"This is probably the tenth spill I've cleaned up to-night." She drew back and kicked the pile of soiled towels aside as she walked to the sink. "Only, this time it was due to an 'I hate my life' hissy fit."

Morgan folded his arms over his dark-green vest and raised his eyebrows.

"Marien's pot roast went horribly wrong, and uh, she didn't handle it well," Vanessa explained as she washed her hands under the faucet. "I told her to go take a breather."

She paused at the memory of Marien's screeching as she dumped the blackened beef on the floor and did a maniacal jig all over it.

Vanessa blinked. "She's a teensy bit stressed."

"I assume the kitchen is closed for the evening, then?" Morgan asked as she dried her hands off on her apron.

"Never for you," she said quickly and then tucked a wisp of hair behind her ear. "I-I saved your dinner, since I knew you were on duty. I built the fire low for one of the ovens so I could keep it warm. I'd hoped you would come by before our stroll tonight."

"You'd sent word that you had something special to give me beforehand." He ran his palm down his goatee. "Naturally, I could not refuse such an intriguing invita-tion."

Vanessa opened the heavy iron door set in the wall and retrieved the foil-wrapped dish. In the dim light, she unwrapped it and tried to decoratively arrange the scrawny frites around the mound of food in the center.

When she turned, Morgan was standing close. He looked down at the plate in her hands and then met her eyes with one eyebrow quirked.

"I helped Marien make shepherd's pie," she said, in an effort to describe what was now not looking very much like its name. "I thought it would be good English comfort food." She frowned at the mixture. "Of course, I may have done you a great disservice as a result."

He angled his head to regard it. "Traditionally, a meal more Irish in origin," he remarked.

She lowered her shoulders. "Oh."

"But quite popular in England"—he eased the plate from her hands—"and a personal favorite of mine. You've done me a great favor, not a disservice."

She smiled, squaring her shoulders again. She untied her apron to toss it aside and then grabbed a bottle and a glass to follow him out to the dining area.

Morgan set down his plate but then looked over at Thomas, who was humming to himself where he sat alone at one of the tables against the outer wall.

"He hasn't moved from that spot for the last hour." She poured some red wine into Morgan's glass and then held the bottle against herself. "I'm kind of concerned about him."

In truth, she was *very* concerned. She had caught Thomas now and then when he was tipsy after one of his shifts, but this was the most inebriated she had ever seen him. The jokes the other soldiers told about his love affair with alcohol were not quite so funny anymore. Because, as with tonight, the way his gaze turned glassy whenever he brooded over his booze left no doubt that his thoughts were swimming in dark waters. And the more he drank, the more some nameless despair—lurking like a pollutant deep in his eyes—began to surface and spread.

Morgan's expression was grim, and he touched her elbow gently to excuse himself past her.

Thomas was leaning so far over that his chest was pressed against the table's edge. When Morgan stopped beside him, Thomas looked up and then straightened unsteadily. "Hey, luh! The good and noble Sir Morgan!" The Newfoundlander grinned, but gazed over the lieutenant's shoulder, as if unable to focus his eyes. "Wanna be joinin' me? It's some bad screech, but I've had drinks o' worse."

Morgan frowned. "You seem to have already had enough for the both of us."

Thomas grabbed the neck of the rum bottle beside him and hefted it high. "It's not enough till it's empty, me cock."

He slammed it down, making the oil lamp on the table hop forward. Then he raised his glass and took a long swallow.

Vanessa cringed. She had tried to warn Thomas away from the homemade hooch that Sven had once produced while experimenting with distillation. It was the only bottle remaining, and for good reason: Rhetta had poured out the others after three residents suffered repeated bouts of diarrhea.

Morgan narrowed his eyes as Thomas hiccupped once. "Are you not on watch tonight, Private Mercer?"

"Nope! Angus swuh—swishhhed—switched me out."

"Was that before or *after* he saw this?" Morgan tilted the nearly empty bottle against the table to squint at it.

Thomas stared at him. "Uh…"

Morgan's voice became stern. "Make it an early night, soldier. I'm assigning you to a cleanup detail in the morning."

"Aw, fuck, Lieutenant!"

Morgan leaned onto a hand on the table and pulled the bottle away with his other, much to Thomas's dismay. He set the rum down on the table behind him and lifted the young soldier by an arm. Thomas swayed on wobbly legs as Morgan guided him to the door.

"Are you all right to find your way?" the Englishman asked.

Thomas waved him off. "Yeah sure, me son, sure," he grumbled. "I knows this place like the hand o' me back. No worries, eh?"

Morgan tossed Vanessa a solemn look.

He walked Thomas out of the room and disappeared into the darkness beyond. Within minutes, he returned. He strolled over to Vanessa and seated himself at the table where his shepherd's pie awaited him.

She twisted her hands together at her stomach and threw one more glance through the doorway. "I take it you found him a chaperone?"

"Henrick will look after him."

The old Dutch soldier was tough, but in a gentle,

grandfatherly way. He would probably even tuck Thomas into bed, to make sure he stayed put.

"Has he always been like this?" she asked. "So…troubled?"

"Yes." A note of sadness rang through Morgan's voice. "And it has progressed over the years in ways that take their toll. But every man needs a mask. His is that of the jester."

She shook her head. "He wears it well."

But it's the cracks in the mask that worry me.

Vanessa set a beautifully ripe Belle de Boskoop next to Morgan's plate that she had reserved especially for him. He nodded his thanks as she stepped over the bench and hopped up to sit on the table. She smoothed her long skirt over her legs and waited for him to taste his meal.

Morgan chewed thoughtfully for a moment before swallowing. "A flavor I had not anticipated." He must have seen the look on her face, because he paused. "It's remarkably good," he assured her.

She smiled and leaned forward to hug her knees. "I cooked the ground lamb and whipped the potatoes, while Marien did everything else," she confessed. "I figured those were the most important parts, and I wanted to ensure your dinner was less of a…um…disaster."

He gave her a half smile. "Fair play to you, then, for it is far from that."

"Well, that's a relief." She used her thumb to wipe a brown smear of gravy off the rim of his plate. "Because it's not going to win any blue ribbons for its looks."

He smiled wider as she licked off her thumb. "Fortunately, a man's stomach, like love, is blind."

She nudged him playfully in the thigh with the toe of her slipper and set one elbow on her knee to rest her chin in her hand as Morgan raised the fork to his mouth again.

How warm and sensuous he was, with a sharp mind and a charmingly dry sense of humor. Elegant and yet intensely masculine. A very compelling package overall.

He slipped the stem of his glass between his fingers and scooped the goblet up to his lips.

Like he should be dressed in a golden-threaded tunic and seated at a round table with a sword at his side.

It was little wonder so many of the resident women would whisper and giggle to each other like a bunch of ninnies when he passed by.

A spark of annoyance popped in her chest.

And, as much as some of the women looked disapprovingly at Vanessa's wardrobe, they certainly had no issues with wearing their necklines lower whenever Morgan was around. Or falling all over themselves if he spoke to them.

She pressed her lips together.

He deserved better than to be regarded as just a tasty treat. Although…he probably would make a nice mouthful. She inhaled slowly. If the right girl struck his fancy, no doubt his libido would be a force to be reckoned with. Whatever damsel he wanted in his bed would probably be gratified to the point of delirium.

All those hard curves and hot flesh…

His strong body in motion, hovering over her in the near dark while his eyes absorbed the deep gray shadows of the room. She'd slide her arms up around his neck to pull him closer as his gaze pinned her in place beneath him. He'd clasp her leg to his naked side while his hips rocked rhythmically between her thighs in time with his rapid breathing. And he'd use his other hand to grip her headboard as it slammed against the wall over and over. *Bang…bang…bang…*

"A riotous daydream."

She sat up and blinked at him. "What?"

"Whatever wild reverie has you in its grasp," Morgan clarified. "I've rarely seen *idle* thoughts put such color in a woman's cheeks." He slid a frite into his mouth and chewed as he watched her.

She pressed her palms to her face. Her skin must have been giving off smoke for how hot it felt!

"It's n-nothing," she said. "I was thinking about…gardening."

"I see." Morgan swiped the napkin across his mouth,

but his eyes remained fixed on hers. "Perhaps I have not given horticulture its due."

She swallowed, pushing aside the image of her yanking on Morgan's shoulders, the muscles across his bare chest flexing in a steady tempo above her.

"Believe me, there's a lot to be said for…gardening," she replied weakly.

A smile tugged at his lips. "Apparently."

Vanessa turned her head as someone walked into the kitchen.

Marien approached hesitantly, and there was an embarrassed sound to her voice when she spoke. "Hoi, Vanessa. Thanks for helping me with the…accident tonight." She tucked her auburn hair behind an ear. "I-I hope it wasn't too much trouble to clean up."

Vanessa shook her head. "No problem."

Marien tucked the hair behind her other ear. "You don't think anyone noticed, do you?"

Noticed? The cook's demented dance on the charred remains of the unfortunate roast had already become legend.

Vanessa smiled thinly. "I'm sure it's all been forgotten."

Marien appeared relieved. "Well, I came back to prep the oliebol dough for tomorrow's breakfast." But then she smiled shyly when she saw Morgan lean back on the bench to look at her. "Oh! Goedenavond, Lieutenant."

He nodded. "I thank you for your extra efforts on the shepherd's pie, Marien. It is cooked to perfection." He glanced at Vanessa with a knowing look.

But Marien accepted the praise with delight. "Really?"

"Quite."

Marien held her shoulders back. "Maybe I'll make that part of our regular Thursday menu, then!"

She strutted past them on her way to the cooking area.

Vanessa grinned at Morgan. "I think you just made a friend for life, Lieutenant," she whispered.

He chuckled. A rush of pleasure swelled through her at the sound. She looked over his face as he went back to his dinner.

"You know"—she leaned toward him and ran her fingers through his bangs, which had begun to curl down his forehead over the last week or so—"you're getting a little shaggy, Englishman."

He paused, looking up at her as he slowly finished chewing his bite. "Am I?"

He gazed at her as she brushed her fingers through the longer raven-black hair near his temple. It was so soft, like feathers gliding over her skin.

She smoothed part of it behind his ear. "I'd say you're a man in need of some kind of trim."

At that, he looked steadily at her, and the tiniest smile started on his lips.

She wrinkled her brow. "What's funny about that?"

He merely shook his head, but his eyes swept the length of her before he turned back to his meal.

"Well?" She leaned onto her hands behind her. "Don't you agree that it would be good for you?"

"Indeed," he said simply. He lifted a forkful of shepherd's pie and sedately put it in his mouth.

"We could do it right here, if you want."

Morgan seemed to swallow a little too quickly. He put a fist to his mouth and coughed into it.

"It wouldn't take us long, only a few minutes," she went on, "and I think you'll feel much better afterward."

He averted his gaze as he set his elbows on the table. "Truly, I would enjoy every part of it. But it's quite all right."

"Seriously, I want to. And there's plenty of room in here for me to get into the right positions, so that I can come at you from all angles. There are even some special techniques we can try out." She held up her hands. "I mean, to be honest, I've only ever done it with women, but I doubt it's much different with a man. I think you'll be happy with the results."

Morgan pinched the bridge of his nose with his fingers. "Vanessa—"

"Don't worry, I promise I won't hurt you. I'll be

careful, and we can take it nice and slow. Just tell me how you want it. You'll have full control."

"I fear I would have nothing of the sort," he said as he closed his eyes and steepled his hands beneath his chin.

"And I've got all the right tools for the job." She peered into the cooking area where Marien was punching a pile of dough near the propane stove. Then she spotted the kitchen shears in the butcher block. "Just give me a second to get ready—"

She started to slide off the table, when Morgan put his hand on her knee. Her heart skidded to a stop at his touch.

"Vanessa, I am more than confident in your…skills," he told her. "Rest assured, should I require the occasional trim"—he gave her a gradual, and strangely mischievous, smile—"I shall look to no one but you."

She shrugged and scooted back onto the table. "Okay, another time, then." She picked up the apple from beside his plate and polished it against her hip. "But believe it or not, I'm very good at it."

When she held the apple out to Morgan, he was watching her closely. He glanced down at the offering and then accepted it from her hand.

"When the time comes, I shall gladly let you have your way with me," he murmured and bit heavily into the Belle.

She smiled and dropped her eyes to her skirt. She plucked at the part draped over her knees, making the fabric flutter against her calves. A breeze blew by and stirred the hair hanging against her shoulders. She glanced out the windows cut high into the stone wall. The sky was black and unbroken tonight, but the kitchen remained warm and snug. The heat still coming from the ovens kept the air's frosty nip at bay.

Cold time of year to move on to unknown parts, though.

She shifted her gaze to her slippers, which were propped beside Morgan on the bench, and nibbled on her lip as she slipped a hand into her skirt pocket.

She'd left the hastily folded map in her room when she changed into the longer skirt that evening. It was currently tucked between the pages of the first book she happened to pull off her shelf: *Around the World in Eighty Days*.

She flicked a stray crumb off the table that she had missed earlier when she was clearing away the residents' dirty dishes. "It sounds like the captain is already planning his next stop." She glanced at Morgan hesitantly. "Has he said anything to you about—about when you're leaving?"

Morgan stopped chewing and held her eyes for a moment. He swallowed and carefully set his fruit in front of him. "No formal timeline, as far as I'm aware."

She rubbed at a stain on the table and tried to steady her voice. "But it's soon, isn't it?"

With the tip of one finger, he traced the outline of the bite taken from his apple. "Yes."

Her stomach began to burn, and she crossed her arms over it. "Any idea where he's moving you?"

"I believe southward to France is a fair assumption." Morgan met her eyes again as he rested his wrists against the worn wooden edge. "We have earmarked a few remote areas in the countryside on the way to the Spanish border."

She picked up a frite from his plate and bit off the end of it. But it sat like a piece of cardboard in her mouth. "I don't understand why you can't stay longer. You all seem to be settling in. And a lot of the residents have come to accept this…situation. And—and whoever your enemies are, they obviously don't have a clue where you are, or they would have shown up by now, right? So there's no real reason to leave."

He had been listening intently as she spoke, his hands perfectly still upon the table. The gentle sound of water running in the sink reached her from the cooking area.

"Morgan, why can't you stay?" She uttered the question with a quaver that she could not control.

The depths of his eyes shifted in the glow of the few kitchen lanterns, like lightning flickering in the heart of distant storm clouds.

"Were it my decision to make, I would be loath to leave you." He eased his fork into the whipped potato topping and rotated the utensil slowly. "But one does not easily change Ethan's mind."

Vanessa's shoulders sagged. *No. I guess one doesn't.*

She fell silent as she grasped the edge of the table on either side of her and stared down at her slippers against the bench. She should have tried harder. She'd had the perfect opening to work on Ethan earlier that afternoon and convince him to stay. But she'd squandered her chance, getting caught up in the pleasure of just being near him, touching him, and learning about him. But now he was leaving. Maybe even this week. And she would never have the opportunity to get through to him. To really understand him.

She rubbed her palms on her knees, dragging her skirt against them.

Or to find out whether he feels anything deeper for me.

And all of it was due to his conviction that he had to run to survive.

She stopped her hands and then bunched her skirt in them. "Morgan, what are Ukes?"

The lieutenant, who had returned to his meal, sat staring at it for a few seconds. But when he lifted his eyes to hers, the flickers of far-off lightning intensified in those storm-filled skies. "You want to know why they pursue us."

She nodded.

Morgan's gaze wandered over her face.

A crash from the cooking area made Vanessa jerk her head up.

Marien was holding her hands high like she was being robbed at gunpoint. Giant gobs of dough lay at her feet next to an overturned mixing bowl. She directed her wide eyes at Vanessa. Then she let out a cry and dashed to the sink, where water cascaded over the edges.

Morgan glanced back toward Marien as she wrenched the faucet handle and then used her apron to frantically mop down the cabinets. He let his fork slide through his fingers to rest on his plate with a soft clink, and he rose to step over the bench. He extended his hand to Vanessa.

"Would you walk with me?"

CHAPTER THIRTY-FIVE

VANESSA

They emerged into the crisp night air—such a contrast to the mild temperatures during the day—and Vanessa rubbed her palms together. As they neared the back gates, Morgan offered her his right arm.

As with all their prior evening strolls, she wrapped her hand around his bicep and savored the muscular warmth of him moving against her while they walked.

They exited the compound, and Morgan glanced up at the northern battlements. Miguel—the slowly surfacing moonlight glinting off his dark, slicked-back hair—stood in Thomas's usual place. The Argentinian must have been the one to take over Thomas's watch.

Morgan nodded at Miguel, who nodded back and slipped his rifle off his shoulder to ready it in his hands. He adjusted his position along the rampart so that he could keep Morgan and Vanessa in sight as they continued along the perimeter of the meadow near the fort wall.

She slipped her free hand into the crook of Morgan's elbow. "I didn't mean to take you away from your dinner."

He looked down at her and smiled. "My mother may scold you for denying me the proper vegetable allotment, but I would never dare."

She laughed and squeezed his arm in her hands. His

muscles barely gave under her fingers.

Damn, he is so solid.

She tucked a lock of hair behind her ear and fiddled with the top button of her blouse. They began to pass by one of the old tourist plaques bolted to its rusty stand. Though the moon had begun to peek out, the evening was still too dark to read the printed words, but Vanessa knew them by heart. The sign marked spot number forty-two on the Fort Adventure Map. It was the exact location where the compound's original architect—the crackpot nobleman with more money than talent—used to set his frilly-fringed chair every day and oversee Fort Van Doorn's construction.

"You said your mom is still in England, back in your hometown outside of London." She trailed her fingers over the plaque's familiar bumpy surface that had warped in the sun over the years. "Do you ever get to talk to her?"

"Communication is problematic." Morgan's forehead creased. "And the prepaid crings—our contact devices—do not extend across the North Sea nor the Channel, due to restricted satellite reception. But I have other means. I will endeavor to connect with her again soon."

He lifted a hand and ran his fingers around the inside of his shirt collar, absently tucking that brown leather cord out of sight, where it had ridden up against his neck again. She had glimpsed his mysterious necklace so often during their walks, but had yet to ask about its significance. He seemed to fuss with it only when the conversation turned to something personal.

"I'll bet she worries about you all the time. I know I would." She paused when he turned his head to look at her. "I mean, if I were she," she said hastily. "Your mother, that is."

Morgan let out a short breath through his nose with a smile. "I have given her great cause to worry, in the past. I once ran with a dodgy lot—some East Enders from London who'd moved to our little village. Most of them were good lads, but our...adventures landed me in the nick a few times. As Ethan would surely say, I was young, dumb, and full of'"—he paused and glanced at her. He cleared his throat—"bravado."

Vanessa laughed. "I bet your mom had her hands full."

Morgan bowed his head as he fingered the pommel of his dagger on his left side. "Yes. At times I was the more troublesome of her two children." His voice took on a grumbling tone. "Though at least I did not turn into an insufferable twat."

Whoa, doesn't sound like he's close with his sibling, then!

She opened her mouth to ask if this were a brother or sister, but Morgan continued as if lost in thought. "My mum has always been a resilient woman. The most trying time was after my father's passing. I was but a boy of six and so offered more encumbrance than consolation, though she would deny it."

They departed from the hilltop's natural curve around the fort and began to descend the gradual slope.

"What's her name?" Vanessa asked as she watched her slippers glide through the overgrown ryegrass.

"Beatrice." Morgan's voice was gentle. "Appropriately, a name meaning 'Bringer of Joy.' "

Vanessa perked up. "Like in *Paradiso*. Beatrice was Dante's guide through Heaven."

Morgan nodded. "She has indeed earned her place in such a realm." He gave her a sidelong glance that bordered on a smirk. "Though I am surprised you have suffered the *Divine Comedy* to rest upon your shelves, considering your unnatural aversion to poetry, based on our previous evenings' discussions."

"Oh, come on, it's not that I don't like poetry," she said, poking her finger against his arm. "I have a lot of favorite verse. But if you pinned me down and made me choose, then I'll go for a real *story* every time."

"You don't believe all poems tell stories?" Morgan nudged her shoulder with his as they walked. "Baudelaire, Tennyson, Angelou—all storytellers in their own ways. All commentators on the human condition, drawing scenes as dramatic as any from H. G. Wells."

"But I like the monsters, the bad guys, the Moriartys and Voldemorts." She held up a hand when Morgan opened his mouth. "And don't throw Shakespeare at me. Or Poe. They're exceptions. But my go-to is novels." She swung her arm out to the side and shook her head. "Stories with danger and heroes and"—she glanced at him and then began picking at his sleeve—"and romance."

"And happy endings, I would imagine," Morgan said quietly.

She lifted her face. He regarded her with what seemed a pensive air, but then his features relaxed in a slight smile. As they passed the small whitewashed brick smokehouse on their left, Vanessa's eyes automatically wandered toward the pair of ghostly pale headstones far in the distance at the edge of the back field, where the compound's little cemetery sat nestled near the end of the forest. Her heart seemed to beat a little weaker, as it always did when she glanced in that direction.

"Or at least endings where the characters can somehow make up for the bad things that happened," she said. "Things they did wrong."

Morgan squeezed his bicep, pressing the back of her hand warmly against his side, and leaned forward to block her view. "Things best left in the past." He brushed her hair back from her cheek. "Sometimes the happiest endings are those we choose to create in spite of the story."

The heaviness in her chest fell away as she met his gaze, and she slipped her other hand into his to clasp it. She'd never told him all the details of her parents' death, but he knew enough to guess.

They began to approach the widest spread of forest that ringed the back field and crowded the landscape with black poplars. The tree population was a topographical anomaly this close to the ocean. But it created a Grimm-fairytale kind of playground that had sparked her imagination as a child and had fostered her love for the dense smell of wet leaves when she had hidden among the shadows of the burred-bark trees. In the spring and summer, the woody giants would wave their broad leaves in the daytime sea breezes like fretful guardians watching over the fort. But now, with December almost upon them, they'd shed their glossy hands for bony fingers and bent like nervous crones awaiting the threat of snow.

As she and Morgan neared the woods, one of the larger bushes shook. Morgan halted and immediately pushed Vanessa behind him. Her stomach compressed like a metal spring. The protective motion was exactly like Ethan's, when he had placed her behind him in the city alley where the merchant had accosted her.

Vanessa bunched the back of Morgan's satin vest in her hands as he pulled his gun and held it at his side. The copse of trees was filled with inky shadows that twisted around the trunks of the black poplars. But the insects continued to chirp and buzz, so the life crawling through the brittle scattered leaves and undergrowth went on undisturbed.

Maybe they know something we don't.

She pressed against Morgan from behind and curled her fingers over his forearm. "Wait."

He glanced back at her, but his hand did not loosen its grip on his gun.

The bushes swayed again. A furry head on a long neck rose above the foliage. The animal turned to stare at Morgan and Vanessa. Its large perked ears swiveled toward them. Morgan's arm relaxed.

"It's a red deer," Vanessa whispered. "You see them a lot around here, especially at this time of night. There aren't many stags, though, mostly hinds like this one. This little forest is the thickest patch for several kilometers, so they wander into it now and then."

The deer stepped out and blinked at them. Its rust-colored coat had already turned grayish-brown for the autumn and had thickened further for the coming winter.

Vanessa kept her voice to a whisper. "They feel safe here. Protected." She paused. "But even the most secluded home is not the best shelter, is it? Someone will always find you."

Maybe that's what Ethan's so sure of.

Morgan carefully replaced his weapon in its holster and glanced at her with his eyebrows lowered.

"Back when we could still use guns for hunting," she went on, "Cornelis used to go after them for the meat. The compound would use half the venison and sell the rest. He tried to teach me, but I don't have the stomach for killing. He did show me how to dress the deer, though. You've probably noticed he's pretty good with a knife."

Morgan lowered his eyebrows further. "A deft hand at charcuterie does little to impress me." He clapped his hands once, and the deer bolted back into the thicket.

"He fought alongside all of you, when those men attacked us," she pointed out. "And I think he held his own."

"One skirmish does not prepare a man to face every enemy."

She shook her head and took his arm as they resumed their stroll. He and Cornie had gotten off to a bad start, all right, back when Morgan had intervened in the garden brawl. They were probably never going to get along.

Morgan guided her past the edge of the darkened forest. "Those Achterwaartsstad townsmen were incautious, which led them to their death. But malice is what brought them to our door." His voice dropped as his steps slowed. "And yet, there are others in the world whose hatred is unrivaled. Men made into monsters by a single act of wrath."

A chill snuck down her spine. She pulled away from him and walked to one of the black poplars. "So are you finally going to tell me about Ethan? About what he's running from?" She flattened her hands behind her on the trunk and leaned against them. "That's why we're really out here, isn't it?"

Morgan approached her slowly, and the faint moonlight shifted across the fluid sheen of his vest until the shadows of the trees swallowed him. His manner was pensive, his voice subdued. "You care for him."

The air became heavy, the watchful steadiness of his gaze only doubling the weight of his words.

She bit her lip and scratched at the bark behind her. "I care for both of you. Very much."

Morgan grew still, and his eyes seemed to dilate slightly as he studied her.

"But I want to know what happened," she said. "I want to know why he hides himself from everyone. What could he have done that makes him—"

That makes him keep his distance from me.

She paused as she tried again. "I can already see some scarring around his mouth and eyes, within the mask. What's so bad about his appearance?"

And why doesn't he understand that I don't care about that?

Morgan backed away until he could lean against the tree across from her. He ran a hand down his goatee and then rested it on his gun. "There is much damage to his body. The scars cover his chest and face, most of all. But it is not his physical condition that is the greater affliction." Morgan looked at her. "Ethan burdens himself with memories that are far worse than any disorder of the flesh. And he contends with them by condemning any influence which he feels creates weakness."

The sudden pressure of his gaze made her hesitate.

Me? Does he mean me?

"How did he…become this way?" she asked.

Morgan took a breath, as if resigned to an uncomfortable, but inevitable, task.

"Two years ago, he destroyed a facility we were occupying in an eastern oblast of Ukraine," he began, his voice so low that she had to lean forward to hear above the steady clicking of beetles nearby. "At the time, we needed them for their resources: medicine, provisions, money. They were civilians, like the people here, and they had banded together to form their own community. But as history has long proven, Ukrainians are a fierce, proud people and are not to be subjugated by any invading force. We did not intend to be their enemy. We did only what was necessary to temporarily survive, as has become our way. We should have anticipated their spirit of resistance and trod more carefully."

Or asked to be allowed in and sheltered, instead of demanding their obedience.

But she kept the comment to herself as Morgan frowned and rubbed his fingers thoughtfully against the grip of his holstered pistol.

"During the course of our stay, there was a plotted uprising—an event for which we are usually well-prepared. But when the situation escalated, many of our soldiers were killed by the Ukrainians. Their deaths were…deliberately brutal, to make a point and to drive us out. Perhaps it is the legacy of a repeatedly victimized people: they learn to employ equally violent deterrents." He met her eyes again. "But once we regained control, Ethan made an example of those who had perpetrated the revolt."

She hugged herself against rising goose bumps. "What did he do to them?"

The crooked tree branches spread their fingerlike shadows across Morgan's face. "Something no man should admit to."

Her mouth went dry at his tone.

"We then decided to relinquish the facility, but not before the remaining residents chose to attack us once more. During the confusion, the Ukrainians were able to secretly evacuate all of the women and children, though many of the men also fled with them. But in our haste to withdraw during the assault, Ethan decided to leave a final lasting impression."

Something about those words made her stomach knot. The sound of bugs scuttling through the dark woods paused, and the night around them became strangely silent.

"We rigged the building with explosives and timed the charges to detonate," he went on as the skeletal shadows on his face seemed to curl in on themselves. "I knew the plan was ill-conceived. I recognized the irrationality of it, Ethan's way of lashing out at his own grief and guilt and calling it justice. But I raised no objection. The mistake became mine as much as his."

Morgan stopped. The dark depths of his eyes churned in the trick of the low light. She gripped the sides of her long skirt in her fists.

"As we were leaving, three of the Ukrainians took us unawares and attacked Ethan," he continued at last. "Fortunately, I was there to help even the odds. But just as we made good our escape, one more man appeared and drove Ethan back inside. I turned, mere seconds too late to grab him. The concussion from the blast flung me several meters away, which was enough to save me from the flames. But Ethan…did not escape."

He swallowed and the churning in his eyes—like writhing storm clouds—worsened.

"I ran back for him. The building had become a furnace, the heat as scorching as hellfire. But then his hand reached forth from the wreckage inside, and I wrapped my shirt around it to drag him out. I smothered the flames engulfing him so that I could turn him over. His lungs rattled like the chains of death itself, a nightmarish sound I shall never forget. But he was alive."

Morgan's voice vanished for a few seconds as he raised a hand and seemed to absently finger the necklace cord hidden under his collar.

"We often need reminders that those we cherish can disappear from our lives. For all our willful resilience, it takes but one rash folly to reveal life's frailty…and one friend's vulnerability to expose our own." He stared at the ground, his fingers still moving against his collar. "Had I lost such a friend—a true brother—due to his *own* undoing, because I did nothing to divert him from his course…" He shook his head, eyes still downcast. "A harsh reminder indeed."

She hugged herself tighter, the cold night air numbing her arms, despite the fiery images of smoke and rubble that buffeted her brain. She knew what it was to lose people she loved and to mourn them like the world was ending. In Morgan's case, he would have blamed himself for his inaction. But in the case of her parents, she was guilty of worse. Her stomach contracted.

She'd acted, and she'd been wrong. That was *her* reminder.

As the chirring of awakening insects began to overcome the quiet, Morgan's voice drew her to him once more.

"We were able to stabilize him, if only barely. We moved on, relying upon past allies with more medically advanced resources along the way. But on our heels came the Ukrainian survivors, feeding upon their own vengeance and our debility. We fought to keep Ethan from succumbing to his injuries, whilst remaining hidden from our enemies. But each time we relocated, the chase renewed."

Vanessa rubbed her elbows. "So the Ukrainians are why you've made your way over to this side of Europe."

Morgan let his arms hang beside him as he walked toward her. "And they are the reason we remain mobile. We are not yet well-situated to confront them head-on, for it is certain they have gathered like-minded transients to expand their forces." He stopped in front of her. "But that is not to say we should not reassess our strategy. Recent realities have had a bearing on our circumstances." His eyes rested on her face before gliding down her neck. "On our preferences."

Her fingers played with a button at her cleavage as a palpable heat spread along the path of his gaze. "Morgan?"

He drifted closer. "Yes?"

"I know you think you don't belong anywhere. That none of you fit anywhere." She shook her head. "But you're wrong. You're needed here."

With a slight smile, he let out a breath through his nose. "A sentiment not shared by others, I'm afraid."

"But if one person needs you," she said as she plucked harder at the button, "isn't that enough?"

Morgan placed his hand upon the tree above her head. His eyes were a deep dusky blue in the shifting shadows.

"In truth," he said, his voice turning softer, "it would

depend upon the person."

The button she was playing with slipped out of its hole, and Morgan's eyes dropped to her fingers. A heady feeling of déjà vu rolled over her, and all at once she was standing with her back to the corridor wall on that first night of the army's occupation. And she was once again trapped helplessly before him as he seemed to look right into her.

"I just think...this is the best place for you." She breathed deeper and began to pick at the next button down. "Surviving doesn't have to mean running away." She lifted her shoulders in a half shrug. "Aren't you tired of leaving things behind?"

"A man so long inured to a vagabond life learns to find solace in the road ahead." He lowered his hand from the tree and seemed to study her. Then, carefully, he brushed the backs of his fingers across her cheek, and she paused in mid-breath. "And yet, what I am beginning to find instead," he murmured, "is that any path leading away from here is no path I wish to travel."

The depths of the forest surrounded them in a sudden ecstatic silence. The smell of him—that seductive mix of spice and leather—wound itself around her. She rested her fingers upon his abdomen, where his vest gave a satin surface to rows of hard, grooved muscles hidden beneath. Her eyelids became all at once heavy while her feet were ready to float off the ground.

Her thoughts tumbled slowly over one another on their way to her mouth. "Morgan..."

He touched his fingertips to the underside of her chin and lifted it. "Yes?"

She leaned into him, into the warm, firm feel of his body as he hovered over her.

Stop it, Vanessa. Stop it now.

She blinked as her mind fought through the haze. She pulled back gently. "Thank you for—for telling me about Ethan. I'm sorry that it was painful for you, but...I think I understand things better now."

Morgan lowered his hand to his side, the heated animation in his features subsiding. "Ethan..." His eyes adopted the darkness of the evening sky, now cloaked in clouds. "Yes…of course."

She grasped her shirt to close it. "Would you mind walking me back to the kitchen? Marien is probably done making a mess of tomorrow's breakfast, but I still have a few chores to finish up. And it's—it's late."

"Too late, it would appear." His voice was low and despondent.

She loosened the grip on her shirt, and a pang of regret shot through her when he stepped back, the enticing scent of him departing like a vanishing fog.

He stood with his hands clasped behind him and tilted his head in invitation for her to pass by. His mood was somber, the angles of his face drawn together once more into an enigmatic mask. She rubbed her arms and turned to walk with him. The night had grown colder and the shadows in the woods thicker. She could not even distinguish the familiar shapes of the wild juniper bushes from which she had taken a few cuttings last week. As they made their way up to the fort, he placed his hand gently upon the small of her back but did not look at her.

A simple kiss. That's all it would have been. One small, shared gratification in response to a mutual attraction that had been building for weeks. And they'd both been ready to explore it just now, to see where it went. So why had she felt so guilty about it?

And that wasn't the only confusing sensation. She now also struggled against the creep of melancholy and rising desperation. It already felt like the excitement that had begun to filter new life into the compound was fading beneath the reality of the army's impending absence. It was like discovering long-lost relations from unknown branches of a family tree, offshoots who'd quickly sprouted and flourished alongside her, only to be pruned away too soon. The soldiers were going to abandon this place like it was no more than a random rock they'd use to cross a stream.

And no one could do anything to change that, except Ethan himself.

CHAPTER THIRTY-SIX

ETHAN

The night was quiet, which made it easy to hear the muffled chuckling and loud whispers coming from the kitchen's high row of windows. Ethan had made his way in from the rear perimeter outside the compound when the incongruous noises caught his attention. He had just performed a quick routine inspection of his sentries, a duty he often shared with Morgan to keep his men alert. But before that, he'd been stewing over his missing map.

It was the one damn document he'd wanted to take another look at that afternoon before he got sidetracked again, and the fucking thing had disappeared. If he could just stay focused, then shit like this wouldn't happen.

If I could just stay away from her, that is…

When he reached the kitchen doorway, he stepped into the warm, cozy light cast by the many lanterns placed throughout the room. Out of habit, he reached up to push back his hood but caught himself, since he hadn't bothered to don the robe this evening. On a table nearby were several stacks of neatly folded napkins and dish towels next to a plastic laundry basket. But he dismissed those details as soon as he stared sternly across the room.

Angelo and John leaned over a sleeping Vanessa, saying something to each other as they pointed at her. She was sitting cross-legged on a bench at one of the tables and was slumped against the wall with her arms folded.

The soldiers, as gleeful as frat boys, had rolled up two napkins and had stuck the twisted ends into her ears so that they hung far out from either side of her head like donkey ears. On her brow the words "Out of Order" were scrawled in bold blue letters.

As if suddenly sensing him there, the men turned their heads. Both of them gave him a grin.

"Capitano, check it out," Angelo said, barely able to keep his voice low. "You can do anything to her and she won't wake up."

Angelo's hair, as usual, was a mass of dark puffy curls that somehow managed to always draw attention to his classically aquiline nose, a feature the young Italian mechanic was very proud of. But his slender frame was utterly contrasted by the stocky build of John standing next to him, who seemed more intent than Angelo on the mischief at hand.

John winked at Ethan and nodded down at Vanessa. "Shit, Cap, it's funny as all get-out," he said, his Texas twang running his words together. "She's dead to the world. I mean, look here."

John pushed up the sleeves of his olive-drab T-shirt, revealing the tri-colored tattoo of his home state wrapped in barbed wire, and carefully lifted one of Vanessa's wrists. Then he slid a glass of what had to be warm water across the table.

"No. *No.*" Ethan held up a finger at John as he dangled her hand over the glass.

Both men's faces showed their disappointment. But John obeyed and set her hand in her lap instead.

Ethan gave them a glare that, even from behind the mask, clearly communicated what he thought of their behavior.

They backed away from Vanessa and proceeded to shuffle past him, each giving a sheepish salute as they went.

Ethan put a gloved hand to John's brick wall of a chest to stop him and then held out his other, palm up. The

Texan sighed, slapped the blue marker into Ethan's hand, and slunk out.

Ethan walked over to where Vanessa sat snoozing with her cheek against her shoulder. He shook his head and bent over her. He plucked the ludicrously lolling napkins from her ears and tossed them and the marker on the table. Lowering himself onto the bench beside her, he let his eyes wander over her. Something about the way she looked so peaceful made her even prettier, despite the absurd lettering now emblazoned on her forehead.

He reached out and lifted part of her long hair, pulling it forward to let it glide across his palm. The strands looked rich and radiant against the black leather of his glove.

How many times had he watched her play with these beautiful locks and twine them around her fingers? And how many times had he wished he could experience this one small piece of her in reality? The very touch of her hair—the casual ability to feel it brushing over his skin— was something that only a few years ago he would have taken for granted.

He stared at her.

She had not moved since he had sat down. For all he knew, she had not moved since John and Angelo had started their game. When she slept, she obviously slept hard, which would explain her reluctance to greet the dawn each day. Perhaps the soldiers were right that there was little that could rouse her.

Only one way to find out.

He tugged at the fingertips of his left glove to pull it off, his eyes never leaving her face.

The sight of his hand—swirled flesh upon a knotted surface—made him flinch reflexively. But he extended it toward her.

If she wakes up, she'll see. She'll see what you are, you asshole.

He hesitated and curled his fingers against his palm.

The image of Vanessa smiling at him in the orchard flowed across his thoughts...the wind blowing through those long tresses…imagining those same tresses woven around his knuckles as he lay with her in a darkened bedroom…

It's not worth the risk.

He clenched his jaw and took the same locks of her hair in his hand. And again pulled them through his fingers. No glove. No barriers.

He closed his eyes at the silky feel against his naked flesh. A long, slow breath left his lungs.

Wrong. It's more than worth it.

He opened his eyes and moved closer to her on the bench. She continued to sleep with her head against her shoulder, never stirring.

A nervous tremor tightened his stomach. Using the barest pressure, like stroking a spider's web, he touched his fingertips to her cheek.

Her skin was so soft it made him ache.

As he spread his palm gingerly on her cheek, his gaze brushed over her lips.

They probably taste as good as they look.

He trailed his fingertips forward along her jawline and traced her bottom lip with his thumb.

His eyes traveled downward. The unbuttoned placket of her blouse was parted enough to show the bulges of her breasts, her cleavage invitingly visible.

And those probably taste even better.

He took a breath as his fingers descended to the opening.

But he jerked his hand away when Vanessa mumbled something unintelligible and nestled her head higher against her shoulder. His heart thumping, he watched to see if she would come to life. But she had already slid back into slumber.

He sat back from her and glanced toward the door. He squared his shoulders and grabbed his glove to jerk it back on.

Pull it together, numbnuts.

It was bad enough he was acting like a teenager at a peepshow. The last fucking thing he needed was a witness.

He gave an impatient sigh and dunked his gloved fingers into the glass beside him. He flicked them at Vanessa, misting her with water. She awoke with a start.

"Hey!" she protested groggily, her eyes still closed as she wiped at her face.

"So I let you keep your own room, and then you sleep in the kitchen," he intoned.

She blinked at him and then yawned, arching her body away from the wall as she stretched. "It was just a catnap." She rubbed at one eye with the heel of her hand. "What are you doing here?"

He ripped his gaze away from her breasts, which had nearly popped open the remaining buttons at her cleavage during her stretch.

"Saving you from certain humiliation. Privates Pierce and Zanetti seemed to have run out of things to keep them entertained. You were an easy target."

She squinched her face suspiciously. "What exactly did they do?"

"Not as much as they'd planned."

She glanced at the twisted napkins on the table. She stuck a pinky in one ear and wiggled it. "I should have known. Those two pranksters are always cooking up something."

When he shifted his eyes upward, she frowned at him and then glanced at the marker on the table.

"They wrote something on my forehead, didn't they?" she asked dryly.

Even though she was receptive to his men's teasing, it was probably best to soften the joke.

"It says 'Do Not Disturb,' " he told her, taking one of the napkins and dipping it into the glass of water.

She giggled as Ethan started to rub off the wording above her eyebrows. "Okay, I'll hand it to them, that's funny."

A smile slipped across his mouth before he could catch it. He wet the napkin again.

"Regardless," he said flatly, "you may want to choose your napping spots more carefully."

"That's what I get for deciding to wake up so early," she bemoaned. "By the time evening rolls around, it all catches up with me and I'm pooped." She fixed him with a very serious look as he worked to remove the ink. "I think it's bad for my health and a detriment to the compound community."

"Let me guess." He dipped a clean end of the napkin in the glass. "That's your latest excuse for pulling the covers over your head in the morning."

"It's not an excuse if it's real science." She pointed a fingertip down onto the bench as he pressed the damp cloth along her brow. "I formed a hypothesis that I'm no good to anyone if I'm in a walking coma by twenty hundred. And the controlled variable in that experiment has been getting up at an ungodly hour of the morning. It wrecks the entire equation every time."

"Did your scientific mother ever buy that bullshit?"

She sighed. "Not once. I still had to wash the dishes after dinner."

He almost chuckled but instead wiped harder at the lettering.

She leaned closer to him as he removed the last of the smudged blue marks over her left eyebrow.

She rested her hand on his knee. "Thank you, Ethan."

He lowered the cloth from her face. She gazed intently at him, and her hand glided from his knee…to his thigh.

He hastily dropped the napkin on the table and rose to his feet. He turned away to leave as he ordered his body to comply with one simple command: *Stop losing your shit every time she touches you.*

"Will you walk me to my room?" she asked.

He squeezed his eyes shut.

Fuck. Fuck. Fuck. Fuck.

"Fine." He started toward the door.

As soon as Vanessa stood, there was a pattering like gentle rain. They both looked at the floor, where handfuls of sunflower seeds had showered down from her lap.

"The boys certainly were busy," she remarked about John and Angelo's final prank. "Good thing I'm not first on cleanup duty tomorrow."

He stood out in the corridor as she put the folded linens away. He leaned on a hand against the archway column nearby and waited as she blew out each lamp in the kitchen.

When she finally emerged, she closed the door solidly behind her, and the moon brightened to cast her in a soft bluish light. Staring, he slowly dropped his hand from the stone pillar.

Her fair hair rippled in thick waves about her face as her eyes reflected the evening's glow, and her long skirt flowed around her from a gentle night breeze. She seemed a being born of fantasy, inhabiting those mystical places in the woods like one of the winsome fairy folk—the tylwyth teg—that his mother used to tell him about as a child. Some of the Welsh lore said that if a human man could ever catch such a playful fairy maiden, then he could carry her off and make her his.

"What is it?" Vanessa asked as the breeze lifted her hair from her shoulders.

"You just—" He shook his head. "Nothing."

He glared at the ground as he began to walk swiftly down the corridor.

She hurried to catch up with him, and she slipped her hand under his left arm. He struggled not to react to the way she pressed close to him as they walked. It was difficult enough to concentrate on where the hell they were going as they traversed the dark hallways, thanks to the distraction of her subtle gingery perfume.

She brushed her fingertips up and down his bicep, as if she were using the chance to explore the curve of his muscles.

Or she's trying to figure out what's wrong about the way the skin feels under the cloth.

An image of his arm—parts of it wrapped in ropes of scarred flesh—reared up in his mind, and he curled his left hand into a fist. In response, Vanessa tightened her fingers more firmly around his bicep, and he fought the urge to push her off him.

They did not speak as they made their way through the compound. But with each turn down a new hallway, he would lock gazes with her as she seemed to glance up at the same time.

Something's on her mind. But since when does she keep her thoughts to herself?

He rolled his shoulders uncomfortably and tried not to look at her again.

At last, they reached her room, and she pulled a key out of her skirt pocket. There was a slow, heavy clunk of metal as she turned the lock, and the sound echoed down the dimly lit passageway.

She faced him, returning the key to her pocket, and leaned back against the door. Her lips were parted as she transfixed him with those dark emerald eyes, and the front of his jeans—already packed full—expanded further.

"Do you want to come inside?" she asked in a quiet voice.

In every way.

"No." He pulled on the chin of his mask and stepped back. "I have an early day. And anything we need to discuss we can discuss tomorrow."

Her face fell. "But I'm wide awake now. And I thought we could just...spend some time together. I keep a bottle of Dornfelder on my mantel. It's a really good German red wine and hard to find anymore."

"No, I really have to—"

"But I owe you for saving me." She flattened her hands on the door behind her and shrugged with a smile. "Twice now."

He thought of the feel of her cheek against his bare fingers. "An even better reason to get some rest," he said, tamping down the twinge of yearning. "I may not be there next time to rescue you from another catnap." He turned to leave, but she stopped him.

"Ethan? Back in the kitchen...How long was it before you woke me?"

He suppressed the sight of those shining locks sliding over his fingers. "Not long."

She opened her mouth, then closed it again. Seconds of silence sat heavy on his ears.

Finally, uneasy, he asked, "What?"

She pressed her shoulders back against the door. "Did you peek?"

His eyes moved from her face down to her partially unbuttoned blouse, but he managed to snap them back up. "I don't know what you mean."

You know exactly what she means.

She ran her fingers down the open center of her shirt, drawing his gaze to either side of it, where her nipples had begun to make a brazen appearance behind the cloth. "Did you try to see what's under here?"

His erection—which had been building strength since they'd arrived at her door—pulsed harder against the unyielding denim. "No."

"That's a shame." Her voice was soft but even. "Because I wore your favorite color."

When she held his gaze, the revelation washed over him and rocked his senses. She had wanted him to look. She had wanted him to touch her. And not because of any hidden motive. Not for any power play or a wish for safety. She had wanted him to do it—

Because she wants me.

"Well…goodnight, then," Vanessa said.

But she did not move as her eyes searched his. She continued to play with the buttons at her cleavage, her breathing slow and deep. Even the waning light could not disguise the fevered flush of her neck. Her gaze lowered to his mouth, where his lips had at least healed more than the skin around them…enough so that they would create a soft contact if he pressed them to hers.

Heat churned in his chest like an engine revving up. His heart began to piston as the blood ran through his veins like hot oil. He clenched his hands into fists and took a hesitant step toward her. "I—" But all at once his body locked up, stalled like a transmission thrown into reverse at high speed. He held his position and ignored the cramping of his stomach. "Goodnight."

Her forehead creased and her fingers paused against her chest as her eyes clung to his. Then, after another moment, she opened the door behind her and slipped inside her room.

He stood motionless as his rib cage seemed to close in on itself and wring the air from his lungs. He stared at her door, regret warring with arousal. With each day that passed, every minute he spent near her dissolved his resistance like a sweet acid. Soon he would have no resolve left, only a fading residue of restraint. He was losing control. He needed to get his army out of there before it was too late. He took a step to turn away, but his eyes swept across the translated sign on the wall beside her door.

Officer's Pleasure.

He looked back at her room. She had probably already unzipped her skirt and dropped it to the floor. And next, fully unbuttoned her blouse to shed the thin material from her shoulders like a nymph rising from a sylvan pond. And the light from the solitary lamp on her windowsill would then lend its warm glow to every exposed bend of her body.

Were her bra and panties made of solid black lace? Or were they black but sheer, so that he could almost see what lay under that single removable layer? And how would she look as she crawled across her bed and lowered herself onto her belly? He could picture her body slowly flexing against the rumpled sheets, the tender crescents of her buttocks peeking out below panties that he could have peeled off with one finger. Maybe right at that moment—while he was standing there in the hall debating with his desires—she was watching the door, waiting for him to change his mind. Waiting for him to come in and wreck that bed with her until it collapsed.

He turned restlessly and strode down the corridor.

Most nights he could avoid dreaming. His subconscious had had its fair share of shit thrown at it over the years, but usually his brain was equipped to counter it, like launching some mental antiballistic payload that reduced everything to blackness and silence. But that night, his mind would not shut the fuck down.

Over and over—his body damp with perspiration and his bedsheets snarled—his eyes would flutter open, trying to snag the last tantalizing fragments of an image. But there was one dream in particular that seared itself into his memory...

CHAPTER THIRTY-SEVEN

ETHAN

Ethan stood in one of the shower stalls and let the warm water cascade over his head. As he rubbed the bar of soap against his chest, white bubbles bloomed and tangled in the dark hair scattered across his flesh. He slowed his movements. Something was off.

He drew a breath and glanced about himself. But he was surrounded by the normal stone walls of the fort that divided the old facilities. The vast empty room echoed with the sound of the showerhead turned on full blast. Thick steam rose around him, sweltering enough that sweat dripped down from his scalp under his hair. He ran his fingers along his jaw. Stubble. He was due for a shave. Should have brought in a razor with him.

He turned around in the spray to feel the water against his back, and he rolled his shoulders contentedly. The heavy curtain of steam parted then, and Vanessa stood in the opening to the stall.

She wore only a set of black lace lingerie, and her thick hair spilled over her shoulders. She floated toward him as her eyes took a leisurely tour of his body. She lifted her fingers to the front center of her bra and languidly unhooked it. His mouth quirked in a smile as she pulled the bra apart and let it slide down off her shoulders. It fell to the damp stone floor behind her. Her breasts were full, and they bounced gently as she walked, her nipples pert and deep pink, like her lips. She tucked her tongue into the corner of her mouth, as he had seen her do a dozen times when she was contemplating something, and his dick instantly responded.

Vanessa stopped close to him, her nipples only centimeters from his flesh, and she glanced downward with a smile. He made no attempt to hide his appreciation, but rather shifted his pelvis forward to give her a better view. She placed her hands on his chest and gently pushed him backward.

The water streamed over her face, soaking her hair, and trickled down her lusciously bare tits. Long bands of hair plastered themselves to her cheeks and neck as she pressed Ethan back against the rough wall, until they both stood out of the showerhead's spray. Vanessa gazed up at him for a moment before reaching down and taking the soap from his hand. Her eyes never left his as she eased the bar up his arm, leaving a thick chain of bubbles. He canted his head and, with a subtle thrust of his hips, grazed her midriff with the tip of his penis.

She smiled wider and pushed the soap across his pecs and down to his stomach, using long stroking motions as she went. She stepped closer and dragged her breasts against his chest, building a rich layer of foam between their bodies. She guided the soap down to his groin and cupped his balls in the same hand. She rubbed the bar against his scrotum slowly, sensuously, lathering him as she gently worked the flesh swollen there.

With a growl, he reached for her.

But he couldn't move his hands.

What the fuck?

His pulse sprinted as Vanessa undulated against him.

He jerked his arms, desperate to make them obey. This was his chance to have her, maybe his only chance. She might not wait much longer. He had to take her now. He knew she wanted him to grasp her breasts, to feel her nipples against his palms, to slide his hands down to her ass and slip his fingers into each tight hole in turn. But he was pinned to the wall, helpless to do anything but feel his body self-destructing under the temptations she forced on him.

She soaped him faster, her other hand joining in, until at last she grabbed his shaft and gave it one long, demanding stroke. He ground his teeth.

His cock couldn't take much more teasing. It was sitting up hard at attention, trapped between their bodies. He closed his eyes at how her belly felt moving against it. Every muscle was tensed, prepared for the second he could get his goddamn body to work.

Vanessa wrapped one hand around the nape of his neck and drew his head down to her. She brought her lips to his and kissed him hungrily as her other hand continued to fondle him. She moaned against his mouth and twirled her tongue around his, sending a dizzying current through his limbs.

And all at once, that shock of energy threw everything into gear.

His arms slid around her, and he pulled her fiercely against him. The bar of soap thudded to the floor as Vanessa's hands roamed up into his dripping hair to grip it in her fists. Their bodies glided against each other, and he spread his fingers against her back as her nipples dug into him.

Then he flipped her around to face the adjacent wall. Her midnight-black panties clung to her wetly as she flattened her palms on the coarse weeping stone before her.

He knelt behind her and pulled the slick lingerie down to her thighs. He seized her ass in his hands and massaged her firm flesh, making himself stiffen to the very fringe of climax. He spread her cheeks and pressed his face to her so that his tongue found the sweet slippery flesh of her pussy. He tickled and probed her, determined to drive his tongue deep enough to make her clench it like a vise. She shuddered against his mouth as he gathered her between his lips and licked the cream from her.

The water from the showerhead started to rain hotter

and harder. It gushed down his side as he rose to his feet.

He gripped Vanessa's hip in his left hand and squeezed. She looked back at him over her shoulder.

"Show me." The sound of his voice joined the unrelenting hiss of the water. "Show me what you want."

Without pause, she spread her legs wider, and the abrupt movement audibly ripped the seams of the panties around her thighs.

He took a breath, shutting his eyes.

No more holding back. No more hiding.

He nestled the head of his cock between her tender folds and trailed his other hand along her side.

I'm where I belong.

And, with the same eager certainty she'd just offered him, he pushed himself in.

She trembled as he stretched her open, her fingers turning clawlike against the wall in front of her. Then he wrapped his hands around her slender waist and began to pump her. He tilted his head back, blissful at how hot and receptive she was, as if she had been thinking about this as much as he had. Wanting it as much as he did. Needing it more than anything.

And knowing it could change everything.

Vanessa gasped and gripped him inside her as he fucked her faster. He bent over against her back and reached around her with both arms. He grasped her breasts, and her soft, wet flesh filled his hands perfectly. He pulled back enough to run his tongue up her spine and bite the nape of her neck. The bitterness of soap in his mouth barely registered as he straightened and grabbed her hips to thrust himself deeper into her. She panted as she again watched him over her shoulder and urgently bounced herself against him. With a self-satisfied smile, he looked down at where their flesh connected over and over, and he listened to the slap of his thighs against hers.

Then a lock of his dark brown hair drifted down to settle on the small of her back.

He slowed and squinted at the hair. It seemed to be smoking, as if singed.

Vanessa let out a soft moan, but he paid little attention as another smoldering lock appeared beside the first. His thrusts at once became jerky and erratic.

Other scorched clumps of hair followed, looking the same. They floated down and stuck to Vanessa's moist skin. He put a hand to his head and felt exposed flesh. More and more of his hair dropped in front of him.

In the next second, the surface of his scalp felt different. Bumpy and uneven. He stopped moving. It was only then that he looked at his other hand, which gripped Vanessa's hip.

The flesh upon it began to blur and melt.

He held both hands in front of his face and watched in shock as the skin slid around on his fingers and down his arms, steaming and twisting like molten plastic. Vanessa, still bent over, turned to look at him behind her.

And her mouth no longer opened in ecstasy. It gaped in horror.

Ethan touched his cheeks and chin and recoiled at the alarming pliability of his own flesh as it grew sticky and gnarled.

Vanessa jerked away and turned to cower back against the shower wall, covering her body with her hands.

He breathed raggedly, swept into a whirlpool of panic and pain. He tried to speak, reaching out to her, but only gurgling came forth. Vanessa pushed herself away from him along the wall, her eyes wide and unblinking. She shoved a fist to her mouth and ran from him. He tried to call her name, but his lips drooped and melded together like strips of softening wax.

The water jetting down from the showerhead turned so scalding it blistered his back. And then, as if the room itself had taken a deep breath, all sound was suspended.

His heart beat once—hard—before noise and blinding light erupted around him.

He clapped his hands to ears that felt like they were disintegrating beneath his fingers and ducked down. He fell to one knee in the shower stall. He shut his eyes, but another flash pierced them regardless. Dark shapes danced in his vision as he swayed from side to side. The entire room was on fire. Flames roared up around him and ran in lines along the tops of the stalls surrounding him.

The heat was so intense that when he looked at his arms, he saw the flesh start to bubble off his very bones. The skin covering his chest flowed down his body like layers of hot custard. He threw his arms around his own torso and staggered to his feet, but nothing could stop the liquefaction. He stared as the thick tissue poured away and puddled on the floor around him.

Vanessa was gone. An inferno engulfed him.

And one final drawn-out scream shredded the air.

CHAPTER THIRTY-EIGHT

ETHAN

It didn't mean anything. Suck it up, dipshit.

Ethan reached into his hood and fiddled again with one of the safety pins at the back of his head that had refused to stay closed all day. He winced as the point of it jabbed his thumb through the leather, but he managed to wrangle it shut. He jerked his mask down from his mouth, where it had risen over his bottom lip, and swung around the corner of the adjoining hall.

Twilight framed the end of the passageway, where it opened up to a perimeter corridor of the garden. But when he glimpsed the fiery glow of the sky in the distance, he balked against a mental image of his flesh oozing off his arms in long, greasy cords.

Cut it the fuck out, Evans!

He had been trying for the last two days to forget the raucous dream about Vanessa in the shower. He had important matters to deal with, and his own selfish inclination to pick it apart was fucking up his focus.

But his body fought him every time his thoughts re-wound to her wet nubile figure against him. The erection was instant, and he had to stop whatever he was doing to get it under control. But it didn't take long for it to subside, because the memory that usually followed was that of his ruinous form, its blood and melted muscle leaking onto the ground.

He had brought his condition upon himself, crafted his own hell by ordering the destruction of the Ukrainian community. It was an act that had visited upon him something of a karmic retribution. In a just man's world, he had deserved it.

But goddamn it, this was not a virtuous world, and the people in it were not principled people. And so how was this punishment justified? Why the fuck should he accept it?

Because you're an evil, vicious bastard, that's why.

Ethan walked faster toward the end of the hall until he burst into the cold evening. The sun had drifted down beneath the horizon, and the orange radiance he had seen before was giving way to more somber hues of gray and violet. Rain was coming.

He stopped at the kitchen doorway and poked his head in.

Vanessa was in the dining area, gathering up plates scattered across the tables. The residents must have just eaten their dinner there. His soldiers, in contrast, all carried their dishes to deposit them by the sinks, rather than make her scurry around to clear them away.

She bustled to a table near the door and sidled along the bench, stacking plates as she went. When she scooped the tower of dishware into her arms, Ethan knocked his knuckles on the doorframe.

Her head snapped up. "Oh, Captain!" She sounded a little short of breath as she balanced the stack of dirty plates against herself. "I'll be there in a sec."

He nodded and folded his arms. As she whirled away, one metal spoon flew off her pile and clattered to the stone floor.

He bent down, picked it up, and then leaned his shoulder against the doorway. He stretched his jaw against the mask and twirled the spoon thoughtfully between his gloved fingers.

Though the sight of her threatened to dredge up the dream, he had no choice if he wanted the information he had requested.

He had steeled himself to approach her that morning and ask if she would do a little investigative work for him. Not only had more of his guns gone missing from the armory and the tunnels, but some of his men were now AWOL. And suspiciously, so were the residents to whom the absent soldiers had been assigned as armed escorts into Achterwaartsstad. Not much of a coincidence, but a whole shitload of unacceptable. Vanessa would be able to find out what kind of "relationships" had developed in the compound and provide him with details to help him track down the deserters. The other residents tended to close ranks. Even now, most would not even meet his eyes.

Ethan flipped the spoon in the air and caught it as he watched Vanessa clean crumbs off a table in the back.

Desertion had never been a problem before. His men were used to being displaced. And they knew better than to threaten the solidarity of this army. Any one soldier's disloyalty could put the rest of them in danger. But now, here, they seemed to be questioning their nomadic life. That was his fault. He'd given them too much latitude, and they'd all gotten soft. Especially him.

I'm losing control. Everything I do is turning to shit. And it's because of this fucking place. We shouldn't be here.

Vanessa threw him a smile as she wiped down one of the benches. He gripped the spoon and dragged his thumb back and forth on it.

Even if it feels right.

Vanessa hurried back into the cooking area to hand her last pile of dishes to another staff member. Then she bounded back toward Ethan, and the light from the many lamps reflected enchantingly off her long tresses as she pushed them behind her. He tugged his hood forward, but his gaze skated down one side of her blue V-shaped neckline. Her cleavage didn't need any help drawing attention to itself, so when she deliberately augmented it with a blouse that embraced her breasts like a second skin, she ensnared every eye that wandered her way.

And there goes the goddamn hard-on again.

He handed her the spoon and straightened off the doorframe. He pulled down on the front of his robe. "Done?"

She looked at the spoon in her hand. She shrugged and tossed it over her shoulder to clang onto the floor. "Sure, let's go. We can talk out by the orchard wall. Looks like it might storm in a little while, but we've got time." She took his arm and pulled on it to lug him along with her.

He stood firmly in place. "Here is fine. What did you find out?"

She tugged on him. "Come on, it's still a nice evening and not too cold yet."

Not too cold? It was a November night in North Holland. His eyes dropped to her skirt, which fell just past her knees. *She must have polar bear blood in her veins.*

"I only have a few minutes," he mumbled.

She wrapped her arm closer around his, and her breast skimmed across his sleeve. "Then I'll make them count," she said with a coy smile.

He bit his tongue at the sudden image of her drenched in water, her hair clinging to her skin as she pressed her bare, lathered body to his.

"All right," he managed, even more self-conscious as his cock continued to prod his jeans under the robe.

"Where's Morgan?" she asked as they stepped out of the one-sided corridor. "I thought he was still playing your conjoined twin these days."

Ethan stared down at the grass, which had begun to yellow as the blades retracted into dormancy. "I needed him elsewhere."

"Just as well. We could use the privacy."

He glanced at her. Privacy for what?

They serpentined around the fenced vegetable beds, a few of the plots dominated by leafy heads of cauliflower and stands of clustered Brussels sprouts. The silhouettes of two of his sentries passed each other along the eastern ramparts beyond, where the sky had deepened to a navy blue. The downpour was headed their way. When they reached the orchard, Vanessa stopped and turned her back to the wall.

"Okay, so I asked around today, like you wanted." She put the heels of her hands behind her on the wall's edge to hike herself up. "And I found out that there are—" She dropped back to the ground with a grunt and then repositioned her hands for another attempt. "Anyway, I found out there are actually—Ow!" She landed with a stumble and shook out her fingers. "Crap, okay, hold on."

Ethan folded his arms.

She stuck the tip of her tongue against a corner of her mouth as she replanted the heels of her hands and bounced on her toes for a moment. She hopped up—

Then slid awkwardly down the wall.

Ethan raised his eyebrows behind the mask.

She pressed her lips together tightly and turned away from him to lay her arms across the wall's top. Her voice was muffled as she dug the toe of one slipper into a stone seam. "Anyway, what people told me—*unh!*" Her foot slipped as she clawed her way onto her stomach. "Was that they thought it was strange—*unh!*—that no one— *unh!*—had seen—" She let out a long growl while both feet scrabbled for purchase.

He shook his head. *Graceful as a swan.*

She dropped back down, spun around, and blew her hair out of her face. "You know, you could do the gentlemanly thing and help a lady out!"

He continued to stand with his arms folded. "I thought you almost had it that time."

She crossed her arms at him in return. With a sigh, he moved closer and grabbed hold of her waist. She yelped as he hoisted her onto the wall. She slid her hands onto his shoulders and squirmed against his fingers.

"Well, now," she said as she bumped her heels against the wall. "That's more like it."

He hesitated as his eyes lowered to where her skirt had ridden above her knees.

Fuck. Those legs. I'd kill for five seconds to follow them all the way up.

He forced his gaze back to her face and cleared his throat. "Just…try not to fall off."

But before he could pull back, she caught his shirt-sleeves. "Maybe you should hold on to me, then." She gave his wrists a squeeze. "Just in case."

Holy hell, she is going to be the end of me.

He dragged his arms free from her hands. "I think you can take your chances." He glanced over her. "Besides, anyone who can ignore all weather and common sense already has luck on her side."

"No luck needed." She shrugged one shoulder. "I'm a spring baby, born in late April. So my father said that I always carry some sunshine around with me. Keeps me warm all year." She rested her hands on the wall and rocked side to side to adjust herself farther back. "When were you born?"

"Winter."

She rolled her eyes. "That figures."

He frowned.

"Well," she said, knocking her knees together leisure-ly, "they do say opposites attract."

She then parted her legs, creating enough space for him to slide his hand between them under her skirt, if he dared. He met her eyes as she gave him the hint of a smile. All at once, in his mind, she was bent over with her palms spread against a damp wall in front of her, her soaked black panties around her thighs.

He nudged himself and squared his shoulders. "You said you had intel for me," he said sharply. "Your report?"

She straightened and put on a mock-serious expression as she saluted him. "Yes, sir, Captain Crabby, sir."

He set his hands on his waist. "Just spit it out, smart-ass."

She gave a laugh, which made her breasts bounce and come dangerously close to escaping that low neckline. "Okay, so you guessed right about the residents who left. There were just those three, as of this afternoon. Two women, one man, all in their twenties, and all of them single. And yeah, based on what the gossip gang has seen them doing around the compound, they were, uh, very friendly with your missing soldiers." She gave him a sidelong look. "I suppose you want a list with all the details?"

"Yes." He paused when she showed him a smirk. "It's not an order. But I'd appreciate it."

"Then it would be my pleasure." Her gaze fell from his, and she started to fidget with the hem of her skirt. "I could bring it by your bedroom tonight," she suggested softly.

A quiver raced through his stomach, and his cock stirred again. "You don't want to do that."

She lifted her eyebrows.

"That is, I'm sure you have better ways to spend your time," he said quickly and stepped back. "Tomorrow's good enough. I'd best get going. I still have some things to finish before I hit the sack."

"What did you do with those residents who had an X by their names?"

He stopped in mid-turn. Her cautious delivery of the question made the words hover in the air between them. "What?"

She picked at the crumbling edge of the wall beside her but wouldn't meet his eyes. "The ones you drew a line through. On the other list I made."

"How do you know I—?" He took a slow step toward her and leaned both hands on the wall to either side of her. "What were you doing in my quarters?"

"I went to see you, but you weren't there."

"That's not an excuse."

Her tone grew firm. "What happened to them?"

"Rhetta is fine," he snapped.

The tendons in her neck were visibly taut as her eyes remained glued to his. "What about the others?"

"Why does it matter?"

"Because I"—she began to repeatedly bunch the side of her skirt in her fist—"because I gave them to you."

"And you think what? That I had their throats ripped out?" Ethan's voice was vinegary. "Had them buried in a mass grave?"

Her eyes widened. "No, I—" She bit her lip for a second. "I guess I shouldn't have assumed the worst."

"You shouldn't have assumed *at all*." Ethan paused and drummed his fingers upon the wall as she sat tensely between his arms. "I relocated them to other provinces, far enough out that they can't get in my way while I'm here." He gripped the stone and inclined his head. "Except for one. And he had it coming."

She nodded hesitantly. "Okay." She dropped her gaze again. "I guess I'm an exception, since I'm still here. Because I seem to do nothing *but* get in your way."

"That's not true."

"Isn't it? You told me yourself, back in town, that I just made things worse."

"That wasn't your fault. I shouldn't have blamed you."

She furrowed her brow. "But you said—"

"Forget what I said." He relaxed the muscles in his arms so that he stopped gripping the wall. "I…shouldn't have treated you like that." His chest felt heavy, his body straining as if tied to a sinking anchor. "You've never been in a situation like that before, so you weren't prepared for it. And when you stopped me…you were just going with your gut." He stared at his knuckles as he knocked them lightly against the stone edge. "I'm sorry I couldn't see that."

She glided her hand onto his beside her. "Thank you. It means so much to hear you say that. I didn't agree with you, but…I thought I'd lost your respect because of it."

His heart lurched at the warmth of her slender fingers upon his glove. "That's never going to happen," he said gently. "You are the biggest smart-ass around"—he smiled when she squinted at him—"but you're no pushover. And you know how to stand up to me."

She eased her hands onto the front of his robe, gathered it in her fists, and pulled him toward her. "I also know what I want."

He felt a slow burn of excitement as his stomach pressed against her knees. "And what exactly is that?"

Show me what you want. His own words from the dream echoed in his mind. He saw her naked, ready for him, accepting him. Vanessa shifted her knees against his stomach, her hands twisting the dark fabric of his robe. His shoulders were rigid, muscles drawn together as he watched her.

"I want you to trust me," she whispered. She opened her legs just enough to drag him closer.

Giving in to a heady rush of anticipation, he placed his palms on the outsides of her thighs and massaged her skirt fabric between his fingers. Every nerve in his body seemed to throb in time with his quickening heartbeat.

She reached out and pushed his hood off his head. Then she leaned forward to put her mouth near his covered ear. "Show me your face."

The world went silent as the blood thrusting through his veins seemed to stop.

"You don't have to hide from me." She drew back marginally and looked over his mask as if she could already see beneath it. "I know that you're burned."

It was like a bucket of ice water had been dumped on him. He wavered as her words seeped through his thoughts. He saw her stumbling back from him in the shower, covering her wet body with her hands...her mouth stretched wide in terror...her eyes full of revulsion...everything spinning out of control as his flesh ruptured and dissolved around him...

He took her wrists and pried her hands from his robe. He straightened his shoulders and met her eyes. "Do you know why?"

"Yes."

His body at once turned uncomfortably hot, melting the glacial numbness. Streaks of fire blazed along every scar, igniting his flesh in a reenactment of the explosion two years ago, when Morgan had pulled him from the wreckage. He had lain upon a ground that felt made of needles, choking up at a smoke-filled sky as blood and ash filled his mouth and every raw muscle convulsed in unison.

"How much were you told?" he asked stiffly as he shifted back from her.

Her gaze was skittish as she chewed her bottom lip. "Only that you did it for revenge. And that you were trapped inside before you could get out."

"Then you don't know anything." The words honed his voice to a razor's edge. "And you don't need to." He blinked as his eyes stung for an instant, and he raised the hood over his head. He receded as far back as possible into its darkness, and his voice was scarcely audible when he spoke. "I am a…flawed man. I've done things that still make me lose sleep. But I'm not looking for redemption." He clenched his jaw. "I'm beyond repair."

She studied him for a moment. Then she reached up and her fingertips strayed across his lips. "No one is completely broken."

He grabbed her hand and pulled it away. "You have no idea what you're saying. My past is my business. I made my choices and then they made *me*. My body—my face—is a fucking curse." He held her gaze sternly. "But I live with it. You don't. Quit deciding you have any right to make demands."

"I'm not demanding," she insisted, her eyes darting between his. "I'm asking you to let me in—"

"Well, stop asking. I've made a lot of mistakes, but I don't want this one to come between us."

The confession escaped before he could catch it. He tensed.

Vanessa pulled back, seeming equally startled. "Us?" she echoed faintly.

An unanticipated yearning welled up at how her eyes caught the shine of the distant kitchen light. He struggled to make his voice emerge. "Yes."

She took a quick breath and seemed to hold it. The creeping shadows in the garden grew and spread around them. Then she dropped her gaze as she began to twine her fingers in the front of his robe. "How can there be an 'us' if you won't be honest with me?"

He lifted her chin with a finger and looked pointedly

at her. "I have never lied to you."

"But you've hidden things. You've avoided me. You won't tell me why you're so dead set on getting away from here."

A bitterness at the back of his tongue made him swallow, but he kept his voice steady. "I—we have to stay on the move. If you already know what happened in Ukraine, then you know that, too."

"I guess the map is true."

"What?"

She pressed her knees together and reached into her pocket to pull out a thick square of tan-colored paper. She turned it in her hands and finally held it toward him. "I saw this on your desk, too."

He snatched it and unfolded the map he'd been carefully using for years to keep track of his wretched route.

"You had no business taking this," he said curtly. "Why did you?"

She shrugged, looking down and picking at her skirt. "Because I was going to ask you about it. But then I realized I already knew the answer." She raised her eyes only briefly. "After that, I kept it because…I thought maybe not having it would slow you down."

His lungs tightened as his fingers loosened around the paper. He should have been angry. He should have given her the full reprimand he would have delivered to any one of his soldiers. But all he could do was watch the way her eyes lost some of their glow. And his mind refused to grasp on any thought except one.

She wants me. For some damn reason, she wants me.

He slowly placed the map on the wall beside her, where one edge of it lifted and fluttered in the rising breeze. "I set something in motion a long time ago, and I've forced my men into this position now, too. We have to move to live. If we stay in one place too long, we sacrifice our survival. Or more accurately, I'd be sacrificing *their* survival. And I won't do that."

"But this place can be your stronghold," she countered. "You can build it up better, to withstand anything.

And no one in the town will contest your ownership of the compound anymore, not even Mayor Visser—"

"For now," he said firmly. "But that will change with time. Those villagers will get braver as they think we're becoming complacent. And there will be more attacks, like the one last month. It *will* happen. And worse, our other enemies *will* catch up with us. So I will not deliberately put my soldiers in the line of fire if I don't have to." He trailed his eyes down her anxious face. "And I will not put you in danger anymore, either. I can't risk your life, no matter how—" His heart seemed to drop as if cut from its cavity, and he cradled her chin in his gloved palm. "No matter how selfish I want to be." He brushed his thumb over her bottom lip, as he had back in the kitchen two nights ago, when he had stolen that one covert caress. "And damn, do I want to be," he whispered.

In the distance, there was an ominous grumble, and the clouds lit up beyond the battlements.

Vanessa opened her mouth hesitantly, as if to speak, but Ethan robbed her of the chance. He took her face in both hands and eased her knees apart with his body. She looked up at him as he pressed close to her against the wall, and she spread her legs wider so that the warmth of her thighs enclosed him. The energy building in his core spiraled together with the static charge in the air as the storm rolled toward them. His mask stretched against him, fighting to restrain him as he leaned in. His hood framed her face, making her join him within its shadows, and she clutched his robe in her fists. She sighed against his lips as he gradually, tentatively brought them to hers.

A wildness flooded his senses, held in check only by how gently she poured herself into his embrace and returned the kiss. He angled his head and drew the tip of his tongue across her lips, so that she opened her mouth to him. He entered her—kissed her deeper, slower, his body animated with a fundamental craving that made every motion exquisite.

He glided one hand down her hair until he reached the small of her back, where he curled his fingers into the slinky fabric of her shirt and dragged it upward. He traced the inside of her lips with his tongue while he tucked his fingertips into the waistband of her skirt, imagining the softness of her skin through the leather of his glove. He ran his other hand along her thigh and under the filmy garment, catching its hem with his thumb and pulling it up across her flesh.

He should have done this that night outside her room, instead of shutting her down and walking away. He should have done so many things before this.

There was another rumble of thunder, closer this time, and a flurry of wind scattered her tresses around him like swirling sunlight. His hand quested higher beneath her skirt until he reached her hip, where he hooked his fingers into the delicate side strap of her panties and gripped it. Vanessa gasped against his mouth, but then trapped him tighter between her legs, her lips joining his again.

At last, they parted just enough to catch their breath, and his heartbeat pulsed heavy in his ears. The outside world slowly came back into focus as the night closed in. She slipped her arms around his neck and pressed her mouth upon his chin to kiss it through the mask. They breathed quietly against each other, until she nudged his nose with hers and showed him a fragile smile.

"What took you so long?" she murmured.

He grunted a laugh. "I obviously don't know how to take a hint." She giggled at that, and he held her cheek to brush his thumb over it. "But I'm learning. If you'll be patient with me."

She passed her lips playfully across his. "Careful, Captain. Now you're sounding like a man who plans on sticking around." She put her hand upon his, which rested against her face, and her smile faded. "So are you?"

A sudden lurch of excitement in the pit of his stomach made him pause. "How can I?"

She squeezed his hand. "*Be* selfish. If you stay, you can protect me. You can protect all of us. Or teach us how to fight, and we can help *you* survive."

"You're not ready for that. It would take a lot of training. And you'd need to trust me. All of you. I don't know if we have that kind of time."

"You know I trust you. And the others will too."

"This place is rundown. There's too much to repair for it to be viable under a siege, if things go sideways—"

"Yes, there are a lot of things we'll need to do. And I'm sure that military mind of yours won't have any trouble thinking them all up." She slid her hands back into his hood to hook them behind his neck, and her voice became velvety. "So why don't you walk me to my room and tell me all about it?" She started a slow smile that made his every muscle draw tight. "We have the whole night to make a nice…long…list."

He glided his gloved hands along her arms. "You're asking for trouble."

She nodded and tugged him toward her. "My favorite kind."

Ethan quickly closed the space between them and sealed her mouth with his again. He renewed his advance, this time sliding both hands beneath her skirt until he could twist his fingers into the frail, ribbonlike sides of her lingerie. He paused only to nip at her bottom lip before he let her tongue back in to stroke his. The feel of her mouth sent a blaze of heat down his body that grew hotter with every soft, wet noise she made. But then the sharp burst of fire began to gutter when a heavy coldness blunted its edge.

And how far do you think you can take this, shithead? This isn't a goddamn fairy tale. She won't want a burned bastard like you. You're only going to fuck up her life…or end it.

Ethan halted, his lips going still. At that, Vanessa paused and drew back from him.

"Ethan?" She placed her hands on his chest. "What's wrong?"

The air began to feel thick, oppressive. He started to respond but couldn't, rendered mute as if a metal collar had been cuffed to his throat.

"Ethan." She shook her head weakly, and her gaze held the vanishing evening light like a wavering mirror.

"What is it?"

He touched his fingers to her cheek. Every soft, fragile curve of her features begged for his answer and made the rising ache in his chest worse. His mind moved as if treading murky water: losing its logic, its direction, disorientation compromising the instinct not to drown. And he was left to founder when the unexpected weight of the moment dragged him under.

"I can't do this," was all he could manage.

The breathless moment broke. They both glanced down as something fluttered between them. The wind had blown the map and flattened it against the front of his robe. Vanessa peeled it off carefully and handed it to him. Her eyes, already glimmering like misted glass, gleamed brighter.

"Well, then." Her voice was barely a whisper. "I guess you're going to need this after all." She gazed at him for a few more seconds before turning her face away.

In an instant, he was left stranded, isolated. It was as if a last ray of daylight had been cut off. And the darkness it had once divided became complete.

The sky gave a deep-chested growl and flared above them.

"You don't understand," he tried again. "It's not—"

"I think I do understand. Better than ever." She put the heels of her hands against the edge of the wall and pushed herself down off it.

"Vanessa," he said too softly for her to hear when she swept by. He didn't move until the first few drops of rain hit his shoulders and roused him from staring at the wall where she had sat. He turned and strode after her as he gripped the map beside him. "Vanessa, wait," he said louder as he followed. "It's not that simple." He drew up behind her and caught her elbow. "You're not listening to—"

When she turned to him, her teeth were gritted. "That's just it, Captain. I *was* listening. More than you do!"

A heavier roll of thunder vibrated the ground, and the

raindrops struck his shoulders harder. A breeze gusted and blew his robe to billow out beside him.

His voice roughened. "I'm not doing this for me."

Vanessa yanked her elbow from his hand and backed away. "Well, you're certainly not doing it for me, either."

He clenched his fists. "That's where you're wrong."

"No. What I was wrong about is thinking that all of this"—she gestured around herself at the fort, the garden—"was starting to mean something to you. That you were going to give this—give *us* a chance." Her face was wet, the rain beginning to drench her hair and run down her cheeks. "But I guess that's just me being naïve again, isn't it? Maybe it's just as well that you're leaving. Because I'm tired of getting my hopes up." She hugged herself and spun away.

He stood motionless, insensible to the grumbling noise overhead. His hood whipped against his masked face as the wind attacked it. He unclenched his fists until his hands hung limply beside him, the map fluttering against his fingers as if desperate to escape its bonds. The rain started in earnest then, bringing down a steel-colored curtain that blocked out Vanessa's frail form as she fled into the corridor across the way.

The rain pounded against him, but still he did not move. He let it soak through every layer of black cloth that enfolded him until he could feel the water streaming down his misshapen body beneath. The tattered map grew limp and sodden, no longer fighting to free itself.

The warm bright glow coming from the kitchen winked out as Vanessa closed the door. And a realization—as if chained to a deep, cold seabed—tore loose and floated to the surface to be pitched upon the raging waves.

She'd just declared defeat. Which meant he'd just lost everything.

CHAPTER THIRTY-NINE

VANESSA

"I dinnae ken what it could be." Angus blinked down at the green lump in Mabayoje's outstretched hand. "A tattie, maybe?"

The tall lieutenant pinched the object to squint at it against the backdrop of the garden just outside the kitchen. "It does not look like any potato I have ever seen." Mabayoje held his clipboard flat to set the conversation piece in the center. "I nearly broke a tooth on it."

"Well, I sneaked this out from me lunch." Thomas pulled a wad of napkins from his pocket.

Morgan, Angus, Frank, and Mabayoje leaned in as he unwrapped it.

"That's a wee bit of herring," Angus said firmly, jabbing a brawny finger at it.

Morgan bent closer to the jellied object. "I don't believe herring are known to have…fur."

"Ach!" Angus said, waving a hand under his nose. "Whate'er it is, it's pure givin' me the boke!"

"Christ on a cucumber!" Thomas cried and dumped the thing on the ground. "It just moved, I swears it!"

Vanessa giggled to herself and brushed the dirt from a newly excavated potato before dropping it onto the others in the pile nearby. Thomas and the officers had all started playing "Figure Out the Food" not long after Rhetta's departure, since every meal had so far presented itself as a puzzle. But the entertainment factor hadn't made up for Rhetta's absence. Having her gone felt like losing another family member to a senseless act. Vanessa shook her head and rose from her knees to grab the spading fork leaning against the wire fence around the vegetable bed. She plunged the tool into the soil at an angle and used her foot to shove the tines deeper.

Ethan was being unfair, and he knew it. She could tell he knew it because of how uptight he would get each time she brought it up.

She stabbed the dirt again and waggled the handle.

Not that she'd had any desire to talk to him over the past week in order to bring it up again, though. Why bother? He was only focused on his own needs. He was leaving her behind, and he didn't care how she felt about that, either. She should be glad to see him march his grumpy self right out the rear gates.

She gritted her teeth and flung a glob of soil aside before prying at the potato plant to expose its roots.

Even if he had been so tender and passionate with her that night, and his lips had felt so very good on hers, and his kiss had filled her with an orgasmic hunger that left her panting, and his arms had felt like the safest, most natural place in the world, like she belonged there…

All her hair swung forward as she jabbed the ground harder.

It had all been for nothing. He was so freakin' stubborn and refused to listen. Who knew if that kiss had even meant anything to him? He'd probably forgotten all about it, just like he was going to forget about her—

"You's all right there, ducky?"

She stopped mid-grunt and looked up.

Thomas, Morgan, and the others had paused their guessing game to stare at her.

She shrugged. "I'm fine. Why?"

The men exchanged glances.

Then she looked down at the soil strewn wildly about her, most of it landing on her. She lifted the spading fork, whose tines had impaled a cluster of potatoes so violently that chunks of them littered the bed.

She stared back at the soldiers. "Oh."

Heat crept into her cheeks, and she knelt next to the tool to wiggle the butchered vegetables free. With a sigh, she grabbed a fistful of hair and shook it, clumps of dirt raining down on the potatoes she'd already wiped clean.

At least it wasn't as bad as her breakfast mishap earlier, when she'd had to retreat to the ladies' facilities to wash the exploded egg bits off her blouse. She'd been rehashing her and Ethan's conversation then, too. She pressed her lips together. Not long ago, thinking about him would have made her take a cold shower for an entirely different reason, but so much for that now.

She sighed even louder and pushed back the plant's yellowed, dying foliage to unearth any last tubers hidden beneath its base.

"What about you?" Mabayoje asked Frank as the guys went back to their pop quiz.

The big Russian sergeant took a cigar from his back pocket and put it between his teeth. He opened his other hand to reveal a mottled brown cube. All the men recoiled.

Morgan spread his thumb and forefinger across his mustache. "I see Marien no longer concerns herself with simulating even the semblance of meat."

Frank frowned deeper than usual as he turned the crumbly cube between his fingers. He handed it to Thomas, who grimaced and eyed the mysterious sample.

Thomas griped, "How can a fella be more gut-foundered comin' out of a meal than when he wents in?" He watched Frank slip his lighter out of another pocket and flick the lid up to puff on his cigar against the flame. "Me boots is lookin' right tasty 'bout now, eh?" Thomas let the cube fall and then drop-kicked it.

"You'd best save them for your supper, Private." Morgan nodded toward the other side of the garden. "It's time you gathered the deserters for their sentencing. The captain is already on his way."

At that, Vanessa snapped her head back up, her fingers buried in the moist soil between a few remaining potatoes. Ethan—his robe gone but his glare intact—was striding past the orchard, heading straight for his officers, who still lingered near the kitchen. Thomas promptly saluted Morgan and trotted off down the nearby corridor toward the entrance to the tunnels. Frank took one long drag on the cigar, making the end glow bright orange, and then turned to grind the butt against the stone wall next to him. As Ethan drew near, his shoulders were rigid, and his gloved hands were fisted at his sides. When he began to maneuver around the flower and vegetable beds, he tugged at the chin of his mask, and his gaze latched on to Vanessa's.

And that's my cue. She quickly gathered the potatoes against herself and rose to cradle them in her apron. *No way I'm sticking around for Captain Cold-Heart to put on a show and punish even more people.*

"Where are they?" she heard Ethan ask as she deliberately kept her eyes on the ground and walked toward the kitchen.

"Thomas is collecting them," Morgan answered.

"And the other matter?"

The jumbled sound of people talking excitedly—like the indistinct babbling of a far-off crowd—drifted and echoed through the halls leading from the front of the compound.

"I believe therein lies your answer," Morgan said.

Vanessa blew a lock of hair from her face and used a shoulder to wipe what felt like a dried smear of mud off her cheek. The noise became louder as several residents emerged from the dark of the main hallway, seeming to flock around someone in the center of the moving mass. Cornelis and Pieter were in the lead but were soon pushing people apart, Cornie pausing only to turn his head and flash her a grin.

Vanessa hesitated as she placed a foot on the threshold of the kitchen, the dank smell of dirt rising heavily to her nostrils from the bulky bundle of potatoes against her. She peered through the cluster of residents. What on earth were they—?

Her arms went slack, and all the potatoes fell and tumbled across the stone walkway. With a cry, Vanessa leaped over the scattered vegetables. She ran down the hallway, past Cornelis, past all the chattering residents, and right into Rhetta's embrace.

The old cook clasped her tightly, letting out a small whimper. When Vanessa pulled back, Rhetta was smiling as brightly as the glittering tears in her eyes. Vanessa hugged her again, her own vision blurring and her heart still pounding.

"Oh, Rhetta," she said, muffled against the cook's shoulder. "I've missed you so much! I looked for you every time I went to Achterwaartsstad, but no one knew where to find you."

Rhetta drew back and wiped at her wet cheeks. She glanced beside her at Henrick, whose salt-and-pepper mustache lifted in a warm smile. "The captain is lucky to have Henrick in his army. Dutch soldiers do not quit a task till it is finished. He searched for many days." She reached out to grasp his hand briefly with a slight blush in her cheeks. "He also knew the right words to say."

Vanessa paused to glance between them. *Well, that's interesting.*

Rhetta turned and held Vanessa at arm's length. "It is good to be home, liefje." But then her smile faded when her eyes moved to something in the distance beyond Vanessa's shoulder. "Even if things are not as they should be."

Vanessa glanced behind her. Ethan stood in front of his officers, his arms folded, but he was gazing at Vanessa. She squeezed Rhetta's hand tighter and firmed her mouth. What could have changed his mind? He had been crystal clear about his decision to banish Rhetta. So only some calculated, strategic reason would make him reverse it. That's how his brain worked. There was no other explanation.

Ethan continued to watch her. Then he gave her a

slow nod.

Her heart skipped. *Unless it was…for me? Was that why he did it?*

That would mean he actually had listened, that he actually did care.

She started to drift forward, her pulse picking up speed, but stopped herself.

No. He's still leaving. So how much does he really care if he's not changing that?

Her shoulders sank as a chill numbed her skin. She faced Rhetta and slipped her arms around her, this time seeking comfort from the reunion.

The residents continued to chitter-chatter happily to each other and press in on Rhetta to ask questions, so Vanessa backed carefully out of the throng to give the others a chance to welcome her. But then the general clamor of the residents changed in tone and became uneasy.

That was when three of the captain's soldiers—none of them wearing any kind of uniform anymore, like she was used to seeing—emerged from the tunnel entrance. Their hands were tied behind them, and Thomas brought up the rear with an unusual blankness to his face. They all crossed the garden to where Ethan waited. Standing shoulder to shoulder behind him were all the officers, their spines stiff and shoulders back as they stared straight ahead. Surrounding the garden from above were the rest of the captain's soldiers—every one of them—spaced apart on the battlements and standing at attention. She and the other residents were still milling in the perimeter corridor near the kitchen, but no doubt there were silent, unmoving soldiers hovering overhead, too. Cornelis appeared at her side, his gaze moving from Ethan to the battlements and then down to her. The grim line of his mouth was probably an exact reflection of hers.

Thomas placed his hands on each of the bound men's shoulders and positioned them a meter apart in a straight line. Then he stood in front of the captain and saluted him. Ethan returned it. Thomas took one step back, pivoted ninety degrees, and took one more step back to stand with his arms at his sides.

Rhetta squeezed her hand and patted it. Vanessa glanced at her and, with a start, relaxed her anxious grip around the cook's fingers. The eeriness of all the military formality was making her whole body tighten up. What was Ethan planning? It couldn't be good.

Ethan approached the three men, whose faces were sweaty in spite of the icy day. The soldiers kept their gazes fixed, their shoulders held square and their bodies still. Their hands were partially fisted against the wrist restraints behind them, as if standing at attention like the rest of Ethan's men.

The compound was hushed, everyone seeming to watch the scene before them like the start of a play, when the curtain begins to rise. The back of Vanessa's neck twinged as its tension expanded into her shoulders. If only she'd exited early and pulled Rhetta with her into the kitchen. Both of them had seen this kind of drama before, after the raid on the fort, and could already figure out the ending.

Ethan stopped in front of the three soldiers. He clasped his hands behind himself and looked at each of them in turn. Finally, he spoke, and his voice seemed to echo through the entire fort.

"I remember when each of you joined this army. And I remember how much you wanted in. All of you recognized what was becoming of your countries, your governments. All of you were forced out, your own people making an example of you for standing against them. But all of you were looking for a second chance. Lucky for you, this whole outfit is made up of second chances. So you got yours, because *we* gave it to you."

He walked over to the first soldier in line and began making his way past them.

"And then we came here. We took over, we dug in. And then apparently, all your training, all your convictions, all your loyalty went out the fucking window. You got comfortable. You started to forget why you're here and what we have to do in order to survive. But most of all, you forgot why you asked to be here, with us. You got selfish."

Vanessa glanced at Rhetta, who seemed to be barely breathing as she watched. Henrick, beside her, was at attention just like the rest of the soldiers, his expression stoic.

"I know why you did it," Ethan went on, "but I don't accept why you did it. You swore an oath to me and to Lieutenant Winchester and to every man here." He paused to look over them again. "This isn't some club you joined that you can drop out of. This is your *family*. And you don't disregard family. You don't forge a bond like this and then ignore it because you changed your mind, found a better option." His tone grew sharper, angrier. "The very fucking least you owed me was a conversation. An explanation. I would have listened, just as I listened when each of you petitioned me to join this army. Would I have been pissed off? Yes. Would I have given you the dressing-down of your life? Your goddamn ears would've bled."

Vanessa shook her head and began to edge toward the kitchen. *Okay, I've seen enough. I can guess where this is going.*

"Would I have considered it a betrayal?" Ethan brought his arms back to his sides, and his voice lowered. "No."

Vanessa halted. *What's this? A plot twist?*

Several residents around her started to murmur to each other, as if equally startled. But the only soldiers who showed any reaction were the three men, whose brows furrowed as they tossed a glance at one another.

"But what you did by stealing from us and then deserting, sneaking off in secret," Ethan told them firmly, "that is a betrayal. You did more than simply disrespect me." He swept an arm around at the soldiers standing along the battlements above. "You turned your backs on every one of your brothers. All of us. With no regard for our history together or our future together." Ethan folded his arms, straightening to his full height, which gave him an imposing presence that always stole her breath. "But this, gentlemen, is your *second* second chance."

Ethan nodded at Thomas, and the Canadian walked behind the soldiers to briskly untie their hands. Then he stuffed the ropes in his pockets and resumed his previous position.

"It's a simple choice: stay with us or leave." Ethan narrowed his eyes at them. "But once you're out, you're out. There will be no more accommodations. So if you stay, your hearts sure as hell better be in it for the long haul. No doubts. No disloyalty. And no dishonesty."

The men each seemed to look directly at Ethan, but otherwise made not the slightest move.

Ethan dropped his arms and raised his voice. "But you all know that I'm not one to ignore this kind of behavior. What you did goes well beyond any minor misconduct. So if you do stay, the disciplining you get will be a shitload more severe than any nonjudicial punishment. In any other outfit, your asses would be court-martialed for your crimes, so I can promise that I won't go light on you. But if you want to be part of this army again, you will accept that punishment willingly. And you'll have to re-earn my trust and the trust of your brothers, so it won't be an easy way back in. You can either show us that you actually value this family, or you can turn around and get the hell out of our sight, because we have no use for you."

The residents had spread throughout the perimeter corridors of the garden, seeming fully engrossed in how the scene was unfolding. Two of the resident women and one young man had strayed into the garden itself to get closer, their faces twisted in agitation.

When Ethan spoke again, his voice was as clear and sharp as a hammer's strike on a bell. "Make your choice."

The soldiers along the battlements were like statues. The residents had stopped whispering to each other and watched, motionless. The women and the man who'd wandered closer stood holding each others' hands. The silence was such that Vanessa could almost hear her blood rushing through her veins.

Slowly, the soldier in the middle of the formation stepped forward. He raised his arm and held a steady hand to his brow.

Ethan settled his gaze on him.

Then the soldier on the end nearest Vanessa did the same and held his salute in silence next to the first man.

The residents all appeared to hold their breath as everyone's focus turned to the last soldier, who was squeezing his fists at his sides as he shifted his weight. But all at once, he lifted his chin higher, the rise and fall of his chest slowing, and he took one step forward. He jerked his arm up in a determined salute.

Ethan moved his eyes across the soldiers, all of them standing stiffly with their hands to their brows and their jaws clenched. His chest expanded even further as he drew a long breath, and, though his gaze eased, his tone remained inflexible. "If you ever have something to say to me in the future, then you say it. I'll listen. Show me respect, and I'll show you the same. Is that understood?"

"Yes, sir!" they chorused, still locked in their poses.

At last, Ethan saluted them in return. "Dismissed."

At that, all the soldiers along the battlements relaxed and started mixing together, many of them springing down the steps into the garden. The male and two female residents who had been waiting nearby suddenly broke apart, each of them running to one of the three soldiers to throw their arms around him. The soldiers embraced them with wide smiles, the couples holding each other with an identical relief.

Cornie rubbed a hand on his mouth, his eyebrows high, and shared a thoughtful look with Pieter, who stood next to him. The sound of bubbling conversation rose from the crowd as everyone watched the captain walk back to his line of officers and nod at Mabayoje.

In a barking voice, the towering lieutenant called for the three soldiers to "fall in." The men gave their partners a squeeze of the hand or shoulder before hurrying to stand at attention as Mabayoje approached. He produced the clipboard and started to call out each man's name, along with a catalog of assignments. None of the duties sounded very pleasant or very easy, so evidently there was no time to waste in beginning the men's punishments!

Stay with his army or leave, Ethan had said. Why not leave, once and for all, to be with the people they'd chosen to love? They'd already started a new life together the minute the soldiers had deserted, so why return?

But then she paused as her stomach pinched. Would she want to be rejected by the only family she had left? To lose that connection forever?

She looked over the faces of all the soldiers plodding through the garden or conversing in pairs as they made their way down the halls. Every one of them had already been cut off from their home countries and transformed into outsiders, like Morgan had said. They *were* a family now. And disownment was a heavy price.

She clutched Rhetta's hand, her chest feeling empty.

But so was abandonment. As happy as the soldiers and their partners probably were that Ethan hadn't inflicted some dire penalty, they were still going to be separated once the army pulled out. A short-lived celebration, in the end.

As fleeting as the feel of Ethan's arms around her.

When she raised her head, Ethan and Morgan were talking nearby in the corridor. Morgan pivoted and began to walk through the garden, though he turned his head to show her a gentle smile. Ethan, seeming uncomfortable, barely glanced at her as he pivoted away. But Rhetta suddenly pulled her arm from Vanessa's and followed him. Vanessa, startled, began to go after her, but the cook was already calling out to him.

"Captain Evans."

Ethan stopped and squinted at her.

Rhetta slowed until she stood before him, with Vanessa loitering at her shoulder. Henrick had trailed behind them as well, the wrinkles in his brow multiplying, but he stood to the side at a modest distance.

Rhetta straightened, her hands trembling only slightly

as she folded them at her stomach, and met Ethan's gaze. "Is that why I am here? Is this my 'second chance'?"

He looked steadily at her. "It is."

She hesitated, but her tone was defiant. "Am I to be punished too?"

The other residents had quieted down to watch, along with some of the soldiers who were within earshot. Cornelis and Pieter had drawn up behind Henrick. Cornelis—his body stiff and his eyes on Ethan—looked like he was ready to pounce.

Ethan took an unhurried step toward Rhetta. "Second chances are not about wiping away your debts. Your actions will be remembered, because they resulted in people losing their lives. You'll always know that they didn't need to die that way, and you'll have to live with your decision." He paused, and his arms tensed against the sleeves of his shirt. "Sometimes that's punishment enough."

"Yes," Rhetta said bitterly, dropping her gaze, "I know this to be true. But even then, I did not think you would bring me back. You do not trust me."

"No, I don't." His eyes jumped briefly to Vanessa. "But whether I like it or not, they need you here."

Vanessa hugged herself as an unexpected longing swelled through her. So he had done it for her, after all.

When he started to leave again, Rhetta asked, "Did you mean what you said, what you told your soldiers?" She lifted her chin. "That you will listen when someone must say something?"

He narrowed his eyes at her. "I meant it."

Rhetta nodded and took a breath. "You claim that your actions are to protect your men, the people you care about. You call your soldiers your family. Well, I did what I had to, to protect my home and family and to fight a tyrant. You are the intruder here. And you showed no respect for us by taking over. I will not apologize to you, and I will not ask to be forgiven."

"Is that it?" Ethan said tartly.

"No."

He paused. Then he crossed his arms, spread his feet, and waited.

Rhetta blinked fiercely and pursed her lips, seeming to steel herself against his intimidating stance. "I will not apologize, but I will also not make trouble while you are here. And I will give *you* a second chance."

The black fabric against Ethan's forehead shifted as he appeared to raise his eyebrows behind the mask.

"You make grand speeches about respect," she continued. "Well, we deserve yours, Captain. I do not think you are all bad men, but you are used to treating others badly, making them enemies. Taking what you need instead of asking. It is an easy thing to be cruel and demanding. It is much harder to be patient and humble."

"I don't think your caretaker was a humble man," Ethan remarked dryly.

Rhetta gave a loud huff. "Dijkstra was a klootzak!"

"If you mean 'dickweed,' then we agree on that."

"You are stronger than us, so we cannot force you out. But you must honor our wish for freedom and fairness, not repression. Then we can have peace."

"A truce, basically."

Rhetta held her head up. "Yes."

"Then I have a condition of my own." Ethan's voice turned thorny. "I'll play nice, but don't ever try to hide shit from me again. I don't tolerate deceit or cowardice. You got a problem with the way I run things, you say it to my face."

A small smile lifted the corner of her mouth, and she relaxed her shoulders. "You will always know what is on my mind, Captain."

Ethan regarded Rhetta for a moment longer, then tugged on the cuff of each glove.

But before he turned, his gaze slid to Vanessa. An aching rose from her belly as his bright eyes seemed to dim, like he was retracting all emotion from them. Shielding himself, as always. She almost opened her mouth to say his name, to reach out to him, but he looked away and began striding down the hallway.

Her body felt leaden, and it wasn't until Cornelis's voice struck her ears that she was roused back to her senses.

"Way to stand up to that pompous eikel, Rhetta," Cornie told her, an equally proud, spiky-haired Pieter beaming next to him. "Damn, it's good to have you back."

Rhetta waved him off with her usual *I-have-better-things-to-think-about* air and took Vanessa's elbow to guide her toward the kitchen.

"Why did you not use the basket, as I've always told you, liefje?" the cook scolded her, shaking her head at all the scattered potatoes in the corridor. "Come, girl, I have taught you better!" She bent down and began gathering them. "Well, we shall have to make a nice stamppot out of the bruised ones." She glanced up at Marien, who was stepping into the kitchen. "Fetch some endive and bacon, if we have them, and be quick about it!"

Marien, seeming overcome with joy at handing back her head-cook crown, nodded with a grin and dashed over the threshold to obey.

Vanessa began to smile, restraining herself from hugging Rhetta again and risking bruising the rest of the tubers. She started to pick up the few near her feet, but as she straightened, she glanced back down the hallway, where Ethan had vanished into its darkness. That hollow sensation overtook her happiness once more. Soon, she'd have to witness his final disappearing act.

CHAPTER FORTY

ETHAN

"Nic, pick out a Snatch I can take into town."

The mechanic looked up from where he had been retrieving a head gasket from one of the open boxes in front of him. "Sure, Capitano!" He smiled and carefully set the part back in the box.

Nicolo swaggered up to him, rubbing his hands together and blowing on them for warmth. He was wearing the thick orange jacket he once bragged about rescuing from a dumpster in a sketchy neighborhood of his hometown Verona. It was too long for his short frame, so that he looked like he was peeking out of a carrot, but the Italian was proud of it nonetheless.

"I have a Snatch already gassed up for you," he informed Ethan as he tugged on his hat brim. Then he snapped his fingers at Angelo, who was wiping down the windshield of a Land Rover Wolf far down the line. "Ascolta! Ascolta!"

When the young Italian saw Nicolo point at the captain, he gave a thumbs-up and tossed the rag onto the polished tan hood.

Ethan crossed his arms and looked at the drone lying on an oil-stained piece of cardboard nearby. "You finally going to get that thing off the ground, Corporal?" he asked gruffly. "I'd like to reactivate our perimeter shield, in case the mayor comes knocking again."

Nicolo nodded, setting his hands on his waist. "Yes, Capitano. I will be doing another test run tonight. The old solar power packs were merda, no good. The laser shield projector drew too much juice. And the mayor's drone is still too light to carry it." He lifted his thumb in the air. "I get her up, and then—" He inverted his thumb and blew out a long raspberry as he lowered his arm.

"She goes down like a two-dollar whore," Ethan finished for him.

"Sì!" Nicolo threw back his head with eyes turned up to the sky and bit his lip. "Mannaggia!" He held both palms out as if in open prayer and then dropped them with a sigh. "I would rather you had stuck the drone up Visser's culo."

Ethan uncrossed his arms. "Well, it's the best we've got right now. Make it work."

Nicolo mumbled something under his breath with a shake of his head, but Ethan ignored him as the black vehicle pulled up in front of them.

Angelo swung the door open and jumped down. He saluted the captain and then gave him a knowing smile as he left.

Ethan squinted after him. But as he stepped up into the Land Rover, he paused and glanced over the truck. He looked at Nicolo. "Is this the same one that—?"

Nicolo nodded, patting the puffy sides of his carrot-jacket. "We've been keeping it nice for you, Capitano." He winked at Ethan. "Even after these months, it still has her perfume in it, eh?"

Ethan pressed his mouth closed. Now he understood Angelo's mysterious smile. Evidently, Ethan's attraction to Vanessa had become common knowledge. It would explain why, as friendly as the soldiers all were with her, they never became *too* friendly.

"I'll be back soon," he muttered.

"Just be sure to—"

"Yes, watch the third gear, I know." He slammed the door shut.

It was already well into December—the first day of winter only a week away—so he had to flip on the defroster as soon as he started up. He shoved the stick into first gear and headed out.

I don't know why the hell I'm doing this.

He thought of the way Vanessa had been on her knees in the garden earlier that morning, tending to her winter squash. And how she did not even look his way when he walked by.

He sighed roughly. *Because it's a peace offering.*

But he was not going to hold his breath that Achter-waartsstad would have anything worthwhile in the way of a gift. Not that he had any clear idea of what to get her anyway. But something told him he would know it when he saw it.

He draped his right wrist over the steering wheel as he rested his other hand on the shifter knob.

He'd at least gotten back on somewhat better terms with her over the last few weeks as the emotional episode in the garden was overwritten by the day-to-day activity of the compound. But she didn't act the same toward him. And that bothered the shit out of him. Especially since he could still feel that kiss. In fact, he couldn't *stop* feeling it. Her lips—soft, eager, submissive—had been irresistible at the time and now torturous in their absence. How the hell could one woman's touch do that to him? And how could he miss the sound of her voice so much? She always had far more to say than he wanted to hear, and yet these days he could barely pry one sentence out of her. Everything felt wrong.

But maybe that was the fucking problem: he shouldn't still be here in North Holland at all. He should have moved on, like he'd planned. He had a rough route in mind. He had every logical reason to leave. All he had to do was give the order. So why hadn't he done it?

He tapped his fingers against the stick shift. *I just need to set this one thing straight. Make it right. And then we go.*

He gradually revved the engine, running up the rpm. He shifted from second to fourth gear and stared at the dirt road ahead of him.

Bringing Rhetta back should have rectified things, but instead, Vanessa remained reticent toward him. At least the general health of his soldiers had improved with the cook's return. The repast that had finally pushed their tolerance past its limits was the night Marien had served what she termed "ham casserole," but which had devolved into a soupy concoction that had to be ladled into bowls. Several of the men had taken one look and then filed out of the dining room. And every one of them had picked up pieces of fruit from Vanessa's basket on their way out the door.

The Land Rover bounded over a rain-eaten patch of road, rattling the doors around him, but he only pressed the gas pedal harder.

And so, the next day, he had ordered Henrick to track down Rhetta and fetch her from her hiding place. The old Dutch soldier had seemed more than eager about the assignment, so evidently there had been something going on between him and the cook. As for the rest of the compound population—including his men—it seemed the minute Rhetta set foot in the gateway, her homecoming had been celebrated like some kind of holiday.

And yet, Vanessa still stayed in her shell, whenever she was near him.

She's preparing herself. She knows I'm leaving any day now. But I don't have a choice.

The Land Rover jounced over a set of deep ruts, jarring him in his seat and kicking up dust through the mesh screens on the side windows. He swerved around a pothole and downshifted with a curse when the vehicle almost lifted off its left tires.

The sooner he could give this gift to her and get her off his conscience, the better. Because she was not the only thing that weighed on his mind and made him want to get as far away from this place as possible: the residents were now being…*nice* to him.

It was an unforeseen byproduct of allowing Rhetta back. Since then, many of the residents greeted him in the halls and expressed words of gratitude for reinstating the cook to her former position. He understood why his own men would be especially happy about it, but the residents seemed to have interpreted it as a gesture of forgiveness and compromise.

Like he was their new benevolent caretaker.

Ethan jerked the wheel to avoid a large boulder at the edge of the road and narrowed his eyes at the town coming into view in the distance.

Whatever the case, the people of the compound seemed to regard him more favorably. Over the years, he had disciplined himself to instill fear in others. To make them whisper when he walked into a room. To react to his presence with meekness and apprehension. The cordiality that now dominated the fort's atmosphere was perplexing.

And fucking annoying.

Ethan tugged on the chin of his mask and downshifted irritably as he reached the town's limits. He pulled alongside the outermost building, not caring this time about what kind of image he projected to the villagers. He had one reason for being there, and he wanted to accomplish his goal as quickly as possible. He ignored the looks—both frightened and leery—that he received as he made his way through the streets. He did, however, pay attention to the few law officers who spotted him, and he stared them down as he passed. He made sure they could see both his weapons clearly within the open sides of his robe. None of the cops confronted him.

He aimed straight for the town's marketplace, where he intended to inspect every store and booth to find the one item that would grab him. It had to be the right gift, nothing commonplace. She deserved more than a casual trinket. He stopped at the same perfume booth that Vanessa had been fixated on before. But he was uncomfortable browsing through the samples, so he turned his attention elsewhere. He passed dozens of jewelry merchants whose booths boasted a wide array of bracelets, rings, and necklaces, but all the goods were gaudy. At one booth, he waved the vendor off as he glared down at a particularly ugly ruby brooch shaped like an apple. Then he moved on to the next. He spent an hour making his way through the streets. He looked in store windows and scanned carts holding scarves, handbags, hats, and more garish jewelry. Every item looked just as shitty as the one before it.

At last, he took a breath and rubbed at his eyes through the mask. *Fuck it. This is a waste of time.*

But as he turned, something caught his eye when it flashed for one brilliant second in the sunlight filtering through the leafless trees.

He hesitated. And then walked slowly down the sidewalk to a cart several meters away. He swept past the goods lining the vendor's makeshift shelves, zeroing in on a solitary item that swung lazily from the primitive fabric awning. He pushed back his hood and reached up to cup his hand behind the dangling necklace. He stared, fascinated, at the small emerald pendant. The dark depths of the square-shaped gemstone glinted as he turned it against his palm.

The vendor, laying out more of his wares on the felt-covered board, paused his busy movements. He set down the two ornamental boxes he was holding and smiled tentatively.

"You like it, sir?" he asked in an amiable but stiff tone.

Ethan ran his hand up the delicate gold chain and unhooked it from the peg under the edge of the cloth roof. "How much for this?"

The man seemed jumpy as his eyes darted first to the SIG Sauer to the right of Ethan's chest and then over to the H&K on his left hip. The merchant licked his lips and shrugged. His nervous breaths were visible in the crisp air, but the strained look of friendliness returned.

"For you, Captain Evans, it is nothing. You take it. It is free for you."

Ethan's shoulders tightened.

He reached into his robe to his front shirt pocket and pulled out several folded bills between two fingers. He flattened them under his glove against the wobbly tabletop, sending some of the trinket boxes tumbling from their shelves. The vendor's eyes went wide. But then he nodded quickly. He waited until the captain had moved his hand far away from the wad of euros before venturing to take it.

Ethan yanked his hood back up, turned, and made his way out of the city.

CHAPTER FORTY-ONE

ETHAN

He stared at the dangling jewel pendant as he stood behind his desk.

Incredible. An exact match.

It was like he was gazing directly into Vanessa's eyes.

The jewelry vendor had most likely been unaware of the expensive workmanship involved in creating such a high-caliber piece. But Ethan had become an expert on the value of anything that could be used as currency, and so he had paid the merchant well for it. Each of his men was allowed a sum of cash for discretionary purposes, including him.

And today, this had seemed the best possible use of his money.

He smiled and twirled the pendant on its chain. But then uncertainty rippled through him. What if she didn't find it as perfect as he did?

And what if I look like a fucking idiot for giving it to her?

It was just a form of apology, something to assuage his guilt. He would be gone soon, and he didn't want to leave any loose ends. The whole episode in the garden had simply been a misunderstanding. She had an inexplicable infatuation with him, and he had merely gotten caught up in it. Kissing her had only made things more complicated.

She might think this means something. She won't under-

stand.

Shit. He should just hide it in the back of his drawer. Forget about the purchase. Chalk it up to a momentary whim. On the road, this bit of jewelry could fetch him a nice stash of euros to use on ammo, gasoline, whisky…

He rested the gem in his gloved palm and lowered the delicate chain into a pile beside it.

But damn. It would look spectacular against her soft skin. And he wanted to see it on her. The black leather background it rested on provided a striking display, but showcased on her flesh it would be breathtaking. And the long golden strands of her hair would complement the scintillating quality of the fine chain.

He breathed in slowly. *It belongs on her.*

There was a knock on the door.

With a start, he closed his hand around the necklace. "What is it?"

"It's me."

Vanessa.

He yanked open the desk drawer, laid the necklace on a notepad, and closed the drawer carefully. He grabbed his robe off his chair and hurled it at the bed as he moved around in front of his desk. He ran a glove down the crooked line of pins at the back of his head and then smoothed both sides of the mask at his cheeks.

He cleared his throat under his breath. "Come in."

The door opened a few centimeters, and Vanessa peeked around it. "Are you busy?"

"No."

"Well, that's a first," she mumbled.

He frowned.

She opened the door wider and glided into the room to stand before him.

Morgan raised his eyebrows and gave him an amused look from the threshold before closing the door.

Vanessa stared at him diffidently as she stood with her hands behind her, like she'd been put on stage and suddenly could not remember her lines.

He settled his shoulders. "Well?"

Damn it. Too abrupt. I won't get many more chances like this.

He curbed his tone and attempted to soften his gaze. "I wasn't expecting you," he tried again. "Something on your mind?"

At that, her shoulders relaxed somewhat, though she only barely maintained eye contact with him. She rocked forward on her toes, fiddling with something behind her back.

"I forgot to mention one of my other skills." She brought her hands around in front of her and held up a black mask in each fist. "I can also sew."

He leaned back against the desk, unprepared for this development. "You made those for me?"

He instantly regretted the question when she almost rolled her eyes.

"No, they're for the other masked superhero I know." But a blush passed her cheeks, as if she'd just mentally reprimanded herself for the snark. "Anyway, I stuck with a classic color. And, of course, your favorite." She dangled the masks between her fingers. "I thought about making one in paisley, just for kicks, but Liam said you'd look like a Mexican wrestler."

He straightened. "Why were you talking to him about it?"

"Because he saw me working on these when he came by the kitchen after his watch. And he thinks my snap closure design is a good idea. So does Raphaël."

"Raph—" He closed his mouth. So now he was getting secondhand fashion advice from his own men. "What snap closure?"

She stepped forward to show him. "See? Instead of using safety pins, or pieces of tape, or chewing gum, or whatever else you seem to find lying around in the morning—"

He threw her a peevish look.

"You have a built-in line of snaps running up the back. That should make it easier to put on and take off, since I tried to shape it to your face and neck."

He took one of the masks from her and turned it over. He looked at her, impressed. "These are extremely well-made."

"They'd better be. I could only work on them during my spare moments, but I did them right. It took a few trips into town, to find exactly the right cloth. I wanted it to be durable yet breathable. And soft enough that it would feel like it was caressing you."

She met his eyes then. He thought of her face cradled between his palms as he parted her legs with his body and leaned into her. Her hands grasping his robe. Her breath whispering across his lips. Exploring her with his fingers as she pulled him closer. The gentle curves of her flesh felt through mere millimeters of leather…

"And look—" She held up the other mask and poked her finger out a neatly stitched opening on the side of it. "No more pretending you can't hear me."

He sighed loudly. "Well, that's one advantage lost."

But inwardly he smiled when the corners of Vanessa's mouth turned up.

"I'd stay to help you try them on for size," she said as she handed him the other mask, "but we both know you're not going to let that happen."

A prickle of remorse made his brain rewind to the conversation that had created this coldness between them.

Fix this. Do something.

He accepted the proffered mask and took a step toward her. But she had already sidled away to head for the exit.

"I plan to make you one more." She turned as she opened the door. "You know, for laundry day." She gave him a small smile, which made the air around her almost shimmer. "But it may take a while, since I don't have a legion of little elves sneaking into my room at night to magically help me. I just hope…you'll be here long enough for me to finish it."

"Vanessa," he said as she started to step out. He gentled his tone, hoping it would convey his sincerity. "Thank you."

She hesitated and seemed unsure about leaving. But, finally, she bestowed upon him another smile, which had the same bewitching effect. "You're welcome, Captain."

And with that, she left.

He stood staring at the door, in a room that now felt disturbingly empty. He tossed one of the masks onto his desk and gazed down at the other in his hands.

She had been thinking about him after all. Maybe he was already halfway to being back in her good graces. He only needed to make up the other half.

He detached the black cloth that was held against his head by the cumbersome pins. As the rough material fell away, he ran his fingers over one cheek. The flesh there was the same knobby, ugly surface that covered the rest of his arms and torso. But one day, he was going to find a way to restore it. There were surgeons on this side of the world that had made huge strides in facial reconstruction. And with enough pressure, they would sure as hell do what he needed them to. He would rectify this insufferable stigma. And then maybe he could come back and—

Stop kidding yourself. No amount of surgery in the world can fix you.

Ethan clenched the cloth in his hands, a flash of dismay seeming to roast his skin. He quickly tossed the old mask aside and pulled on the new one. After pressing together each snap against the back of his head, he stretched his face against the fabric to settle into it.

Holy shit. It's perfect.

He was awestruck by how precise she had gotten the dimensions. The material, which had a subtle stretchy character, fit his face and neck like one of his gloves. And yet it allowed him all the freedom of movement he had never had with his own makeshift covering. And—though he would never admit it to Vanessa—the sounds coming to him were much clearer. He could even breathe easier, for, not only had she made the opening for his mouth exactly frame his lips, she had painstakingly created small holes for his nostrils. She had evidently set her mind to including every detail that would make the mask as practical as possible.

She had gone to a lot of trouble for him.

When he opened the door, Morgan stood looking thoughtfully down the hallway. Vanessa must have just turned the corner at the end of it.

He felt another pinch of disappointment that he had not caught her in time to coax even a few more words out of her.

Ethan leaned against the doorway and smoothed the soft fabric against his neck.

Morgan turned to him. He crossed his arms and shifted his weight onto one foot as he looked over Ethan's face. "She did a rather nice job on you."

He tugged on the material at his chin to adjust it. "She showed them to you, I take it?"

"Indeed. They were a...now, how did she put it?" Morgan cocked his head with a musing look. "A 'special delivery for Captain Curmudgeon' I believe was the literal phrasing."

Ethan scowled behind the mask. Morgan slapped a hand to Ethan's shoulder and began to walk down the hallway.

CHAPTER FORTY-TWO

ETHAN

Ethan strode down the corridor leading to the kitchen. Chances were good Vanessa would still be there at this time of the evening. He had her schedule more or less memorized without consciously trying to do so.

The chilled night air felt good and was the perfect trial for one of the new masks Vanessa had given him that afternoon. He adjusted the cloth at his neck, pleased once more at how comfortable it was against his skin, thanks to her careful choice of fabric and construction. And maybe her polar-bear immunity was starting to rub off on him, because the briskness of the season was actually...invigorating. He inhaled the hallway's earthy smell of old stone—dry on a crisp night such as this—and a smile passed his lips.

On his way, several of his soldiers hailed him. But then, so did many of the residents. Again, these were the same people who had previously averted their eyes or hurried in a different direction whenever he approached, a reaction to which he had become accustomed. And which he preferred. But now that they acknowledged him with a nod or a wave, his response was a puzzled stare.

What the fuck am I doing wrong?

He shook his head and tugged on the bottom of each glove as he walked.

When he reached the cheerfully lit kitchen, the scent of warm cookie spice surrounded him. Evidently, Rhetta's speculaas had gone over well, because there was no sign of the Dutch cookies she had baked earlier. They had become a favorite of his soldiers and never lasted long once they came out of the ovens. Morgan had been good enough to save Ethan a few of the biscuits, as the Englishman called them, before the horde had descended.

Dinner was long since over, but several stragglers loitered in the dining room. They were composed of both soldiers and residents. He paused at the sight. Evidently, they had all begun eating together regularly since Rhetta's return. Most days, Ethan did not join his men for meals. Instead, he holed himself up in his room to plan for their departure. He had not witnessed this…camaraderie firsthand. The growing assimilation could not be blamed entirely on the cook's reappearance, though. It was becoming increasingly obvious that there was an organic process taking place throughout the compound. A cross-pollination of perspectives. As a result, his men and the residents were starting to mature alongside each other with an attitude of understanding.

Better rip those roots out before they go too deep.

He nodded at the soldiers who looked up and gave him a friendly salute. Then he stopped and tapped his gloved fingers against a table edge as he scanned the room.

Upon seeing him, Rhetta set down the dirty broiler pan she held and came out from the cooking area. She wiped her hands on a dishcloth draped over her shoulder before patting a hand to the frazzle-haired gray bun at the back of her head.

"Captain Evans," she said in a formal tone, as if addressing a supervisor. "Vanessa has left for the evening." When he hesitated, she added, "She will probably be in the garden. It is where she likes to go after she is done with her chores. If not there, then the dining hall. With a book, naturally."

"Naturally," he echoed, awkwardly shifting his weight.

Why does everyone assume that everything I do is related to her?

"Would you like to stay for a minute?" Rhetta gestured toward a table nearby. "There are a few appelflappen left from yesterday's dessert. I can heat them for you. And there is still cream to go with them."

"No, I...have something to do." He turned to leave but then paused. "Thank you, Rhetta."

She glanced over him and pursed her lips with undisguised disapproval. "You do not eat enough, Captain. You should join us for dinner more often, instead of sitting behind that desk day and night. You cannot lead your soldiers if you are unwell." She nodded briskly. "I will make a good stew for you tomorrow."

He stared at her as she went back to her work.

What is happening?

There was still a part of him that condemned his decision to let her return. She had cooperated in an egregious act that had cost three men their lives, one of them from her own people. But ever since she'd approached him that day Henrick had brought her back, her interactions with him had been upfront and respectful. No more subterfuge or subversion, but instead, a tolerant civility. Maybe it was being around Vanessa's incessant starry-eyed outlook for so long, but he grudgingly recognized Rhetta's mistake as just that: a mistake. On the night of the raid, she had acted rashly. Ignorantly. But not maliciously. She'd acted in defense of her home and her family. Maybe it was time to stop penalizing people for that.

Ethan stepped back out of the cookie-scented comfort of the kitchen. He nodded at Darshan as he passed the Sikh in the corridor. Instead of the camouflage pagri from earlier that day, Darshan had on his black turban, which he typically wore when assigned to nighttime guard duty, so he must have been going on watch. Most of the men were out on nocturnal maneuvers, which Mabayoje and Frank periodically organized to keep the soldiers acclimated to working and fighting in the dark. That left only a handful of his army at the compound for these few hours.

Morgan—switching into high gear when the fort's defenses were diminished like this—busily patrolled the outside perimeter to make sure all sentries were in place and alert.

As he had done on his way to the kitchen, Ethan scoured the garden and orchard with his eyes, but there was no sign of Vanessa. He was about to set his course for the dining hall when he saw her step from behind a stone arch on the north side of the garden.

She cupped a hand around her mouth to call up to a soldier on the battlement above her. Edvard—his big, bulky form outlined against the backdrop of a moonlit sky—pivoted. The giant Swede was one of only a few guards on duty along the ramparts. Edvard seemed to give Vanessa a toothy, boyish smile and shifted his rifle to his other shoulder. He shook his head and said something down to her. Then she waved at him and turned. Tim was tucked into her other arm. When she saw the captain walking toward her, she dipped beneath a nearly leafless tree branch to make her way through the orchard.

A long sky-blue skirt swayed against her as she moved, giving the illusion of a waterfall spilling over the winter-wilted grass. She also wore a creamy pink peasant top with the neckline pulled low off her shoulders, in spite of the oncoming chill of night. Perhaps she was ready to retreat to the warmth of her own room, so he had found her in time.

"What was that all about?" He glanced up at the Swedish soldier, who had returned to his post.

She shrugged. "Seeing if Edvard needed anything. He's been a little under the weather." She ran a hand over Tim as the rabbit stretched toward the captain and wriggled his nose. "He didn't even finish his third steak at lunch. And I'm afraid he may have passed it on to Miguel, because he came to me about getting a cup of my honey-and-herb cure-all tea."

"Mothering my men again?"

"When they need it."

Ethan nodded at Tim, who began nibbling on

Vanessa's blouse sleeve. "Aren't rabbits supposed to be asleep by now?"

"Tim makes his own schedule." She put her other arm under the animal and pressed a kiss between his ears. "When he's ready to rest, he'll disappear. We still can't figure out where his burrow is. He keeps his secrets as well as you do."

He chose to ignore the comment and watched instead as the rabbit put a paw on her elbow and strained toward Ethan. His one crooked ear swiveled back as the other perked forward.

"He likes you," she remarked.

"Wow. Great."

"I think you owe him a petting. Everyone else has petted him. Even Frank."

He looked at her with an absolute lack of enthusiasm. "I'll pass."

"Don't be such a sourpuss. You'll hurt his feelings. Pet the bunny."

"I'm not petting the bunny."

Vanessa held Tim up and hid her face behind him. "Come on, Captain Cranky-Pants," she said in a deep voice as she bobbed the rabbit in the air, "pet me!"

Tim stopped twitching his nose and gave Ethan that single-toothed, dimwitted stare. His brown eyes were open wide, the black patch of fur over his left one making him look like a startled pirate. Jesus, he was a goofy-looking bastard.

Finally, after Vanessa jiggled Tim another time, Ethan gave in. He ran a gloved hand smoothly over the animal, flattening his white-tipped ebony ears and petting the full length of him. Even through the leather, he could tell the rabbit's fur was extremely soft. He could see how the most hardened soldier would be pacified by the therapeutic action. Ethan ran his hand over Tim again. Silky. Like when he had touched Vanessa's hair with his bare fingers…

He yanked his hand back. "There. Satisfied?"

She sighed and held Tim against her chest. "Spoken

like a true Grumpelstiltskin."

Ethan turned with her as she began to stroll through the middle of the orchard.

She peeked at him as she walked. "The mask looks good on you, by the way."

He rubbed a hand from his cheek to the back of his head, where he lightly fingered the line of snaps. "Feels good, too. Feels like it's"—he glanced at her and cracked a hesitant smile—"caressing me."

She seemed to flush slightly as she bowed her head and trailed her fingers through Tim's fur of midnight and snowy patterns. The rabbit closed his eyes and settled himself deeper into her arms, his broken ear bouncing with her gentle movements.

"I'm almost jealous," Ethan said, and frowned as the animal let out a soft snore.

"Why?" She mussed Tim's fur between his ears as she walked. "You could have traded places with him last month, remember?"

His shoulders prickled unpleasantly, and he kept his eyes on the ground with his fists tight. "Nice to see you're not holding a grudge," he muttered.

Her voice instantly softened. "I'm sorry, I didn't mean it that way." She shrugged, and one of Tim's skinny hind legs slipped through to dangle against her. "It's just that you…We shared something that night. And now you can't seem to even acknowledge it."

Acknowledge it? I can't stop reliving it. Or wanting more of it.

"I think it's better we move on." He squinted off to the side as he smoothed the mask at his neck.

"That's what you're best at," she said, almost too low for him to hear.

His shoulders tightened again. "Look, as you've been so quick to remind me, we're not here by your invitation. No one wants us around. We're intruders."

"Yeah, but things are different now. I think you know that, too." She adjusted her arms around Tim and scooped his leg up into her embrace as the rabbit yawned contentedly. "Your men all want to be a part of this place. And even some of the most stubborn residents have warmed up to the idea."

"We have no right to be here."

"No, at first you didn't," she agreed, "but maybe now you've earned the right. Maybe this is where you're supposed to be."

He felt a twinge of discomfort as she held his gaze. This was circling dangerously close to their last conversation in the garden. "You can't simply create a home for us, like we're stray puppies."

"I'm not creating anything. It's already here for you. Can't you see that?"

"These soldiers are outsiders, like I am. They don't know how to settle down in one place."

"I think they're getting the hang of it." She nodded toward the rear gates, where one of the men from the compound was lighting the cigarette of a sentry. Both of them leaned against the corridor wall as they talked and smoked.

The captain twisted back to her. *Damn it, why does she make me argue with her?*

"My men have chosen this lifestyle."

"And you haven't let them choose otherwise since."

He batted a branch out of his way. "I have never forced anyone to join me. And no one's tying their hands."

"I'm sure of that." She ducked around the low-hanging boughs of the apple tree. "I can see it on their faces. They follow you because they respect you. But look at how they act now. They might not want to say it to you directly yet, but consider that maybe they don't want the same things anymore."

He walked in silence, his eyes sweeping restlessly over the ground in front of him.

"Do you?" she asked.

He stopped and looked back at her.

She stood beneath the branches of her Belle de Boskoop tree, her hand on Tim's back as he slept snuggled against her. "There's an old Dutch proverb Rhetta likes to use, that even *I* can remember," she said slowly as she gazed down at the rabbit and gently pulled his crooked ear through her fingers. "Een mens zijn zin is een mens zijn leven. A man's meaning is a man's life." She raised her head. "So what's your purpose, Captain? What is it *you* really want?"

He could not answer at first. Her eyes seemed to pick up the glow reaching out from the open doorway of the kitchen far behind him. At last, the question crouching at the back of his mind sprang forward. "Why are you working so hard to keep us here?"

She bent down and eased the rabbit out of her arms and onto the ground. Tim seemed bewildered at losing his warm napping place, but then he unhurriedly hopped through the sparse carpet of grass.

Vanessa straightened and met Ethan's eyes. "You know why."

His heartbeat seemed to pause the same way it did when he was dug into a battlefield, and he knew a shell was about to hit.

She looked down and tugged on her pinky finger as she approached him. "I tried to leave so many times before you ever came here. I told you about my parents, but I didn't tell you all of it. I didn't tell you that every stone in this rundown fort reminds me of how I betrayed them. It felt like a prison, because I treated it like something to escape. I thought I'd only be able to live a new life if I went out and looked for it. And then I'd find that one person to start it with." She tilted her face up and knitted her brows. "But this place—no matter what happened—is my home. And now, for the first time in so long, I want to stay." Vanessa hugged herself, and the ruffled neckline of her pink peasant blouse slipped farther off her shoulders. "It's you, Ethan. You're my reason to stay. Because I want this to be your home, too."

An explosion deep inside him vibrated his core.

She really means that.

Sharp heat, like shrapnel, tore through his gut.

How the fuck do I deserve something this good?

Ethan opened his mouth for a second and then shut it as his thoughts scrambled to line up. Then: "I have something for you."

He had not intended to bring it up so abruptly, but the entire conversation had knocked him back and left him disoriented, his ears ringing in the aftermath. He pivoted and walked to stand near the orchard wall. He reached into the pocket of his jeans and withdrew the necklace, which he had wrapped meticulously in a piece of tissue paper he'd found in Commissary #2. The paper was blue, her favorite color.

He hesitated as he felt Vanessa draw up behind him. *It's just a simple gesture. An apology. Nothing more.*

He continued to stare down at the small mounded packet as he turned it over in his fingers.

She touched the back of his elbow. "What is it?"

He took a breath and turned to look at her. He concealed the packet in his palm at his side. Her eyes, so green and alluring in the evening light, searched his.

He knocked his fist against his leg as he squeezed the packet tighter. "I thought—" His chest burned; his lungs were cramped and heavy. Instead of finishing, he held out his palm to offer her the small wrapped item.

Carefully, she picked it up. He held his breath as she unwrapped it. She furrowed her forehead at the open tissue paper in her hands and then raised her face to him.

"I thought you might like it." He tried to say it casually, despite the way his pulse skipped faster through his veins.

She looked down at it again. Every muscle in his body coiled.

Shit. She hates it. This was a fucking stupid idea.

She lifted the dark-emerald pendant by its glittering chain and let it revolve in the faint light coming from the kitchen. She let out a rush of breath. "Ethan, it's magnificent."

Ripples of cool weightlessness spread through him, and he relaxed his shoulders.

She bit her lip while she drew a slow breath and shook her head. "I've never seen anything so beautiful."

He watched her as she admired the sparkling square gem. *I have.*

"I wanted to show you that I…appreciate you," he said.

She beamed at him. He stood mesmerized, as if the sun had leapt out in front of him and banished the surrounding darkness in one bright burst. She handed him the necklace and turned her back to him. As she lifted her hair off her neck with a hand, she looked back at him. He shifted to one foot, his neck muscles tensing again. He had assumed she would simply thank him so he could tactfully excuse himself and go to his quarters for the night. But she never let him off easy.

He regarded the necklace as if he'd been handed an explosive to defuse, and he shifted to the other foot as she watched him. He could not do anything with these gloves on. He would have to remove them in order to handle the delicate clasp. Vanessa's eyes darted to his hands. And without a word, she faced forward and lifted her chin high. After another pause, he tugged off both his gloves and slipped his arm between her neck and bent elbow as she continued to hold her hair up. He brought the two ends of the chain together behind her, concentrating on the small golden fastener instead of his damaged fingers.

As soon as he closed the clasp, he stared at the nape of her neck, which looked flushed and soft. And very kissable. He straightened and hurriedly pulled on his gloves.

Vanessa turned and stepped closer. She took his hands in hers. The pendant rested tantalizingly above her cleavage, perfectly nestled in its new home. "Ethan, I love it." Her smile gone, she seemed to study his face behind the mask. "I will never take it off."

She said it so ardently, so intimately—her words a heartfelt oath—that he faltered. With her tempting, limber form so near, his will began to drain away like loose sand from a fractured hourglass. The impulse to wrap himself around her surged through his body.

She released his hands and glided her fingers onto his waist. The tingle of goose bumps raced over his skin. The dark emerald depths of the necklace's gemstone were identical to her eyes and shone with the same exquisite shimmer. Her breasts swelled higher with each breath she took, the low neckline of her blouse promising him easy access to the supple flesh beneath. The gingerbread scent of her, trapped within those radiant locks, floated to him and intoxicated him.

Every one of his senses screamed for her, demanded her. He balled his hands into fists, his knuckles popping under the force. He ordered himself to gain control, to ignore the hunger that thrummed through each expanding blood vessel and made that primal part of him pulsate. But as the arousal flooded through him, it slammed into the last psychological strut bracing his restraint, and the barricades within him crashed into rubble.

Goddamn her.

He pulled her against him and covered her mouth with his. His pulse pounded as he slid his tongue deep and felt hers writhe around it. The thrill of touching her again, having her again, swept him into a familiar madness, but this time the kiss was different. This time it was unstoppable. He dove in with animal need, letting his instincts take over. He enveloped her and surrendered to her. The undulation of her body dictated where his hands went, what curves he clutched, seeking out all the succulent portions he longed to explore with more than his fingers.

Vanessa lurched forward and shoved him back against the wall so hard that the rough stone dug into him through his clothes. He wanted to tear the mask from his face. The feel of its interference infuriated him. But she returned his kiss so desperately, so zealously—just shy of devouring him—that the obstruction seemed nonexistent to her. All of his cravings broke free from the corners inside him where they had been straining at the leash, and he let his passions assault him unchecked. The feel of a woman in his arms again—this one woman—enflamed the primitive desire for consummation that had grown so distant over the years.

His hands moved over her body, down across her buttocks, and gripped the backs of her thighs to lift her onto her toes as he held her. He pressed his mouth to her neck as she clung to him. Her flesh shivered against his tongue, and he closed his eyes. She tasted even sweeter than he had imagined: the saccharine gush of a ripened peach. He couldn't wait to work his way down and find every one of her flavors.

He turned his nose into her hair and breathed her in as he freed one hand to place it on her breast. With a slow squeeze, he rubbed his thumb across her raised nipple, which nearly crested the rim of her strapless bra. She moaned in that same helpless way as she had back in the dining hall during their match, when he had pictured her arching her body up against him while he ravished her. Sliding his jaw along hers, he thrust his groin to make her moan again. And again. She put her hand on his, upon her breast, and kneaded his fingers to make him grasp her harder. He cupped the arc of her ass cheek in his other hand and massaged it through the skirt as she squirmed insistently against his erection like she'd already mounted him, intent on making him take her.

And who gave a shit that people might be watching. Damn all strategies and consequences. Damn the past. This was all he needed. This one moment.

He cradled her face in his hands and drew her lips to his again as he let the greed overwhelm him. He could have her. Keep her. Make her his and make her happy. This could be his life, if—

Fingers. Hands on his flesh. His *bare* flesh.

The world shuddered, started to crumble. His mind balked, thrashing as if dragged screaming from a rapturous dream.

Vanessa's hands. She'd slipped them into the back of his jeans. And she must have wormed them under the T-shirt beneath his long-sleeved top, infiltrating all his layers. A single reckless deed committed in the throes of lust.

And it was the only lit fuse that could detonate every anxiety at once, like a stockpile of gunpowder.

His pulse exploded through his veins. He grabbed her hands from behind him and jerked back.

She stared up at him, her breath still coming fast. "Ethan, what? Why did you stop?"

"What the hell is wrong with you?" His own voice boomed in his ears.

She swallowed, still panting. "What do you mean?"

"You touched me." The words nearly died on his tongue. "Why the fuck did you touch me?"

She shook her head. "I-I'm sorry, I thought—"

"No, that's what you fucking never do." His breath burned his lungs. "The last time you wanted me to show myself to you, I asked one goddamn thing of you: I told you to leave it alone."

She gripped his hands. "And I told you that you don't have to hide from me. I don't care what you look like."

"So as usual, you decided not to give a shit about what I say." Waves of fire rolled through him, ravaging every limb and every melted line of his face under the mask. "I told you that I won't—that I can't—" His muscles bucked against the phantom flames, and he pulled his hands from hers. "Damn it, you never quit until you see how far you can push me."

"But you want this too, don't you?" Her eyes were pleading. "To have nothing in our way? Nothing to hold us back?"

"*You* just held us back," he said roughly. "*You* made the wrong move. I told you where the line was, but you crossed it anyway, like it didn't even matter. Everything is not about what you believe is right and how you think things should be. I'm tired of this goddamn game, and I'm not playing it anymore just because you want me to fuck you."

Her body stiffened, and the look on her face sent a shock radiating through him like a kick to the solar plexus.

"What?" She took an unsteady step backward.

"No," he began numbly, as if he couldn't catch his

breath, "I didn't mean—"

"That's all you think I want?" Her face was pale. "Of course I want to be close to you and feel you, but...is that how you think of me?"

The urges she had stoked in him still thundered through his body, and her absence made the night air seem jarringly colder as it took its place between them.

Vanessa shook her head slowly. "I thought I was getting through to you, making a connection. All the things we've talked about and done together...And then last month, the way you kissed me—I thought you felt something deeper, like I did." She grasped the emerald pendant at her throat. "Like I *do*."

"No, Vanessa"—he took a step and reached for her—"I wasn't—"

She shoved his hands away. "Don't. I feel like an idiot, as it is." Her eyes began to glimmer in the faint light. "You should have been honest with me, so that I didn't keep making a fool of myself. You should have told me this wasn't real for you, that you thought I was only trying to be your...piece of ass."

"No, goddamn it. Listen to me, I never said that I didn't—" He clenched his jaw as so many raw emotions grappled and tumbled inside his chest. "You don't understand."

She gritted her teeth. "Then make me understand. Tell me what you really feel." Her voice sounded thick, her eyes now brimming with tears. "Do I even mean anything to you?"

She waited for him to answer, but his mind was caught in a spinning loop of images: Sitting in quiet conversation with her on a rampart wall each day at dusk, holding her close as they slipped into the shadows of a deserted hallway, listening to her chime-like laugh whenever they shared a joke...

He would have treated her with nothing less than a reverential lust, returning her affections with the fury of a man committed to her every need, to her protection, her pleasure. He would have done all of that, had he not made himself the thing he now was, both inside and out.

His breathing became painful, like the tip of a knife dragging across his lungs. *I am not what she needs. I can never be what she needs.*

A gradual buzzing in the background became louder as a dark object appeared overhead. The repaired stolen drone bobbed in the air above them. Then, after a grinding *thunk*, harsh orange beams of light shot out from all sides and cascaded in a dome over the compound.

When he looked back down at Vanessa, her eyes had caught the fire of the glowing vault and reflected it back at him.

"Ethan, answer me." She grasped his shirt, and her chin started to tremble. "Do you want me or not?"

Tell her the truth. Tell her you're a piece of shit. Tell her you're doing this for her.

He took a searing breath as he clenched his fists. "This was a mistake."

Her fingers loosened their grip, and she stared up at him as the tears dangled upon her bottom lashes. "What?"

He forced the words out, his voice dense like curing concrete. "I'm leaving in January."

She blinked, and the drops rolled down her cheeks in shining streaks of fire. "What about us?"

He took another breath and nearly choked on it. "There is no 'us.' "

With that, he pulled away and began to stride along the wall toward the front of the garden. He stared at the ground, where the grass glowed with a sickly reddish tint from the burning shield above. The night seemed to rush in and encircle him with eddies of darkness that even the lurid light of the security beams could not lessen. As he stretched out the distance between himself and the orchard, he heard a soft sob echo through the complex. He squeezed his eyes shut and walked faster.

Off to his left, there was movement in the shadows of one of the corridors. He hesitated, his muscles pulled taut. Then he recognized Morgan's dark outline against a stone arch. His friend must have finished his rounds and come to give the captain his report, when he stumbled upon the scene in the orchard. Ethan's stomach jerked like someone had stabbed a steel spike right through it.

The soft cloth had now plastered itself to his face, soaked with a sweat that served only to remind him of the disaster he had just caused. He wanted nothing more than to get to his quarters and rip the mask apart.

CHAPTER FORTY-THREE

ETHAN

Fuck breakfast. And fuck lunch, too.

He didn't need to see Vanessa look at him with those injured eyes. Injury that he had inflicted. He hadn't slept, which made him give even less of a fuck about everything going on that day. He couldn't concentrate. The officers' briefing had gone to shit. He'd thrown the duty roster across the room. Then he'd stormed back to his quarters so he could sit behind his desk and stare blankly at the fucking mangled map on which his rain-soaked notes had dried in long bloody smears. But all he could picture was Vanessa from last night, left alone in the orchard to contend with his bullshit.

Near dinnertime, he finally pulled his robe back on and emerged from his hole. In one of the hallways, a group of his men were joking with each other as they came up behind him. Ethan glanced at them as they started to pass by, and he caught Jakub's arm.

When the young Pole turned and looked up at Ethan, he snapped to attention and saluted. "Captain Evans! I am sorry, I did not see you there!"

"At ease," Ethan told him as the soldier stood frozen. "Are you headed to the chow hall?"

Jakub nodded as he tucked his sandy bangs under his beret. "Yes, Captain."

"Do you know if…they're at full staff tonight?"

Jakub cocked his head. "Sir?"

Ethan cleared his throat. "Is the Brouwer girl working?"

"Oh! Miss Vanessa!" Jakub said with a broad smile. "No, she is off today." But then he seemed embarrassed as he asked carefully, "You have not seen her, sir? Not since…?"

Ethan stiffened his shoulders and said in a cool voice, "Since what, Private?"

Jakub paled and saluted again. "N-nothing, sir."

"Dismissed." He barely mumbled the word as he turned and walked on.

Once inside the kitchen, he seated himself at the table where Mabayoje, Frank, Angus, and Thomas were all gathered. All of them talked and laughed animatedly. But their apparent high spirits only drove his mind deeper into the gloom of his thoughts. He leaned on his elbows, steepling his fingers in front of him, and tried to block out the bubbly conversations around him.

A few of his men—joined at their tables by several residents—tossed him a glance now and again. The soldiers gave him respectful, albeit seemingly sympathetic, smiles. Ethan looked away, his skin burning beneath the mask, and pulled his hood farther forward.

Does everyone know my fucking business now?

They were not the first to give him that look today. Though none of his men would dare say it to his face, word had obviously spread about the ill-fated encounter with Vanessa in the garden the night before.

And how Captain Cock-Up had fucked himself out of ever getting close to her again.

Rumbles of appreciation rippled through the room as members of the kitchen staff brought out trays laden with food-filled crockery. The delicious aromas filled the kitchen more strongly, now that the meal had been dished out. He sat back as he and the others at his table were presented with plates of herbed, buttered potatoes and rutabagas. Baskets holding a variety of freshly baked breads were placed out, as well as bowls of a thick, hearty stew.

As Marien set a dish in front of Angus, the Scotsman tossed his long brown braid back over his shoulder and leaned forward to inhale the meaty fragrance steaming up from the bowl.

"Ah, that is some good fairn, lass!" His bushy beard puffed out farther as he grinned. "What kind of stew is it?"

"Hazenpeper," Marien answered as she set a bowl in front of Frank.

"Oh?"

"Rabbit," she clarified with a bright smile. "Enjoy!" And she turned to go back to the cooking area.

Ethan pushed back his hood and picked up his spoon to dip it into the bowl. But he paused after he raised the utensil to his mouth. The others at his table sat staring at their suppers, their brows furrowed and frowns on all their faces, especially Frank's. Ethan lowered his spoon and glanced around. Several other soldiers, including Liam, Miguel, and Edvard, regarded their dinners with the same uncomfortable expressions. Some of the men pushed their bowls away. Darshan, who was a vegetarian, dined instead on a collection of cheese and spiced vegetables. But the Sikh, too, looked more disdainful of the main meal than usual. The room grew quiet as more of the stew was distributed.

What the—?

Then Ethan felt a flare of annoyance as it finally dawned on him.

Oh, for the love of Christ.

He set his spoon down hard. "It's not Tim!"

At that, he had everyone's attention, and there was a long pause. Then all of the men smiled and dove back in. The noise of conversation and clinking utensils resumed. Ethan let out an aggravated sigh and shoved a spoonful of stew in his mouth. Morgan walked in then and seated himself across from Ethan as a bowl was brought to him. The Englishman stared down at it for a moment, and his brow wrinkled.

Ethan swallowed and shook his head. "Relax. That resident kid who wants to be a doctor—Abel—caught these out in the back field. Our butt-ugly fluffy friend is still running free." Then his voice dropped to a grumble. "And undermining my authority."

Morgan directed an amused smile at him and unfurled a napkin to drape across his thigh. The lieutenant dipped his spoon into the stew.

"I noticed the light under your door remained steady last night, as Frank took his shift following mine." Morgan scooped the stew away from himself before eating it, in that oh-so-proper way that seemed he should be sticking out his pinky. "Am I to assume you are functioning on a paltry few hours' sleep today?"

"I'm fine," Ethan said in an ornery voice, ripping off a piece of white crusty bread to drop it in his bowl. "I had a lot of things on my mind."

"Understandable."

Ethan's grip tightened around the spoon handle. "Regarding our next steps as to where we move the army," Ethan clarified crisply. "We've already stayed here far too long as it is, and I don't believe for a minute that the Ukes have stopped following us. They've proven to be more resourceful than we anticipated. And, since we don't yet have the ability to hunt them down and strike at them first, we need to continue our evasive tactics."

Morgan listened while he chewed a piece of the pumpernickel bread he'd chosen. "With all due respect," Morgan said after a pause, "it is possible that we are running from figments. In the space of nine months, there has been no evidence to suggest that they have any knowledge of our whereabouts. Otherwise, as is their perverse custom, they would have made their presence known."

Ethan fell silent, poking his spoon at a sliver of mushroom against the inside of his bowl. It was true that not one of the Ukrainian runners had caught up with them in almost a year. That fact alone may have been a positive sign that his army had finally eluded them. But at any point, one of those Uke bloodhounds could show up on their doorstep with a crimson strip of nylon tied around one arm. The usual tracking device would be implanted in a new part of the runner's body—a trick they used to keep Ethan from immediately knowing where to cut it out—and the man would repeat the same morbid message:

You cannot burn us. You cannot kill us. We will bury you screaming beneath the bodies of your men.

"I don't trust it to be that easy," Ethan muttered. "It's never that easy."

Morgan said nothing to that but merely turned his attention back to his bowl and stirred his stew.

Ethan speared a large chunk of tender rutabaga from his plate and talked around his mouthful. "As soon as we get the last shipment of goods from this other black-market dealer, we can get the hell out of here."

"That will not be for another month, at a minimum."

Ethan stopped chewing. "Are you shitting me? We placed that order two weeks ago."

Morgan lifted his eyes and raised his wineglass. "We are fortunate they took our order at all. Not many are willing to conduct such long-distance transactions with a client now evidently categorized as a high-risk venture."

"They get paid damn well to deal with clients like us."

"Apparently, their opinion differs." Morgan took a sip of wine.

Ethan pressed his mouth closed and tapped his spoon against his plate. "This is holding us up. We need to keep moving, so we might have to cut our losses."

Morgan held his gaze. "We may not again have opportunity to procure what we require for many months."

"We have enough. We'll work around it. We need to be gone by the end of January."

"It might be more prudent to wait until spring, so that we avoid the inhospitable winter conditions during travel that—"

"No," Ethan said sharply, and Morgan squinted at him. "It has to be January."

Morgan paused but shifted his gaze away. "When shall we begin preparations for departure?"

Ethan frowned at the subtle disapproval in his friend's tone. "Soon."

Morgan gathered a hunk of meat onto his spoon. "What is our destination?"

"South."

Morgan lowered his spoonful back into his bowl without eating it. "South."

A twinge of irritation made Ethan clench his jaw. "Yes, south."

"You forced a bout of insomnia for most of the night—sequestered in the name of strategy—and all your hours of deliberation culminated in…south?"

Ethan threw his utensil into his bowl with a clatter. All heads in the room turned. He grabbed his napkin off his lap and whipped the cloth down on the table. "I don't appreciate being ridiculed, Lieutenant." He met Morgan's anchored gaze. "We have more than one option available. I'm weighing the advantages of each, based on what supplies we have, what supplies we need, and where we will be the most undetected. Is that strategic enough for you?"

Morgan did not look away. "Yes, sir."

Ethan pushed his bowl aside with an arm and leaned forward. He interlocked his fingers in front of him to rub at his eyes through the mask with both thumbs. "Look"— he took a breath and laid his forearms on the table—"I know this is an unfamiliar situation for us. We're not used to digging into a place and then finding our-selves…reluctant to dig back out. And I'm the one responsible for bringing us here. It was my fuckup. It's up to me to fix this. It's tough on all of us."

Morgan watched him quietly before his stoic gaze finally eased. His friend knew how to take Ethan's temper in stride, better than anyone. And the Englishman also understood when he was trying to apologize.

"But we can't stay," Ethan continued. "It's not our nature. It's not our purpose."

Morgan set his spoon down carefully beside his dish and then rested his hands on his knees. "What is our purpose?"

"Survival. You know that."

Morgan shook his head. "And what are we sacrificing in the name of it?"

Ethan slid his arms back across the table as he straightened. "What do you mean?"

The lieutenant held his hands out to the sides, to indicate everything around him. "What are we sacrificing?"

Ethan didn't know what to say. His mind threw Vanessa's face at him, showed him again how she had clutched his shirt the night before and demanded his answer. Her eyes—bright and full of anguish—had begged him to acknowledge her feelings and express his in return. It was a painful entreaty that had called on him to surrender to the simple human act of admitting that he felt something too. And that he wanted what she wanted.

Ethan clenched and unclenched his hand around his napkin upon the table as he fought to shove the images aside. When he spoke, his voice came out hoarse. "This is not our home, Morgan. We don't belong here. We don't belong with these people. We can't change that."

"Are you so certain?"

Ethan glanced at the soldiers who sat elbow-to-elbow with the resident men and women, all of them smiling and talking. The early evening light that streamed in through the high-cut windows shed a bluish glow over the heads of the diners. But a gradual yellow luminance began to overcome it as first one lantern and then another flared to life. Marien, Anna, and the other kitchen staff moved among the soldiers to light the lamps upon the tables, the women laughing with each other at a casual joke. Rhetta swept into the dining area then, to the enthusiastic applause of many. She bore a fresh browned cake on a tray, which filled the room with the fragrance of warm butter. Thomas and Liam both eagerly rushed to her side and helped her find a home for the dessert on the table near them.

Morgan picked up his spoon and resumed his meal in silence.

Ethan slowly pulled his bowl back in front of him—his stomach shrunken to a sour knot—and forced himself to eat.

CHAPTER FORTY-FOUR

VANESSA

Vanessa squirmed and reached under her backside to feel around the floor for the angled object that had been poking into her for the last ten minutes. She had ignored it at first. Now she was tired of being tolerant.

She pulled the object out to stare at it. It was part of a wooden peg that must have finally rotted off the old gears of the gristmill. She tilted her head back against the rickety pine railing behind her to gaze up at the toothy wheels turning lazily in the shadows of the peaked dome of the windmill cap. It might have come from the bovenwiel, the top wheel of the horizontal wind shaft attached to the external blade assembly. It had to do the work of rotating the big wooden spindle that ran the entire height of the derelict smock mill—so it had had a lot of strain put on it over the years.

She dropped the piece behind her through the space between the vertical shaft and the hole in the floor. The useless remnant bounced dully against the revolving pinions down the length of the shaft to the various floors below. Poor defunct grain windmill. The old gray worker should have quit moving before the rest of its parts fell off.

Not like the captain. He's probably afraid he'll crumble away to nothing if he stays still.

She pressed her lips together and sat up straighter. She

smoothed her long, flowing skirt over her bent legs and set the spine of the open book in the crease between her knees. But it was no good. She still didn't care what was on the pages. She slammed the book closed and tossed it away, nearly knocking over the glowing lantern she had brought with her. Staring up at the small moonlit window in the wall beneath the mill's curved cap, she breathed in slowly.

She had seen Ethan earlier in the day, but she knew he would only avoid her if she approached him. So she didn't bother trying. She had decided, instead, to keep the hurt and confusion to herself. What had happened in the orchard the night before was a wound that would not heal if she kept letting him open it.

He doesn't want me. I needed an answer, and I got it. End of story.

The thud of plodding footsteps rose from the level below and continued up the ladder nearby.

Cornelis poked his silver-haired head through the square opening in the floor and looked at her. "Is this a private party, or can anyone crash?"

"Crash away," she told him as he squeezed his shoulders through and climbed the rest of the way into the small room.

"Brought you these, courtesy of Rhetta." He walked over and set a foil-wrapped plate in her lap. "Figured you could use some comfort food."

She lowered her legs to stretch them out and peeled back one corner of the foil. She looked up at Cornelis, startled.

"I thought these were long gone, after yesterday." She pulled out one of the lightly browned speculaas and nipped off the end of it.

"She saw you moping around all day and so baked them specially, to cheer you up." He squatted and snatched one of the crispy spice cookies before easing himself down next to her. "And you'd better appreciate these. She had to fight off an Italian, a Swede, and a Canadian to save them for you."

Vanessa laughed. Thomas had probably fought the hardest, since Rhetta said she often caught him stuffing four of them in his face the minute she turned her back.

Vanessa popped the rest of the cookie into her mouth and picked up the next. She turned it in the lamplight with a smile. Rhetta had made them into the traditional windmill shapes, which Vanessa liked the best. Few of the kitchen staff could ever successfully get the dough out of the ancient wooden speculaas mold whenever they tried their hand at it. And because of the fleeting nature of the cookies whenever Rhetta made them, the cook herself typically did not bother to imprint them with designs.

But she always made an exception for Vanessa.

Cornelis tugged on the railing behind his head. "Can't believe your parents had to put this in around the koningsspil, to protect you. But they never could keep you out of this part of the mill."

"Okay, that was *one* time. And I was seven. I insisted on hugging everything that made me happy." She shrugged. "And this windmill made me happy." She glanced back at the big spindle. "Especially this magical turny thingy."

"As I remember your father telling it, they were still picking splinters out of your arms a week later."

Vanessa giggled. "I'm a hard hugger."

"Don't I know it?" Cornelis brushed her hair away from her cheek with his finger. "Remember what we used to call this place? Especially this top floor? That is, once we were older and started sneaking around so we could—"

"The lovemill," she said quickly, smiling and blushing at the same time. "I remember."

He stretched his legs out beside hers and knocked his shoes against her slippers.

"Grain mill's a perfect place for a little privacy," he remarked with a grin, then biting off half his cookie. "Considering we did plenty of 'grinding' back then, ourselves."

"Perfect privacy for thinking things through, too." Vanessa's smile faded as she picked at a gouge in the wooden floorboard next to her. "I guess I needed that tonight."

Cornelis's jaw slowed and he swallowed. "I heard what happened last night. You want to talk about it?"

She sighed and scowled at him. "I don't think so. You don't approve of my choice in men."

"Not this one," he agreed. "I don't trust him. And I think he's going to hurt a lot of people if he stays." Cornelis looked pointedly at her. "Especially you."

Too late for that.

She folded the foil back over the plate. "You don't think any of them are worthwhile, do you?"

At that, he paused. "A few of them are better than I first thought," he admitted. "Thomas, Miguel, John. Not the worst people I've ever met."

She raised an eyebrow. "John? Your American 'guard dog' who follows you to work, as you so politely put it?"

Cornie frowned at her. "Outside of comparing everything to Texas all the time, he's tolerable. That asshole Irishman—Liam—could use some work, though." Then his voice turned grumpy. "Not to mention Morgan, who walks around like we should be throwing rose petals at his feet."

Vanessa rolled her eyes as he folded his arms and seemed to pout.

After a moment, he leaned his head back against the railing as the turning gear wheels above creaked sedately in the quiet. "The old beast just won't quit, will it?" he mused.

Vanessa flicked a corner of the foil back and forth. "It'll probably outlast all of us."

Cornie sat forward and reached for the book lying next to the flickering lamp. He flipped through it. "Greek myths," he mumbled. "Haven't seen this in your collection before. I didn't think you were into that stuff."

"I picked it up from the bookstore in town, on one of my trips when I was—"

Trying to find just the right cloth for Ethan's masks.

She hesitated. "It looked lonely on its empty little

shelf, so I gave it a home."

He paged backward to the middle of the book. He handed it to her with his thumb pressed to the center.

"Here. Found your place," he said as she took it. "I need to get you a proper bookmark one of these days, so you quit dog-earing the poor things to death."

Vanessa stared at the chapter's title page: "Persephone and Hades: The Myth of Spring and Winter."

She almost gave a bitter laugh.

Cornelis's eyes drifted to her blouse, parted at the neck, and he squinted. He slipped his hand behind the square emerald pendant against her chest and examined it on his palm. "Where did this come from?"

Dejection—like ice-cold claws—latched around her heart and nearly punctured it.

"It was a gift," she said softly. "From the captain."

Cornelis let the jewel slide off his palm. "He spent a lot of money on that gift." His voice was edgy. "What did he expect in return?"

"Nothing." She dropped her gaze. *Unfortunately.*

She peeked at him to see his reaction. As expected, his crystal-blue eyes sparked with disapproval.

"A man like that acts on instinct. And a present like that means more than you think." Cornelis's voice was low, cautious. "If he does decide he wants something—"

She closed the book firmly. "It's not like that. He doesn't want anything from me." Her shoulders sank. "Believe me."

"When are you going to see him for what he is? What does it take to wake you up?"

But Cornelis's voice was not harsh, not scolding. She met his gaze, and the cool blue of his eyes was highlighted by the worried creases around them. He placed his hand over hers on the book's cover.

"Let him go, Ness. It was never meant to be. When he moves on and leaves you with a broken heart, you'll see I was right." He shook his head at her. "A man like him doesn't appreciate someone like you. He doesn't *understand* someone like you."

She blinked her eyes as they began to sting, but then nodded and looked away.

"Are you going to be all right?" he asked gently.

She managed a faint smile. "I always am."

He cocked his head, seeming to study her closely. "I'm here if you need me, schatje."

This time, her smile was sincere. "You always are."

Cornelis leaned in and pressed his lips tenderly to the side of her head for a long moment. Then he climbed to his feet and made his way to the floor hatch to disappear down the ladder.

His footsteps faded as he descended to the lower levels of the windmill until the only sound was the steady creaking of the wooden wind shaft as it dutifully turned the spindle behind her.

Vanessa wriggled her fingers under the foil on the plate and extracted one more of the speculaas. She bit into it and chewed glumly. She picked up the book and flipped again to the dog-eared chapter. She skimmed through it until she reached the last page of the story. It did ultimately work out between the title characters in the end. But it was still a piece of fiction. And things didn't happen like that in real life.

Even so, she had felt Ethan's passion, the truth of his need. Her heart had lured his into the open, if only for a moment, while his body had called to her and commanded her with a carnal appetite that mirrored her own. It *had* been real. And so had the look she'd seen burning in his bright green eyes. It was the look of a man reaching out to her in spite of the tormented voice that told him he couldn't. She had not imagined the emotion in his gaze or the fire in his touch.

But it had been *her* touch that had sent him back into his black armor. The scarring she'd felt across his bare skin was ridged and malformed, rough but smooth at the same time, and had been more extensive than she'd imagined. An expanse of scourged flesh. And yet, it was not the mutation he considered it. Not to her. That's what she'd tried to show him. And that's when the voice inside him had won.

She ran a hand slowly over the cover of the book and

then lifted her fingers to stroke the delicate square jewel upon her chest. She curled her fist around it.

No. Their story was not over. It couldn't be. She just needed to make him see that too.

The lantern flickered as a breeze slinked in and swatted the flame. Vanessa gazed through the open window at the night sky beyond and turned the half-eaten speculaas between her fingers.

It was time for him to stop hiding from her. Despite his resistance, he'd already given her glimpses beneath his mask. And she liked the man she saw. She wanted more of that. More of *him*. She was not going to let him leave her life as suddenly as he had entered it. Not without a no-holds-barred face-off. She would have to convince him that he belonged here. And if he still wouldn't stay, then—

"Ow!" She slapped a hand to her scalp after something bounced off it and skipped across the floor.

She bent forward and scooped up the small jagged object. It looked like another chunk off one of the revolving pinions above. She twisted her body and peered up into the shadows overhead. But then she turned again to the discarded wooden piece and rolled it in her palm. She closed her hand around the windmill fragment with a laugh.

If Ethan won't stay still, then I won't stop moving either!

January was on the way. The weather would get worse, so she'd need to make sure she dug out every piece of warm clothing she had and try to cram it all into her travel satchel. No telling what France was like in the winter, but she had spring in her veins, and that trumped any frigid conditions. Whether he liked it or not—and whether he invited her or not—if Ethan wanted to move on, she would be along for the ride.

She crossed her ankles, shoved the rest of the spiced cookie into her mouth, and tore the foil cover off the nearby plate. She smiled as she chewed.

Nope. This story's not finished. It's just getting started.

EPILOGUE

"Do not grumble at me," the young woman said sharply as her eyes snapped back to the boy's face. "Keep still, or I will tie this around your throat instead!"

The biker frowned at her impatiently and twisted the throttle to rev the engine. He chastised her in rapid-fire Ukrainian. "Your fingers are slow, like my old baba. I could have already been south in Regensburg by now!"

The woman jerked the knot tight against his arm and he yelped. She thumped him smartly in the temple with her index finger. "You are barely away from your baba's apron. Do not think you are important."

The boy frowned again and adjusted the bloodred nylon strip farther up his bicep.

But as he started to pull on his helmet, the woman slapped the back of her hand against his shoulder. "Do you have yours?"

He set the helmet on the tank in front of him, and his voice turned curt. "He gave it to me last night, when I stepped forward to be next. Why do you think I am sitting here if I am not ready?"

"Show me."

The teenager let out a rough sigh and hooked a finger into the side of his mouth to pull down his lip. The woman bent closer until she could see the porcelain crown on his bottom molar. And embedded in the tooth above it, the tiny blunt metal spike to pierce it.

She straightened with a nod, and he let his lip pop back into place. "Do not use it early. Be sure he is where you can talk to him."

At that, his lips stretched in a sneer. "I will spit in his face as I die."

She showed him a tight smile. "You will honor our murdered countrymen."

He knocked his face shield down into place and then nodded at the two other bikers nearby, one of whom also sat astride a sport bike and could barely touch the ground with his toes. They bobbed their heads in acknowledgment and pulled on their helmets, the icy wind sending the loose ends of their own nylon armbands into a wild crimson dance. The boy leaned his chest against the tank, hiked his feet onto the foot pegs, and gunned the throttle. His rear tire threw out a fountain of dirt as he and the others tore off through the barren aisles of hop trellises that had been picked clean months before.

She pulled the tracker from her coat pocket and switched it on with her thumb. The green, blue, and yellow dots at the center of the screen moved in parallel for a few seconds before splitting off into three different directions across the digital topography of Germany.

Her thoughts were interrupted with "Ruslana!"

She turned her head as their leader swung himself down from the idling KrAZ Spartan several meters away. He slammed the door shut on the armored personnel carrier and ambled toward her.

"Hadeon." She pocketed the tracker and walked to meet him. She glanced down at the rectangular outline of the splint beneath his pant leg. "How is your ankle feeling?"

"We will camp here tonight," he said gruffly, jerking on his coat with his left hand and then buttoning the empty sleeve on his right to the front of his jacket. "The others will follow soon."

Ruslana put her hand on her hip. "Do not ignore me. Your ankle."

Hadeon tossed his head so that the wind caught his gray hair and pushed it back from his lined, frowning face. "It is fine. You worry about me, when it is the hounds who need your attention."

"I have already sent them off," she replied evenly.

Hadeon grunted and tilted his head to squint at the

sky. "It will snow in a while."

"They are fast boys," she countered, watching him work the buttons at the top of his jacket. "They each have their own route and will stop as they need. They have long roads ahead of them, if they are to cover so much territory this time."

Hadeon's Ukrainian words were clipped when he spoke. "Should have gone sooner."

She stepped forward and batted his hand away from the collar of his coat. "You should not question me." She tugged firmly on the sides of his collar to pull it up around his neck. "I know what is best for our cause. Your son did not marry a stupid woman."

"No." He let his hand fall away, and he gave her a slight smile. "He married a lioness."

She quirked her mouth as if with displeasure, but her cheeks warmed nonetheless. "The captain will soon hear all of us roar. We will find him this time, and we will have justice. The Russians, with all their soldiers and all their machines, cannot defeat the Ukrainian heart, the many times they have tried." She smoothed Hadeon's empty right sleeve against him. "The captain is but one man with a few fools who follow him. He will not win."

Hadeon nodded, scratching the stubble on his jaw as he squinted at something in the distance. "And he cannot run forever. As our greatest leaders have said, his grave will be the only quiet place for him in this world."

Ruslana turned to glance at the armed men who began to appear within the hop field. They trod carefully between the tall wooden poles, where the trellis wires, strung high above their heads, held up empty meters of twine that new green hop bines would begin to climb in the spring.

Ruslana rolled the elastic band from her wrist and gathered her shoulder-length hair behind her to secure it against her head. She stared off as she combed her fingers through it. Her husband used to say it was the baked brown color of the korovai bread that was made for their wedding only a few years ago and that when she stayed in the sun too long, some strands would lighten to mimic the korovai's feathery, swirling decorations. She lowered her arms, and the wind pushed her tears past the corners of her eyes.

A hand rested upon her shoulder, and she lifted her face to her father-in-law. His strong, tapered chin and rounded features were so like those of her husband, who would have aged as handsomely.

"Danilo's spirit will be at rest soon." Hadeon's eyes were bright and reflected the shine of the approaching headlights as more of their comrades arrived. "*All* of them will be. The captain will pay for every single death cry that went up that day."

Ruslana gritted her teeth as the stinging wind swept back new tears. "Hung up like pigs and swallowed by fire. There was not even enough to bury." She took a sharp breath. "And then to destroy our home, everything we had left—"

Hadeon gripped her shoulder harder and bent his head to level his gaze at her. "He cannot burn us. He cannot kill us."

Ruslana held her shoulders back and lifted her chin slowly. Her voice shook, but she finished the words with a bitter pride. "We will bury him screaming beneath the bodies of his men."

Acknowledgments

I would like to thank my husband John, whose patience and support over the years has been remarkable, and Becky, who has read and advised on at least four iterations of this book without a single complaint.

I would also like to thank my editor, David Antrobus, for all his insights and amazing work in helping me to polish this first novel.

And, of course, the cover is a beautiful work of art, thanks to the incredible design talents of Sinisa Poznanovic, whom I found through Upwork.

I have had so many helpful and wonderful guides along this journey, and I am grateful to each and every person who took the time to provide feedback on the story, characters, and cultures. In particular, I would like to thank the following people:

For reading through the entire manuscript (sometimes twice!) and/or for unflinching support throughout the process:

- Jenn Abudayeh
- Debra Belanger
- Lori Sanders Foley
- Christianne Hale
- Georgette Hardin
- Desiree Holt
- Tim Kerins
- LoriAnne

- Debbie S G
- Charan Saini
- Walter Seidenschwarz
- Nashwa Shalaby

For advice and suggestions on the book's many characters, cultures, and languages:
- Aderonke Babajide
- Karin Vreeswijk Beaty
- Jaspreet S. Dhau
- Irene and Franco
- Luigi L.
- Anika Laracker
- Matthew LeDrew
- Danny McGeachy
- Tosin Odesanya
- Harjinder Singh
- Santiago Vidal

About the Author

Karen Yakey writes novels for adult readers who enjoy a cocktail of romance, humor, and action with a dark-drama chaser. Though her literary leanings harken back to a master's degree in literature, linguistics, and communications, she has spent twenty-three years in global corporations within the tech world and financial services, which helps feed an appetite for diverse experiences. A self-professed queen of beer-brewing and brisket-smoking, she has pulled up her Texas roots to plant them in Florida. Owing to a love of traveling throughout Europe, she has sought to imbue this story with an honest sense of how a simple human connection can bridge any border or culture.

The blog on her website at www.KarenYakey.com is where her introspective, often hyperbolic, humor goes to play, and pessimism has no place there. Please reach out anytime, sign up for her newsletter, and feel free to follow her on:

- Twitter and Instagram (KarenYakey)
- Facebook (facebook.com/KarenYakey)